THE SEA LIONS

OR

THE LOST SEALERS

BY

J. FENIMORE COOPER

"Daughter of Faith, awake, arise, illume
The dread unknown, the chaos of the tomb
Melt, and dispel, ye spectre doubts that roll
Cimmerian darkness o'er the parting soul"
CAMPBELL

Fredonia Books
Amsterdam, The Netherlands

The Sea Lions; The Lost Sealers

by
J. Fenimore Cooper

ISBN: 1-58963-783-6

Fredonia Books
Amsterdam, The Netherlands
http://www.fredoniabooks.com

PREFACE.

If anything connected with the hardness of the human heart could surprise us, it surely would be the indifference with which men live on, engrossed by their worldly objects, amid the sublime natural phenomena that so eloquently and unceasingly speak to their imaginations, affections, and judgments. So completely is the existence of the individual concentrated in self, and so regardless does he get to be of all without that contracted circle, that it does not probably happen to one man in ten that his thoughts are drawn aside from this intense study of his own immediate wants, wishes, and plans, even once in the twenty-four hours, to contemplate the majesty, mercy, truth, and justice of the Divine Being that has set him, as an atom, amid the myriads of the hosts of heaven and earth.

The physical marvels of the universe produce little more reflection than the profoundest moral truths. A million of eyes shall pass over the firmament on a cloudless night, and not a hundred minds shall be filled with a proper sense of the power of the dread Being that created all that is there—not a hundred hearts glow with the adoration that such an appeal to the senses and understanding ought naturally to produce. This indifference, in a great measure, comes of familiarity; the things that we so constantly have before us becoming as a part of the air we breathe, and as little regarded.

One of the consequences of this disposition to disregard the Almighty Hand, as it is so plainly visible in all around us, is that of substituting our own powers in its stead. In this period of the world, in enlightened countries, and in the absence of direct idolatry, few men are so hardy as to deny the existence and might of a Supreme Being; but, this fact admitted, how few really feel that profound reverence for him that the nature of our relations justly demands! It is the want of a due sense of humility, and a sad misconception of what we are, and for what we were created, that misleads us in the due estimate of our own insignificance, as compared with the majesty of God.

Very few men attain enough of human knowledge to be fully aware how much remains to be learned, and of that which they never can hope to acquire. We hear a great deal of god-like minds, and of the far-reaching faculties we possess; and it may all be worthy of our eulogiums, until we compare ourselves in these, as in other particulars, with Him who produced them. Then, indeed, the utter insignificance of our means becomes too apparent to admit of a cavil. We know that we are born, and that we die; science has been able to grapple with all the phenomena of these two great physical facts, with the exception of the most material of all—those which should tell us what is life, and what is death. Something that we cannot comprehend lies at the root of every distinct division of natural phenomena. Thus far shalt thou go and no farther, seems to be imprinted on every great fact of creation. There is a point attained in each and all of our acquisitions, where a mystery that no human mind can scan takes the place of demonstration and conjecture. This point may lie more remote with some intellects than with others; but it exists for all, arrests the inductions of all, conceals all.

We are aware that the more learned among those who disbelieve in the divinity of Christ suppose themselves to be sustained by written authority, contending for errors of translation, mistakes and misapprehensions in the ancient texts. Nevertheless, we are inclined to think that nine-tenths of those who refuse the old and accept the new opinion, do so for a motive no better than a disinclination to believe that which they cannot comprehend. This pride of reason is one of the most insinuating of our foibles, and is to be watched as a most potent enemy.

How completely and philosophically does the venerable Christian creed embrace and modify all these workings of the heart! We say philosophically, for it were not possible for mind to give a juster analysis of the whole subject than St. Paul's most comprehensive but brief definition of Faith. It is this Faith which forms the mighty feature of the church on earth. It equalizes capacities, conditions, means, and ends, holding out the same encouragement and hope to the least, as to the most gifted of the race ; counting gifts in their ordinary and more secular points of view.

It is when health, or the usual means of success abandon us, that we are made to feel how totally we are insufficient for the achievement of even our own purposes, much less to qualify us to reason on the deep mysteries that conceal the beginning and the end. It has often been said that the most successful leaders of their fellow-men have had the clearest views of their own insufficiency to attend their own objects. If Napoleon ever said, as has been attributed to him, "*Je propose et je dispose*," it must have been in one of those fleeting moments in which success blinded him to the fact of his own insufficiency. No man had a deeper reliance on fortune, cast the result of great events on the decrees of fate, or more anxiously watched the rising and setting of what he called his "star." This was a faith that could lead to no good ; but it clearly denoted how far the boldest designs, the most ample means, and the most vaulting ambition, fall short of giving that sublime consciousness of power and its fruits that distinguish the reign of Omnipotence.

In this book the design has been to portray man on a novel field of action, and to exhibit his dependence on the hand that does not suffer a sparrow to fall unheeded. The recent attempts of science, which employed the seamen of the four greatest maritime states of Christendom, made discoveries that have rendered the polar circles much more familiar to this age than to any that has preceded it, so far as existing records show. We say "existing records ;" for there is much reason for believing that the ancients had a knowledge of our hemisphere, though less for supposing that they ever braved the dangers of the high latitudes. Many are, just at this moment, much disposed to believe that "Ophir" was on this continent ; though for a reason no better than the circumstance of the recent discoveries of much gold. Such savans should remember that "peacocks" came from ancient Ophir. If this be in truth that land, the adventurers of Israel caused it to be denuded of that bird of beautiful plumage.

Such names as those of Parry, Sabine, Ross, Franklin, Wilkes, Hudson, Ringgold, &c., &c., with those of divers gallant Frenchmen and Russians, command our most profound respect ; for no battles or victories can redound more to the credit of seamen than the dangers they all en-

countered, and the conquests they have all achieved   One
of those named, a resolute and experienced seaman, it is
thought must, at this moment, be locked in the frosts of
the arctic circle, after having passed half a life in the endeavor to push his discoveries into those remote and frozen
regions.   He bears the name of the most distinguished of
the philosophers of this country ; and nature has stamped
on his features—by one of those secret laws which just as
much baffle our means of comprehension, as the greatest
of all our mysteries, the incarnation of the Son of God—a
resemblance that, of itself, would go to show that they are
of the same race.   Any one who has ever seen this imprisoned navigator, and who is familiar with the countenances
of the men of the same name who are to be found in numbers amongst ourselves, must be struck with a likeness
that lies as much beyond the grasp of that reason of which
we are so proud, as the sublimest facts taught by induction, science, or revelation.   Parties are, at this moment,
out in search of him and his followers ; and it is to be
hoped that the Providence which has so singularly attem-
pered the different circles and zones of our globe, placing
this under a burning sun, and that beneath enduring frosts,
will have included in its divine forethought a sufficient care
for these bold wanderers to restore them, unharmed, to
their friends and country.   In a contrary event, their
names must be transmitted to posterity as the victims to a
laudable desire to enlarge the circle of human knowledge,
and with it, we trust, to increase the glory due to God.

THE SEA LIONS.

CHAPTER I.

—— "When that's gone,
He shall drink naught but brine."—*Tempest.*

WHILE there is less of that high polish in America that is obtained by long intercourse with the great world, than is to be found in nearly every European country, there is much less positive rusticity also. There, the extremes of society are widely separated, repelling rather than attracting each other ; while among ourselves, the tendency is to gravitate toward a common centre. Thus it is, that all things in America become subject to a mean law that is productive of a mediocrity which is probably much above the average of that of most nations ; possibly of all, England excepted ; but which is only a mediocrity after all. In this way, excellence in nothing is justly appreciated, nor is it often recognized ; and the suffrages of the nation are pretty uniformly bestowed on qualities of a secondary class. Numbers have sway, and it is as impossible to resist them in deciding on merit as it is to deny their power in the ballot-boxes ; time alone, with its great curative influence, supplying the remedy that is to restore the public mind to a healthful state, and give equally to the pretender and to him who is worthy of renown his proper place in the pages of history.

The activity of American life, the rapidity and cheapness of intercourse, and the migratory habits both have induced, leave little of rusticity and local character in any particular sections of the country. Distinctions, that an acute observer may detect, do certainly exist between the Eastern and the Western man, between the Northerner and the Southerner, the Yankee and Middle States' man ; the Bostonian, Manhattanese, and Philadelphian ; the Tuckahoe and the Cracker; the Buckeye or Wolverine, and the Jersey Blue. Nevertheless, the world cannot probably produce another instance of a people who are derived from so many different races, and who occupy so large an extent of country, who are so homogeneous in appearance, characters, and opinions. There is no question that the institutions have had a material influence in producing this uniformity, while they have unquestionably lowered the standard to which opinion is submitted, by referring the decisions to the many, instead of making the appeal to the few, as is elsewhere done. Still, the direction is onward, and though it may take time to carve on the social column of America that graceful and ornamental capital which it forms the just boast of Europe to possess, when the task shall be achieved, the work will stand on a base so broad as to secure its upright attitude for ages.

Notwithstanding the general character of identity and homogeneity that so strongly marks the picture of American society, exceptions are to be met with, in particular districts, that are not only distinct and incontrovertible, but which are so peculiar as to be worthy of more than a passing remark in our delineations of national customs. Our present purpose leads us into one of these secluded districts, and it may be well to commence the narrative of certain deeply interesting incidents that it is our intention to attempt to portray, by first referring to the place and people where and from whom the principal actors in our legend had their origin.

Every one at all familiar with the map of America knows the position and general form of the two islands that shelter the well-known harbor of the great emporium of the commerce of the country. These islands obtained their names from the Dutch, who called them Nassau and Staten; but the English, with little respect for the ancient house whence the first of these appellations is derived, and consulting only the homely taste which leads them to a practical rather than to a poetical nomenclature in all things, have since virtually dropped the name of Nassau, altogether substituting that of Long Island in its stead.

Long Island, or the island of Nassau, extends from the mouth of the Hudson to the eastern line of Connecticut; forming a sort of sea-wall to protect the whole coast of the latter little territory against the waves of the broad Atlantic. Three of the oldest New York counties, as their names would imply, Kings, Queens, and Suffolk, are on this island. Kings was originally peopled by the Dutch, and still possesses as many names derived from Holland as from England, if its towns, which are of recent origin, be taken from the account. Queens is more of a mixture, having been early invaded and occupied by adventurers from the other side of the Sound; but Suffolk, which contains nearly, if not quite, two-thirds of the surface of the whole island, is and ever has been in possession of a people derived originally from the Puritans of New England. Of these three counties, Kings is much the smallest, though, next to New York itself, the most populous county in the State; a circumstance that is owing to the fact that two suburban offsets of the great emporium, Brooklyn and Williamsburg, happen to stand within its limits, on the waters of what is improperly called the East River; an arm of the sea that has obtained this appellation in contradistinction to the Hudson, which, as all Manhattanese well know, is as often called the North River as by its proper name. In consequence of these two towns, or suburbs of New York, one of which contains nearly a hundred thousand souls, while the other must be drawing on toward twenty thousand, Kings County has lost all it ever had of peculiar or local character. The same is true of Queens, though in a diminished degree; but Suffolk remains Suffolk still, and it is with Suffolk alone that our present legend requires us to deal. Of Suffolk, then, we propose to say a few words by way of preparatory explanation.

Although it has actually more sea-coast than all the rest of New York united, Suffolk has but one seaport that is ever mentioned beyond the limits of the county itself. Nor is this port one of general commerce, its shipping being principally employed in the hardy and manly occupation of whaling. As a whaling town, Sag Harbor is the third or fourth port in the country, and maintains something like that rank in importance. A whaling haven is nothing without a whaling community. Without the last it is almost hopeless to look for success. New York can, and has often fitted whalers for sea, having sought officers in the regular whaling ports; but it has been seldom that the enterprises have been rewarded with such returns as to induce a second voyage by the same parties.

It is as indispensable that a whaler should possess a certain *esprit de corps*, as that a regiment, or a ship of war, should be animated by its proper spirit. In the whaling communities, this spirit exists to an extent and in a degree that is wonderful, when one remembers the great expansion of this particular branch of trade within the last five-and-twenty years. It may be a little lessened of late, but at the time of which we are writing, or about the year 1820, there was scarcely an individual who followed this particular calling out of the port of Sag Harbor, whose general standing on board ship was not as well known to all the women and girls of the place as it was to his shipmates. Success in taking the whale was a thing that made itself felt in every fibre of the prosperity of the town ; and it was just as natural that the single-minded population of that part of Suffolk should regard the bold and skilful harpooner or lancer with favor, as it is for the belle at a watering-place to bestow her smiles on one of the young heroes of Contreras or Cherubusco. His peculiar merit, whether with the oar, lance, or harpoon, is bruited about, as well as the number of whales he may have succeeded in "making fast to," or those which he caused to "spout blood." It is true that the great extension of the trade within the last twenty years, by drawing so many from a distance into its pursuits, has in a degree lessened this local interest and local knowledge of character ; but at the time of which we are about to write both were at their height, and Nantucket itself had not more of this "intelligence office" propensity, or more of the true whaling *esprit de corps*, than were to be found in the district of country that surrounded Sag Harbor.

Long Island forks at its eastern end, and may be said to have two extremities. One of these, which is much the shortest of the two legs thus formed, goes by the name of Oyster Pond Point ; while the other, that stretches much farther in the direction of Block Island, is the well-known cape called Montauk. Within the fork lies Shelter Island, so named from the snug berth it occupies. Between Shelter Island and the longest or southern prong of the fork are the waters which compose the haven of Sag Harbor— an estuary of some extent ; while a narrow but deep arm of the sea separates this island from the northern prong, that terminates at Oyster Pond.

The name of Oyster Pond Point was formerly applied to a long, low, fertile, and pleasant reach of land that extended several miles from the point itself, westward, toward the spot where the two prongs of the fork united. It was not easy, during the first quarter of the present century, to find a more secluded spot on the whole island than Oyster Pond.

Recent enterprises have since converted it into the ter-
minus of a railroad ; and Greer Port, once called Sterling,
is a name well known to travellers between New York and
Boston ; but in the earlier part of the present century it
seemed just as likely that the *Santa Casa* of Loretta should
take a new flight and descend on the point, as that the improvement that has actually been made should in truth
occur at that out-of-the-way place. It required, indeed, the
keen eye of a railroad projector to bring this spot in connection with anything ; nor could it be done without having recourse to the water by which it is almost surrounded.
Using the last, it is true, means have been found to place
it in a line between two of the great marts of the country,
and thus to put an end to all its seclusion, its simplicity,
its peculiarities, and we had almost said, its happiness.

It is to us ever a painful sight to see the rustic virtues
rudely thrown aside by the intrusion of what are termed
improvements. A railroad is certainly a capital invention
for the traveller, but it may be questioned if it is of any other
benefit than that of pecuniary convenience to the places
through which it passes. How many delightful hamlets,
pleasant villages, and even tranquil country towns, are losing their primitive characters for simplicity and content-
ment by the passage of these fiery trains, that drag after
them a sort of bastard elegance, a pretension that is destructive of peace of mind, and an uneasy desire in all who
dwell by the wayside to pry into the mysteries of the whole
length and breadth of the region it traverses !

We are writing of the year of our Lord one thousand
eight hundred and nineteen. In that day Oyster Pond
was, in one of the best acceptations of the word, a rural
district. It is true that its inhabitants were accustomed to
the water, and to the sight of vessels, from the two-decker
to the little shabby-looking craft that brought ashes from
town to meliorate the sandy lands of Suffolk. Only five
years before an English squadron had lain in Gardiner's
Bay, here pronounced "Gar'ner's," watching the Race, or
eastern outlet of the Sound, with a view to cut off the trade
and annoy their enemy. That game is up forever. No
hostile squadron, English, French, Dutch, or all united, will
ever again blockade an American port for any serious length
of time—the young Hercules passing too rapidly from the
gristle into the bone any longer to suffer antics of this nature to be played in front of his cradle. But such was not
his condition in the war of 1812, and the good people of

Oyster Pond had become familiar with the checkered sides of two-deck ships, and the venerable and beautiful ensign of Old England, as it floated above them.

Nor was it only by these distant views, and by means of hostilities, that the good folk of Oyster Pond were acquainted with vessels. New York is necessary to all on the coast, both as a market and as a place to procure supplies ; and every creek, or inlet, or basin, of any sort, within a hundred leagues of it, is sure to possess one or more craft that ply between the favorite haven and the particular spot in question. Thus was it with Oyster Pond. There is scarce a better harbor on the whole American coast than that which the narrow arm of the sea that divides the point from Shelter Island presents ; and even in the simple times of which we are writing Sterling had its two or three coasters, such as they were. But the true maritime character of Oyster Pond, as well as that of all Suffolk, was derived from the whalers, and its proper nucleus was across the estuary, at Sag Harbor. Thither the youths of the whole region resorted for employment, and to advance their fortunes, and generally with such success as is apt to attend enterprise, industry, and daring, when exercised with energy in a pursuit of moderate gains. None became rich in the strict signification of the term, though a few got to be in reasonably affluent circumstances ; many were placed altogether at their ease, and more were made humbly comfortable. A farm in America is well enough for the foundation of family support, but it rarely suffices for all the growing wants of these days of indulgence, and of a desire to enjoy so much of that which was formerly left to the undisputed possession of the unquestionably rich. A farm, with a few hundreds *per annum* derived from other sources, makes a good base of comfort ; and if the hundreds are converted into thousands, your farmer or agriculturist becomes a man not only at his ease, but a proprietor of some importance. The farms on Oyster Pond were neither very extensive, nor had they owners of large incomes to support them ; on the contrary, most of them were made to support their owners ; a thing that is possible, even in America, with industry, frugality, and judgment. In order, however, that the names of places we may have occasion to use shall be understood, it may be well to be a little more particular in our preliminary explanation.

The reader knows that we are now writing of Suffolk

County, Long Island, New York. He also knows that our opening scene is to be on the shorter, or most northern, of the two prongs of that fork which divides the eastern end of this island, giving it what are properly two capes. The smallest territorial division that is known to the laws of New York, in rural districts, is the "township," as it is called. These townships are usually larger than the English parish, corresponding more properly with the French canton. They vary, however, greatly in size, some containing as much as a hundred square miles, which is the largest size, while others do not contain more than a tenth of that surface.

The township in which the northern prong, or point of Long Island, lies, is named Southold, and includes not only all of the long, low, narrow land that then went by the common names of Oyster Pond, Sterling, etc., but several islands also which stretch off in the Sound, as well as a broader piece of territory near Riverhead. Oyster Pond, which is the portion of the township that lies on the "point," is, or *was*—for we write of a remote period in the galloping history of the State—only a part of Southold, and probably was not then a name known in the laws at all.

We have a wish, also, that this name should be pronounced properly. It is not called Oyster *Pond*, as the uninitiated would be very apt to get it, but *Oyster* Pùnd, the last word having a sound similar to that of the cockney's "pound" in his "two pùnd two." This discrepancy between the spelling and the pronunciation of proper names is agreeable to us, for it shows that a people are not put in leading-strings by pedagogues, and that they make use of their own in their own way. We remember how great was our satisfaction once, on entering Holmes' Hole, a well-known bay in this very vicinity, in our youth, to hear a boatman call the port "Hum'ses Hull." It is getting to be so rare to meet with an American, below the higher classes, who will consent to cast this species of veil before his schoolday acquisitions, that we acknowledge it gives us pleasure to hear such good, homely, old-fashioned English as "Gar'ner's Island," "Hum'ses Hull," and "*Oyster* Pùnd."

This plainness of speech was not the only proof of the simplicity of former days that was to be found in Suffolk, in the first quarter of the century. The eastern end of Long Island lies so much out of the track of the rest of the world, that even the new railroad cannot make much im-

pression on its inhabitants, who get their pigs and poultry,
butter and eggs, a little earlier to market than in the days
of the stage-wagons, it is true, but they fortunately, as yet,
bring little back except it be the dross that sets everything
in motion, whether it be by rail, or through the sands, in
the former toilsome mode.

The season, at the precise moment when we desire to
take the reader with us to Oyster Pond, was in the delightful month of September, when the earlier promises of the
year are fast maturing into performance. Although Suffolk, as a whole, can scarcely be deemed a productive
county, being generally of a thin, light soil, and still covered with a growth of small wood, it possesses, nevertheless, spots of exceeding fertility. A considerable portion
of the northern prong of the fork has this latter character,
and Oyster Pond is a sort of garden compared with much
of the sterility that prevails around it. Plain but respectable dwellings, with numerous out-buildings, orchards, and
fruit-trees, fences carefully preserved, a painstaking til-
lage, good roads, and here and there a "meeting-house,"
gave the fork an air of rural and moral beauty that, aided
by the water by which it was so nearly surrounded, contributed greatly to relieve the monotony of so dead a level.
There were heights in view, on Shelter Island, and bluffs
toward Riverhead, which, if they would not attract much
attention in Switzerland, were by no means overlooked in
Suffolk. In a word, both the season and the place were
charming, though most of the flowers had already faded ;
and the apple, and the pear, and the peach, were taking the
places of the inviting cherry. Fruit abounded, notwithstanding the close vicinity of the district to salt water, the
airs from the sea being broken, or somewhat tempered, by
the land that lay to the southward.

We have spoken of the coasters that ply between the
emporium and all the creeks and bays of the Sound, as
well as of the numberless rivers that find an outlet for their
waters between Sandy Hook and Rockaway. Wharves were
constructed, at favorable points, *inside* the prong, and occasionally a sloop was seen at them loading its truck, or discharging its ashes or street manure ; the latter being a
very common return cargo for a Long Island coaster. At
one wharf, however, now lay a vessel of a different mould,
and one which, though of no great size, was manifestly intended to go *outside*. This was a schooner that had been
recently launched, and which had advanced no farther in

its first equipment than to get in its two principal spars, the rigging of which hung suspended over the mast-heads, in readiness to be "set up" for the first time. The day being Sunday, work was suspended, and this so much the more, because the owner of the vessel was a certain Deacon Pratt, who dwelt in a house within half a mile of the wharf, and who was also the proprietor of three several parcels of land in that neighborhood, each of which had its own buildings and conveniences, and was properly enough dignified with the name of a farm. To be sure, neither of these farms was very large, their acres united amounting to but little more than two hundred; but, owing to their condition, the native richness of the soil, and the mode of turning them to account, they had made Deacon Pratt a warm man for Suffolk.

There are two great species of deacons; for we suppose they must all be referred to the same *genera*. One species belong to the priesthood, and become priests and bishops; passing away, as priests and bishops are apt to do, with more or less of the savor of godliness. The other species are purely laymen, and are *sui generis*. They are, *ex-officio*, the most pious men in a neighborhood, as they sometimes are, as it would seem to us, *ex-officio*, also the most grasping and mercenary. As we are not in the secrets of the sects to which these lay deacons belong, we shall not presume to pronounce whether the individual is elevated to the deaconate because he is prosperous, in a worldly sense, or whether the prosperity is a consequence of the deaconate; but, that the two usually go together is quite certain; which being the cause, and which the effect, we leave to wiser heads to determine.

Deacon Pratt was no exception to the rule. A tighter-fisted sinner did not exist in the county than this pious soul, who certainly not only wore, but wore out the "form of godliness," while he was devoted, heart and hand, to the daily increase of worldly gear. No one spoke disparagingly of the deacon, notwithstanding. So completely had he got to be interwoven with the church—"meeting," we ought to say—in that vicinity, that speaking disparagingly of him would have appeared like assailing Christianity. It is true, that many an unfortunate fellow-citizen in Suffolk had been made to feel how close was the gripe of his hand, when he found himself in its grasp; but there is a way of practising the most ruthless extortion, that serves not only to deceive the world, but which would really seem to mislead the extortioner himself. Phrases take the place of deeds, sentiments those of facts, and grimaces those of benevolent looks, so ingeniously and so impudently that the wronged often fancy that they are the victims of a severe dispensation of Providence, when the truth would have shown that they were simply robbed.

We do not mean, however, that Deacon Pratt was a robber. He was merely a hard man in the management of his affairs, never cheating, in a direct sense, but seldom conceding a cent to generous impulses, or to the duties of kind. He was a widower, and childless, circumstances that rendered his love of gain still less pardonable ; for many a man who is indifferent to money on his own account, will toil and save to lay up hoards for those who are to come after him. The deacon had only a niece to inherit his effects, unless he might choose to step beyond that degree of consanguinity, and bestow a portion of his means on cousins. The church—or, to be more literal, the " meeting "—had an eye to his resources, however ; and it was whispered it had actually succeeded, by means known to itself, in squeezing out of his tight grasp no less a sum than one hundred dollars, as a donation to a certain theological college. It was conjectured by some persons that this was only the beginning of a religious liberality, and that the excellent and godly-minded deacon would bestow most of his property in a similar way, when the moment should come that it could be no longer of any use to himself. This opinion was much in favor with divers devout females of the deacon's congregation, who had daughters of their own, and who seldom failed to conclude their observations on this interesting subject with some such remark as, " Well, in *that* case, and it seems to me that everything points that way, Mary Pratt will get no more than any other poor man's daughter."

Little did Mary, the only child of Israel Pratt, an elder brother of the deacon, think of all this. She had been left an orphan in her tenth year, both parents dying within a few months of each other, and had lived beneath her uncle's roof for nearly ten more years, until use, and natural affection, and the customs of the country, had made her feel absolutely at home there. A less interested, or less selfish being than Mary Pratt, never existed. In this respect she was the very antipodes of her uncle, who often stealthily rebuked her for her charities and acts of neighborly kindness, which he was wont to term waste. But

Mary kept the even tenor of her way, seemingly not hearing such remarks, and doing her duty quietly, and in all humility.

Suffolk was settled originally by emigrants from New England, and the character of its people is to this hour of modified New England habits and notions. Now one of the marked peculiarities of Connecticut is an indisposition to part with anything without a *quid pro quo*. Those little services, offerings and conveniences that are elsewhere parted with without a thought of remuneration, go regularly upon the day-book, and often reappear on a "settlement," years after they have been forgotten by those who received the favors. Even the man who keeps a carriage will let it out for hire; and the manner in which money is accepted, and even asked for by persons in easy circumstances, and for things that would be gratuitous in the Middle States, often causes disappointment, and sometimes disgust. In this particular Scottish and Swiss thrift, both notorious, and the latter particularly so, are nearly equalled by New England thrift; more especially in the close estimate of the value of services rendered. So marked, indeed, is this practice of looking for requitals, that even the language is infected with it. Thus, should a person pass a few months by invitation with a friend, his visit is termed "boarding;" it being regarded as a matter of course that he pays his way. It would scarcely be safe, indeed, without the precaution of "passing receipts" on quitting, for one to stay any time in a New England dwelling, unless prepared to pay for his board. The free and frank habits that prevail among relatives and friends elsewhere, are nearly unknown there, every service having its price. These customs are exceedingly repugnant to all who have been educated in different notions; yet they are not without their redeeming qualities, that might be pointed out to advantage, though our limits will not permit us, at this moment so to do.

Little did Mary Pratt suspect the truth; but habit, or covetousness, or some vague expectation that the girl might yet contract a marriage that would enable him to claim all his advances, had induced the deacon never to bestow a cent on her education, or dress, or pleasures of any sort, that the money was not regularly charged against her in that nefarious work he called his "day-book." As for the self-respect, and the feelings of caste, which prevent a gentleman from practising any of these tradesmen's tricks, the deacon knew nothing of them. He would have set the man down as a fool who deferred to any notions so unprofitable. With him not only every *man*, but every *thing*, "had its price," and usually it was a good price too. At the very moment when our tale opens, there stood charged in his book, against his unsuspecting and affectionate niece, items in the way of schooling, dress, board, and pocket money, that amounted to the considerable sum of one thousand dollars, money fairly expended. The deacon was only intensely mean and avaricious, while he was as honest as the day. Not a cent was overcharged; and, to own the truth, Mary was so great a favorite with him that most of his charges against *her* were rather of a reasonable rate than otherwise.

CHAPTER II.

"Mary, I saw your niece do more favors
To the count's serving-man, than ever she bestowed
Upon me; I saw it i' the orchard!"—*Twelfth Night.*

ON the Sunday in question, Deacon Pratt went to meeting as usual, the building in which divine service was held that day, standing less than two miles from his residence; but, instead of remaining for the afternoon's preaching, as was his wont, he got into his one-horse chaise, the vehicle then in universal use among the middle classes, though now so seldom seen, and skirred away homeward as fast as an active, well-fed, and powerful switch-tailed mare could draw him; the animal being accompanied in her rapid progress by a colt of some three months' existence. The residence of the deacon was unusually inviting for a man of his narrow habits. It stood on the edge of a fine apple-orchard, having a door-yard of nearly two acres in its front. This door-yard, which had been twice mown that summer, was prettily embellished with flowers, and was shaded by four rows of noble cherry-trees. The house itself was of wood, as is almost uniformly the case in Suffolk, where little stone is to be found, and where brick constructions are apt to be thought damp; but it was a respectable edifice, with five windows in front, and of two stories. The siding was of unpainted cedar-shingles; and, although the house had been erected long previously to the Revolution, the siding had been renewed but once, about ten

years before the opening of our tale, and the whole building was in a perfect state of repair. The thrift of the
deacon rendered him careful, and he was thoroughly convinced of the truth of the familiar adage which tells us that
"a stitch in time saves nine." All around the house and
farm was in perfect order, proving the application of the
saying. As for the view, it was sufficiently pleasant, the
house having its front toward the east, while its end
windows looked, the one set in the direction of the Sound,
and the other in that of the arm of the sea, which belongs
properly to Peconic Bay, we believe. All this water, some of
which was visible over points and among islands, together
with a smiling and fertile, though narrow stretch of fore-
ground, could not fail of making an agreeable landscape.

It was little, however, that Deacon Pratt thought of
views, or beauty of any sort, as the mare reached the open
gate of his own abode. Mary was standing in the stoop,
or porch of the house, and appeared to be anxiously
awaiting her uncle's return. The latter gave the reins to
a black, one who was no longer a slave, but who was a
descendant of some of the ancient slaves of the Pratts,
and in that character consented still to dawdle about the
place, working for half price. On alighting, the uncle
approached the niece with somewhat of interest in his
manner.

"Well, Mary," said the former, "how does he get on
now ?"

"Oh! my dear sir, he cannot possibly live, I think, and
I do most earnestly entreat that you will let me send across
to the Harbor for Dr. Sage."

By the Harbor was meant Sag's, and the physician
named was one of merited celebrity in old Suffolk. So
healthy was the country in general, and so simple were the
habits of the people, that neither lawyer nor physician
was to be found in every hamlet, as is the case to-day.
Both were to be had at Riverhead, as well as at Sag Harbor ; but, if a man called out "Squire," or "Doctor," in
the highways of Suffolk, sixteen men did not turn round
to reply, as is said to be the case in other regions ; one
half answering to the one appellation, and the second
half to the other. The deacon had two objections to
yielding to his niece's earnest request ; the expense being
one, though it was not in this instance the greatest ; there
was another reason that he kept to himself, but which will
appear as our narrative proceeds.

A few weeks previously to the Sunday in question, a sea-going vessel, inward bound, had brought up in Gardiner's Bay, which is a usual anchorage for all sorts of craft. A worn-out and battered seaman had been put ashore on Oyster Pond, by a boat from this vessel, which sailed to the westward soon after, proceeding most probably to New York. The stranger was not only well advanced in life, but he was obviously wasting away with disease.

The account given of himself by this seaman was sufficiently explicit. He was born on Martha's Vineyard, but, as is customary with the boys of that island, he had left home in his twelfth year, and had now been absent from the place of his birth a little more than half a century. Conscious of the decay which beset him, and fully convinced that his days were few and numbered, the seaman, who called himself Tom Daggett, had felt a desire to close his eyes in the place where they had first been opened to the light of day. He had persuaded the commander of the craft mentioned to bring him from the West Indies, and to put him ashore as related, the Vineyard being only a hundred miles or so to the eastward of Oyster Pond Point. He trusted to luck to give him the necessary opportunity of overcoming these last hundred miles.

Daggett was poor, as he admitted, as well as friendless and unknown. He had with him, nevertheless, a substantial sea-chest, one of those that the sailors of that day uniformly used in merchant-vessels, a man-of-war compelling them to carry their clothes in bags, for the convenience of compact stowage. The chest of Daggett, however, was a regular inmate of the forecastle, and, from its appearance, had made almost as many voyages as its owner. The last, indeed, was heard to say that he had succeeded in saving it from no less than three shipwrecks. It was a reasonably heavy chest, though its contents, when opened, did not seem to be of any very great value.

A few hours after landing this man had made a bargain with a middle-aged widow, in very humble circumstances, and who dwelt quite near to the residence of Deacon Pratt, to receive him as a temporary inmate ; or, until he could get a " chance across to the Vineyard." At first Daggett kept about, and was much in the open air. While able to walk he met the deacon, and singular—nay, unaccountable as it seemed to the niece—the uncle soon contracted a species of friendship for, not to say intimacy with, this stranger. In the first place, the deacon was a little particular in not having intimates among the necessitous, and the Widow White soon let it be known that her guest had not even a "red cent." He had chattels, however, that were of some estimation among seamen ; and Roswell Gardiner, or "Gar'ner," as he was called, the young seaman *par excellence* of the Point, one who had been not only a-whaling, but who had also been a-sealing, and who at that moment was on board the deacon's schooner, in the capacity of master, had been applied to for advice and assistance. By the agency of Mr. Gar'ner, as the young mate was then termed, sundry palms, sets of sail-needles, a fid or two, and various other similar articles, that obviously could no longer be of any use to Daggett, were sent across to the "Harbor," and disposed of there, to advantage, among the many seamen of the port. By these means the stranger was, for a few weeks, enabled to pay his way, the board he got being both poor and cheap.

A much better result attended this intercourse with Gardiner than that of raising the worn-out seaman's immediate ways and means. Between Mary Pratt and Roswell Gardiner there existed an intimacy of long standing for their years, as well as of some peculiar features, to which there will be occasion to advert hereafter. Mary was the very soul of charity in all its significations, and this Gardiner knew. When, therefore, Daggett became really necessitous, in the way of comforts that even money could not command beneath the roof of the Widow White, the young man let the fact be known to the deacon's niece, who immediately provided sundry delicacies that were acceptable to the palate of even disease. As for her uncle, nothing was at first said to him on the subject. Although his intimacy with Daggett went on increasing, and they were daily more and more together in long and secret conference, not a suggestion was ever made by the deacon in the way of contributing to his new friend's comforts. To own the truth, to give was the last idea that ever occurred to this man's thoughts.

Mary Pratt was observant, and of a mind so constituted that its observations usually led her to safe and accurate deductions. Great was the surprise of all on the Point when it became known that Deacon Pratt had purchased and put into the water the new sea-going craft that was building on speculation at Southold. Not only had he done this, but he had actually bought some half-worn copper, and had it placed on the schooner's bottom, as high as the bends, ere he had her launched. While the whole neighborhood was "exercised" with conjectures on the motive which could induce the deacon to become a ship-owner in his age, Mary did not fail to impute it to some secret but powerful influence that the sick stranger had obtained over him. He now spent nearly half his time in private communications with Daggett; and, on more than one occasion, when the niece had taken some light article of food over for the use of the last, she found him and her uncle examining one or two dirty and well-worn charts of the ocean. As she entered, the conversation invariably was changed; nor was Mrs. White ever permitted to be present at one of these secret conferences.

Not only was the schooner purchased, and coppered, and launched, and preparations made to fit her for sea, but "young Gar'ner" was appointed to command her! As respects Roswell Gardiner, or "Gar'ner," as it would be almost thought a breach of decorum, in Suffolk, not to call him, there was no mystery. Six-and-twenty years before the opening of our legend, he had been born on Oyster Pond itself, and of one of its best families. Indeed, he was known to be a descendant of Lyon Gardiner, that engineer who had been sent to the settlement of the lords Saye, and Seal, and Brook, since called Saybrook, near two centuries before, to lay out a town and a fort. This Lyon Gardiner had purchased of the Indians the island in that neighborhood which still bears his name. This establishment on the island was made in 1639; and now, at an interval of two hundred and nine years, it is in possession of its ninth owner, all having been of the name and blood of its original patentee. This is great antiquity for America, which, while it has produced many families of greater wealth and renown, and importance, than that of the Gardiners, has seldom produced any of more permanent local respectability. This is a feature in society that we so much love to see, and which is so much endangered by the uncertain and migratory habits of the people, that we pause a moment to record this instance of stability, so pleasing and so commendable, in an age and country of changes.

The descendants of any family of two centuries' standing will, as a matter of course, be numerous. There are exceptions, certainly; but it is the rule. Thus is it with

Lyon Gardiner and his progeny, who are now to be numbered in scores, including persons in all classes of life,
though it carries with it a stamp of caste to be known in
Suffolk as having come direct from the loins of old Lyon
Gardiner. Roswell, of that name, if not of that ilk, the island
then being the sole property of David Johnson Gardiner,
the predecessor and brother of its present proprietor, was
allowed to have this claim, though it would exceed our
genealogical knowledge to point out the precise line by
which this descent was claimed. Young Roswell was of
respectable blood on both sides, without being very brill-
iantly connected or rich. On the contrary, early left an
orphan, fatherless and motherless, as was the case with
Mary Pratt, he had been taken from a country academy
when only fifteen, and sent to sea, that he might make
his own way in the world. Hitherto his success had not
been of a very flattering character. He had risen, notwithstanding, to be the chief mate of a whaler, and bore
an excellent reputation among the people of Suffolk.
Had it only been a year or two later, when speculation
took hold of the whaling business in a large way, he would
not have had the least difficulty in obtaining a ship. As
it was, however, great was his delight when Deacon Pratt
engaged him as master of the new schooner, which had
been already named the Sea Lion, or Sea Lyon, as Roswell
sometimes affected to spell the word, in honor of his old
progenitor, the engineer.

Mary Pratt had noted all these proceedings, partly with
pain, partly with pleasure, but always with great interest.
It pained her to find her uncle, in the decline of life, engaging in a business about which he knew nothing. It
pained her still more to see one whom she loved from
habit, if not from moral sympathies, wasting the few hours
that remained for preparing for the last great change in
attempts to increase possessions that were already much
more than sufficient for his wants. This consideration, in
particular, deeply grieved Mary Pratt ; for she was profoundly pious, with a conscience that was so sensitive
as materially to interfere with her happiness, as will presently be shown, while her uncle was merely a deacon. It
is one thing to be a deacon, and another to be devoted to
the love of God, and to that love of our species which we
are told is the consequence of a love of the Deity. The
two are not incompatible ; neither are they identical. This
Mary had been made to see, in spite of all her wishes to

be blind as respects the particular subject from whom she had learned the unpleasant lesson. The pleasure felt by our heroine, for such we now announce Mary Pratt to be, was derived from the preferment bestowed on Roswell Gardiner. She had many a palpitation of the heart when she heard of his good conduct as a seaman, as she always did whenever she heard his professional career alluded to at all. On this point Roswell was without spot, as all Suffolk knew and confessed. On Oyster Pond he was regarded as a species of sea lion himself, so numerous and so exciting were the incidents that were related of his prowess among the whales. But there was a dark cloud before all these glories in the eyes of Mary Pratt, which for two years had disinclined her to listen to the young man's tale of love, which had induced her to decline accepting a hand that had now been offered to her, with a seaman's ardor, a seaman's frankness, and a seaman's sincerity, some twenty times at least, and which had induced her to struggle severely with her own heart, which she had long found to be a powerful ally of her suitor. That cloud came from a species of infidelity that is getting to be so widely spread in America as no longer to work in secret, but which lifts its head boldly among us, claiming openly to belong to one of the numerous sects of the land. Mary had reason to think that Roswell Gardiner denied the divinity of Christ, while he professed to honor and defer to him as a man far elevated above all other men, and as one whose blood had purchased the redemption of his race !

We will take this occasion to say that our legend is not polemical in any sense, and that we have no intention to enter into discussions or arguments connected with this subject, beyond those which we may conceive to be necessary to illustrate the picture which it is our real aim to draw —that of a confiding, affectionate, nay, devoted woman's heart, in conflict with a deep sense of religious duty.

Still, Mary rejoiced that Roswell Gardiner was to command the Sea Lion. Whither this little vessel, a schooner of about one hundred and forty tons measurement, was to sail, she had not the slightest notion ; but, go where it might, her thoughts and prayers were certain to accompany it. These are woman's means of exerting influence, and who shall presume to say that they are without results, and useless ? On the contrary, we believe them to be most efficacious ; and thrice happy is the man who, as he treads the mazes and wiles of the world, goes accompanied by the petitions of such gentle and pure-minded beings at home as seldom think of approaching the throne of grace without also thinking of him and of his necessities. The Romanists say, and say it rightly too, could one only believe in their efficacy, that the prayers they offer up in behalf of departed friends are of the most endearing nature ; but it would be difficult to prove that petitions for the souls of the dead can demonstrate greater interest, or bind the parties more closely together in the unity of love, than those that are constantly offered up in behalf of the living.

The interest that Mary Pratt felt in Roswell's success needs little explanation. In all things he was most agreeable to her, but in the one just mentioned. Their ages, their social positions, their habits, their orphan condition, even their prejudices—and who that dwells aside from the world is without them, when most of those who encounter its collisions still cherish them so strongly ? all united to render them of interest to each other. Nor was Deacon Pratt at all opposed to the connection ; on the contrary, he appeared rather to favor it.

The objections came solely from Mary, whose heart was nearly ready to break each time that she was required to urge them. As for the uncle, it is not easy to say what could induce him to acquiesce in, to favor indeed, the addresses to his niece and nearest relative, of one who was known not to possess five hundred dollars in the world. As his opinions on this subject were well known to all on Oyster Pond, they had excited a good deal of speculation ; "exercising" the whole neighborhood, as was very apt to be the case whenever anything occurred in the least out of the ordinary track. The several modes of reasoning were something like these :

Some were of opinion that the deacon forsaw a successful career to, and eventful prosperity in the habits and enterprise of the young mate, and that he was willing to commit to his keeping, not only his niece, but the three farms, his " money at use," and certain shares he was known to own in a whaler, and no less than three coasters, as well as an interest in a store at Southold ; that is to say, to commit them all to the keeping of " young Gar'ner," when he was himself dead ; for no one believed he would part with more than Mary, in his own lifetime.

Others fancied he was desirous of getting the orphan off

his hands, in the easiest possible way, that he might make a bequest of his whole estate to the theological institution that had been coquetting with him now, for several years, through its recognized agents, and to which he had already made the liberal donation of one hundred dollars. It was well ascertained that the agents of that institution openly talked of getting Deacon Pratt to sit for his portrait, in order that it might be suspended among those of others of its benefactors.

A third set reasoned differently from both the foregoing. The "Gar'ners" were a better family than the Pratts, and the deacon being so "well to do," it was believed by these persons that he was disposed to unite money with name, and thus give to his family consideration from a source that was somewhat novel in its history. This class of reasoners was quite small, however, and mainly consisted of those who had rarely been off of Oyster Pond, and who passed their days with "Gar'ner's Island" directly before their eyes. A few of the gossips of this class pretended to say that their own young sailor stood next in succession after the immediate family actually in possession should run out, of which there was then some prospect ; and that the deacon, sly fellow, knew all about it ! For this surmise, to prevent useless expectations in the reader, it may be well to say at once, there was no foundation whatever, Roswell's connection with the owner of the island being much too remote to give him any chance of succeeding to that estate, or to anything else that belonged to him.

There was a fourth and last set among those who speculated on the deacon's favor toward "young Gar'ner," and these were they who fancied that the old man had opened his heart toward the young couple, and was disposed to render a deserving youth and a beloved niece happy. This was the smallest class of all ; and, what is a little remarkable, it contained only the most reckless and least virtuous of all those who dwelt on Oyster Pond. The parson of the parish, or the Pastor as he was usually termed, belonged to the second category, that good man being firmly impressed that most, if not all, of Deacon Pratt's worldly effects would eventually go to help propagate the gospel.

Such was the state of things when the deacon returned from meeting, as related in the opening chapter. At his niece's suggestion of sending to the Harbor for Dr. Sage, he had demurred, not only on account of the expense, but for a still more cogent reason. To tell the truth, he was exceedingly distrustful of any one's being admitted to a communication with Daggett, who had revealed to him matters that he deemed to be of great importance, but who still retained the key to his most material mystery. Nevertheless, decency, to say nothing of the influence of what folks "would say," the Archimedean lever of all society of puritanical origin, exhorted him to consent to his niece's proposal.

"It is such a roundabout road to get to the Harbor, Mary," the uncle slowly objected, after a pause.

"Boats often go there, and return in a few hours."

"Yes, yes—*boats ;* but I'm not certain it is lawful to work boats of a Sabbath, child."

"I believe, sir, it was deemed lawful to do good on the Lord's day."

"Yes, if a body was certain it *would* do any good. To be sure, Sage is a capital doctor—as good as any going in these parts—but, half the time, money paid for doctor's stuff is thrown away."

"Still, I think it our duty to try to serve a fellow-creature that is in distress ; and Daggett, I fear, will not go through the week, if indeed he go through the night. '

"I should be sorry to have him die !" exclaimed the deacon, looking really distressed at this intelligence. "Right sorry should I be to have him die—just yet."

The last two words were uttered unconsciously, and in a way to cause the niece to regret that they had been uttered at all. But they had come, notwithstanding, and the deacon saw that he had been too frank. The fault could not now be remedied, and he was fain to allow his words to produce their own effect.

"Die he will, I fear, uncle," returned Mary, after a short pause ; "and sorry should I be to have it so without our feeling the consolation of knowing we had done all in our power to save him, or to serve him."

"It is so far to the Harbor, that no good might come of a messenger ; and the money paid *him* would be thrown away, too."

"I dare say Roswell Gar'ner would be glad to go to help a fellow-creature who is suffering. *He* would not think of demanding any pay."

"Yes, that is true. I will say this for Gar'ner, that he is as reasonable a young man, when he does an odd job, as any one I know. I like to employ him."

Mary understood this very well. It amounted to neither

more nor less than the deacon's perfect consciousness that the youth had, again and again, given him his time and his services gratuitously ; and that, too, more than once, under circumstances when it would have been quite proper that he should look for a remuneration. A slight color stole over the face of the niece as memory recalled to her mind these different occasions. Was that sensitive blush owing to her perceiving the besetting weakness of one who stood in the light of a parent to her, and toward whom she endeavored to feel the affection of a child? We shall not gainsay this, so far as a portion of the feeling which produced that blush was concerned ; but, certain it is, that the thought that Roswell had exerted himself to oblige *her* uncle, obtruded itself somewhat vividly among her other recollections.

"Well, sir," the niece resumed, after another brief pause, "we can send for Roswell, if you think it best, and ask him to do the poor man this act of kindness."

"Your messengers after doctors are always in such a hurry! I dare say Gar'ner would think it necessary to hire a horse to cross Shelter Island, and then perhaps a boat to get across to the Harbor. If no boat was to be found, it might be another horse to gallop away round the head of the Bay. Why, five dollars would scarce meet the cost of such a race!"

"If five dollars were needed, Roswell would pay them out of his own pocket, rather than ask another to assist him in doing an act of charity. But, no horse will be necessary ; the whale-boat is at the wharf, and is ready for use at any moment."

"True, I had forgotten the whale-boat. If that is home the doctor might be brought across at a reasonable rate ; especially if Gar'ner will volunteer. I dare say Daggett's effects will pay the bill for attendance, since they have answered, as yet, to meet the Widow White's charges. As I live, here comes Gar'ner at this moment, and just as we want him."

"I knew of no other to ask to cross the bays, sir, and sent for Roswell before you returned. Had you not got back as you did, I should have taken on myself the duty of sending for the doctor."

"In which case, girl, you would have made yourself liable. I have too many demands on my means to be scattering dollars broadcast. But, here is Gar'ner, and I dare say all will be made right."

Gardiner now joined the uncle and niece, who had held this conversation in the porch, having hastened up from the schooner the instant he received Mary's summons. He was rewarded by a kind look and a friendly shake of the hand, each of which was slightly more cordial than those that prudent and thoughtful young woman was accustomed to bestow on him. He saw that Mary was a little earnest in her manner, and looked curious, as well as interested, to learn why he had been summoned at all. Sunday was kept so rigidly at the deacon's that the young man did not dare visit the house until after the sun had set; the New England practice of commencing the Sabbath of a Saturday evening, and bringing it to a close at the succeeding sunset, prevailing among most of the people of Suffolk, the Episcopalians forming nearly all the exceptions to the usage. Sunday evening, consequently, was in great request for visits, it being the favorite time for the young people to meet, as they were not only certain to be unemployed, but to be in their best. Roswell Gardiner was in the practice of visiting Mary Pratt on Sunday evenings ; but he would almost as soon think of desecrating a church, as think of entering the deacon's abode, on the Sabbath, until after sunset, or "sun*down*," to use the familiar Americanism that is commonly applied to this hour of the day. Here he was now, however, wondering, and anxious to learn why he had been sent for.

"Roswell," said Mary earnestly, slightly coloring again as she spoke, "we have a great favor to ask. You know the poor old sailor who has been staying at the Widow White's this month or more—he is now very low; so low, we think he ought to have better advice than can be found on Oyster Pond, and we wish to get Dr. Sage over from the Harbor. How to do it has been the question, when I thought of you. If you could take the whale-boat and go across, the poor man might have the benefit of the doctor's advice in the course of a few hours."

"Yes," put in the uncle, "and I shall charge nothing for the use of the boat ; so that, if *you* volunteer, Gar'ner, it will leave so much toward settling up the man's accounts, when settling-day comes."

Roswell Gardiner understood both uncle and niece perfectly. The intense selfishness of the first was no more a secret to him than was the entire disinterestedness of the last. He gazed a moment, in fervent admiration, at Mary ; then he turned to the deacon, and professed his readiness to "volunteer." Knowing the man so well, he took care distinctly to express the word, so as to put the mind of this votary of Mammon at ease.

"Gar'ner will *volunteer*, then," rejoined the uncle, "and I shall charge nothing for the use of the boat. This is 'doing as we would be done by,' and is all right, considering that Daggett is sick and among strangers. The wind is fair, or nearly fair, to go and to come back, and you'll make a short trip of it. Yes, it will cost nothing, and may do the poor man good."

"Now go at once, Roswell," said Mary, in an entreating manner; "and show the same skill in managing the boat that you did the day you won the race against the Harbor oarsmen."

"I will do all that a man can, to oblige you, Mary, as well as to serve the sick. If Dr. Sage should not be at home, am I to look for another physician, Mr. Pratt?"

"Sage *must* be at home—we can employ no other. Your old, long-established physicians understand how to consider practice, and don't make mistakes—by the way, Gar'ner, you needn't mention *my* name in the business at all. Just say that a sick man, at the Widow White's, needs his services, and that you had *volunteered* to take him across. *That* will bring him—I know the man."

Again Gardiner understood what the deacon meant. He was just as desirous of not paying the physician as of not paying the messenger. Mary understood him, too, and, with a face more sad than anxiety had previously made it, she walked into the house, leaving her uncle and lover in the porch. After a few more injunctions from the former, in the way of prudent precaution, the latter departed, hurrying down to the water-side in order to take the boat.

CHAPTER III.

"All that glisters is not gold,
  Often have you heard that told ;
Many a man his life hath sold,
  But my outside to behold."
        —Merchant of Venice.

No sooner was Deacon Pratt left alone, than he hastened to the humble dwelling of the Widow White. The disease of Daggett was a general decay, that was not attended with much suffering. He was now seated in a homely armchair, and was able to converse. He was not aware, indeed, of the real danger of his case, and still had hopes of surviving many years. The deacon came in at the door, just as the widow had passed through it, on her way to visit another crone, who lived hard by, and with whom she was in the constant habit of consulting. She had seen the deacon in the distance, and took that occasion to run across the road, having a sort of instinctive notion that her presence was not required when the two men conferred together. What was the subject of their frequent private communications, the Widow White did not exactly know ; but what she imagined, will in part appear in her discourse with her neighbor, the Widow Stone.

"Here's the deacon, ag'in !" cried the Widow White, as she bolted hurriedly into her friend's presence. "This makes the third time he has been at *my* house since yesterday morning. What *can* he mean ?"

"Oh! I dare say, Betsy, he means no more than to visit the sick, as he pretends is the reason of his many visits."

"You forget it is Sabba' day !" added the Widow White, with emphasis.

"The better day, the better deed, Betsy."

"I know that ; but it's dreadful often for a *man* to visit the sick—three times in twenty-four hours !"

"Yes ; 'twould have been more nat'ral for a woman, a body must own," returned the Widow Stone, a little dryly. "Had the deacon been a woman, I dare say, Betsy, you would not have thought so much of his visits."

"I should think nothing of them at all," rejoined the sister widow, innocently enough. "But it is dreadful odd in a *man* to be visiting about among the sick so much—and he a deacon of the meeting !"

"Yes, it is not as common as it might be, particularly among deacons. But, come in, Betsy, and I will show you the text from which the minister preached this morning. It's well worth attending to, for it touches on our forlorn state." Hereupon, the two relicts entered an inner room, where we shall leave them to discuss the merits of the sermon, interrupted by many protestations on the part of the Widow White, concerning the "dreadful" character of Deacon Pratt's many visits to *her* cottage, "Sabba' days" as well as week days.

In the meanwhile, the interview between the deacon himself, and the sick mariner, had its course. After the first salutations, and the usual inquiries, the visitor, with some parade of manner, alluded to the fact that he had sent for a physician for the other's benefit.

"I did it of my own head," added the deacon ; "or, I might better say, of my own heart. It was unpleasant to me to witness your sufferings, without doing something to alleviate them. To alleviate sorrow, and pain, and the throes of conscience, is one of the most pleasant of all the Christian offices. Yes, I have sent young Gar'ner across the bays, to the Harbor ; and three or four hours hence we may look for him back, with Dr. Sage in his boat."

"I only hope I shall have the means to pay for all this expense and trouble, deacon," returned Daggett, in a sort of doubting way, that, for a moment, rendered his friend exceedingly uncomfortable. "Go, I know I must, sooner or later ; but could I only live to get to the Vineyard, it would be found that my share of the old homestead would make up for all my wants. I *may* live to see the end of the other business."

Among the other tales of Daggett, was one which said that he had never yet received his share of his father's property ; an account that was true enough, though the truth might have shown that the old man had left nothing worth dividing. He had been a common mariner, like the son, and had left behind him a common mariner's estate. The deacon mused a moment, and then he took an occasion to advert to the subject that had now been uppermost in his thoughts ever since he had been in the habit of holding secret conferences with the sick man. What that subject was, will appear in the course of the conversation that ensued.

"Have you thought of the chart, Daggett," asked the deacon, "and given an eye to that journal ?"

"Both, sir. Your kindness to me has been so great, that I am not a man apt to forget it."

"I wish you would show me, yourself, the precise place on the chart, where them islands are to be found. There is nothing like seeing a thing with one's own eyes."

"You forget my oath, Deacon Pratt. Every man on us took his bible oath not to point out the position of the islands, until a'ter the year 1820. Then, each and all on us is at liberty to do as he pleases. But, the chart is in my chest, and not only the islands, but the key, is so plainly laid down, that any mariner could find 'em. With that chest, however, I cannot part, so long as I live. Get me well, and I will sail in the Sea Lion, and tell your captain Gar'ner all he will have occasion to know. The man's fortune will be made who first gets to either of them places."

"Yes, I can imagine that, easy enough, from your accounts, Daggett—but, how am I to be certain that some other vessel will not get the start of me?"

"Because the secret is now my own. There was but seven on us, in that brig, all told. Of them seven, four died at the islands of the fever, homeward bound; and of the other three, the captain was drowned in the squall I told you of, when he was washed overboard. That left only Jack Thompson and me; and Jack, I think, must be the very man whose death I see'd, six months since, as being killed by a whale on the False Banks."

"Jack Thompson is so common a name, a body never knows. Besides, if he was killed by that whale, he may have told the secret to a dozen before the accident."

"There's his oath ag'in it. Jack was sworn, as well as all on us, and he was a man likely to stand by what he swore to. This was none of your custom-house oaths, of which a chap might take a dozen of a morning, and all should be false; but it was an oath that put a seaman on his honor, since it was a good-fellowship affair, all round."

Deacon Pratt did not *tell* Daggett that Thompson might have as good reasons for disregarding the oath as he had himself; but he *thought* it. These are things that no wise man utters on such occasions; and this opinion touching the equality of the obligation of that oath was one of them.

"There is another hold upon Jack," continued Daggett, after reflecting a moment. "He never could make any fist of latitude and longitude at all, and he kept no journal. Now, should he get it wrong, he and his friends might hunt a year without finding either of the places."

"You think there was no mistake in the pirate's account of that key, and of the buried treasure?" asked the deacon, anxiously.

"I would swear to the truth of what *he* said, as freely as if I had seen the box myself. They was necessitated, as you may suppose, or they never would have left so much gold, in sich an uninhabited place; but leave it they did, on the word of a dying man."

"Dying?—You mean the pirate, I suppose?"

"To be sure I do. We was shut up in the same prison,

3

and we talked the matter over at least twenty times, before he was swung off. When they were satisfied I had nothing to do with the pirates, I was cleared ; and I was on my way to the Vineyard, to get some craft or other, to go a'ter these two treasures (for one is just as much a treasure as t'other) when I was put ashore here. It's much the same to me, whether the craft sails from Oyster Pond or from the Vineyard."

"Of course. Well, as much to oblige you, and to put your mind at rest, as anything else, I've bought this Sea Lion, and engaged young Roswell Gar'ner to go out in her, as her master. She'll be ready to sail in a fortnight, and, if things turn out as you say, a good voyage will she make. All interested in her will have reason to rejoice. I see but one thing needful just now, and that is, that you should give me the chart at once, in order that I may study it well, before the schooner sails."

"Do you mean to make the v'y'ge yourself, deacon ?" asked Daggett, in some surprise.

"Not in person, certainly," was the answer. "I'm getting somewhat too old to leave home for so long a time ; and, though born and brought up in sight of salt-water, I've never tried it beyond a trip to York, or one to Boston. Still, I shall have my property in the adventure, and it's nat'ral to keep an eye on *that*. Now, the chart well studied beforehand would be much more useful, it seems to me, than it can possibly be if taken up at a late hour."

"There will be time enough for Captain Gar'ner to overhaul his chart well, afore he reaches either of his ports," returned the mariner, evasively. "If I sail with him, as I suppose I *must*, nothing will be easier than for me to give all the courses and distances."

This reply produced a long and brooding silence. By this time the reader will have got a clew to the nature of the secret that was discussed so much and so often between these two men. Daggett, finding himself sick, poor, and friendless, among strangers, had early cast about him for the means of obtaining an interest with those who might serve him. He had soon got an insight into the character of Deacon Pratt, from the passing remarks of the Widow White, who was induced to allude to the uncle in consequence of the charitable visits of the niece. One day, when matters appeared to be at a very low ebb with him, and shortly after he had been put ashore, the sick mariner requested an interview with the deacon himself. The request had been reluctantly granted; but, during the visit, Daggett had managed so well to whet his visitor's appetite for gain, that henceforth there was no trouble in procuring the deacon's company. Little by little had Daggett let out his facts, always keeping enough in reserve to render himself necessary, until he had got his new acquaintance in the highest state of feverish excitement. The schooner was purchased, and all the arrangements necessary to her outfit were pressed forward as fast as prudence would at all allow. The chart, and the latitude and longitude, were the circumstances over which Daggett retained the control. These he kept to himself, though he averred that he had laid down on the charts that were in his chest the two important points which had been the subjects of his communications.

Although this man had been wily in making his revelations, and had chosen his confidant with caution and sagacity, most of that which he related was true. He had belonged to a sealer that had been in a very high southern latitude, where it had made some very important discoveries touching the animals that formed the objects of its search. It was possible to fill a vessel in those islands in a few weeks; and the master of the sealer, Daggett having been his mate, had made all his people swear on their "bible oaths" not to reveal the facts, except under prescribed circumstances. His own vessel was full when he made the discoveries, but misfortune befell her on her homeward-bound passage, until she was herself totally lost in the West Indies, and that in a part of the ocean where he had no business to be.

In consequence of these several calamities, Daggett and one more man were the sole living depositories of the important information. These men separated, and, as stated, Daggett had reason to think that his former shipmate had been recently killed by a whale. The life and movements of a sailor are usually as eccentric as the career of a comet. After the loss of the sealing-vessel, Daggett remained in the West Indies and on the Spanish Main for some time, until, falling into evil company, he was imprisoned on a charge of piracy, in company with one who better deserved the imputation. While in the same cell the pirate had made a relation of all the incidents of a very eventful life. Among other things revealed was the fact that, on a certain occasion, he and two others had deposited a very considerable amount of treasure on a key that he described very minutely, and which he now bestowed on Daggett as some compensation for his present unmerited sufferings, his companions having both been drowned by the upsetting of their boat on the return from the key in question. Subsequently, this pirate had been executed, and Daggett liberated. He was not able to get to the key without making friends and confidants on whom he could rely, and he was actually making the best of his way to Martha's Vineyard with that intent, when put ashore on Oyster Pond. In most of that which this man had related to the deacon, therefore, he had told the truth, though it was the truth embellished, as is so apt to be the case with men of vulgar minds. He might have been misled by the narrative of the pirate, but it was his own opinion that he had not been. The man was a Scot, prudent, wary, and sagacious; and in the revelations he made he appeared to be governed by a conviction that his own course was run, and that it was best that his secret should not die with him. Daggett had rendered him certain services, too, and gratitude might have had some influence.

"My mind has been much exercised with this matter of the hidden gold," resumed the deacon, after the long pause already mentioned. "You will remember that there may be lawful owners of that money, should Gar'ner even succeed in finding it."

"'Twould be hard for 'em to prove their claims, sir, if what McGosh told me was true. Accordin' to his account, the gold came from all sides—starboard and larboard, as a body might say—and it was jumbled together, and so mixed, that a young girl could not pick out her lover's keepsake from among the other pieces. 'Twas the 'arnin's of three years' cruisin', as I understood him to say; and much of the stuff had been exchanged in port, especially to get the custom-house officers and king's officers out of its wake. There's king's officers among them bloody Spaniards, Deacon Pratt, all the same as among the English."

"Be temperate in your language, friend; a rough speech is unseemly, particularly on the Lord's day."

Daggett rolled the tobacco over his tongue, and his eyes twinkled with a sort of leer, which indicated that the fellow was not without some humor. He submitted patiently to the rebuke, however, making no remonstrance against its reception.

"No, no," he added presently, "a starn chase, they say,

is a long chase; and the owners of them doubloons, if owners they can now be called, must be out of sight long before this. Accordin' to McGosh, some of the gold r'aally captured had passed back through the hands of them that sent it to sea, and they did not know their own children!"

"It is certainly hard to identify coin, and it would be a bold man who should stand up in open court, and make oath to its being the same he had once held. I have heaid of the same gold's having answered the purposes of twenty banks, one piece being so like another."

"Ay, ay, sir, gold is gold; and any of it is good enough for me, though doubloons is my favor*ites*. When a fellow has got half-a-dozen doubloons alongside of his ribs he can look the landlord full in the eye; and no one thinks of saying to sich as he, 'It's time to think of shipping ag'in.'"

From the nature of this discourse, it will not be easy for the reader to imagine the real condition of Daggett. At the very moment he was thus conversing of money, and incidentally manifesting his expectations of accompanying Roswell Gardiner in the expedition that was about to sail, the man had not actually four-and-twenty hours of life in him. Mary Pratt had foreseen his true state, accustomed as she was to administer to the wants of the dying; but no one else appeared to be aware of it, not even the deacon. It was true that the fellow spoke, as it might be, from his throat only, and that his voice was hollow, and sometimes reduced to a whisper; but he ascribed this, himself, to the circumstance that he had taken a cold. Whether the deacon believed this account or not, it might be difficult to say; but he appeared to give it full credit. Perhaps his mind was so much occupied with the subject of his discussion with Daggett that it did not sufficiently advert to the real condition of the man.

Twice that afternoon did Deacon Pratt go between the cottage of the Widow White and his own dwelling. As often did the relict fly across the way to express her wonder to the Widow Stone at the frequency of the rich man's visits. The second time that he came was when he saw the whale-boat rounding the end of Shelter Island, and he perceived, by means of his glass, that Dr. Sage was in it. At this sight the deacon hurried off to the cottage again, having something to say to Daggett that could no longer be delayed.

"The whale-boat will soon be in," he observed, as soon as he had taken his seat, "and we shall shortly have the doctor here. That young Gar'ner does what he has to do, always, with a jerk! There was no such haste, but he seems to be ever in a hurry!"

"Do what is to be done at once, and then lie by, is the sailor's rule, deacon," rejoined the mariner. "Squalls, and gusts, and reefin', and brailin' up, and haulin' down, won't wait for the seaman's leisure. *His* work must be done at once, or it will not be done at all. I'm not afeard of the doctor; so let him come as soon as he pleases. Medicine can't hurt a body, if he don't take it."

"There's one thing I wish to say to you, Daggett, before Dr. Sage comes in. Talking too much may excite you, especially talking of matters that are of interest; and you may give him a false impression of your state should you get the pulse up and the cheek flushed by over-talking."

"I understand you, deacon. My secret is my secret, and no doctor shall get it out of me as long as I know what I say. I'm not so friendly with them as to seek counsel among doctors."

"Then it's the Lord's day," added the Pharisee, "and it is not seemly to dwell too much on worldly interests on the Sabbath."

A novice might have been surprised, after what had passed, at the exceeding coolness with which the deacon uttered this sentiment. Daggett was not so in the least, however; for he had taken the measure of his new confidant's conscience, and had lived long enough to know how marked was the difference between professions and practice. Nothing, indeed, is more common than to meet with those who denounce that in others which is of constant occurrence with themselves; and who rail at vices that are so interwoven with their own moral being as to compose integral portions of their existence. As for the deacon, he really thought it would be unseemly, and of evil example, for Daggett to converse with Dr. Sage touching these doubloons on the Lord's day; while he had felt no scruples himself, a short hour before, to make them the theme of a long and interesting discussion in his own person. It might not repay us for the trouble to look for the salve that the worthy man applied to his own conscience by way of reconciling the apparent contradiction; though it probably was connected with some fancied and especial duty on his part of taking care of the sick man's secrets. Sickness, it is well known, forms the apology for many an error, both of omission and commission

Dr. Sage now arrived ; a shrewd, observant, intelligent man, who had formerly represented the district in which he lived in Congress. He was skilful in his profession, and soon made up his mind concerning the state of his patient. As the deacon never left him for a moment, to him he first communicated his opinion, after the visit, as the two walked back toward the well-known dwelling of the Pratts.

"This poor man is in the last stages of a decline," said the physician, coolly, "and medicine can do him no good. He *may* live a month ; though it would not surprise me to hear of his death in an hour."

"Do you think his time so short ! " exclaimed the deacon ; "I was in hopes he might last until the Sea Lion goes out, and that a voyage might help to set him up."

"Nothing will ever set him up again, deacon, you may depend on that. No sea-voyage will do him any good ; and it is better that he should remain on shore, on account of the greater comforts he will get. Does he belong on Oyster Pond ? "

"He comes from somewhere east," answered the deacon, careful not to let the doctor know the place whence the stranger had come, though to little purpose, as will presently be seen. "He has neither friend nor acquaintance here ; though I should think his effects sufficient to meet all charges."

"Should they not be, he is welcome to my visit," answered the doctor, promptly ; for he well understood the deacon's motive in making the remark. "I have enjoyed a pleasant sail across the bays with young Gar'ner, who has promised to take me back again. I like boating, and am always better for one of these sailing excursions. Could I carry my patients along, half of them would be benefited by the pure air and the exercise."

"It's a grateful thing to meet with one of your temperament, doctor ; but Daggett——"

"Is this man named Daggett ? " interrupted the physician.

"I *believe* that is what he calls himself, though a body never is certain of what such people say."

"That's true, deacon ; your rambling, houseless sailor is commonly a great liar—at least, so have I always found

him. Most of their log-books will not do to read ; or, for
that matter, to be written out, in full. But if this man's
name is really Daggett, he must come from the Vineyard.
There are Daggetts there in scores ; yes, he must be a
Vineyard man."

"There are Daggetts in Connecticut, as I know, of a certainty——"

"We all know that, for it is a name of weight there ; but
the Vineyard is the cradle of the breed. The man has a
Vineyard look about him, too. I dare say, now, he has
not been home for many a day."

The deacon was in an agony. He was menaced with the
very thing he was in the hope of staving off, or a discussion
on the subject of the sick man's previous life. The doctor
was so mercurial and quick of apprehension, that, once
fairly on the scent, he was nearly certain he would extract
everything from the patient. This was the principal reason why the deacon did not wish to send for him ; the expense, though a serious objection to one so niggardly, being of secondary consideration when so many doubloons
were at stake. It was necessary, however, to talk on
boldly, as any appearance of hesitation might excite the
doctor's distrust. The answers, therefore, came instantaneously.

"It may be as you say, doctor," returned the deacon ; "for
them Vineyard folks (Anglicé folk) are great wanderers."

"That are they. I had occasion to pass a day there, a
few years since, on my way to Boston, and I found five
women on the island to one man. It must be a particularly
conscientious person who could pass a week there, and escape committing the crime of bigamy. As for your bach-
elors, I have heard that a poor wretch of that description,
who unluckily found himself cast ashore there, was married
three times the same morning."

As the doctor was a little of a wag, Deacon Pratt did not
deem it necessary religiously to believe all that now escaped
him ; but he was glad to keep him in this vein, in order to
prevent his getting again on the track of Daggett's early
life. The device succeeded, Martha's Vineyard being a
standing joke for all in that quarter of the world, on the
subject of the ladies.

Mary was in the porch to receive her uncle and the physician. It was unnecessary for her to ask any questions,
for her speaking countenance said all that was required,
in order to obtain an answer.

"He's in a bad way, certainly, young lady," observed the doctor, taking a seat on one of the benches, "and I can give no hope. How long he may live is another matter. If he has friends whom he wishes to see, or if he has any affairs to settle, the truth should be told him at once, and no time lost."

"He knows nothing of his friends," interrupted the deacon, quite thrown off his guard by his own eagerness, and unconscious, at the moment, of the manner in which he was committing himself on the subject of a knowledge of the sick man's birth-place, "not having been on the Vineyard, or heard from there, since he first left home, quite fifty years since."

The doctor saw the contradiction, and it set him thinking, and conjecturing, but he was too discreet to betray himself. An explanation there probably was, and he trusted to time to ascertain it.

"What has become of Captain Gar'ner?" he asked, looking curiously around, as if he expected to find him tied to the niece's apron-string.

Mary blushed, but she was too innocent to betray any real confusion.

"He has gone back to the schooner, in order to have the boat ready for your return."

"And that return must take place, young lady, as soon as I have drunk two cups of your tea. I have patients at the Harbor who must yet be visited this evening, and the wind goes down with the sun. Let the poor man take the draughts I have left for him—they will soothe him, and help his breathing—more than this my skill can do nothing for him. Deacon, you need say nothing of this visit —I am sufficiently repaid by the air, the sail, and Miss Mary's welcome. I perceive that she is glad to see me, and that is something, between so young a woman and so old a man. And now for the two cups of tea."

The tea was drunk, and the doctor took his leave, shaking his head as he repeated to the niece, that the medical science could do nothing for the sick man.

"Let his friends know his situation at once, deacon," he said, as they walked toward the wharf where the whale-boat was all ready for a start. "There is not an hour to lose. Now I think of it, the Flash, Captain Smith, is to take a cargo of oil to Boston, and sails to-morrow. I can write a line by her, as it is ten to one she will go into the Hole. All our craft get into that Hole, or into Tarpaulin

Cove, before they venture across the Shoals ; and a letter addressed to any person of the name of Daggett might find the right man. I'll write it this very evening."

The announcement of this intention threw the deacon into a cold-sweat, but he did not think it prudent to say aught against it. He had bought the Sea Lion, engaged Roswell Gardiner, and otherwise expended a large sum of money, in the expectation of handling those doubloons, to say nothing of the furs ; and here was a chance of all his calculations being defeated by the interference of impertinent and greedy relatives! There was no remedy but patience, and this the deacon endeavored to exercise.

Deacon Pratt did not accompany the doctor beyond the limits of his own orchard. It was not deemed seemly for a member of the meeting to be seen walking out on the Sabbath, and this was remembered in season to prevent neighborly comments. It is true the *doctor* might furnish an apology ; but your strictly religious people, when they undertake the care of other people's consciences, do not often descend to these particulars.

No sooner had Gardiner and the physician re-embarked, than the deacon returned to the cottage of the Widow White. Here he had another long and searching discourse with the sick mariner. Poor Daggett was wearied with the subject ; but Dr. Sage's predictions of an early termination of the case, and the possibility that kinsmen might cross over from the " Vineyard," in order to learn what the long-absent man had in his possession, acted on him as keen incentives. By learning the most material facts now, the Sea Lion might get so far ahead of all competitors as to secure the prizes, even should Daggett let others into the secret, and start another vessel on the same expedition. His own schooner was nearly ready for sea, whereas time would be needed in order to make an entire outfit.

But Daggett did not appear to be disposed to be more communicative than heretofore. He went over the narrative of the discovery of the sealing-island, and gave a graphic account of the number and tame condition of the animals who frequented it. A man might walk in their midst without giving the smallest alarm In a word, all that a gang of good hands would have to do would be to kill and skin, and secure the oil. It would be like picking up dollars on a sea-beach. Sadly ! sadly ! indeed, was the deacon's cupidity excited by this account ; a vivid picture of whales or seals having some such effect on the imagination of a true Suffolk County man, or more properly on that of an East-ender, as those who live beyond Riverhead are termed, as a glowing account of a prairie covered with wheat has on that of a Wolverine or a Buckeye; or an enumeration of cent. per cent. has on the feelings of a Wall-street broker. Never before had Deacon Pratt been so much "exercised" with a love of Mammon. The pirate's tale, which was also recapitulated with much gusto, scarce excited him as much as Daggett's glowing account of the number, condition, and size of the seals.

Nothing was withheld but the latitudes and longitudes. No art of the deacon's, and he practised many, could extort from the mariner these most material facts, without which all the rest were useless; and the old man worked himself into a fever almost as high as that which soon came over Daggett in the effort to come at these facts—but all in vain.

At that hour the pulse of the sick man usually quickened; but on this occasion it fairly thumped. He had excited himself as well as his listener; and the inconsiderate manner in which both had yielded up their energies to these enticing images of wealth contributed largely to increase the evil. At length exhaustion came to put an end to the scene, which was getting to be dramatic as well as revolting.

So conscious was the deacon on returning home that evening, that his mind was not in such a condition as it behooved him to keep it on the Lord's day, that he was afraid to encounter the placid eye of his devout and single-minded niece. Instead of joining her and uniting in the services that were customary at that hour, he walked in the adjoining orchard until near nine o'clock. Mammon was uppermost in the place of the Deity, and habit offered too strong a barrier to permit him to bring, as it were, the false god openly into the presence of the true.

CHAPTER IV.

"Oh! mourn not for them, their grief is o'er,
 Oh! weep not for them, they weep no more;
 For deep is their sleep, though cold and hard
 Their pillow may be in the old kirk-yard."—BAYLY.

EARLY on the succeeding morning the whole household of Deacon Pratt, himself included, were up and doing. It was as the sun came up out of the waters that Mary and her uncle met in the porch, as if to greet each other.

"Yonder comes the Widow White, and seemingly in a great hurry," said the niece, anxiously. "I am afraid her patient is worse!"

"He seemed better when I left him last evening, though a little tired with talking," returned the uncle. "The man *would* talk, do all I could to stop him. I wanted to get but two or three words from him, and he used a thousand, without once using the few I wished most to hear. A talking man is that Daggett, I can tell you, Mary!"

"He'll never talk ag'in, deacon!" exclaimed the Widow White, who had got so near as to hear the concluding words of the last speaker—"He'll never say good or evil more!"

The deacon was so confounded as to be speechless. As for Mary, she expressed her deep regrets that the summons should have been so sudden, and that the previous preparation was so small; matters that gave her far more concern than any other consideration. They were not long left to conjectures, the voluble widow soon supplying all the facts that had occurred. It appeared that Daggett died in the night, the widow having found him stiff and cold on visiting his bedside a few minutes before. That this somewhat unexpected event, as to the time at least, was hastened by the excitement of the conversation mentioned, there can be little doubt, though no comment was made on the circumstance. The immediate cause of death was suffocation from the effects of suppuration, as so often occurs in rapid consumption.

It would be representing Deacon Pratt as a worse man than he actually was, to say that this sudden death had no effect on his feelings. For a short time it brought him back to a sense of his own age, and condition, and prospects. For half an hour these considerations troubled him, but the power of Mammon gradually resumed its sway, and the unpleasant images slowly disappeared in others that he found more agreeable. Then he began seriously to bethink him of what the circumstances required to be done.

As there was nothing unusual in the death of Daggett, the investigations of the coroner were not required. It was clearly a natural, though a sudden death. It remained, therefore, only to give directions about the funeral, and to have an eye to the safe-keeping of the effects of the deceased. The deacon assumed the duty of taking charge of everything. The chest of Daggett was removed to his house for safe-keeping, the key having been taken from the pocket of his vest, and the necessary orders were given for the final disposition of the body.

The deacon had another serious, and even painful half hour, when he first looked upon the corpse. There it lay, a senseless shell, deserted by its immortal tenant, and totally unconscious of that subject which had so lately and so intensely interested them both. It appeared as if the ghastly countenance expressed its sense of the utter worthlessness of all earthly schemes of wealth and happiness. Eternity seemed stamped upon the pinched and sunken features ; not eternity in the sense of imperishable matter, but in the sense of the fate of man. Had all the gold of the Indies laid within his reach, the arm of Daggett was now powerless to touch it. His eye could no longer gloat upon treasure, nor any part of his corporeal system profit by its possession. A more striking commentary on the vanity of human wishes could not, just then, have been offered to the consideration of the deacon. His moral being was very strangely constituted From early childhood he had been accustomed to the cant of religion ; and, in many instances, impressions had been made on him that produced effects that it was easy to confound with the fruits that real piety brings forth. This is a result that we often find in a state of society in which appearances are made to take the place of reality. What is more, it is a result that we may look for equally among the formalists of established sects, and among the descendants of those who once deserted the homes of their fathers in order to escape from the impiety of so meretricious an abuse of the substance of godliness. In the case of the latter, appearances occupy the mind more than that love of God which is the one great test of human conversion from sin to an improving state of that holiness, without which we are told no man shall see his Creator ; without which, indeed, no man could endure to look upon that dread Being face to face.

The deacon had all the forms of godliness in puritanical perfection. He had never taken the "name of his God in vain," throughout the course of a long life ; but he had abstained from this revolting and gratuitous sin, more because it was a part of the teachings of his youth so to do, and because the neighbors would have been shocked at its commission, than because he felt the deep reverence for his Maker, which it became the insignificant being that was the work of his hand to entertain ; and which would, of itself, most effectually have prevented any wanton use of his holy name, let the neighbors feel or think as they might on the subject. In this way Deacon Pratt might be said to have respected most of the commands of the decalogue ; not, however, because the spirit of God impelled him, through love, to reverence and obey, but because he had been brought up in a part of the country where it was considered seemly and right to be moral, to the senses, at least, if not to the all-seeing eye above. It was in this way that the deacon had arrived at his preferment in the meeting. He had all the usual sectarian terms at the end of his tongue ; never uttered a careless expression ; was regular at meeting ; apparently performed all the duties that his church required of its professors, in the way of mere religious observances ; yet was he as far from being in that state which St. Paul has described succinctly as "for me to live is Christ, and to die is gain," as if he had been a pagan. It was not the love of God that was active in his soul, but the love of self ; and he happened to exhibit his passion under these restrained and deceptive forms, simply because he had been born and educated in a state of society where they composed an integral part of existence. Covetousness was the deacon's besetting sin ; and, as it is a vice that may be pretty well concealed, with a little attention to appearances, it was the less likely to expose him to comments than almost any other sin. It is true, that the neighborhood sometimes fancied him "close," or, as they expressed it, "cluss," and men got to look sharply to their own interests in their dealings with him ; but, on the whole, there was perhaps more reason to apprehend, in such a community, that the example of so good a man should be accepted as authority, than that his acts should impeach his character, or endanger his standing.

Very different were the situation, feelings, and motives of the niece. She devoutly loved God, and, as a consequence, all of those whom he had created and placed around her. Her meek and gentle spirit led her to worship in sincerity and truth ; and all that she thought, said, and did, was under the correction of the principles such motives could best produce. Her woman's love for Roswell Gardiner alone troubled her otherwise happy and peaceful existence. That, indeed, had caused her more than once to falter in her way ; but she struggled with the weakness, and had strong hopes of being able to overcome it. To accept of any other man as a husband was, in her eyes, impossible ; with the feelings she was fully conscious of entertaining toward him, it would have been both indelicate and unjust ; but to accept *him*, while he regarded the Redeemer as only man, however pure and exalted, she felt would be putting herself willingly, or wilfully, into the hands of the great enemy of her salvation Often and often had she prayed for her lover, even more devoutly, and with hotter tears, than she had ever prayed for herself ; but, so far as she could discover, without any visible fruits. His opinions remained unchanged, and his frank nature forbade him from concealing their state from Mary. In this way, then, was unhappiness stealing on the early and innocent hours of one who might, otherwise, have been so contented and blessed. It formed a somewhat peculiar feature in her case, that her uncle favored the views of her suitor. This rendered the trials of the niece so much the more severe, as she had no other judgment to sustain her than her own, fortified as that was, however, by the consciousness of right, and the support of that great Power which never deserts the faithful.

Such was the state of feeling among some of the principal actors of our tale, when the sudden death of Daggett occurred. The body was not removed from the house of the Widow White, but the next morning it was conveyed to the "grave-yard"—"church-yard" would have sounded too episcopal—and interred in a corner that was bestowed on the unhonored and unknown. It was then, only, that the deacon believed he was the sole depository of the important secrets. He had the charts in his possession, and no more revelations could pass the lips of Daggett. Should

the friends of the deceased sailor hear of his death, and
come to look after his effects, there was very little probability of their finding anything among them to furnish a
clew to either the new sealing-ground, or to the buried
treasure of the pirate.   In order to be secured, he even
went a little beyond his usual precautions, actually discharging all indebtedness of the deceased to the Widow
White out of his own pocket, by giving to her the sum of
ten dollars.   This was handsome compensation in her eyes
as well as in his, and he quieted the suspicions so great
and unusual an act of liberality would be apt to awaken,
by saying, "he would look to the friends, or if they failed
him, to the effects, for his returns ; for it was better he
should lose by the stranger, than a lone widow."   He also
paid for the coffin, the digging of the grave, and the other
light expenses of the interment.   In a word, the deacon
endeavored to hush all impertinent inquiries by applying
the salve of silver, wherever it was needed.

The chest had been removed to a large, light closet, that
communicated with the deacon's own room.   When all his
accounts were settled, thither he repaired, armed with the
key that was to expose so much treasure to his longing
eyes.   Some slight qualms arose, after he had locked himself in the room, touching the propriety of his opening the
chest.   It was not his, certainly ; but he put such a construction on the nature of the revelations of Daggett, as he
thought would fully justify him in proceeding.   He had
purchased the schooner expressly to go in quest of the
seals and the treasure.   This he had done with Daggett's
knowledge and acquiescence ; nor did he conceive that his
own rights were lessened by the mariner's decease.   As for
himself, the deacon had never believed that the Martha's
Vineyard man could accompany the expedition, so that his
presence or absence could have no influence on his own
rights.   It is true, the deacon possessed no direct legal
transfer of the charts ; but he inferred that all the previous
circumstances gave him sufficient claims to justify him in,
at least, looking into their contents.

It was a solemn, as well as an anxious moment to the
deacon, when he first raised the lid of the chest.   Solemn,
because it was not possible to forget the recent decease of
its late owner, and anxious, inasmuch as he had no certainty that he should find, even on the charts, the places of
which he sought the latitudes and longitudes.   Certainly,
nothing like treasure presented itself to his eyes, when all

that Daggett had left behind him lay exposed to view. The chest of a common sailor is usually but ill-furnished, unless it may be just after his return from a long and well-paid voyage, and before he has had time to fall back on his purchases of clothes, as a fund to supply his cravings for personal gratification. This of Daggett's formed no exception to the rule. The few clothes it contained were of the lightest sort, having been procured in warm climates, and were well worn, in addition. The palms, needles, and shells, and carving in whalebone, had all been sold to meet their owner's wants, and nothing of that sort remained. There were two old, dirty, and ragged charts, and on these the deacon laid his hands, much as the hawk, in its swoop, descends on his prey. As it did, however, a tremor came over him, that actually compelled him to throw himself into a chair, and to rest for a moment.

The first of the charts opened, the deacon saw, at a glance, was that of the antarctic circle. There, sure enough, was laid down in ink, three or four specks for islands, with lat.—°,—″, and long.—°,—″, written out, at its side. We are under obligations not to give the figures that stand on the chart, for the discovery is deemed to be important, by those who possess the secret, even to the present hour. We are at liberty to tell the whole story, with this one exception ; and we shall proceed to do so, with a proper regard to the pledges made in the premises.

The deacon scarcely breathed, as he assured himself of the important fact just mentioned, and his hands trembled to such a degree as to fairly cause the paper of the chart to rattle. Then he had recourse to an expedient that was strictly characteristic of the man. He wrote the latitude and longitude in a memorandum-book that he carried on his person ; after which he again sat down, and with great care erased the islands and the writing from the chart, with the point of a penknife. This done, his mind felt infinitely relieved. Nor was this all. Charts purchased for the schooner were lying on a table in his own room, and he projected on one of them, as well as his skill would allow, the sealing-islands he had just removed from the chart left by Daggett. There he also wrote, in pencil, the important figures that we are commanded not to reveal.

The second chart was then opened. It was of the West Indies, and particularly of certain keys. One of these last was pointed out in a way to leave no doubt that it was meant for the key indicated by the pirate. The same pro-

4

hibition existing as to this key that exists in respect to the sealing-island, we cannot be more explicit. The writing near this key being in pencil, it was effectually removed by means of india-rubber. When this was done, the deacon used the precaution to rub some material on the clean place made by his knife, on the other chart, when he believed no eye could detect what had just been done. Having marked the proper key on his own chart of the West Indies, he replaced the charts of Daggett in the chest, and locked all up again. The verbal accounts of the sick mariner he had already transferred to paper, and he now believed himself secure of all the information that was necessary to render him the richest man in Suffolk !

When they next met, Mary was surprised at the gayety of her uncle, and that so soon after a funeral. He had a lightened heart, however ; for, after leading him on, step by step, until he had gone so far as to purchase and fit out the schooner, Daggett had pertinaciously refused to enter into those minute particulars which it is even now forbidden us to state, and a want of which would have rendered his previous expenditures useless. Death, however, had lifted the veil, and the deacon now believed himself secure in this knowledge.

An hour or two later, Deacon Pratt and his niece were seated, in company with two others, at the dinner-table. The fare was simple, but good. Fish enters largely into the domestic consumption of all those who dwell near the water, in that part of country ; and, on that particular oc-casion, the uncle had, in the lightness of his heart, in-dulged in what, for him, was a piece of extravagance. In all such regions there are broken-down, elderly men, who live by taking fish. Liquor has usually been their great enemy, and all have the same generic character of laziness, shiftless and ill-regulated exertions, followed by much idleness, and fits of intemperance, that in the end com-monly cause their death. Such a man fished between Oyster Pond and Shelter Island, being known to all who dwelt within his beat, by the familiar appellation of Bait-ing Joe.

Shortly after the discovery of the latitudes and longi-tudes on the charts, the deacon had gone to the wharf, in his impatience to see how Roswell Gardiner got on with the Sea Lion. The young man, with his gang of hands, was hard at work, and a very material difference was to be observed in the state of the schooner, from that in which

she was described in our opening chapter. Her rigging
had all been set up, every spar was in its place, and altogether she had a look of preparation and completeness.
Her water was taking in, and from time to time a country
wagon, or an ox-cart, delivered alongside articles belonging to her stores. Of cargo, proper, there was none, or
next to none ; a sealer carrying little besides salt, and her
stores. In a word, the work was rapidly advancing, and
"Captain Gar'ner" told his impatient owner that the
craft would be ready to put to sea in all that week.

"I have succeeded in engaging the first officer I wanted,"
added the young man, "and he is now busy in looking up
and shipping hands, at Stonington. We must get half a
dozen reliable men on the main, and then we can take
some of our neighbors here as beginners, just to please
them."

"Yes, ship a goodly number of green hands," said the
deacon, zealously. "They work at cheap 'lays,' and
leave the owners the greater profits. Well, well, Captain
Gar'ner, things seem to be doing well in your hands, and
I will leave you. About two hours after dinner I shall
want to have a word with you in private, and will thank
you just to step across to the house, where you will be certain to find me. Baiting Joe seems to have hooked something there, in 'arnest."

"That has he ! I'll answer for it that he has a sheepshead at the end of his line that will weigh eight or ten
pounds."

The words of Gardiner proved true, for Joe actually
pulled in a fish of the description and weight he had just
mentioned. It was this sight that, in the lightness of his
heart, tempted the deacon to a little extravagance. Joe
was called ashore, and after a good deal of chaffering, the
deacon bought the prize for half a dollar. As Mary was
celebrated for her skill in preparing this particular fish,
the deacon, before he left the wharf with the sheepshead
hanging from one hand, fairly invited "Captain Gar'ner"
so to time his visit to the house, as to be present at the
feast.

Nor was this all. Before the deacon had settled with
Joe, the Rev. Mr. Whittle came on the wharf, confess-
edly in quest of something to eat. The regular occupations of this divine were writing sermons, preaching,
holding conferences, marrying, christening, and burying,
and hunting up "something to eat." About half of his

precious time was consumed in the last of these pursuits. We do not wish to represent this clergyman as
having an undue gastronomic propensity ; but, as having a
due one, and a salary that was so badly paid, as quite to
disable him from furnishing his larder, or cellar, with anything worth mentioning, in advance. Now, he was short
of flour ; then, the potatoes were out ; next, the pork was
consumed ; and always there was a great scarcity of gro-
ceries, and other necessaries of that nature. This neglect
on the part of the parishioners, coupled with a certain im-
providence on that of the pastor, left the clergyman's family completely in that state which is usually described as
being in the "from hand to mouth" condition, and which
consequently occupied so large a portion of the good
man's time in "providing."

Deacon Pratt felt a little conscious and awkward, at encountering the Rev. Mr. Whittle. It was not the fish that
caused the first any concern. Fifty times had he met and
gone by his pastor, running about with a perplexed and
hungry look, when his own hands, or chaise, or wagon, as
the case might be, contained enough to render the divine's
family happy and contented for a week. No compunc-
tions of that sort ever troubled the deacon's breast. But he
had missed the afternoon's meeting in the last Sabbath, a
delinquency for which he felt an awkwardness in account-
ing, while he saw its necessity. The salutations passed as
usual, the one party thinking intently on the absence from
service, and the other of the sheepshead. Now, it happily
occurred to the deacon to invite his pastor also to partake
of the fish. There was enough for all ; and, though no
one on Oyster Pond was much in the habit of entertaining at dinner, it was by no means unusual for the parishioners to have their pastor for a guest. This lucky invitation so occupied the parties that nothing was said about
an occurrence so very unusual as the deacon's absence
from "meeting" the "last Sabba' day afternoon."

By these simple means the party at table consisted of the
deacon himself, Mary, Roswell Gardiner, and the Rev. Mr.
Whittle. The fish was excellent, being so fresh and so
skilfully prepared ; and Mary was highly complimented by
all who ate of it for her share in the entertainment. But
Mary Pratt seemed sad. She had not yet recovered from
the melancholy feelings awakened by the recent death
and funeral ; and then her thoughts recurred, with few
interruptions, to the long voyage of Roswell, and most

especially to the unhappy state of religious belief in which
he would undertake so hazardous an expedition. Several
times had she hinted to the clergyman her desire that he
would "talk to Roswell;" but the good man, though well
enough inclined, had really so much to do in "providing,"
that it was not a very easy matter for him to go beyond
the beaten track, in order to probe the consciences of particular individuals. He promised fairly, but always forgot
to perform; and in this he imitated closely the example set
him by his parishioners in reference to his own salary.

Roswell Gardiner, therefore, remained in his unbelief;
or, what was tantamount to it, under the influence of a set
of opinions that conflicted with all that the Church had
taught since the time of the apostles—at least so thought
Mary, and so think we.

On the contrary, the pastor and the deacon were particularly gay for men of their habitual sobriety. Although
those were not the days of temperance, *par excellence*,
neither of the guests was what might be termed even
a moderate drinker. For a novelty in a sailor, Roswell
Gardiner seldom touched anything but water, while the
other two took their rum and water; but it was in moderation, as all the gifts of God should be used. As for the
intemperate cry which makes it a sin to partake of any
liquor, however prudently, it was then never heard in the
land. On the whole, the clergy of all denominations might
be set down as brandy-and-water men, a few occasionally
carrying out their principle to exaggeration. But the
Rev. Mr. Whittle was a sober man, and, though he saw no
great harm in enlivening his heart and cheering his spirits
with brandy taken in small quantities, he was never known
to be any the worse for his libations. It was the same with
the deacon, though *he* drank rum and water of choice;
and no other beverage, Mary's currant-wine and cider excepted, was ever seen on his table.

One thing may be said of liquor, whether it be in its
favor or not: it usually brings out all there is of the face-
tious in a man, rendering him conversable and pleasant;
for the time being at least. This was apt to be peculiarly
the case with the Rev. Mr. Whittle and his deacons. In
their ordinary intercourse with their fellow-creatures these
good people had taken up the idea that, in order to be
religious, their countenances must be sombre, and that
care and anxiety should be stamped on their faces, just as
if they had no confidence in the efficacy of the redemption.

Few, indeed, are they who vindicate their professions by living at peace with God and man! At Oyster Pond it was much the fashion to imagine that the more a person became impressed with the truths of *his*, and particularly with those of *her*, lost condition, the more it became the party to be cynical, and to pry into, and comment, on the backslidings of the entire community. This weakness, however, was characteristic of neither the pastor nor the deacon, each of whom regarded his professions too much in the light of a regular " business transaction," to descend into these little abuses. As for Mary, good creature, her humility was so profound as to cause her to believe herself among the weakest and least favored of all who belonged to meeting.

" I was sorry that my late journey into Connecticut prevented my seeing the poor man who was so suddenly taken away from the house of Widow White," observed the Rev. Mr. Whittle, some little time after he had made his original attack on the sheepshead. "They tell me it was a hopeless case from the first?"

"So Dr. Sage considered it," answered the deacon. "Captain Gar'ner volunteered to go across for the doctor in *my* boat,"—with a heavy emphasis on the possessive pronoun—"and we had him to look at the patient. But, if the salt-water *be* good for consumptive people, as, some pretend, I think there is generally little hope for seamen whose lungs once give way."

" The poor man was a mariner, was he ? I did not know his calling, but had rather got the impression that he was a husbandman. Did he belong to Oyster Pond ? "

" No ; we have none of the name of Daggett here, which is a tribe on the Vineyard. Most of the Daggetts are seafaring folks (folk, *Anglicè*), and this man was one of that class, *I believe ;* though I know nothing of him, or his pursuits, except by a word, here and there, dropped in discourse."

The deacon thought himself safe in venturing this little departure from the literal truth, inasmuch as no one had been present, or he *thought* no one had ever been present at his many secret conferences with the deceased mariner. Little, however, did he understand the character of the Widow White, if he flattered himself with holding any discourse under her roof in which she was not to participate in its subject. So far from this having been the case, the good woman had contrived to obtain, not only a listening-place, but a peeping-hole, where she both heard and saw most of that which passed between her guest and the deacon. Had her powers of comprehension been equal to her will, or had not her mind been prepossessed with the notion that the deacon *must* be after herself, old Suffolk would have rung with the marvels that were thus revealed. Not only would an unknown sealing-island have been laid before the East-enders, but twenty such islands, and keys without number, each of which contained more hidden treasure than "Gar'ner's Island," Oyster Pond, the Plumb and Fisher's, and all the coasts of the Sound put together ; enriched as each and all of these places were thought to be, by hidden deposits of Kidd.

Nothing but an accident had prevented these rumors from being circulated. It happened that on only one occasion Daggett was explicit and connected in his narrative. At all other times his discourse was broken, consisting more in allusions to what had been previously said than in direct and clear revelations. The widow, most unfortunately for her means of information, was with "neighbor Stone" when the connected narrative was given, and all that she knew was disjointed, obscure, and a little contradictory. Still, it was sufficient to set her thinking intensely, and sufficient to produce a material influence on the future fortunes of the Sea Lion, as will appear in the sequel.

"It is always a misfortune for a human being to take his departure away from home and friends," observed the Rev. Mr. Whittle. "Here was an immortal soul left to take its last great flight, unsupported, I dare say, except by the prayers of a few pious neighbors. I regret having been absent during the time he was here. Getting home of a Friday only, I was compelled to devote Saturday to preparations for the Sabbath ; and Sabbath-night, as I understand it, he departed."

"We are all in the hands of Divine Providence," said the deacon, with a sober mien, "and it is our duty to submit. To my thinking, Oyster Pond catches more than its share of the poor and needy, who are landed from vessels passing east and west, and add considerably to our burdens"

This was said of a spot as much favored by Divine Providence, in the way of abundance, as any other in highly-favored America Some eight or ten such events as the landing of a stranger had occurred within the last half century, and this was the only instance in which either of them had cost the deacon a cent. But, so little was he accustomed, and so little was he disposed to give, that even a threatened danger of that sort amounted, in his eyes, nearly to a loss.

"Well," exclaimed the literal Roswell Gardiner, "I think, deacon, that we have no great reason to complain. Southold, Shelter Island, and all the islands about here, for that matter, are pretty well off as to poor, and it is little enough that we have to pay for their support."

"That's the idea of a young man who never sees the tax-gatherers," returned the deacon. "However, there are islands, Captain Gar'ner, that are better off still, and I hope you will live to find them."

"Is our young friend to sail in the Sea Lion in quest of any such?" inquired the pastor, a little curiously.

The deacon now repented him of the allusion. But his heart had warmed with the subject, and the rum-and-water had unlocked some of its wards. So timid and nervous had he become, however, that the slightest indication of anything like a suspicion that his secrets were known, threw him into a sweat.

"Not at all—not at all—the captain goes on well-known and beaten ground—Sam, what is wanting, now?"

"Here is Baiting Joe comed up from the wharf, wanting to see master," returned a gray-headed negro, who had formerly been a slave, and who now lived about the place, giving his services for his support.

"Baiting Joe! He is not after his sheepshead, I hope. If he is, he is somewhat late in the day."

"Ay, ay," put in the young sailor, laughing. "Tell him, Sam, that no small part of it is bound to the southward, meaning to cross the line in my company, and that right soon."

"I paid Joe his half-dollar, certainly—*you* saw me pay him, Captain Gar'ner."

"I don't think it's any sich thing, master. There is a stranger with Joe, that he has ferried across from Shelter Island, and *he's* comed up from the wharf too. Yes—that's it, master."

A stranger! Who could it be? A command was given to admit him, and no sooner did Mary get a sight of his person, than she quietly arose to procure a plate, in order that he, too, might have his share of the fish.

CHAPTER V.

" Stranger ! I fled the home of grief,
    At Connocht Moran's tomb to fall ;
I found the helmet of my chief,
    His bow still hanging on our wall."—CAMPBELL.

"AMPHIBIOUS ! " exclaimed Roswell Gardiner, in an aside
to Mary, as the stranger entered the room, following Baiting Joe's lead. The last only came for his glass of rum-
and-water, served with which, by the aid of the negro, he
passed the back of his hand across his mouth, napkin-
fashion, nodded his " good-day," and withdrew. As for the
stranger, Roswell Gardiner's term being particularly significant, it may be well to make a brief explanation.

The word "amphibious " is, or rather *was*, well applied
to many of the seamen, whalers, and sealers, who dwelt on
the eastern end of Long Island, or the Vineyard, around
Stonington, and perhaps we might add, in the vicinity of
New Bedford. The Nantucket men had not base enough,
in the way of terra firma, to come properly within the category. The class to which the remark strictly applied
were sailors without being seamen, in the severe signification of the term. While they could do all that was indispensably necessary to take care of their vessels, were surpassed by no other mariners in enterprise and daring, and
hardihood, they knew little about "crowning cables,"
"carrick-bends," and all the mysteries of "knotting,"
"graffing," and "splicing." A regular Delaware Bay seaman would have turned up his nose in contempt at many
of their ways, and at much of their real ignorance ; but,
when it came to the drag, or to the oar, or to holding out
in bad weather, or to any of the more manly qualities of
the business, he would be certain to yield his respect to
those at whom it had originally been his disposition to
laugh. It might best describe these men to say that they
bore some such relation to the thoroughbred tar, as the
volunteer bears to the regular soldier.

As a matter of course, the stranger was invited to take
his seat at the table. This he did without using many
phrases ; and Mary had reason to believe, by his appetite,
that he thought well of her culinary skill. There was very
little of the sheepshead left when this, its last assailant,

shoved his plate back, the signal that he could do no more.
He then finished a glass of rum-and-water, and seemed to
be in a good condition to transact the business that had
brought him there. Until this moment, he had made no
allusion to the motive of his visit, leaving the deacon full
of conjectures.

"The fish of Peconic and Gar'ner's is as good as any I
know," coolly observed this worthy, after certainly having
established some claim to give an opinion on the subject.
"We think ourselves pretty well off, in this respect, on the
Vineyard——"

"On the Vineyard!" interrupted the deacon, without
waiting to hear what was to follow.

"Yes, sir, on Martha's Vineyard, for that's the place I
come from. Perhaps I ought to have introduced myself
a little more particularly. I come from Martha's Vineyard, and my name is Daggett."

The deacon fairly permitted the knife, with which he
was spreading some butter, to fall upon his plate. "Daggett" and the "Vineyard" sounded ominously. Could it
be that Dr. Sage had managed to get a message so far, in
so short a time ; and had this amphibious inhabitant of the
neighboring island come already to rob him of his treasure ?
The perceptions of the deacon, at first, were far from clear ;
and he even imagined that all he had expended on the Sea
Lion was thrown away, and that he might be even called
on to give some sort of an account, in a court of chancery,
of the information obtained from the deceased. A little
reflection, however, sufficed to get the better of this weakness, and he made a civil inclination of his head, as much
as to tell the stranger, notwithstanding his name and place
of residence, that he was welcome. Of course, no one but
the deacon himself knew of the thoughts that troubled
him, and after a very brief delay, the guest proceeded with
his explanations of the object of his visit.

"The Daggetts are pretty numerous on the Vineyard,"
continued the stranger, "and when you name one of them,
it is not always easy to tell just what family he belongs to.
One of our coasters came into the Hull (Holmes' Hole was
meant) a few weeks since, and reported that she spoke an
inward-bound brig, off New Haven, from which she heard
that the people of that craft had put ashore, at Oyster Pond,
a seafaring man who belonged to the Vineyard, and who
was bound home arter an absence of fifty years, and whose
name was Thomas Daggett. The word passed through the

island, and a great stir it made among all us Daggetts. There's plenty of our Vineyard people wandering about the 'arth, and sometimes one drops in upon the island, just to die. As most of them that come back bring something with them, it's gen'rally thought a good sign to hear of their arrival. After casting about, and talking with all the old folks, it has been concluded that this Thomas Daggett must be a brother of my father's, who went to sea about fifty years since, and has never been seen or heard of since. He's the only person of the name for whom we can't account, and the family have got me to come across to look him up."

"I am sorry, Mr. Daggett, that you are so late," answered the deacon, slowly, as if unwilling to give pain. "Had you come last week, you might have seen and conversed with your relation ; or had you come early this morning, only, you might have attended his funeral. He came among us a stranger, and we endeavored to imitate the conduct of the good Samaritan. I believe he had all the comforts that Oyster Pond can give ; and, certainly, he had the best advice. Dr. Sage, of Sag Harbor, attended him in his last illness—Dr. Sage, of the Harbor ; doubtless you have heard *him* mentioned ?"

"I know him by reputation, and make no doubt all was done that could be done. As the sloop I named lay by the brig some time, in a calm, the two captains had a long talk together ; and ours had prepared us to hear of our kinsman's speedy dissolution. He was in a decline when he landed, and we suppose that no human skill could have saved him. As he had so skilful a physician, and one who came so far, I suppose my uncle must have left property ?"

This was a home thrust ; but, fortunately for the deacon, he had already prepared himself with an answer.

"Seafaring men, that are landed on points and capes from inward-bound vessels, are not very apt to be overloaded with worldly goods," he said, smiling. "When a man prospers in that calling, he usually comes ashore at a wharf, in some large place, and gets into his coach to ride up to some grand tavern ! I have remarked, pastor, that seafaring men love comforts and free-living, unaccountably, when they can fairly get a chance at 'em."

"That is natural, deacon—quite natural ; and what is natural, is very likely to happen. The natural man loves all sorts of indulgences, and these among others."

As there was no gainsaying this commonplace commentary on the species, it was permitted to pass unanswered.

"I hope my kinsman has not been a burden to any on Oyster Pond?" said the nephew, inquiringly.

"I cannot say that he has," returned the deacon. "He was at little cost at first, and got along by selling a few odd things that he owned. As Providence had placed him in the dwelling of a poor widow, I thought it might be pleasing to the friends—and every man has *some* friends, I suppose—to settle with *her*. This I did, this very morning, taking her receipt in full, as you can see, " passing the paper to the stranger. "As a sort of security for my advances, I had the chest of the deceased removed to this house ; and it is now upstairs, ready to be examined. It feels light, and I do not think much silver or gold will be found in it."

To own the truth, the Vineyard seaman looked a little disappointed. It was so natural that a man who has been absent fifty years should bring back the fruits of his labor, that he had expected some slight reward for the trouble he was now taking, to be bestowed in this particular form. This, however, was not the specific object of his visit, as will appear as we proceed. Keeping in view his real motive, the nephew continued his inquiries, always putting his questions a little indirectly, and receiving answers that were as evasive and cautious as his own interrogatories. All this was characteristic of the wary people from which both had sprung, who seldom speak, in a matter of business, without bearing in mind all the possible constructions of what they are saying. After a discourse of some fifteen minutes, in which the history of the chest, in its outlines, was fully given, and during which the stranger produced written evidence of his right to interfere, it was determined to make an inventory, on the spot, of the property left by Daggett, for the benefit of all who might have any interest in it. Accordingly, the whole party, including Mary, was soon assembled in the deacon's own room, with the sea chest placed invitingly in the centre. All eyes were fastened on the lid, in curious anticipations of the contents ; for, the deacon excepted, all supposed that those contents were a profound secret. The widow White could have told them better, she having rummaged that chest a dozen times, at least, though without abstracting even a pin. Curiosity had been her ruling motive, far more than cupidity. It is true, the good woman had a prudent regard to her own interests, and felt some anxiety to learn the prospects of her receiving the stipulated price for board—only $1.50 per week—but the sales of the needles, and palms, and carved whalebone, having kept her accounts reasonably square, solicitude on this particular interest was not at its height. No; curiosity, pure female curiosity, a little quickened by the passion which is engendered among the vulgar by the possession of a slight degree of instruction, was really at the bottom of her researches. Not only had she handled every article in the chest, but she had read, and re-read, every paper it contained, half a dozen letters included, and made her own surmises on their nature. Still, the good woman was very little the wiser for her inquiries. Of the great secret she knew absolutely nothing, unless the broken hints collected in her many listenings, could be so considered. But here her ignorance ceased. Every hole in a shirt, every patch in a pair of trowsers, and every darn in a stocking, had been examined, and its probable effect on the value of the garment duly estimated. The only thing that had escaped her scrutiny was a small till that was locked. Into that she could not look, and there were moments when she would have parted with a finger in order to overhaul it.

"This jacket might sell for a dollar," had the widow White calculated, "but for the hole in the elbow; and that well patched, would bring seventy-five cents. Them trowsers must have cost two dollars, but they aren't worth half-price now. That pea-jacket is the best article in the chest, and, sent across to the Harbor, about the time the ships are going out, it would bring enough to maintain Daggett a month!"

Such had been the character of the widow's visitations to the chest, though no one knew anything of her discoveries, not even her sister-relict, neighbor Stone.

"Here is the key," said the deacon, producing that instrument from the drawer of a table, as if he had laid it carefully aside for some such moment. "I dare say it will be found to fit, for I remember to have seen Daggett use it once or twice myself."

Roswell Gardiner, as the youngest man, and the one on whom the laboring oar ought to fall, now took the key, applied it to the lock, turned it without difficulty, and then lifted the lid. Disappointment appeared on every face but that of the deacon, at the meagre prospect before the company. Not only was the chest more than half empty, but

the articles it did contain were of the coarsest materials ;
well-worn sea clothes that had seen their best days, and
which had never been more than the coarse, common attire
of a forecast hand.

"There is little here to pay a man for crossing from the
Vineyard," observed Roswell Gardiner, a little dryly ; for
he did not half like the appearance of cupidity that shone
through the nephew's tardy concern for the fate of the
uncle. "The last voyage has not been prosperous, I fear,
or the owners failed before the vessel got in ! What is to
be done with all this dunnage, deacon ? "

"It would be best to take out the contents, article by
article," answered the other, "and examine each and all.
Now that we have made a beginning with the inventory,
it is best to go through with it."

.The young man obeyed, calling out the name of each
article of dress, as he raised it from its receptacle, and
passing it over to him who stood there in the character of
a sort of heir-at-law. The last gave each garment a sharp
look, and prudently put his hand into every pocket, in order to make sure that it was empty, before he laid the article on the floor. Nothing was discovered for some time,
until a small key was found in the fob of a pair of old
"go-ashore" pantaloons. As there was the till to the
chest already mentioned, and a lock on that till, the heir-
at-law kept the key, saying nothing touching its existence.

"The deceased does not appear to have been much af-
flicted with this world's wealth," said the Rev. Mr. Whittle,
whose expectations, to own the truth, had been a little
disappointed. "This may have been all the better for
him, when the moment of departure drew near."

"I dare say he would have borne the burden cheerfully,"
put in Roswell Gardiner, "to have been a little more comfortable. I never knew a person, seaman or landsman,
who was ever the worse for having things snug about him,
and for holding on to the better end of his cheer, as long
as he could."

"*Your* notion of what is best for man as he draws near
to his end, Captain Gar'ner, is not likely to be of the most
approved nature. The sea does not produce many very
orthodox divines."

The young sailor colored, bit his lip, cast a glance at
Mary, and began a nearly inaudible whistle. In a moment
he forgot the rebuke he had received, and laughingly went
on with the inventory.

"Well," he cried, "this is rather a poorer outfit than Jack is apt to carry! *In*fit, I suppose it should be called, as the poor fellow who owned it was inward bound, when he brought up on Oyster Pond. You'll hardly think it worth while, Captain Daggett, to take this dunnage across to the Vineyard?"

"It is scarce worth the trouble, though friends and relations may set a value on it that strangers do not. I see a couple of charts there—will you hand them this way, if you please? They may have a value with a seafaring man, as old mariners sometimes make notes that are worth as much as the charts themselves."

This was said very naturally and simply; but it gave the deacon a good deal of concern. Nor was this feeling at all lessened by the earnest, not to say eager, manner in which Daggett, as we shall now call this member of the family, spread the chart on the bed, and began to pry into its records. The particular chart first opened in this way, was the one including the antarctic circle, and, of course, was that from which the deacon had been at so much pains to erase the sealing islands that the deceased mariner had laid down with so great precision and care. It was evident that the Martha's Vineyard man was looking for something that he could not find, and that he felt disappointment. Instead of looking at the chart, indeed, he may be said to have been peering at it, in all its holes and crannies, of which there were not a few, in consequence of the torn condition of the paper. Several minutes elapsed ere the investigation terminated, the stranger seeming, all that time, to feel no interest in the remainder of his relation's wardrobe.

"This is an old chart, and of the date of 1802," observed Daggett, raising himself erect, as a man who has long been bent takes the creaks out of his back. "So old a chart as to be of little use nowaday. Our sealers have gone over so much of the ground to the southward of the two capes, as to be able to do much better than this now."

"Your uncle had the appearance of an old-fashioned sailor," coldly observed the deacon; "and it may be that he most liked old-fashioned charts."

"If such was the case he must have pretty well forgotten his Vineyard schooling. There is not a woman there who doesn't know that the latest chart is commonly the best. I own I'm disapp'inted somewhat; for the master of the sloop gave me to understand he had heard from the master of the brig that some valuable information was to be found on the old gentleman's charts."

The deacon started, as here was an indication that the deceased had talked of his knowledge to others, as well as to himself! It was so natural for a man like Daggett to boast of what his charts were worth, that he saw the extreme probability that a difficulty might arise from this source. It was his cue, however, to remain silent, and let the truth develop itself in due course. His attention was not likely to be drawn aside by the shirts and old clothes, for the stranger began a second time to examine the chart, and what was more, in the high latitudes at no great distance from the very spot where the sealing islands had been placed, and from which they had been so carefully erased.

" It is unaccountable that a man should wear out a chart like this, and leave so few notes on it !" said the Vineyard man, much as one complains of a delinquency. " Here is white water noted in the middle of the ocean, where I dare say no other white water was seen but that which is made by a fish, and nothing is said of any islands. What do you think of this, Captain Gar'ner ?" laying his finger on the precise spot where the deacon had been at work so long that very morning erasing the islands. " This looks well-fingered, if nothing else, eh ?"

" It's a shoal laid down in dirt," answered Roswell Gardiner, laughing. " Let's see ; that's about lat. —° —", and long. —° —". There can be no known land thereaway, as even Captain Cook did not succeed in getting as far south. That's been a favorite spot with the skipper for taking hold of his chart. I've known one of those old-fashioned chaps put his hand on a chart, in that way, and never miss his holding-ground for three years on a stretch. Mighty go-by-rule people are some of our whaling-masters, in particular, who think they know the countenances of some of the elderly fish, who are too cunning to let a harpoon get fast to 'em."

" You've been often in them seas, I some think, Captain Gar'ner ?" said the other, inquiringly.

" I was brought up in the business, and have a hankering for it yet," returned the young man, frankly. " Nor do I care so much for charts. They are well enough when a vessel is on her road ; but, as for whales or seals, the man who wishes to find either, in these times, has to look for them, as I tell my owner. According to reports, the time has been when a craft had only to get an offing to fall in with something that was worth putting a harpoon into; but those days are gone, Captain Daggett ; and whales are to be looked after, out at sea, much as money is to be looked for ashore here."

"Is the craft I saw at the wharf fitting out for a whaler, then ?"

"She is going after luck, and will accept of it, in whatever form it may turn up."

"She is rather small for the whaling business, though vessels of that size *have* done well, by keeping close in upon our own coast."

"We shall know better what she will do after she has been tried," returned Gardiner, evasively. "What do you think of her for the Banks of Newfoundland ?"

The Martha's Vineyard man gave his brother-tar a quick, impatient glance, which pretty plainly said, "tell that to the marines," when he opened the second chart, which as yet had been neglected.

"Sure enough," he muttered, in a low tone, though loud enough to be heard by the keenly attentive deacon ; "here it is—a chart of the West Indies, and of all the keys !"

By this casual, spontaneous outbreaking, as it might be, the deacon got another clew to the stranger's knowledge, that gave him increased uneasiness. He was now convinced that, by means of the masters of the brig and the sloop, such information had been sent to the relatives of Daggett as had prepared them to expect the very revelations on which he hoped to establish his own fortunes. To what extent these revelations had been made, of course he could only conjecture ; but there must have been a good deal of particularity to induce the individual who had come over to Oyster Pond to look into the two charts so closely. Under the circumstances, therefore, he felicitated himself on the precaution he had so early taken to erase the important notations from the paper.

"Captain Gar'ner, your eyes are younger than mine," said the Vineyard man, holding the chart up to the light— "will you be good enough to look here ?—does it not seem as if that key had been noted, and the words rubbed off the chart ?"

This caused the deacon to peer over Roswell Gardiner's shoulder, and glad enough was he to ascertain that the stranger had placed his finger on a key that must lie several hundred miles from that which was supposed to hold the buried treasure of the pirates. Something like an

5

erasure did appear at the indicated point ; but the chart was so old and dirty, that little satisfaction could be had by examining it. Should the inquirer settle down on the key he evidently had in his eye, all would be well, since it was far enough from the spot really noted.

" It is strange that so old a seafaring man should wear out a chart, and make no observations on it! ' repeated the stranger, who was both vexed and at a loss what to conjecture. " All my charts are written over and marked off, just as if I meant to get out an edition for myself."

" Men differ in their tastes and habits," answered Roswell Gardiner carelessly. " Some navigators are forever finding rocks, and white water, and scribbling on their charts, or in the newspapers, when they get back ; but I never knew any good come of it. The men who make the charts are most to be trusted. For my part, I would not give a sixpence for a note made by a man who passes a shoal or a rock, in a squall or a gale."

" What would you say to the note of a sealer who should lay down an island where the seals lie about on the beach like pigs in a pen, sunning themselves ? Would you not call a chart so noted, a treasure ? "

" That would alter the case, sure enough," returned Gardiner, laughing ; " though I should not think of looking into this chest for any such riches. Most of our masters navigate too much at random to make their charts of any great value. They can find the places they look for themselves, but don't seem to know how to tell other people the road. I have known my old man lay down a shoal that he fancied he saw, quite a degree out of the way. Now such a note as that would do more harm than good. It might make a foul wind of a fair one, and cause a fellow to go about, or wear ship, when there was not the least occasion in the world for doing anything of the sort."

" Ay, ay ; this will do for nervous men, who are always thinking they see danger ahead ; but it is different with islands that a craft has actually visited. I do not see much use, Deacon Pratt, in your giving yourself any further trouble. My uncle was not a very rich man, I perceive, and I must go to work and make my own fortune if I wish more than I've got already. If there is any demand against the deceased, I am ready to discharge it."

This was coming so much to the point that the deacon hardly knew what to make of it. He recollected his own ten dollars, and the covetousness of his disposition so far got the better of his prudence as to induce him to mention the circumstance.

"Dr. Sage may have a charge—no doubt has one, that ought to be settled, but your uncle mainly paid his way as he went on. I thought the widow who took care of him was entitled to something extra, and I handed her ten dollars this morning, which you may repay to me or not, just as you please."

Captain Daggett drew forth his wallet and discharged the obligation on the spot. He then replaced the charts, and, without opening the till of the chest, he shut down the lid, locked it, and put the key in his pocket, saying that he would cause the whole to be removed, much as if he felt anxious to relieve the deacon of an encumbrance. This done, he asked a direction to the dwelling of the Widow White, with whom he wished to converse ere he left the Point.

"I shall have the questions of so many cousins to answer when I get home," he said, smiling, "that it will never do for me to go back without taking all the talk I can get with me. If you will be kind enough to show me the way, Captain Gar'ner, I will promise to do as much for you when you come to hunt up the leavings of some old relation on the Vineyard."

Roswell Gardiner very cheerfully complied, not observing the look of dissatisfaction with which his owner listened to the request. Away the two went, then, and were soon at the widow's door. Here the young man left his companion, having duty to attend to on board the Sea Lion. The Widow White received her guest with lively interest, it forming one of the greatest pleasures of her existence to be imparting and receiving intelligence.

"I dare say you found my uncle a companionable man," observed the captain, as soon as amicable relations were established between the parties, by means of a few flattering remarks on one side and on the other. "The Vineyard folks are generally quite conversable."

"That he was, Captain Daggett; and when the deacon had not been over to perplex him, and wake up the worldly spirit in him, he was as well inclined to preparation as any sick person I ever waited on. To be sure it *was* different arter the deacon had paid him one of his visits."

"Was Deacon Pratt in the habit of coming to read and pray with the sick?"

"He pray! I don't believe he as much as went through a single sentence of a prayer in all his visits. Their whull talk was about islands and seals when they was by themselves."

"Indeed!" exclaimed the nephew, manifesting a new interest in the discourse. "And what could they find to say on such subjects? Islands and seals were a strange topic for a dying man?"

"I know it," answered the widow, sharply. "I know'd it at the time; but what could a lone woman do to set 'em right; and he a deacon of the meetin' the whull time? If they *would* talk of worldly things at such times, it wasn't for one like me to put 'em right."

"Then this discourse was held openly in your presence —before your face, as it might be, ma'am?"

"I can't say that it was just that; nor was it altogether when my back was turned. They talked, and I overheard what was said, as will happen when a body is about, you know."

The stranger did not press the point, having been brought up in what might almost be termed a land of listeners. An island that is cut off from much communication with the rest of the earth, and from which two-thirds of the males must be periodically absent, would be very likely to reach perfection in the art of gossiping, which includes that of the listener.

"Yes," he answered, "one picks up a good deal, he doesn't know how. So they talked of islands and seals?"

Thus questioned, the widow cheerfully opened her stores of knowledge. As she proceeded in her account of the secret conferences between Deacon Pratt and her late inmate her zeal became quickened, and she omitted nothing that she had ever heard, besides including a great deal that she had not heard. But her companion was accustomed to such narratives, and knew reasonably well how to make allowances. He listened with a determination not to believe more than half of what she said, and by dint of long experience, he succeeded in separating the credible portions of the woman's almost breathless accounts, from those that ought to have been regarded as incredible, with a surprising degree of success. The greatest difficulty in the way of comprehending the Widow White's report, arose from the fact that she had altogether missed the preliminary and most explicit conference. This left so much to be understood and inferred, that, in her own efforts to supply the deficiencies, she made a great deal of confusion in the statements. Captain Daggett was fully assured that the deacon knew of the existence of the seal-ing-island, at least; though he was in doubt whether the rumor that had been brought to him, touching the buried treasure, had also been imparted to this person. The pur-chase and equipment of the Sea Lion, taken in connection with the widow's account, were enough of themselves to convince one of his experience and foresight, that an ex-pedition after seal was then fitting out on the information derived from his deceased relative. Of this much he had no doubt; but he was not able to assure himself quite so satisfactorily, that the key was to be looked at by the way.

The interview between Captain Daggett and the Widow White lasted more than an hour. In that time the former had gleaned all the information the latter could give, and they parted on the best terms in the world. It is true that the captain gave the widow nothing—he had acquitted his conscience on this score, by repaying the deacon the money the last had advanced—but he listened in the most exemplary manner to all she had to say; and, with a cer-tain class of vehement talkers, the most favored being in the world is your good listener. Interest had given the stranger an air of great attention, and the delighted woman had poured out her torrent of words in a way that grati-fied, in the highest degree, her intense desire to be im-parting information. When they separated, it was with an understanding that letters, on the same interesting subject, should pass between them.

That afternoon, Captain Daggett found means to remove the chest of his late kinsman, across the bays, to Sag Harbor, whither he proceeded himself by the same con-veyance. There, he passed an hour or two in making inquiries touching the state of equipment, and the proba-ble time of the departure of the Sea Lion. The fitting out of this schooner was the cause of a good deal of dis-course in all that region, and the Martha's Vineyard man heard numberless conjectures, but very little accurate in-formation. On the whole, however, he arrived at the conclusion that the Sea Lion would sail within the next ten days; that her voyage was to be distant; that her ab-sence was expected to exceed a twelvemonth; and that it was thought she had some other scheme in view in addition to that of sealing. That night, this hardy mariner—half agriculturist as he was—got into his whale-boat, and sailed for the Vineyard all alone, taking the chest with him. This was nothing, however ; for quite often before had he been off at sea, in his boat alone, looking out for inward-bound vessels to pilot.

CHAPTER VI.

"Launch thy bark, mariner !
　　Christian, God speed thee !
Let loose the rudder-bands,
　　Good angels lead thee !
Set thy sails warily,
　　Tempests will come ;
Steer thy course steadily,
　　Christian, steer home ! "—MRS. SOUTHEY.

THE visit of Captain Daggett, taken in connection with all that he had said and done, while on Oyster Pond, and at Sag Harbor, had the effect greatly to hasten the equipments of the Sea Lion. Deacon Pratt knew the characters of the seamen of the island too well, to trifle in a matter of so much moment. How much the Vineyard folks had been told, in reference to his great secrets, he did not know ; but he felt assured that they knew enough, and had learned enough in this visit to quicken all their desires for riches, and to set them in motion toward the antarctic circle. With such a people, distance and difficulties are of no account ; a man who has been cradling oats to-day, in his own retired fields, where one would think ambition and the love of change could never penetrate, being ready to quit home at twenty-four hours' notice, assuming the marlin-spike as he lays aside the fork, and setting forth for the uttermost confines of the earth, with as little hesitation as another might quit his home for an ordinary journey of a week. Such, did the deacon well know, was the character of those with whom he had now to deal, and he foresaw the necessity of the utmost caution, perseverance, diligence, and activity.

Philip Hazard, the mate mentioned by Roswell Gardiner, was enjoined to lose no time ; and the men engaged for the voyage soon began to cross the Sound, and to make their appearance on board the schooner. As for the craft herself, she had all that was necessary for her wants below hatches ; and the deacon began to manifest some impatience for the appearance of two or three men of particular. excellence, of whom Phil Hazard was in quest, and whom Captain Gardiner had made it a point should be obtained. Little did the worthy owner suspect that the Vineyard people were tampering with these very hands, and keeping them from coming to terms, in order that they might fit out a second Sea Lion, which they had now been preparing for near a month ; having purchased her at New Bedford, with a view to profit by the imperfect information that had reached them, through the masters of the brig and sloop. The identity in the name was accidental, or, it might be better to say, had been naturally enough suggested by the common nature of the enterprise ; but, once existing, it had been the means of suggesting to the Vineyard company a scheme of confounding the vessels, out of which they hoped to reap some benefit, but which it would be premature now fully to state.

After a delay of several days, Hazard sent across from Stonington a man by the name of Watson, who had the reputation of being a first-class sealer. This accession was highly prized ; and, in the absence of his mates, both of whom were out looking for hands, Roswell Gardiner, to whom command was still novel, consulted freely with this experienced and skilful mariner. It was fortunate for the schemes of the deacon that he had left his young master still in the dark, as respected his two great secrets. Gardiner understood that the schooner was to go after seals, sea-lions, sea-elephants, and all animals of the genus *phoca ;* but he had been told nothing concerning the revelations of Daggett, or of the real motives that had induced him to go so far out of his usual course, in the pursuit of gain. We say it was fortunate that the deacon had been so wary ; for Watson had no intention whatever to sail out of Oyster Pond, having been actually engaged as the second officer of the rival Sea Lion, which had been purchased at New Bedford, and was then in active state of forwardness in its equipments, with a view to compete with the craft that was still lying so quietly and unconsciously alongside of Deacon Pratt's wharf. In a word, Watson was a spy, sent across by the Vineyard-men, to ascertain all he could of the intentions of the schooner's owner, to worm himself into Gardiner's confidence, and to report, from time to time, the state of things generally, in order that the East-enders might not get the start of his real employers. It is a common boast of Americans that there are no spies in their country. This may be true in the every-day signification of the term, though it is very untrue in all others. This is probably the most spying country in christendom, if the looking into other people's concerns be meant. Extensive and recognized systems of *espionage* exist among merchants; and nearly every man connected with the press has enlisted himself as a sort of spy in the interests of politics—many, in those of other concerns, also. The reader, therefore, is not to run away with impressions formed under general assertions that will scarce bear investigation, and deny the truth of pictures that are drawn with daguerreotype fidelity, because they do not happen to reflect the cant of the day. The man Watson, who had partially engaged to go out in the Sea Lion, Captain Roswell Gardiner, was not only a spy, but a spy sent covertly into an enemy's camp, with the meanest motives, and with intentions as hostile as the nature of the circumstances would permit.

Such was the state of things on Oyster Pond for quite a week after the nephew had been to look after the effects of the deceased uncle. The schooner was now quite ready for sea, and her master began to talk of hauling off from the wharf. It is true, there was no very apparent reason why this step, preliminary to sailing, should be taken in that port, where there were so few opportunities for her people to run into excesses; but it sounded ship-shape, and Captain Gardiner had been heard to express an intention to that effect. The men arrived but slowly from the main, and something like impatience was manifested by the young commander, who had long before got all his green hands, or youths from the neighborhood, on board, and was gradually breaking them into the ways of a vessel. Indeed, the best reason he could give to himself for "hauling off," was the practice it might give to these lads with the oars.

"I don't know what Hazard and Green are about," called out Roswell Gardiner to his owner, the first being on the quarter-deck of the Sea Lion, and the last on the wharf, while Watson was busy in the main-rigging; "they've been long enough on the main to ship a dozen crews for a craft of this size, and we are still short two hands, even if this man sign the papers, which he has not yet done. By the way, Watson, it's time we saw your handwriting."

"I'm a poor scholar, Captain Gar'ner," returned the cunning mariner, "and it takes time for me to make out even so small a matter as my name."

"Ay, ay; you are a prudent fellow, and I like you all the better for it. But you have had leisure, and a plenty of it too, to make up your mind. You must know the schooner from her keel up by this time, and ought to be able to say now that you are willing to take luck's chances in her."

"Ay, ay, sir; that's all true enough, so far as the craft is concerned. If this was a West India v'y'ge, I wouldn't stand a minute about signing the articles; nor should I make much question if the craft was large enough for a common whalin' v'y'ge; but sealin is a different business, and one onprofitable hand may make many an onprofitable lay."

"All this is true enough; but we do not intend to take any unprofitable hands, or to have any unropfitable lays. You know me——"

"Oh! if all was like *you*, Captain Gar'ner, I wouldn't stand even to wipe the pen. *Your* repitation was made in the southward, and no man can dispute your skill."

"Well, both mates are old hands at the business, and we intend that all the 'ables' shall be as good men as you are yourself."

"It *needs* good men, sir, to be operatin' among some of them sea-elephants! Sea-dogs; for sea-dogs is my sayin'. They tell of seals getting scurce; but I say, it's all in knowin' the business.—'There's young Captain Gar'ner,' says I, 'that's fittin' out a schooner for some onknown part of the world,' says I, 'maybe for the South Pole, for-ti-know, or for some sich out-of-the-way hole; now he'll come back *full*, or I'm no judge o' the business,' says I."

"Well, if this is your way of thinking, you have only to clap your name to the articles, and take your lay."

"Ay, ay, sir; when I've seed my shipmates. There isn't the business under the sun that so much needs that every man should be true, as the sea-elephant trade. Smaller animals may be got along with, with a narvous crew, per-haps; but when it comes to the raal old bulls, or bull-dogs, as a body might better call 'em, give me stout hearts, as well as stout hands."

"Well, now, to my notion, Watson, it is less dangerous to take a sea-elephant than to fasten to a regular old bull-whale, that maybe has had half a dozen irons in him al-ready."

"Yes, sir, *that's* sometimes skeary work, too; though I don't think so much of a whale as I do of a sea-elephant, or of a sea-lion. 'Let me know my shipmates,' say I, 'on a sealin' expedition.'"

"Captain Gar'ner," said the deacon, who necessarily overheard this discourse, "you ought to know at once whether this man is to go in the schooner or not. The mates believe he is, and may come across from the main without a hand to take his place, should he leave us. The thing should be settled at once."

"I'm willing to come to tarms this minute," returned Watson, as boldly as if he were perfectly sincere ; "only let me understand what I undertake. If I know'd to what islands the schooner was bound, it might make a difference in my judgment"

This was a well-devised question of the spy's, though it failed of its effect, in consequence of the deacon's great caution in not having yet told his secret, even to the master of his craft. Had Gardiner known exactly where he was about to go, the desire to secure a hand as valuable as Watson might have drawn from him some imprudent revelation ; but knowing nothing himself, he was obliged to make the best answer he could.

"Going," he said ; "why, we are going after seals, to be sure ; and shall look for them where they are most to be found. As experienced a hand as yourself ought to know where that is."

"Ay, ay, sir," answered the fellow, laughing—"it's just neither here nor there—that's all."

"Captain Gar'ner," interrupted the deacon, solemnly, "this is trifling, and we must come to terms with this man, or write to Mr. Hazard to engage another in his place. Come ashore, sir ; I have business with you up at the house."

The serious manner in which this was uttered took both the captain and the man a little by surprise. As for the first, he went below to conceal his good-looking throat beneath a black handkerchief, before he followed the deacon where it was most probable he should meet with Mary While he was thus occupied, Watson came down out of the main rigging and descended into the forecastle. As the young captain was walking fast toward the dwelling of Deacon Pratt, Watson came on deck again, and hailed Baiting Joe, who was fishing at no great distance from the wharf. In a few minutes Watson was in Joe's boat, bag and all—he had not brought a chest on board—and was under way for the Harbor. From the Harbor he sailed the same evening, in a whale-boat that was kept in readiness for him, carrying the news over to Holmes's Hole that the Sea Lion, of Oyster Pond, would certainly be ready to go out as early as the succeeding week. Although Watson thus seemingly deserted his post, it was with a perfect understanding with his real employers. He had need of a few days to make his own preparations before he left the 41st degree of north latitude to go as far south as a vessel could proceed. He did not, however, leave his post entirely vacant. One of Deacon Pratt's neighbors had undertaken, for a consideration, to let the progress of events be known, and tidings were sent by every opportunity, reporting the movements of the schooner, and the prospects of her getting to sea. These last were not quite as flattering as Roswell Gardiner had hoped and believed, the agents of the Vineyard company having succeeded in getting away two of Hazard's best men ; and as reliable sealers were not to be picked up as easily as pebbles on a beach, the delay caused by this new stroke of management might even be serious. All this time the Sea Lion, of Holmes's Hole, was getting ahead with untiring industry, and there was every prospect of her being ready to go out as soon as her competitor. But to return to Oyster Pond.

Deacon Pratt was in his porch ere Roswell Gardiner overtook him. There the deacon gave his young friend to understand he had private business of moment, and led the way at once into his own apartment, which served the purposes of office, bedroom, and closet ; the good man being accustomed to put up his petition to the throne of Mercy there, as well as transact all his temporal affairs. Shutting the door, and turning the key, not a little to Roswell's surprise, the old man faced his companion with a most earnest and solemn look, telling him at once that he was now about to open his mind to him in a matter of the last concern. The young sailor scarce knew what to think of it all ; but he hoped that Mary was, in some way, connected with the result.

"In the first place, Captain Gar'ner," continued the deacon, "I must ask you to take an oath."

"An oath, deacon ! This is quite new for the sealing business—as ceremonious as Uncle Sam's people."

"Yes, sir, an oath ; and an oath that must be most religiously kept, and on this Bible. Without the oath, our whole connection must fall through, Captain Gar'ner."

"Rather than that should happen, deacon, I will cheerfully take two oaths ; one to clench the other."

"It is well. I ask you, Roswell Gar'ner, to swear on this Holy Book that the secrets I shall now reveal to you shall not be told to any other, except in a manner prescribed by myself ; that in no other man's employment will you profit by them ; and that you will in all things connected with them be true and faithful to your engagements to me and to my interests—so help you God !"

Roswell Gardiner kissed the book, while he wondered much, and was dying with curiosity to know what was to follow. This great point secured, the deacon laid aside the sacred volume, opened a drawer, and produced the two all-important charts, to which he had transferred the notes of Daggett.

"Captain Gar'ner," resumed the deacon, spreading the chart of the antarctic sea on the bed, "you must have known me and my ways long enough to feel some surprise at finding me, at my time of life, first entering into the shipping concern."

"If I've felt any surprise, deacon, it is that a man of your taste and judgment should have held aloof so long from the only employment that I think fit for a man of real energy and character."

"Ay, this is well enough for you to say, as a seaman yourself ; though you will find it hard to persuade most of those who live on shore into your own ways of thinking."

"That is because people ashore think and act as they have been brought up to do. Now just look at that chart, deacon ; see how much of it is water, and how little of it is land. Minister Whittle told us only the last Sabbath, that nothing was created without a design, and that a wise dispensation of Divine Providence was to be seen in all the works of nature. Now if the land was intended to take the lead of the water, would there have been so much more of the last than of the first, deacon ? That was the idea that came into my mind when I heard the minister's words ; and had not Mary——"

"What of Mary ?" demanded the deacon, seeing that the young man paused.

"Only I was in hopes that what you had to say, deacon, might have some connection with her."

"What I have to say is better worth hearing than fifty Marys. As to my niece, Gar'ner, you are welcome to her, if she will have you ; and why she does not is to me unaccountable. But, you see that chart—look at it well, and tell me if you find anything new or remarkable about it."

"It looks like old times, deacon, and here are many places that I have visited and know. What have we here? Islands laid down in pencil, with the latitude and longitude in figures! Who says there is land thereaway, Deacon Pratt, if I may be so free as to ask the question?"

"I do—and capital good land it is for a sealing craft to get alongside of. Them islands, Gar'ner, may make your fortune, as well as mine. No matter how I know they are there—it is enough that I *do* know it, and that I wish you to carry the Sea Lion to that very spot, as straight as you can go ; fill her up with elephant's oil, ivory, and skins, and bring her back again as fast as she can travel."

"Islands in that latitude and longitude!" said Roswell Gardiner, examining the chart as closely as if it were of very fine print indeed—" I never heard of any such land before !"

"'Tis there, notwithstanding ; and like all land in distant seas that men have not often troubled, plentifully garnished with what will pay the mariner well for his visit."

"Of that I have little doubt, should there be actually any land there. It may be a Cape Fly Away that some fellow has seen in thick weather. The ocean is full of such islands !"

"This is none of them. It is bony fidy 'arth, as I know from the man who trod it. You must take good care, Gar'-ner, and not run the schooner on it,"—with a small, chuck-ling laugh, such as a man little accustomed to this species of indulgence uses when in high good-humor. "I am not rich enough to buy and fit out Sea Lions for you to cast 'em away."

"That's high latitude, deacon, to carry a craft into. Cook himself fell short of *that* somewhat !"

"Never mind Cook—he was a king's navigator—my man was an American sealer ; and what he has once seen he knows where to find again. There are the islands—three in number; and there you will find 'em, with animals on their shores as plenty as clam-shells on the south beach."

"I hope it may be so. If land is there, and you'll risk the schooner, I'll try to get a look at it. I shall want you to put it down in black and white, however, that I'm to go as high as this."

"You shall have any authority a man may ask. On that point there can be no difficulty between me and you. The

risk of the schooner must be mine, of course ; but I rely
on you to take as good care of her as a man can. Go
then, direct to that point, and fill up the schooner. But,
Gar'ner, my business doesn't end with this ! As soon as
the schooner is full you will come to the southward, and
get her clear of everything like ice as fast as possible."

"That I should be very likely to do, deacon, though you
had said nothing on the subject."

"Yes, by all accounts them are stormy seas, and the
sooner a body is shut of them the better. And now, Gar'-
ner, I must swear you again. I have another secret to tell
you, and an oath must go with each. Kiss this sacred volume once more, and swear to me never to reveal to another
that which I am about to reveal to you, unless it may be
in a court of law, and at the command of justice, so help
you God !"

"What, a second oath, deacon !—You are as bad as the
custom-houses, which take you on all tacks, and don't
believe you when you've done. Surely, I'm sworn in already."

"Kiss the book, and swear to what I have put to you,"
said the deacon, sternly, "or never go to sea in a craft of
mine. Never to reveal what I shall now tell you, unless
compelled by justice, so help you God !"

Thus cornered, Roswell Gardiner hesitated no longer,
but swore as required, kissing the book gravely and reverently. This was the young man's first command, and he
was not going to lose it on account of so small a matter as
swearing to keep his owner's secrets. Having obtained
the pledge, the deacon now produced the second chart,
which was made to take the place of the other on the bed.

"There !" he exclaimed, in a sort of triumph—"that is
the real object of your voyage !"

"That key ! Why, deacon, that is in north latitude—°
—", and you make a crooked road of it, truly, when you
tell me to go as far south as—°—", in order to reach it."

"It is well to have two strings to a body's bow. When
you hear what you are to bring from that key, you will
understand why I send you south, before you are to come
here to top off your cargo."

"It must be with turtle, then," said Roswell Gardiner,
laughing. "Nothing grows on these keys but a few stunted
shrubs, and nothing is ever to be found on them but turtle.
Once in a while a fellow may pick up a few turtle, if he
happen to hit the right key."

"Gar'ner," rejoined the deacon, still more solemnly—"that island, low and insignificant as it is, contains treasure. Pirates made their deposits here a long time ago, and the knowledge of that fact is now confined to myself."

The young man stared at the deacon as if he had some doubts whether the old man were in his right mind. He knew the besetting weakness of his character well, and had no difficulty in appreciating the influence of such a belief as that he had just expressed, on his feelings; but it seemed so utterly improbable that he, living on Oyster Pond, should learn a fact of this nature, which was concealed from others, that, at first, he fancied his owner had been dreaming of money until its images had made him mad. Then he recollected the deceased mariner, the deacon's many conferences with him, the interest he had always appeared to take in the man, and the suddenness, as well as the time, of the purchase of the shooner; and he at once obtained a clew to the whole affair.

"Daggett has told you this, Deacon Pratt," said Gardiner, in his off-hand way. "And he is the man who has told you of those sealing-islands too!"

"Admitting it to be so, why not Daggett as well as any other man?"

"Certainly, if he knew what he was saying to be true—but the yarn of a sailor is not often to be taken for gospel."

"Daggett was near his end, and cannot be classed with those who talk idly in the pride of their health and strength—men who are ever ready to say, 'Tush, God has forgotten.'"

"Why was this told to you, when the man had natural friends and relatives by the dozen over on the Vineyard?"

"He had been away from the Vineyard and them relatives fifty years; a length of time that weakens a body's feelings considerably. Take you away from Mary only a fourth part of that time, and you would forget whether her eyes are blue or black, and altogether how she looks."

"If I should, a most miserable and contemptible dog should I account myself! No, deacon, twice fifty years would not make me forget the eyes or the looks of Mary!"

"Ay, so all youngsters think, and feel, and talk. But let 'em try the world, and they'll soon find out their own foolishness. But Daggett made me his confidant because Providence put me in his way, and because he trusted to

be well enough to go in the schooner, and to turn the expedition to some account in his own behalf."

"Had the man the impudence to confess that he had
been a pirate, and helped to bury treasure on this key?"

"That is not, by any means, his history. Daggett was
never a pirate himself, but accident placed him in the same
prison and same room as that in which a real pirate was
confined. There the men became friends, and the con-
demned prisoner, for such he was in the end, gave this
secret to Daggett as the last service he could do him."

"I hope, deacon, you do not expect much in the way of
profit from this part of the voyage?"

"I expect the most from it, Gar'ner, as you will too,
when you come to hear the whole story."

The deacon then went into all the particulars of the revelations made by the pirate to his fellow-prisoner, much
as they had been given by Daggett to himself. The young
man listened to this account at first with incredulity, then
with interest; and finally with a feeling that induced him
to believe that there might be more truth in the narrative
than he had originally supposed possible. This change was
produced by the earnest manner of the deacon as much as
by the narrative itself; for he had become graphic under
the strong impulses of that which, with him, was a master
passion. So deep had been the impression made on the
mind of the old man by Daggett's account, and so intense
the expectations thereby awakened, that he omitted nothing, observed the most minute accuracy in all his details,
and conveyed just as distinct impressions to his listener, as
had been conveyed to himself, when the story was first told
to him.

"This is a most extr'or'nary account, take it on whatever
tack you will!" exclaimed Roswell Gardiner, as soon as a
pause in the deacon's story enabled him to put in another
word. "The most extr'or'nary tale I ever listened to!
How came so much gold and silver to be abandoned for so
long a time?"

"Them three officers hid it there, fearing to trust their
own crew with it in their vessel. Their pretence was to stop
for turtle, just as you must do; whilst the hands were turt-
ling, the captain and his mates walked about the key, and
took occasion to make their deposits in that hole on the
coral rock, as you have heard me say. Oh! it's all too natural not to be true!"

Roswell Gardiner saw that the old man's hopes were too

keenly excited to be easily cooled, and that his latent covet-ousness was thoroughly awakened. Ot all the passions to which poor human nature is the slave, the love of gold is that which endures the longest, and is often literally car-ried with us to the verge of the grave. Indeed, in minds so constituted originally as to submit to an undue love of money, the passion appears to increase, as others more de-pendent on youth, and strength, and enterprise, and am-bition, gradually become of diminished force, slowly but surely usurping the entire sway over a being that was once subject to many masters. Thus had it been with the deacon. Nearly all his passions now centred in this one. He no longer cared for preferment in politics, though once it had been the source of a strong desire to represent Suffolk at Albany ; even the meeting, and its honors, were loosening their hold on his mind ; while his fellow-men, his kindred in-cluded, were regarded by him as little more than so many competitors, or tools.

"A lie may be made to seem very natural," answered Roswell Gardiner, "if it has been put together by one who understands knotting and splicing in such matters. Did this Daggett name the amount of the sum that he supposed the pirates may have left on that key?"

"He did," returned the deacon, the whole of his narrow and craving soul seeming to gleam in his two sunken eyes as he answered. "According to the account of the pirate, there could not have been much less than thirty thousand dollars, and nearly all of it in good doubloons of the coin of the kings—doubloons that will weigh their full sixteens to the pound—ay, and to spare!"

"The Sea Lion's cargo, well chosen and well stowed, would double that, deacon, if the right animals can only be found."

"Maybe so—but just think, Gar'ner—this will be in good, bright coined gold!"

"But what right can we have to that gold, even admit-ting that it is there, and can be found ?"

"Right!" exclaimed the deacon, staring. "Does not that which Divine Providence gives man become his own ?"

"By the same rule it might be said Divine Providence gave it to the pirates. There must be lawful owners to all this money, if one could only find them."

"Ay, if one could only find them. Harkee, Gar'ner ; have you spent a shilling or a quarter lately ?"

"A good many of both, deacon," answered the young

6

man, again betraying the lightness of his heart with a laugh. "I wish I had more of your saving temper, and I might get rich. Yes, I spent a quarter only two hours since, in buying fish for the cabin, of old Baiting Joe."

"Well, tell me the impression of that quarter. Had it a head, or only pillars? What was its date, and in whose reign was it struck? Maybe it was from the mint at Philadelphia—if so, had it the old eagle or the new? In a word, could you swear to that quarter, Gar'ner, or to any quarter you ever spent in your life?"

"Perhaps not, deacon. A fellow doesn't sit down to take likenesses, when he gets a little silver or gold."

"Nor is it very probable that any one could say—'that is my doubloon.'"

"Still there must be a lawful owner to each piece of that money, if any such money be there," returned Roswell Gardiner, a little positively. "Have you ever talked with Mary, deacon, on this subject?"

"I talk of such a matter with a woman! Do you think I'm mad, Gar'ner? If I wanted to have the secret run through old Suffo'k, as fire runs over the salt meadows in the spring, I might think of such a thing; but not without. I have talked with no one but the master of the craft that I am about to send out in search of this gold, as well as in search of the sealing-islands, I have shown you. Had there been but *one* object in view, I might not have ventured so much; but with *two* before my eyes, it would seem like flying in the face of Divine Providence to neglect so great an opportunity!"

Roswell Gardiner saw that arguments would avail nothing against a cupidity so keenly aroused. He abstained, therefore, from urging any more of the objections that suggested themselves to his mind, but heard all that the deacon had to tell him, taking full notes of what he heard. It would seem that Daggett had been sufficiently clear in his directions for finding the hidden treasure, provided always that his confidant the pirate had been as clear with him, and had not been indulging in a mystification. The probability of the last had early suggested itself to one of Deacon Pratt's cautious temperament; but Daggett had succeeded in removing the impression by his forcible statements of his friend's sincerity. There was as little doubt of the sincerity of the belief of the Martha's Vineyard mariner, as there was of that of the deacon himself.

The day that succeeded this conference, the Sea Lion

hauled off from the wharf, and all communications with her were now made only by means of boats. The sudden disappearance of Watson may have contributed to this change—men being more under control with a craft at her moorings than when fast to a wharf. Three days later the schooner lifted her anchor, and with a light air made sail. She passed through the narrow but deep channel which separates Shelter Island from Oyster Pond, quitting the waters of Peconic altogether. There was not an air of departure about her, notwithstanding. The deacon was not much concerned ; and some of Roswell Gardiner's clothes were still at his washerwoman's, circumstances that were fully explained, when the schooner was seen to anchor in Gardiner's Bay, which is an outer roadstead to all the ports and havens of that region.

CHAPTER VII.

"Walk in the light ! so shalt thou know
That fellowship of love,
His spirit only can bestow
Who reigns in light above.
Walk in the light ! and sin, abhor'd,
Shall ne'er defile again ;
The blood of Jesus Christ, the Lord,
Shall cleanse from every stain."—BERNARD BARTON.

ABOUT an hour after the Sea Lion, of Oyster Pond, had let go her anchor in Gardiner's Bay, a coasting sloop approached her, coming from the westward. There are two passages by which vessels enter or quit Long Island Sound, at its eastern termination. The main channel is between Plum and Fisher's Islands, and from the rapidity of its currents, is known by the name of the Race. The other passage is much less frequented, being out of the direct line for sailing for craft that keep mid-sound. It lies to the southward of the Race, between Plum Island and Oyster Pond Point, and is called by the Anglo-Saxon appellation of Plum Gut. The coaster just mentioned had come through this latter passage ; and it was the impression of those who saw her from the schooner, that she was bound up into Peconic, or the waters of Sag Harbor. Instead of luffing up into either of the channels that would have carried her into these places, however, she kept off, crossing

Gardiner's Bay, until she got within hail of the schooner. The wind being quite light, there was time for the following short dialogue to take place between the skipper of this coaster and Roswell Gardiner, before the sloop had passed beyond the reach of the voice.

"Is that the Sea Lion, of Oyster Pond?" demanded the skipper, boldly.

"Ay, ay," answered Roswell Gardiner, in the sententious manner of a seaman.

"Is there one Watson of Martha's Vineyard, shipped in that craft?"

"He was aboard here for a week, but left us suddenly. As he did not sign articles, I cannot say that he run."

"He changed his mind, then," returned the other, as one expresses a slight degree of surprise at hearing that which was new to him. "Watson is apt to whiffle about, though a prime fellow, if you can once fasten to him, and get him into blue water. Does your schooner go out to-morrow, Captain Gar ner?"

"Not till next day, I think," said Roswell Gardiner, with the frankness of his nature, utterly free from the slightest suspicion that he was communicating with one in the interests of rivals. "My mates have not yet joined me, and I am short of my complement by two good hands. Had that fellow Watson stuck by me, I would have given him a look at water that no lead ever sounded."

"Ay, ay; he's a whiffler, but a good man on a sea-elephant. Then you think you'll sail day a'ter to-morrow?"

"If my mates come over from the main. They wrote me yesterday that they had got the hands, and were then on the lookout for something to get across in. I've come out here to be ready for them, and to pick 'em up, that they needn't go all the way up to the Harbor."

"That's a good traverse, and will save a long pull. Perhaps they are in *that* boat."

At this allusion to a boat, Roswell Gardiner sprang into his main rigging, and saw, sure enough, that a boat was pulling directly toward the schooner, coming from the main, and distant only a short half mile. A glass was handed to him, and he was soon heard announcing cheerfully to his men, that "Mr. Hazard and the second officer were in the boat, with two seamen," and that he supposed they should *now* have their complement. All this was overheard by the skipper of the sloop, who caught each syllable with the most eager attention.

"You'll soon be travelling south, I'm thinking, Captain Gar'ner?" called out this worthy, again, in a sort of felicitating way. "Them's your chaps, and they'll set you up."

"I hope so, with all my heart, for there is nothing more tiresome than waiting when one is all ready to trip. My owner is getting to be impatient too, and wants to see some skins in return for his dollars."

"Ay, ay, them's your chaps, and you'll be off the day a'ter to-morrow, at the latest. Well, a good time to you, Captain Gar'ner, and a plenty of skinning. It's a long road to travel, especially when a craft has to go as far south as yours is bound!"

"How do you know, friend, whither I am bound? You have not asked me for my sealing-ground, nor is it usual, in our business, to be hawking it up and down the country."

"All that is true enough, but I've a notion, notwithstanding. Now as you'll be off so soon, and as I shall not see you again, for some time at least, I will give you a piece of advice. If you fall *in* with a consort, don't fall *out* with her and make a distant v'y'ge a cruise for an enemy, but come to tarms, and work in company; lay for lay; and make fair weather of what can't be helped."

The men on board the sloop laughed at this speech, while those on board the schooner wondered. To Roswell Gardiner and his people the allusions were an enigma, and the former muttered something about the stranger's being a dunce, as he descended from the rigging and gave some orders to prepare to receive the boat.

"The chap belongs to the Hole," rejoined the master of the schooner; "and all them Vineyard fellows fancy themselves better blue-jackets than the rest of mankind: I suppose it must be because their island lies further out to sea than anything we have here inside of Montauk."

Thus ended the communications with the stranger. The sloop glided away before a light south wind, and, favored by an ebb-tide, soon rounded the spit of sand that shelters the anchorage; and, hauling up to the eastward, she went on her way toward Holmes's Hole. The skipper was a relative of half of those who were interested in fitting out the rival Sea Lion, and had volunteered to obtain the very information he took with him, knowing how acceptable it would be to those at home. Sooth to say, a deep but wary excitement prevailed on the Vineyard, touching not only the sealing islands, but also in respect to the buried treasure. The information actually possessed by the relations of the deceased mariner was neither very full nor very clear. It consisted principally of sayings of Daggett, uttered during his homeward-bound passage, and transmitted by the master of the brig to him of the sloop in the course of conferences that wore away a long summer's afternoon, as the two vessels lay becalmed within a hundred fathoms of each other. These sayings, however, had been frequent and intelligible. All men like to deal in that which makes them of importance ; and the possession of his secrets had just the effect on Daggett's mind that was necessary to render him boastful. Under such impulses his tongue had not been very guarded ; and facts leaked out which, when transmitted to his native island, through the medium of half-a-dozen tongues and as many fancies, amounted to statements sufficient to fire the imaginations of a people much duller than those of Martha's Vineyard. Accustomed to converse and think of such expeditions, it is not surprising that a few of the most enterprising of those who first heard the reports should unite and plan the adventure they now actually had in hand. When the intelligence of what was going on on Oyster Pond reached them, everything like hesitation or doubt disappeared ; and from the moment of the nephew's return in quest of his uncle's assets, the equipment of the " Humses' Hull " craft had been pressed in a way that would have done credit to that of a government cruiser. Even Henry Eckford, so well known for having undertaken to cut the trees and put upon the waters of Ontario two double-bank frigates, if frigates they could be termed, each of which was to mount its hundred guns, in the short space of sixty days, scarce manifested greater energy in carrying out his contract, than did these rustic islanders in preparing their craft to compete with that which they were now certain was about to sail from the place where their kinsman had breathed his last.

These keen and spirited islanders, however, did not work quite as much in the dark as our accounts, unexplained, might give the reader reason to suppose. It will be remembered that there was a till to the chest which had not been examined by the deacon. This till contained an old mutilated journal, not of the last, but of one or two of the earlier voyages of the deceased ; though it had detached entries that evidently referred to different and distant periods of time. By dint of study, and by putting to-

gether sundry entries that at first sight might not be supposed to have any connection with each other, the present
possessor of that chest had obtained what he deemed to
be very sufficient clews to his uncle's two great secrets.
There were also in the chest several loose pieces of paper,
on which there were rude attempts to make charts of all
the islands and keys in question, giving their relative
positions as it respected their immediate neighbors, but in
no instance giving the latitudes and longitudes. In addition to these significant proofs that the reports brought
through the two masters were not without a foundation,
there was an unfinished letter, written by the deceased,
and addressed as a sort of legacy, "to any, or all of
Martha's Vineyard, of the name of Daggett." This address was sufficiently wide, including, probably, some hundreds of persons ; a clan, in fact ; but it was also sufficiently
significant The individual into whose hands it first fell,
being of the name, read it first, as a matter of course,
when he carefully folded it up, and placed it in a pocket-
book, which he was much in the habit of carrying in his
own pocket. On what principle this letter, unfinished and
without a signature, with nothing indeed but its general
and comprehensive address to point out its origin as well
as its destination, was thus appropriated to the purposes
of a single individual, we shall not stop to inquire. Such
was the fact, however, and none connected with the equipment of the Sea Lion, of Holmes's Hole, knew anything of
the existence of that document, its present possessor excepted. He looked it over occasionally, and deemed the
information it conveyed of no trifling import, under all the
circumstances of the case.

Both the enterprises of which we have given an opening
account were perfectly characteristic of the state of society
in which they were brought into existence Deacon Pratt,
if he had any regular calling, was properly a husbandman,
though the love of money had induced him to invest his
cash in nearly every concern around him, which promised
remunerating returns. The principal owners of the Sea
Lion, of Holmes's Hole, were husbandmen also ; folks who
literally tilled the earth, cradled their own oats and rye,
and mowed their own meadows. Notwithstanding, neither
of these men, those of the Vineyard any more than he of
Oyster Pond, had hesitated about investing of his means
in a maritime expedition, just as if they were all regular
shipowners of the largest port in the Union. With such

men, it is only necessary to exhibit an account with a fair
prospect of large profits, and they are ever ready to enter
into the adventure, heart, hand, and pocket.   Last season,
it may have been to look for whales on the coast of Japan ;
the season before that, to search for islands frequented by
the seals ; this season, possibly, to carry a party out to hunt
for camelopards, set nets for young lions, and beat up the
quarters of the rhinoceros on the plains of Africa ; while
the next, they may be transporting ice from Long Pond to
Calcutta and Kingston—not to say to London itself.   Of
such materials are those descendants of the Puritans composed ; a mixture of good and evil ; of the religion which
clings to the past, in recollection rather than in feeling,
mingled with a worldly-mindedness that amounts nearly to
rapacity ; all cloaked and rendered decent by a conventional respect for duties, and respectable and useful, by
frugality, enterprise, and untiring activity.

Roswell Gardiner had not mistaken the persons of those
in the boat.   They proved to be Phil Hazard, his first officer ; Tim Green, the second mate ; and the two sealers
whom it had cost so much time and ingenuity to obtain.
Although neither of the mates even suspected the truth,
no sooner had they engaged the right sort of man than he
was tampered with by the agents of the Martha's Vineyard
concern, and spirited away by means of more tempting
proposals, before he had got quite so far as to sign the articles.   One of the motives for sending Watson across to
Oyster Pond had been to induce Captain Gardiner to believe he had engaged so skilful a hand, which would effectually prevent his attempting to procure another, until,
at the last moment, he might find himself unable to put to
sea for the want of a complement.   A whaling or a sealing
voyage requires that the vessel should take out with her
the particular hands necessary to her specific object,
though, of late years, the seamen have got so much in the
habit of "running," especially in the Pacific, that it is only
the craft that strictly belong to what may be termed the
whaling communities, that bring back with them the people they carry out, and not always them.

But here had Roswell Gardiner his complement full,
and nearly everything ready to sea.   He had only to go
up to the Harbor and obtain his clearance, have a short
interview with his owner, a longer with Mary, and be off
for the antarctic circle, if indeed the ice would allow him
to get so far south.   There were now sixteen souls on

board the Sea Lion, a very sufficient number for the voyage on which she was about to sail. The disposition or rating of the crew was as follows, viz. :

1. Roswell Gardiner, master.	9. Joshua Short, seaman.
2. Philip Hazard, chief mate.	10. Stephen Stimson, do.
3. Timothy Green, second do.	11. Bartlett Davidson, do.
4. David Weeks, carpenter.	12. Peter Mount, landsman.
5. Nathan Thompson, seaman.	13. Arcularius Mott, do.
6. Sylvester Havens, do.	14. Robert Smith, do.
7. Marcus Todd, do.	15. Cato Livingston, cook.
8. Hiram Flint, do.	16. Primus Floyd, boy.

This was considered a good crew, on the whole. Every man was a native American, and most of them belonged to old Suffolk. Thompson, and Flint, and Short, and Stimson, four capital fellows in their way, came from the main ; the last, it was said, from as far east as Kennebunk. No matter ; they were all reasonably young, hale, active fellows, with a promise of excellent service about every man of them. Livingston and Floyd were colored persons, who bore the names of the two respectable families in which they or their progenitors had formerly been slaves. Weeks was accustomed to the sea, and might have been rated indifferently as a carpenter or as a mariner. Mount and Mott, though shipped as landsmen, were a good deal accustomed to the water also, having passed each two seasons in coasters, though neither had ever yet been really *outside*, or seen blue water.

It would not have been easy to give to the Sea Lion a more efficient crew ; yet there was scarce a real seaman belonging to her—a man who could have been made a captain of the forecastle on board a frigate or a ship of the line. Even Gardiner, the best man in his little craft in nearly every respect, was deficient in many attainments that mark the thorough sea-dog. He would have been remarkable anywhere for personal activity, for courage, readiness, hardihood, and all those qualities which render a man useful in the business to which he properly belonged ; but he could hardly be termed a skilful leadsman, knew little of the finesse of his calling, and was wanting in that in-and-in breeding which converts habit into an instinct, and causes the thorough seaman to do the right thing, blow high or blow low, in the right way, and at the right moment. In all these respects, however, he was much the best man on board ; and he was so superior to the rest as

fully to command all their respect. Stimson was probably
the next best seaman, after the master.

The day succeeding that on which the Sea Lion received
the remainder of her people, Roswell Gardiner went up to
the Harbor, where he met Deacon Pratt, by appointment.
The object was to clear the schooner out, which could be
done only at that place. Mary accompanied her uncle, to
transact some of her own little domestic business ; and it
was then arranged between the parties, that the deacon
should make his last visit to his vessel in the return-boat
of her master, while Roswell Gardiner should take Mary
back to Oyster Pond, in the whale-boat that had brought
her and her uncle over. As Baiting Joe, as usual, had
acted as ferryman, it was necessary to get rid of him, the
young sailor desiring to be alone with Mary. This was easily enough effected, by a present of a quarter of a dollar.
The boat having two lugg sails, and the wind being light
and steady, at southwest, there was nothing to conflict with
Roswell Gardiner's wishes.

The young sailor left the wharf at Sag Harbor about ten
minutes after the deacon had preceded him, on his way to
the schooner. As the wind was so light and so fair, he soon
had his sheets in, and the boat gliding along at an easy
rate, which permitted him to bestow nearly all his attention
on his charming companion. Roswell Gardiner had sought
this occasion, that he might once more open his heart to
Mary, and urge his suit for the last time, previously to so
long an absence. This he did in a manly, frank way, that
was far from being unpleasant to his gentle listener, whose
inclinations, for a few minutes, blinded her to the reso-
lutions already made on principle. So urgent was her
suitor, indeed, that she should solemnly plight her faith
to him, ere he sailed, that a soft illusion came over the
mind of one as affectionate as Mary, and she was half inclined to believe her previous determination was unjusti-
fiable and obdurate. But the head of one of her high
principles, and clear views of duty, could not long be deceived by her heart, and she regained the self-command
which had hitherto sustained her in all her former trials,
in connection with this subject.

"Perhaps it would have been better, Roswell," she said,
"had I taken leave of you at the Harbor, and not incurred the risk of the pain that I foresee I shall both give
and bear, in our present discourse. I have concealed nothing from you ; possibly I have been more sincere than

prudence would sanction. You know the only obstacle there is to our union; but that appears to increase in strength the more I ask you to reflect on it—to try to remove it."

"What would you have me do, Mary? Surely, not to play the hypocrite, and profess to believe that which I certainly do not, and which, after all my inquiries, I *cannot* believe."

"I am sorry it is so, on every account," returned Mary, in a low and saddened tone. "Sorry, that one of so frank, ingenuous a mind, should find it impossible to accept the creed of his fathers, and sorry that it must leave so impassable a chasm between us forever."

"No, Mary; that can never be! Nothing but death can separate us for so long a time! While we meet, we shall at least be friends; and friends love to meet and to see each other often."

"It may seem unkind, at a moment like this, Roswell, but it is in truth the very reverse, if I say we ought not to meet each other here, if we are bent on following our own separate ways toward a future world. My God is not your God; and what can there be of peace in a family, when its two heads worship different deities? I am afraid that you do not think sufficiently of the nature of these things."

"I did not believe you to be so illiberal, Mary! Had the deacon said as much, I might not have been surprised; but, for one like you to tell me that my God is not your God, is narrow indeed."

"Is it not so, Roswell? And, if so, why should we attempt to gloss over the truth by deceptive words? I am a believer in the Redeemer, as the Son of God; as one of the Holy Trinity; while you believe in him only as a man —a righteous and just, a sinless man, if you will, but as a man only. Now is not the difference in these creeds immense? Is it not, in truth, just the difference between God and man? I worship my Redeemer; regard him as the equal of the Father—as a part of the Divine Being; while you look on him as merely a man without sin—as a man such as Adam probably was before the fall."

"Do we know enough of these matters, Mary, to justify us in allowing them to interfere with our happiness?"

"We are told that they are all-essential to our happiness —not in the sense you may mean, Roswell, but in one of far higher import—and we cannot neglect them without paying the penalty."

"I think that you carry these notions too far, dearest Mary, and that it is possible for man and wife most heartily to love each other, and to be happy in each other, without their thinking exactly alike on religion. How many good and pious women do you see, who are contented and prosperous as wives and mothers, and who are members of meeting, but whose husbands make no profession of any sort!"

"That may be true, or not. I lay no claim to a right to judge of any other's duties, or manner of doing what they ought to do. Thousands of girls marry without *feeling* the very obligations that they profess to reverence; and when, in after life, deeper convictions come, they cannot cast aside the connections they have previously formed, if they would; and probably would not if they could. That is a different thing from a young woman, who has a deep sense of what she owes to her Redeemer, becoming deliberately, and with a full sense of what she is doing, the wife of one who regards her God as merely a man—I care not how you qualify this opinion, by saying a pure and sinless man; it will be man still. The difference between God and man is too immense to be frittered away by any such qualifications as that."

"But, if I find it *impossible* to believe all you believe, Mary, surely you would not punish me for having the sincerity to tell you the truth, and the whole truth."

"No, indeed, Roswell," answered the honest girl, gently, not to say tenderly. "Nothing has given me a better opinion of your principles, Roswell—a higher notion of what your upright and frank character really is, than the manly way in which you have admitted the justice of my suspicions of your want of faith—of faith, as I consider faith can alone exist. This fair dealing has made me honor you, and esteem you, in addition to the more girlish attachment that I do not wish to conceal from you, at least, I have so long felt."

"Blessed Mary!" exclaimed Roswell Gardiner, almost ready to fall down on his knees and worship the pretty enthusiast who sat at his side, with a countenance in which intense interest in his welfare was beaming from two of the softest and sweetest blue eyes that maiden ever bent on a youth in modest tenderness, whatever disposition he might be in to accept her God as his God. "How can one so kind in all other respects, prove so cruel in this one particular!"

"Because that one particular, as you term it, Roswell, is all in all to her," answered the girl, with a face that was now flushed with feeling. "I must answer you as Joshua told the Israelites of old—'Choose you, this day, whom you will serve ; whether the gods which your fathers served, that were on the other side of the flood, or the gods of the Amorites, in whose land ye dwell ; *but as for me and my house, we will serve the Lord.*'"

"Do you class me with the idolators and pagans of Palestine ?" demanded Gardiner, reproachfully.

"You have said it, Roswell. It is not I, but yourself, who have thus classed you. You worship your reason, instead of the only true and living God. This is idolatry of the worst character, since the idol is never seen by the devotee, and he does not know of its existence."

"You consider it then idolatry for one to use those gifts which he has received from his Maker, and to treat the most important of all subjects as a rational being, instead of receiving a creed blindly, and without thought ?"

"If what you call thought could better the matter ; if it were sufficient to comprehend and master this subject, there might be force in what you say. But what is this boasted reason after all ? It is not sufficient to explain a single mystery of the creation, though there are thousands. I know there are, nay there *must* be, a variety of opinions among those who look to their reasons, instead of accepting the doctrine of revelation, for the character of Christ ; but I believe all who are not open infidels admit that the atonement of his death was sufficient for the salvation of men ; now can you explain this part of the theory of our religion any more than you can explain the divine nature of the Redeemer ? Can you *reason* any more wisely touching the fall than touching the redemption itself ? I know I am unfit to treat of matters of this profound nature," continued Mary, modestly, though with great earnestness and beauty of manner ; "but, to me, it seems very plain that the instant circumstances lead us beyond the limits of our means of comprehension, we are to *believe* in, and not to reason on, revelation. The whole history of Christianity teaches this. Its first ministers were uneducated men ; men who were totally ignorant until enlightened by their faith ; and all the lessons it teaches are to raise faith, and faith in the Redeemer, high above all other attainments, as the one great acquisition that includes and colors every other. When such is the fact, the heart does not make a stumbling-block of everything that the head cannot understand."

"I do not know how it is," answered Roswell Gardiner, influenced, though unconvinced; "but when I talk with you on the subject, Mary, I cannot do justice to my opinions, or to the manner in which I reason on them with my male friends and acquaintance. I confess it does appear to me illogical, unreasonable—I scarce know how to designate what I mean—but, improbable, that God should suffer himself, or his Son, to be crucified by beings that he himself created, or that he should feel a necessity for any such course, in order to redeem beings he had himself brought into existence."

"If there be any argument in the last, Roswell, it is an argument as much against the crucifixion of a man, as against the crucifixion of one of the Trinity itself I understand you to believe that such a being as Jesus of Nazareth did exist; that he was crucified for our redemption; and that the atonement was accepted, and acceptable before God the Father. Now is it not just as difficult to understand how, or why, this should be, as to understand the common creed of Christians?"

"Surely there is a vast difference between the crucifixion of a subordinate being, and the crucifixion of one who made a part of the Godhead itself, Mary! I can imagine the first, though I may not pretend to understand its reasons, or why it was necessary it should be so; but I am certain you will not mistake my motive when I say I cannot imagine the other."

"Make no apologies to me, Roswell; look rather to that dread Being whose teachings, through chosen ministers, you disregard. As for what you say, I can fully feel its truth. I do not pretend to *understand* why such a sacrifice should be necessary, but I *believe* it, *feel* it; and believing and feeling it, I cannot but adore and worship the Son, who quitted heaven to come on earth, and suffered, that we might possess eternal life. It is all mystery to me, as is the creation itself, our existence, God himself, and all else that my mind is too limited to comprehend. But, Roswell, if I believe a part of the teachings of the Christian church, I must believe all. The apostles, who were called by Christ in person, who lived in his very presence, who knew nothing except as the Holy Spirit prompted, worshipped him as the Son of God, as one 'who thought it not robbery to be equal with God;' and shall

I, ignorant and uninspired, pretend to set up my feeble means of reasoning, in opposition to their written instructions!"

"Yet must each of us stand or fall by the means he possesses, and the use he makes of them."

"That is quite true, Roswell; and ask yourself the use to which you put your own faculties. I do not deny that we are to exercise our reason, but it is within the bounds set for its exercise. We may examine the evidence of Christianity and determine for ourselves how far it is supported by reasonable and sufficient proofs, beyond this we cannot be expected to go, else might we be required to comprehend the mystery of our own existence, which just as much exceeds our understanding as any other. We are told that man was created in the image of his Creator, which means that there is an immortal and spiritual part of him that is entirely different from the material creature. One perishes, temporarily at least—a limb can be severed from the body and perish, even while the body survives; but it is not so with that which has been created in the image of the Deity. That is imperishable, immortal, spiritual, though doomed to dwell awhile in a tenement of clay. Now why is it more difficult to believe that pure divinity may have entered into the person of one man, than to *believe*, nay to *feel*, that the image of God has entered into the persons of so many myriads of men? You not only overlook all this, Roswell, but you commit the, to me inexplicable, mistake of believing a part of a mystery, while you hesitate about believing all. Were you to deny the merits of the atonement altogether, your position would be much stronger than it is in believing what you do. But, Roswell, we will not embitter the moment of separation by talking more on this subject now. I have other things to say to you, and but little time to say them in. The promise you have asked of me to remain single until your return, I most freely make. It costs me nothing to give you *this* pledge, since there is scarce a possibility of my ever marrying another."

Mary repeated these words, or rather this idea in other words, to Roswell Gardiner's great delight; and again and again he declared that he could now penetrate the icy seas with a light heart, confident he should find her, on his return, disengaged, and, as he hoped, as much disposed to regard him with interest as she then was. Nevertheless, Gardiner did not deceive himself as to Mary's intentions.

He knew her and her principles too well to fancy that her resolution would be very likely to falter. Notwithstanding their long and intimate knowledge of each other, at no time had she ever betrayed a weakness that promised to undermine her high sense of duty ; and as time increased her means of judging of what those duties were, her submission to them seemed to be stronger and stronger. Had there been anything stern or repulsive in Mary's manner of manifesting the feeling that was uppermost in her mind, one of Roswell Gardiner's temperament would have been very apt to shake off her influence ; but, so far from this being the case, she ever met him and parted from him with a gentle and ingenuous interest in his welfare, and occasionally with much womanly tenderness. He knew that she prayed for him daily, as fervently as she prayed for herself ; and even this, he hoped, would serve to keep alive her interest in him during his absence. In this respect our young sailor showed no bad comprehension of human nature, nothing being more likely to maintain an influence of this sort than the conviction that on ourselves depends the happiness or interests of the person beloved.

CHAPTER VIII.

"And I have loved thee, Ocean ! and my joy
 Of youthful sports was on thy breast to be
 Borne, like thy bubbles, onward , from a boy
 I wanton'd with thy breakers—they to me
 Were a delight ; and if the freshening sea
 Made them a terror—'twas a pleasing fear ;
 For I was, as it were, a child of thee,
 And trusted to thy billows, far and near,
 And laid my hand upon thy mane—as I do here."—BYRON.

IT was past the turn of the day when Roswell Gardiner reached his vessel, after having carefully and with manly interest in all that belonged to her, seen Mary to her home and taken his final leave of her. Of that parting we shall say but little. It was touching and warm-hearted, and it was rendered a little solemn by Mary Pratt's putting into her lover's hand a pocket-bible, with an earnest request that he would not forget to consult its pages. She added at the same time, that she had carefully marked those passages which she wished him most to study and reflect on. The book was accepted in the spirit in which it was offered, and carefully placed in a little case that contained about a hundred volumes of different works.

As the hour approached for lifting the anchor, the nervousness of the deacon became very apparent to the commander of his schooner. At each instant the former was at the latter's elbow, making some querulous suggestion, or asking a question that betrayed the agitated and unsettled state of his mind. It really seemed as if the old man at the last moment had not the heart to part with his property, or to trust it out of his sight. All this annoyed Roswell Gardiner, disposed as he was, at that instant, to regard every person and thing that in any manner pertained to Mary Pratt with indulgence and favor.

"You will be particular about them islands, Captain Gar'ner, and not get the schooner ashore," said the deacon, for the tenth time at least. "They tell me the tide runs like a horse in the high latitudes, and that seamen are often stranded by them, before they know where they are."

"Ay, ay, sir; I'll try and bear it in mind," answered Gardiner, vexed at being importuned so often to recollect that which there was so little likelihood of his forgetting. "I am an old cruiser in those seas, deacon, and know all about the tides. Well, Mr. Hazard, what is the news of the anchor?"

"We are short, sir, and only wait for orders to go on, and get clear of the ground."

"Trip at once, sir; and so farewell to America—or to this end of it, at least."

"Then the keys, they tell me, are dangerous navigation, Gar'ner, and a body needs have all his eyes about him."

"All places have their dangers to your sleepy navigator, deacon; but the man who keeps his eyes open has little to fear. Had you given us a chronometer, there would not have been one-half the risk there will be without one."

This had been a bone of contention between the master of the Sea Lion and his owner. Chronometers were not, by any means, in as general use at the period of our tale as they are to-day; and the deacon abhorred the expense to which such an article would have put him. Could he have got one at a fourth of the customary price he might have been tempted; but it formed no part of his principles of saving to anticipate and prevent waste by liberality.

No sooner was the schooner released from the ground than her sails were filled, and she went by the low spit of

sand already mentioned, with the light southwest breeze
still blowing in her favor, and an ebb tide. Everything
appeared propitious, and no vessel probably ever left home
under better omens. The deacon remained on board until
Baiting Joe, who was to act as his boatman, reminded him
of the distance and the probability that the breeze would
go down entirely with the sun. As it was, they had to contend with wind and tide, and it would require all his own
knowledge of the eddies to get the whale-boat up to
Oyster Pond in anything like reasonable time. Thus admonished, the owner tore himself away from his beloved
craft, giving "young Gar'ner" as many "last words" as
if he were about to be executed. Roswell had a last
word on his part, however, in the shape of a message to
Mary.

"Tell Mary, deacon," said the young sailor, in an aside,
"that I rely on her promise, and that I shall think of her,
whether it be under the burning sun of the line, or among
the ice of the antarctic."

"Yes, yes; that's as it should be," answered the deacon,
heartily. "I like your perseverance, Gar'ner, and hope the
gal will come round yet, and I shall have you for a nephew.
There's nothing that takes the women's minds like money.
Fill up the schooner with skins and ile, and bring back
that treasure, and you make as sure of Mary for a wife as
if the parson had said the benediction over you."

Such was Deacon Pratt's notion of his niece, as well as
of the female sex. For months he regarded this speech as
a *coup de maitre*, while Roswell Gardiner forgot it in half an
hour; so much better than the uncle did the lover comprehend the character of the niece.

The Sea Lion, of Oyster Pond, had now cast off the last
ligament which connected her with the land. She had no
pilot, none being necessary, or usual, in those waters; all
that a vessel had to do being to give Long Island a sufficient berth in rounding its eastern extremity. The boat
was soon shut in by Gardiner's Island, and thenceforth
nothing remained but the ties of feeling to connect those
bold adventurers with their native country. It is true that
Connecticut, and subsequently Rhode Island, was yet visible on one hand, and a small portion of New York on the
other; but as darkness came to close the scene, even that
means of communication was soon virtually cut off. The
light on Montauk, for hours, was the sole beacon for these
bold mariners, who rounded it about midnight, fairly meet-

ing the long, rolling swell of the broad Atlantic. Then the craft might be said to be at sea for the first time.

The Sea Lion was found to perform well. She had been constructed with an eye to comfort, as well as to sailing, and possessed that just proportion in her hull which carried her over the surface of the waves like a duck. This quality is of more importance to a small than to a large vessel, for the want of momentum renders what is termed "burying" a very deadening process to a light craft. In this very important particular Roswell was soon satisfied that the shipwright had done his duty.

As the wind still stood at southwest, the schooner was brought upon an easy bowline, as soon as she had Montauk light dead to windward. This new course carried her out to sea, steering south-southeast, a little easterly, under everything that would draw. The weather appearing settled, and there being no signs of a change, Gardiner now went below and turned in, leaving the care of the vessel to the proper officers of the watch, with an order to call him at sunrise. Fatigue soon asserted its power, and the young man was shortly in as profound a sleep as if he had not just left a mistress whom he almost worshipped for an absence of two years, and to go on a voyage that probably would expose him to more risks and suffering than any other enterprise then attempted by seafaring men. Our young sailor thought not of the last at all, but he fell asleep dreaming of Mary.

The master of the Sea Lion of Oyster Pond was called precisely at the hour he had named. Five minutes sufficed to bring him on deck, where he found everything as he had left it, with the exception of the schooner itself. In the six hours he had been below, his vessel had moved her position out to sea nearly forty miles. No land was now to be seen, the American coast being very tame and unpicturesque to the eye, as the purest patriot, if he happen to know anything of other parts of the world, must be constrained to admit. A low, monotonous coast, that is scarcely visible at a distance of five leagues, is certainly not to be named in the same breath with those glorious shores of the Mediterranean, for instance, where nature would seem to have exhausted herself in uniting the magnificent with the bewitching. On this continent, or on our own portion of it at least, we must be content with the useful, and lay no great claims to the beautiful; the rivers and bays giving us some compensation in their ad-

mirable commercial facilities, for the sameness, not to say
tameness, of the views. We mention these things in passing, as a people that does not understand its relative
position in the scale of nations, is a little apt to fall into
errors that do not contribute to its character or respectability; more especially when they exhibit a self-love
founded altogether on ignorance, and which has been
liberally fed by flattery.

The first thing a seaman does on coming on deck, after
a short absence, is to look to windward, in order to see
how the wind stands, and what are the prospects of the
weather. Then he turns his eyes aloft to ascertain what
canvas is spread, and how it draws. Occasionally, the
order of these observations is changed, the first look being
sometimes bestowed on the sails, and the second on the
clouds. Roswell Gardiner, however, cast his first glance
this morning toward the southward and westward, and
perceived that the breeze promised to be steady. On looking aloft, he was well satisfied with the manner in which
everything drew ; then he turned to the second mate, who
had the watch, whom he addressed cheerfully, and with a
courtesy that is not always observed among sailors.

"A fine morning, sir," said Roswell Gardiner, "and a
good-by to America. We've a long road to travel, Mr.
Green, but we've a fast boat to do it in. Here is an offing
ready-made to our hands. Nothing in sight to the westward ; not so much as a coaster even ! It's too early for the
outward-bound craft of the last ebb, and too late for those
that sailed the tide before. I never saw this bight of the
coast clearer of canvas."

"Ay, ay, sir ; it does seem empty, like. Here's a chap,
however, to leeward, who appears inclined to try his rate
of sailing with us. Here he is, sir, a very little abaft the
beam ; and, as near as I can make him out, he's a fore-
tawsail schooner, of about our own dimensions ; if you'll
just look at him through this glass, Captain Gar'ner, you'll
see he has not only our rig, but our canvas set."

"You are right enough, Mr. Green," returned Roswell,
after getting his look. "He is a schooner of about our
tonnage, and under precisely our canvas. How long has the
fellow bore as he does now ?"

"He came out from under Block Island a few hours since,
and we made him by moonlight. The question with me
is, where did that chap come from ? A Stunnin'tun man
would have naturally passed to windward of Block Island ;

and a Newport or Providence fellow would not have fetched so far to windward without making a stretch or two on purpose. That schooner has bothered me ever since it was daylight ; for I can't place him where he is by any traverse my poor l'arnin' can work !"

" She does seem to be out of her way. Possibly it is a schooner beating up for the Hook, and finding herself too close in, she is standing to the southward to get an offing again."

" Not she, sir. She came out from behind Block, and a craft of her size that wanted to go to the westward, and which found itself so close in, would have taken the first of the flood and gone through the Race like a shot. No, no, Captain Gar'ner ; this fellow is bound south as well as ourselves, and it is quite onaccountable how he should be just where he is—so far to windward, or so far to leeward, as a body might say. A south-southeast course, from any place behind Point Judith, would have taken him off near No Man's Land, and here he is almost in a line with Block Island !"

" Perhaps he is out of New London, or some of the ports on the main, and being bound to the West Indies he has been a little careless about weathering the island. It's no great matter, after all."

" It is some such matter, Captain Gar'ner, as walkin' round a meetin'-us' when your ar'n'd is at the door in front. But there was no such craft in at Stunnin'tun or New London, as I know from havin' been at both places within the last eight-and-forty hours."

" You begin to make me as curious about this fellow as you seem to be yourself, sir. And now I think the matter all over, it is somewhat ext'or'nary he should be just where he is. It is, however, a very easy thing to get a nearer look at him, and it's no great matter to us, intending as we do to make the islands off the Cape de Verde, if we do lose a little of our weatherly position—keep the schooner away a point, and get a small pull on your weather braces— give her a little sheet too, fore and aft, sir. So, that will do—keep her steady at that—southeast and by south. In two hours we shall just about speak this out-of-the-way joker."

As every command was obeyed, the Sea Lion was soon running off free, her bowlines hanging loose, and all her canvas a rap full. The change in her line of sailing brought the sail to leeward, a little forward of her beam ;

but the movement of the vessel that made the freest wind was consequently the most rapid. In the course of half an hour the stranger was again a little abaft the beam, and he was materially nearer than when first seen. No change was made in the route of the stranger, who now seemed disposed to stand out to sea, with the wind, as it was, on an easy bowline, without paying any attention to the sail in sight.

It was noon ere the two schooners came within hail of each other. Of course, as they drew nearer and nearer, it was possible for those on board of each to note the appearance, equipments, and other peculiarities of his neighbor. In size, there was no apparent difference between the vessels, and there was a somewhat remarkable resemblance in the details.

"That fellow is no West India drogger," said Roswell Gardiner, when less than a mile from the stranger. "He carries a boat on deck, as we do, and has one on each quarter too. Can it be possible that he is bound after seals, as well as we are ourselves!"

"I believe you're right, sir," answered Hazard, the chief mate, who was now on deck. "There's a sealing look about the gentleman, if I know my own complexion. It's odd enough, Captain Gar'ner, that two of us should come together, out here in the offing, and both of us bound to the other end of the 'arth!"

"There is nothing so very remarkable in *that*, Mr. Hazard, when we remember that the start must be properly timed for those who wish to be off Cape Horn in the summer season. We shall neither of us get there much before December, and I suppose the master of yon schooner knows that as well as I do myself. The position of this craft puzzles me far more than anything else about her. From what port can a vessel come, that she should be just here, with the wind at southwest?"

"Ay, sir," put in Green, who was moving about the decks, coiling ropes and clearing things away, "that's what I tell the chief mate. Where can a craft come from, to be just here, with this wind, if she don't come from Stunnin'tun. Even from Stunnin'tun she'd be out of her way; but no such vessel has been in that port any time these six weeks. Here, you Stimson, come this way a bit. Didn't you tell me something of having seen a schooner at New Bedford, that was about our build and burden, and that you understood had been bought for a sealer?"

"Ay, ay, sir," answered Stimson, as bluff an old sea-dog as ever flattened in a jib-sheet, "and that's the craft, as I'm a thinkin', Mr. Green. She had an animal for a figure-head, and that craft has an animal, as well as I can judge at this distance."

"You are right enough there, Stephen," cried Roswell Gardiner, "and that animal is a seal. It's the twin-brother of the sea lion we carry under our own bowsprit. There's some proof in that, tastes agree sometimes, even if they do differ generally. What became of the schooner you saw?"

"I heard, sir, that she was bought up by some Vineyard men, and was taken across to Hum'ses Hull. They sometimes fit out a craft there, as well as on the main. I should have crossed myself to see what they was at, but I fell in with Mr. Green, and shipped aboard here."

"An adventure by which, I hope, you will not be a loser, my hearty," put in the captain. "And you think that is the craft which was built at New Bedford, and fitted out on the Vineyard?"

"Sartain of it, sir; for I know the figure-head, and all about her build."

"Hand me the trumpet, Mr. Green; we shall soon be near enough for a hail, and it will be easy to learn the truth."

Roswell Gardiner waited a few minutes for the two schooners to close, and was in the very act of applying the trumpet to his mouth, when the usual salutation was sent across the water from the stranger. During the conversation that now took place, the vessels gradually drew nearer to each other, until both parties laid aside their trumpets, and carried on the discourse with the unaided voice.

"Schooner, ahoy!" was the greeting of the stranger, and a simple "Hilloa!" the answer.

"What schooner is that, pray?"

"The Sea Lion, of Oyster Pond, Long Island; bound to the southward, after seal, as I suppose you know by our outfit."

"When did you leave Oyster Pond—and how did you leave your owner, the good Deacon Pratt?"

"We sailed yesterday afternoon, on the first of the ebb, and the deacon left us as we weighed anchor. He was well, and full of hope for our luck. What schooner is that, pray?"

"The Sea Lion, of Hum'ses Hull; bound to the southward, after seals, as you probably knew by *our* outfit. Who commands that schooner?"

"Captain Roswell Gar'ner; who commands aboard you, pray?"

"Captain Jason Daggett," showing himself more plainly, by moving out of the line of the main-rigging. "I had the pleasure of seeing you when I was on the P'int, looking after my uncle's dunnage, you may remember, Captain Gar'ner. 'Twas but the other day, and you are not likely to have forgotten my visit."

"Not at all, not at all, Captain Daggett; though I had no idea *then* that you intended to make a voyage to the southward so soon. When did you leave the Hole, sir?"

"Day before yesterday, a'ternoon. We came out of the Hull about five o'clock."

"How had you the wind, sir?"

"Sou'west, and sou'west and by south. There has been but little change in that these three days."

Roswell Gardiner muttered something to himself; but he did not deem it prudent to utter the thoughts that were just then passing through his mind aloud.

"Ay, ay," he answered, after a moment's pause, "the wind has stood there the whole week; but I think we shall shortly get a change. There is an easterly feeling in the air."

"Waal, let it come. With this offing, we could clear Hatteras with anything that wasn't worse than a southeaster. There's a southerly set in here down the coast for two or three hundred miles."

"A heavy southeaster would jam us in here between the shoals in a way I shouldn't greatly relish, sir. I like always to get to the eastward of the Stream, as soon as I can, in running off the land."

"Very true, Captain Gar'ner—very true, sir. It *is* best to get outside the Stream, if a body *can*. Once there, I call a craft at sea. Eight-and-forty hours more of this wind would just about carry us there. Waal, sir, as we're bound on the same sort of v'y'ge, I'm happy to have fallen in with you; and I see no reason why we should not be neighborly, and 'gam' it a little, when we've nothing better to do. I like that schooner of yours so well, that I've made my own to look as nearly resembling her as I could. You see our paint is exactly the same."

"I have observed that, Captain Daggett; and you might say the same of the figure-heads."

"Ay, ay; when I was over on the P'int, they told me the name of the carver in Boston, who cut your seal, and

I sent to him to cut me a twin. If they lay in a ship-yard, side by side, I don't think you could tell one from the other."

"So it seems, sir. Pray, haven't you a man aboard there of the name of Watson?"

"Ay, ay—he's my second mate. I know what you mean, Captain Gar'ner—you're right enough, 'tis the same hand who was aboard you; but wanting a second officer, I offered him the berth, and he thought that better than taking a foremast lay in your craft."

This explanation probably satisfied all who heard it, though the truth was not more than half told. In point of fact, Watson was engaged as Daggett's second mate *before* he ever laid eyes on Roswell Gardiner, and had been sent to watch the progress of the work on Oyster Pond, as has been previously stated. It was so much in the natural order of events for a man to accept preferment when offered, however, that even Gardiner himself blamed the delinquent for the desertion far less than he had previously done. In the meantime, the conversation proceeded.

"You told us nothing of your having that schooner fitting when you were on the Point," observed Roswell Gardiner, whose thoughts just then happened to advert to this particular fact.

"My mind was pretty much taken up with the affairs of my poor uncle, I suppose, Captain Gar'ner. Death must visit each of us once; nevertheless, it makes us all melancholy when he comes among friends."

Now Roswell Gardiner was not in the least sentimental, nor had he the smallest turn toward indulging in moral inferences from ordinary events; but this answer seemed so proper that it found no objection in his mind. Still, the young man had his suspicions on the subject of the equipment of the other schooner, and suspicions that were now active and keen, and which led him directly to fancy that Daggett had also some clew to the very objects he was after himself. Singular as it may seem at first, Deacon Pratt's interests were favorably affected by this unexpected meeting with the Sea Lion of Holmes's Hole. From the first, Roswell Gardiner had been indisposed to give full credit to the statements of the deceased mariner, ascribing no small part of his account to artifice, stimulated by a desire to render himself important. But, now that he found one of this man's family embarked in an enterprise similar to his own, his views of its expediency were sensibly changed. Perfectly familiar with the wary economy with which every interest was regulated in that part of the world, he did not believe a company of Martha's Vineyard men would risk their money in an enterprise that they had not good reasons for believing would succeed. Although it exceeded his means to appreciate fully the information possessed by the Vineyard folks, and covetousness did not quicken his faculties on this subject, as they had quickened those of the deacon, he could see enough to satisfy his mind that either the sealing-islands, or the booty of the pirates, or both, had a reality, in the judgment of others, which had induced them also to risk their money in turning their knowledge to account. The effect of this conviction was very natural. It induced Roswell to regard the charts, and his instructions, and all connected with his voyage, as much more serious matters than he had originally been inclined to do. Until now, he had thought it well enough to let the deacon have his fancies, relying on his own ability to obtain a cargo for the schooner, by visiting sealing stations where he had been before ; but now he determined to steer at once for Daggett's Islands, as he and his owner named the land revealed to them, and ascertain what could be done there. He thought it probable the other Sea Lion might wish to keep him company ; but the distance was so great that a hundred occasions must occur when it would be in his power to shake off such a consort, should he deem it necessary.

For several hours the two schooners stood on in company, keeping just without hailing distance apart, and sailing so nearly alike as to render it hard to say which craft had the best of it. There was nothing remarkable in the fact that two vessels, built for the same trade, should have a close general resemblance to each other ; but it was not common to find them so moulded, sparred, and handled, that their rate of sailing should be nearly identical. If there was any difference, it was slightly in favor of the Sea Lion of the Vineyard, which rather drew ahead of her consort, if consort the other Sea Lion could be termed, in the course of the afternoon.

It is scarcely necessary to say that many were the speculations that were made on board these rival vessels —competitors now for the commonest glories of their pursuits, as well as in the ultimate objects of their respective voyages. On the part of Roswell Gardiner and his two mates, they did not fail, in particular, to comment on the singularity of the circumstance that the Sea Lion of the Vineyard should be so far out of her direct line of sailing.

"Although we have had the wind at sow-west" (*sow-west* always, as pronounced by every seaman, from the Lord High Admiral of England, when there happens to be such a functionary, down to the greenest hand on board the greenest sealer) "for these last few days," said Hazard, "anybody can see we shall soon have easterly weather. There's an easterly feel in the air, and all last night the water had an easterly glimmer about it. Now why a man who came out of the Vineyard Sound, and who had nothing to do but just to clear the west eend of his own island, and then lay his course off yonder to the southward and eastward, should bear up cluss (Anglice, close) under Block, and stretch out to sea, for all the world as if he was a Stunnin'tun chap, or a New Lunnoner, that had fallen a little to leeward, is more than I can understand, Captain Gar'ner! Depend on it, sir, there's a reason for't. Men don't put schooners into the water, nowadays, and give them costly outfits, with three whale-boats, and sealin' gear in abundance, just for the fun of making fancy traverses on or off a coast, like your yacht gentry, who never know what they would be at, and who never make a v'y'ge worth speaking on."

"I have been turning all this over in my mind, Mr. Hazard," answered the young master, who was amusing himself at the moment with strapping a small block, while he threw many a glance at the vessel that was just as close under his lee as comported with her sailing. "There is a reason for it, as you say; but I can find no other than the fact that she has come so much out of her way, in order to fall in with *us;* knowing that we were to come around Montauk at a particular time."

"Well, sir, that may have been her play! Men bound the same way often wish to fall into good company, to make the journey seem the shorter, by making it so much the pleasanter."

"Those fellows can never suppose the two schooners will keep in sight of each other from forty-one degrees north all the way to seventy south, or perhaps further south still! If we remain near each other a week, 'twill be quite out of the common way."

"I don't know that. sir. I was once in a sealer that. do

all she could, couldn't get shut of a curious neighbor.
When seals are scarce, and the master don't know where
to look for 'em, he is usually glad to drop into some vessel's
wake, if it be only to pick up her leavin's."

"Outfits are not made on such chances as that. These
Vineyard people know where they are going as well as we
know ourselves ; perhaps better."·

"There is great confidence aboard here, in the master,
Captain Gar'ner. I overheard the watch talking the matter over early this morning ; and there was but one
opinion among *them*, I can tell you, sir."

"Which opinion was, Mr. Hazard——"

"That a lay aboard this craft would be worth a lay and
a half aboard any other schooner out of all America !
Sailors go partly on skill and partly on luck. I've known
hands that wouldn't ship with the best masters that ever
sailed a vessel, if they didn't think they were lucky as well
as skilful."

"Ay, ay, it's all *luck !* Little do these fellows think of
Providence—or of *deserving*, or *undeserving*. Well, I hope
the schooner will not disappoint them—or her master,
either. But, whaling and sealing, and trusting to the
chances of the ocean, and our most flattering hopes, may
mislead us after all."

"Ay, ay, sir ; nevertheless, Captain Gar'ner *has* a name,
and men will trust to it ! "

Our young master could not but be flattered at this,
which came at a favorable moment to sustain the resolu-
tions awakened by the competition with the rival schooner.
Although so obviously competitors, and that in a matter of
trade, the interest which above all others is apt to make
men narrow-minded and hostile to each other, though the
axiom would throw this particular reproach on *doctors*,
there were no visible signs that the two vessels did not
maintain the most amicable relations. As the day advanced the wind fell, and after many passages of nautical
compliments, by means of signals and the trumpet, Roswell Gardiner fairly lowered a boat into the water, and
went a "gamming," as it is termed, on board the other
schooner.

Each of these little vessels was well provided with boats,
and those of the description in common use among whalers. A whale-boat differs from the ordinary jolly-boat,
launch, or yawl—gigs, barges, dinguis, etc., etc., being
exclusively for the service of vessels of war—in the follow-

ing particulars, viz :—It is sharp at both ends in order
that it may "back off" as well as "pull on ;" it steers
with an oar instead of with a rudder, in order that the
bows may be thrown round to avoid danger when not in
motion ; it is buoyant and made to withstand the shock of
waves at both ends ; and it is light and shallow, though
strong, that it may be pulled with facility. When it is
remembered that one of these little egg-shells—little as
vessels, though of good size as boats—is often dragged
through troubled waters at the rate of ten or twelve knots,
and frequently at even a swifter movement, one can easily
understand how much depends on its form, buoyancy and
strength. Among seamen it is commonly thought that a
whale-boat is the safest craft of the sort in which men can
trust themselves in rough water.

Captain Daggett received his guest with marked civility,
though in a quiet, eastern way. The rum and water were
produced and a friendly glass was taken by one after the
other. The two masters drank to each other's success,
and many a conventional remark was made between
them on the subject of sea-lions, sea-elephants, and the
modes of capturing such animals. Even Watson, semi-
deserter as he was, was shaken cordially by the hand, and
his questionable conduct overlooked. The ocean has
many of the aspects of eternity, and often disposes mariners to regard their fellow-creatures with an expansiveness
of feeling suited to their common situations. Its vastness
reminds them of the time that has neither beginning nor
end ; its ceaseless movement, of the never-tiring impulses
of human passions ; and its accidents and dangers, of the
Providence which protects all alike, and which alone pre-
vents our being abandoned to the dominion of chance.

Roswell Gardiner was a kind-hearted man, moreover,
and was inclined to judge his fellows leniently. Thus it
was that his "good evening" at parting to Watson was
just as frank and sincere as that he bestowed on Captain
Daggett himself.

CHAPTER IX.

"Roll on, thou deep and dark blue ocean—roll !
Ten thousand fleets sweep over thee in vain ;
Man marks the earth with ruin—his control
Stops with the shore ;—upon the watery plain
The wrecks are all thy deeds, nor doth remain
A shadow of man's ravage, save his own,
When for a moment, like a drop of rain,
He sinks into thy depths with bubbling groan,
Without a grave, unknell'd, uncoffin'd, and unknown."—BYRON.

THAT evening the sun set in clouds, though the eastern horizon was comparatively clear. There was, however, an unnatural outline to objects, by which their dimensions were increased, and in some degree rendered indefinite. We do not know the reason why the wind at east should produce these phenomena, nor do we remember ever to have met with any attempt at a solution ; but of the fact, we are certain, by years of observation. In what is called "easterly weather," objects are seen through the medium of a refraction that is entirely unknown in a clear north-wester ; the crests of the seas emit a luminous light that is far more apparent than at other times ; and the face of the ocean, at midnight, often wears the aspect of a cloudy day. The nerves, too, answer to this power of the eastern winds. We have a barometer within that can tell when the wind is east without looking abroad, and one that never errs. It is true that allusions are often made to these peculiarities, but where are we to look for the explanation ? On the coast of America the sea breeze comes from the rising sun, while on that of Europe it blows from the land ; but no difference in these signs of its influence could we ever discover on account of this marked distinction.

Roswell Gardiner found the scene greatly changed when he came on deck next morning. The storm, which had been brewing so long, had come at last, and the wind was blowing a little gale from the southeast. The quarter from which the air came had compelled the officer of the watch to haul up on the larboard tack, or with the schooner's head to the southward and westward ; a course that might do for a few days, provided it did not blow too heavily. The other tack would not have cleared the shoals, which stretched away to a considerable distance to the eastward.

Hazard had got in his flying-jib, and had taken the bonnets off his foresail and jib, to prevent the craft burying. He had also single-reefed his mainsail and fore-topsail. The Sea Lion of the Vineyard imitated each movement, and was brought down precisely to the same canvas as her consort, and on the same tack. At that moment the two vessels were not a cable's length asunder, the Oyster Ponders being slightly to leeward. Their schooner, however, had a trifling advantage in sailing when it blew fresh and the water was rough ; which advantage was now making itself apparent, as the two craft struggled ahead through the troubled element.

"I wish we were two hundred miles to the eastward," observed the young master to his first officer, as soon as his eye had taken in the whole view. "I am afraid we shall get jammed in on Cape Hatteras. That place is always in the way with the wind at southeast and a vessel going to the southward. We are likely to have a dirty time of it, Mr. Hazard."

"Ay, ay, sir, dirty enough," was the careless answer. "I've known them that would go back and anchor in Fort Pond Bay, or even in Gardiner's, until this southeaster has blown itself out."

"I couldn't think of that ! We are a hundred miles southeast of Montauk, and if I run the craft into any place, it shall be into Charleston, or some of the islands along that coast. Besides, we can always ware off the land, and place ourselves a day's run further to the southward, and we can then give the shoals a wide berth on the other tack. If we were in the bight of the coast between Long Island and Jersey, 'twould be another matter ; but, out here, where we are, I should be ashamed to look the deacon in the face, if I didn't hold on."

"I only made the remark, Captain Gar'ner, by way of saying something. As for getting to the southward, close in with our own coast, I don't know that it will be of much use to a craft that wishes to stand so far to the eastward, since the trades must be met well to windward, or they had better not be met at all. For my part, I would as soon take my chance of making a passage to the Cape de Verds or their neighborhood, by lifting my anchor from Gardiner's Bay, three days hence, as by meeting the next shift of wind down south, off Charleston or Tybee."

"We should be only five hundred miles to windward, in the latter case, did the wind come from the southwest.

again, as at this season of the year it is very likely to do. But it is of no consequence ; men bound where we have got to go, ought not to run into port every time the wind comes out foul. You know as well as I do, Mr. Hazard, that away down south, yonder, a fellow thinks a gale of wind is a relief, provided it brings clear water with it. I would rather run a week among islands, than a single day among icebergs. One knows where to find land, for that never moves ; but your mountains that float about, are here to-day, and there to-morrow."

"Quite true, sir," returned Hazard ; "and men that take their lays in sealers, are not to expect anything but squalls. I'm ready to hold on as long as our neighbor yonder : he seems to be trimming down to it, as if in raal earnest to get ahead."

This was true enough. The Sea Lion of the Vineyard was doing her best, all this time ; and though unable to keep her station on her consort's weather bow, where she had been most of the morning, she was dropped so very slowly as to render the change nearly imperceptible. Now it was, that the officers and crews of these two crafts watched their "behavior," as it is technically termed, with the closest vigilance and deepest interest. Those in the Oyster Pond vessel regarded the movements of their consort, much as a belle in a ball-room observes the effect produced by the sister belles around her ; or a rival physician notes the progress of an operation that is to add new laurels, or to cause old ones to wither. Now, the lurch was commented on ; then, the pitch was thought to be too heavy ; and Green was soon of opinion that their competitor was not as easy on her spars as their own schooner. In short, every comparison that experience, jealousy, or skill could suggest, was freely made ; and somewhat as a matter of course, in favor of their own vessel. That which was done on board the Sea Lion of Oyster Pond, was very freely emulated by those on board her namesake of the Vineyard. They made *their* comparisons, and formed *their* conclusions, with the same deference to self-esteem, and the same submission to hope, as had been apparent among their competitors. It would seem to be a law of nature that men should thus flatter themselves, and perceive the mote in the eye of their neighbor, while the beam in their own escapes.

Had there been an impartial judge present, he might have differed from both sets of critics. Such a person would have seen that one of these schooners excelled in this quality, while the other had an equal advantage in another. In this way, by running through the list of properties that are desirable in a ship, he would, most probably, have come to the conclusion that there was not much to choose between the two vessels; but that each had been constructed with an intelligent regard to the particular service in which she was about be employed, and both were handled by men who knew perfectly well how to take care of craft of that description.

The wind gradually increased in strength, and sail was shortened in the schooners, until each was finally brought down to a close-reefed foresail. This would have been heaving the vessels to, had they not been kept a little off, in order to force them through the water. To lie-to, in perfection, some after-sail might have been required; but neither master saw a necessity, as yet, of remaining stationary. It was thought better to wade along some two knots, than to be pitching and lurching with nothing but a drift, or leeward set. In this, both masters were probably right, and found their vessels farther to windward in the end, than if they had endeavored to hold their own, by lying-to. The great difficulty they had to contend with, in keeping a little off, was the danger of seas coming on board; but, as yet, the ocean was not sufficiently aroused to make this very hazardous, and both schooners, having no real cargoes, were light and buoyant, and floated dry. Had they encountered the sea there was, with full freights in their holds, it might have been imprudent to expose them even to this remote chance of having their decks swept. Water comes aboard of small vessels, almost without an exception, in head winds and seas; though the contrivances of modern naval architecture have provided defences that make merchant vessels, now, infinitely more comfortable, in this respect, than they were at the period of which we are writing.

At the end of three days, Roswell Gardiner supposed himself to be about the latitude of Cape Henry, and some thirty or forty leagues from the land. It was much easier to compute the last, than the first of these material facts. Of course, he had no observations. The sun had not been visible since the storm commenced, and nearly half the time, during the last day, the two vessels were shut in from one another, by mists and a small rain. It blew more in squalls than it had done, and the relative positions of the schooners were more or less affected by the circumstance. Sometimes, one would be to windward, and ahead ; then, the other would obtain a similar advantage. Once or twice they seemed about to separate, the distance between them getting to be so considerable, as apparently to render it impossible to keep in company ; then the craft would change places, by a slow process, passing quite near to each other again. No one could tell, at the moment, precisely why these variations occurred ; though the reasons, generally, were well understood by all on board them. Squalls, careless steering, currents, eddies, and all the accidents of the ocean, contribute to create these vacillating movements, which will often cause two vessels of equal speed, and under the same canvas, to seem to be of very different qualities. In the nights, the changes were greatest, often placing the schooners leagues asunder, and seemingly separating them altogether. But Roswell Gardiner became satisfied that Captain Daggett stuck by him intentionally ; for on all such occasions if *his* schooner happened to be out of the way, he managed to close again, ere the danger of separating became too great to be overcome.

Our mariners judged of their distance from the land, by means of the lead. If the American coast is wanting in the sublime and picturesque, and every traveller must admit its defects in both, it has the essential advantage of graduated soundings. So regular is the shoaling of the water, and so studiously have the fathoms been laid down, that a cautious navigator can always feel his way in to the coast, and never need place his vessel on the beach, as is so often done, without at least knowing that he was about to do so. Men become adventurous by often-repeated success ; and the struggles of competition, the go-ahead-ism of the national character, and the trouble it gives to sound in deep water, all contribute to cast away the reckless and dashing navigator, on this as well as on other coasts, and this to his own great surprise ; but, whenever such a thing *does* happen, unless in cases of stress of weather, the reader may rest assured it is because those who have had charge of the stranded vessel have neglected to sound. The milestones on a highway do not more accurately note the distances, than does the lead on nearly the whole of the American coast. Thus Roswell Gardiner judged himself to be about thirty-two or three marine leagues from the land, on the evening of the third day of that gale of wind.

He placed the schooner in the latitude of Cape Henry on less certain data, though that was the latitude in which he supposed her to be, by dead reckoning.

"I wish I knew where Daggett makes himself out," said the young master, just as the day closed on a most stormy and dirty-looking night. "I don't half like the appearance of the weather; but I do not wish to ware off the land, with that fellow ahead and nearer to the danger, if there be any, than we are ourselves."

Here Roswell Gardiner manifested a weakness that lies at the bottom of half our blunders. He did not like to be outdone by a competitor, even in his mistakes. If the Sea Lion of Holmes' Hole could hold on, on that tack, why might not the Sea Lion of Oyster Pond do the same? It is by this process of human vanity that men sustain each other in wrong, and folly obtains the sanction of numbers, if not that of reason. In this practice we see one of the causes of the masses becoming misled, and this seldom happens without their becoming oppressive.

Roswell Gardiner, however, did not neglect the lead. The schooner had merely to luff close to the wind, and they were in a proper state to sound. This they did twice during that night, and with a very sensible diminution in the depth of the water. It was evident that the schooner was getting pretty close in on the coast, the wind coming out nearly at south, in squalls. Her commander held on, for he thought there were indications of a change, and he still did not like to ware so long as his rival of the Vineyard kept on the larboard tack. In this way, each encouraging the other in recklessness, did these two craft run nearly into the lion's jaw, as it might be; for, when the day reappeared, the wind veered round to the eastward, a little northerly, bringing the craft directly on a lee shore, blowing at the time so heavily as to render a foresail reefed down to a mere rag, more canvas than the little vessels could well bear. As the day returned, and the drizzle cleared off a little, land was seen to leeward, stretching slightly to seaward, both ahead and astern! On consulting his charts, and after getting a pretty good look at the coast from aloft, Roswell Gardiner became satisfied that he was off Currituck, which placed him near six degrees to the southward of his port of departure, and about four to the westward. Our young man now deeply felt that a foolish rivalry had led him into an error, and he regretted that he had not wore the previous evening, when he might have had an offing that would have enabled him to stand in either direction, clearing the land. As things were, he was not by any means certain of the course he ought to pursue.

Little did Gardiner imagine that the reason why Daggett had thus stood on, was solely the wish to keep him company ; for that person, in consequence of Gardiner's running so close in toward the coast, had taken up the notion that the Sea Lion of Oyster Pond meant to pass through the West Indies, visiting the key which was thought to contain treasure, and of which he had some accounts that had aroused all his thirst for gold, without giving him the clew necessary to obtain it. Thus it was that a mistaken watchfulness on one side, and a mistaken pride on the other, had brought these two vessels into as dangerous a position as could have been obtained for them by a direct attempt to place them in extreme jeopardy.

About ten, the gale was at its height, the wind still hanging at east, a little northerly. In the course of the morning, the officers on board both schooners, profiting by lulls and clear moments, had got so many views of the land from aloft, as to be fully aware of their respective situations. All thoughts of competition and watchfulness had now vanished. Each vessel was managed with a reference solely to her safety ; and, as might have been foreseen when true seamen handled both, they had recourse to the same expedients to save themselves. The mainsails of both crafts were set balance-reefed, and the hulls were pressed up against the wind and sea, while they were driven ahead with increased momentum.

"That mainmast springs like a whalebone whip-handle, sir," said Hazard, when this new experiment had been tried some ten minutes or more. "She jumps from one sea to another, like a frog in a hurry to hop into a puddle!"

"She must stand it, or go ashore," answered Gardiner, coolly, though in secret he was deeply concerned. "Did Deacon Pratt forgive me, should we lose the schooner, I never could forgive myself!"

"Should we lose the schooner, Captain Gar'ner, few of us would escape drowning, to feel remorse or joy. Look at that coast, sir—it is clear now, and a body can see a good bit of it—never did I put eyes upon a less promising landfall for strangers to make."

Roswell Gardiner did look as desired, and he fully agreed with Hazard in opinion. Ahead and astern the land trended to seaward, placing the schooners in a curve of the coast, or what seamen term a bight, rendering it quite impossible for the vessels to lay out past either of the headlands in sight. The whole coast was low, and endless lines of breakers were visible along it, flashing up with luminous crests that left no doubt of their character, or of the dangers that they so plainly denoted. At times, columns of water shot up into the air like enormous jets, and the spray was carried inland for miles. Then it was that gloom gathered around the brows of the seamen, who fully comprehended the nature of the danger that was so plainly indicated. The green hands were the least concerned, "knowing nothing and fearing nothing," as the older seamen are apt to express their sense of this indifference on the part of the boys and landsmen.

According to the calculations of those on board the Sea Lion of Oyster Pond, they had about two miles of drift before they should be in the breakers. They were on the best tack, to all appearances, and that was the old one, or the same leg that had carried them into the bight. To ware now, indeed, would be a very hazardous step, since every inch of room was of importance. Gardiner's secret hope was that they might find the inlet that led into Currituck, which was then open, though we believe it has since been closed, in whole or in part, by the sands. This often happens on the American coast, very tolerable passages existing this year for vessels of an easy draught, that shall be absolutely shut up, and be converted into visible beach, a few years later. The waters within will then gain head, and break out, cutting themselves a channel that remains open until a succession of gales drives in the sands upon them from the outside once more.

Gardiner well knew he was on the most dangerous part of the whole American coast, in one sense at least. The capacious sounds that spread themselves within the long beaches of sand were almost as difficult of navigation as any shoals to the northward ; yet would he gladly have been in one, in preference to clawing off breakers on their outside. As between the two schooners, the Vineyard men had rather the best of it, being near a cable's length to windward, and so much farther removed from destruction. The difference, however, was of no great account in the event of the gale continuing, escape being utterly impossible for either in that case. So critical was the situation of both craft becoming, indeed, that neither could now afford to yield a single fathom of the ground she held.

All eyes were soon looking for the inlet, it having been determined to keep the Sea Lion of Oyster Pond away for it, should it appear to leeward, under circumstances that would allow of her reaching it. The line of breakers was now very distinctly visible, and each minute did it not only appear to be, but it was in fact nearer and nearer. Anchors were cleared away, and ranges of cable overhauled, anchoring being an expedient that a seaman felt bound to resort to, previously to going ashore, though it would be with very little hope of ground-tackles holding.

The schooner had been described by Hazard as "jumping" into the sea. This expression is not a bad one, as applied to small vessels in short seas, and it was particularly apt on this occasion. Although constructed with great care forward as to buoyancy, this vessel made plunges into the waves she met that nearly buried her ; and, once or twice, the shocks were so great, that those on board her could with difficulty persuade themselves they had not struck the bottom. The lead, nevertheless, still gave water sufficient, though it was shoaling fast, and with a most ominous regularity. Such was the actual state of things when the schooner made one of her mad plunges, and was met by a force that seemed to check her forward movement as effectually as if she had hit a rock. The mainmast was a good spar in some respects, but it wanted wood. An inch or two more in diameter might have saved it ; but the deacon had been induced to buy it to save his money, though remonstrated with at the time. This spar now snapped in two, a few feet from the deck, and falling to leeward, it dragged after it the head of the foremast, leaving the Sea Lion of Oyster Pond actually in a worse situation, just at that moment, than if she had no spars at all.

Roswell Gardiner now appeared in a new character. Hitherto he had been silent, but observant ; issuing his orders in a way not to excite the men, and with an air of unconcern that really had the effect to mislead most of them on the subject of his estimate of the danger they were in. Concealment, however, was no longer possible, and our young master came out as active as circumstances required, foremost in every exertion, and issuing his orders amid the gale trumpet-tongued. His manner, so full of animation, resolution, and exertion, probably prevented despair from getting the ascendency at that important moment. He was nobly sustained by both his mates ; and three or four

of the older seamen now showed themselves men to be relied on to the last.

The first step was to anchor. Fortunately, the foresight
of Gardiner had everything ready for this indispensable
precaution. Without anchoring, ten minutes would probably have carried the schooner directly down upon the
breakers, leaving no hope for the life of any on board her,
and breaking her up into chips. Both bowers were let go
at once, and long ranges of cable given. The schooner was
snubbed without parting anything, and was immediately
brought head to sea. This relieved her at once, and there
was a moment when her people fancied she might ride out
the gale where she was, could they only get clear of the
wreck. Axes, hatchets, and knives were freely used, and
Roswell Gardiner saw the mass of spars and rigging float
clear of him with a delight he did not desire to conceal.
As it drove to leeward, he actually cheered. A lead was
instantly dropped alongside, in order to ascertain whether
the anchors held. This infallible test, however, gave the
melancholy certainty that the schooner was still drifting
her length in rather less than two minutes.

The only hope now was that the flukes of the anchors
might catch in better holding-ground than they had yet
met with. The bottom was hard sand, however, which
never gives a craft the chance that it gets from mud. By
Roswell Gardiner's calculations, an hour, at the most,
would carry them into the breakers ; possibly less time.
The Sea Lion of Holmes' Hole was to windward a cable's
length when this accident happened to her consort, and
about half a mile to the southward. Just at that instant
the breakers trended seaward, ahead of that schooner, rendering it indispensable for her to ware. This was done,
bringing her head to the southward, and she now came
struggling directly on toward her consort. The operation
of waring had caused her to lose ground enough to bring her
to leeward of the anchored craft, and nearer to the danger.

Roswell Gardiner stood on his own quarter-deck, anxiously watching the drift of the other schooner, as she drew
near in her labored way, struggling ahead through billows
that were almost as white as the breakers that menaced
them with destruction to leeward. The anchored vessel,
though drifting, had so slow a movement that it served to
mark the steady and rapid set of its consort toward its
certain fate. At first, it seemed to Gardiner that Daggett
would pass just ahead of him, and he trembled for his

cables, which occasionally appeared above water, stretched like bars of iron, for the distance of thirty or forty fathoms. But the leeward set of the vessel under way was too fast to give her any chance of bringing this new danger on her consort. When a cable's length distant, the Sea Lion of the Vineyard *did* seem as if she might weather her consort ; but, ere that short space was passed over, it was found that she fell off so fast, by means of her drift, as to carry her fairly clear of her stern. The two masters, holding with one hand to some permanent object by which to steady themselves, and each pressing his tarpauling firmly down on his head with the other, had a minute's conversation when the schooners were nearest together.

"Do your anchors hold ?" demanded Daggett, who was the first to speak, and who put his question as if he thought his own fate depended on the answer.

"I'm sorry to say they do not. We drift our length in about two minutes."

"That will put off the evil moment an hour or two. Look what a wake *we* are making !"

Sure enough, that wake was frightful ! No sooner was the head of the Sea Lion of the Vineyard fairly up with the stern of the Sea Lion of Oyster Pond, than Gardiner perceived that she went off diagonally, moving quite as fast to leeward as she went ahead. This was so very obvious that a line drawn from the quarter of Roswell's craft, in a quartering direction, would almost have kept the other schooner in its range from the moment that her bow hove heavily past.

"God bless you !—God bless you !" cried Roswell Gardiner, waving his hand in adieu, firmly persuaded that he and the Vineyard master were never to meet again in this world. "The survivors must let the fate of the lost be known. At the pinch, I shall out boats, if I can."

The other made no answer. It would have been useless, indeed, to attempt it ; since no human voice had power to force itself up against such a gale, the distance that had now to be overcome.

"That schooner will be in the breakers in half an hour," said Hazard, who stood by the side of young Gardiner. "Why don't he anchor ! No power short of Divine Providence can save her."

"And Divine Providence will do it—thanks to Almighty God for his goodness !" exclaimed Roswell Gardiner. "Did you perceive that, Mr. Hazard ?"

The "*that*" of our young mariner was, in truth, a most momentous omen. The wind had lulled so suddenly that the rags of sails which the other schooner carried actually flapped. At first our seamen thought she had been becalmed by the swell; but the change about themselves was too obvious to admit of any mistake. It blew terribly, again, for a minute; then there was another lull. Gardiner sprang to the lead-line to see the effect on his own vessel. She no longer dragged her anchor!

"God is with us!" exclaimed the young master—"blessed forever be his holy name!"

"And that of his only and *true* Son," responded a voice from one at his elbow.

Notwithstanding the emergency, and the excitement produced by this sudden change, Roswell Gardiner turned to see from whom this admonition had come. The oldest seaman on board, who was Stimson, a Kennebunk man, and who had been placed there to watch the schooner's drift, had uttered these unusual words. The fervor with which he spoke produced more impression on the young master than the words themselves; the former being very unusual among seafaring men, though the language was not so much so. Subsequently, Gardiner remembered that little incident, which was not without its results.

"I do believe, sir," cried Hazard, "that the gale is broken. It often happens on our own coast that the southeasters chop round suddenly, and come out nor'westers. I hope this will not be too late to save the Vineyard chap, though he slips down upon them breakers at a most fearful rate."

"There goes his foresail again—and here is another lull!" rejoined Gardiner. "I tell you, Mr. Hazard, we shall have a shift of wind—nothing short of which could save either of us from these breakers."

"Which comes from the marcy of God Almighty, through the intercession of his only Son!" added Stimson, with the same fervor of manner, though he spoke in a very low tone of voice.

Roswell Gardiner was again surprised, and for another moment he forgot the gale and its dangers. Gale it was no longer, however, for the lull was now decided, and the two cables of the schooner were distended only when the roll of the seas came in upon her. This wash of the waves still menaced the other schooner, driving her down toward the breakers, though less rapidly than before.

"Why don't the fellow anchor!" exclaimed Gardiner, in his anxiety, all care for himself being now over. "Unless he anchor, he will yet go into the white water and be lost!"

"So little does he think of that, that he is turning out his reefs," answered Hazard. "See! there is a hand aloft loosening his topsail—and there goes up a whole mainsail already!"

Sure enough, Daggett appeared more disposed to trust to his canvas than to his ground-tackle. In a very brief space of time he had his craft under whole sail, and was struggling in the puffs to claw off the land. Presently the wind ceased altogether, the canvas flapping so as to be audible to Gardiner and his companions at the distance of half a mile. Then the cloth was distended in the opposite direction, and the wind came off the land. The schooner's head was instantly brought to meet the seas, and the lead dropped at her side showed that she was moving in the right direction. These sudden changes, sometimes destructive, and sometimes providential as acts of mercy, always bring strong counter-currents of air in their train.

"Now we shall have it!" said Hazard; "a true nor'-wester, and butt-end foremost!"

This opinion very accurately described that which followed. In ten minutes it was blowing heavily, in a direction nearly opposite to that which had been the previous current of the wind. As a matter of course, the Sea Lion of the Vineyard drew off the land, wallowing through the meeting billows that still came rolling in from the broad Atlantic; while the Sea Lion of Oyster Pond tended to the new currents of air, and rode, as it might be, suspended between the two opposing forces, with little or no strain on her cables. Gardiner expected to see his consort stand out to sea, and gain an offing; but, instead of this, Captain Daggett brought his schooner quite near to the disabled vessel, and anchored. This act of neighborly kindness was too unequivocal to require explanation. It was the intention of the Vineyard men to lie by their consort until she was relieved from all apprehensions of danger. The "butt-end" of the "nor'wester" was too large to admit of intercourse until next morning, when that which had been a small gale had dwindled to a good, steady breeze, and the seas had gone down, leaving comparatively smooth water all along the coast. The line of white water which marked the breakers was there, and quite visible; but it no longer excited apprehension. The jury-masts on board

the disabled craft were got up ; and what was very convenient, just at that moment, the wreck came floating out
on the ebb, so near to her as to enable the boats to secure
all the sails and most of the rigging. The main-boom,
too, an excellent spar, was towed alongside and saved.

CHAPTER X.

" The shadow from thy brow shall melt,
 The sorrow from thy strain :
But where thy earthly smile hath dwelt,
 Our hearts shall thirst in vain."—MRS. HEMANS.

As soon as it would do to put his boats in the water, or
at daylight next morning, Captain Daggett came alongside
of his consort. He was received with a seaman's welcome,
and his offers of services were accepted, just as frankly as,
under reversed circumstances, they would have been made.
In all this there was a strange and characteristic admixture
of neighborly and Christian kindness, blended with a keen
regard of the main chance. If the former duties are rarely
neglected by the descendants of the Puritans, it may be
said with equal truth, that the latter are never lost sight of.
Speculation and profit are regarded as so many integral
portions of the duty of man ; and, as our kinsmen of Old
England have set up an idol to worship, in the form of
aristocracy, so do our kinsmen of New England pay homage to the golden calf. In point of fact, Daggett had a
double motive in now offering his services to Gardiner:
the one being the discharge of his moral obligations, and
the other a desire to remain near the Sea Lion of Oyster
Pond, lest she should visit the key, of which he had some
very interesting memorandums, without having enough to
find the place unless led there by those who were better
informed on the subject of its precise locality than he was
himself.

The boats of Daggett assisted in getting the wreck alongside, and in securing the sails and rigging. Then his people aided in fitting jury masts ; and by noon both vessels
got under way and stood along the coast to the southward
and westward. Hatteras was no longer terrible, for the
wind still stood at northwest, and they kept in view of
those very breakers which, only the day before, they would
have given the value of both vessels to be certain of never

seeing again.   That night they passed the formidable cape,
a spit of sand projecting far to seaward, and which is on a
low beach, and not on any mainland at all.   Once around
this angle in the coast, they had a lee, hauling up to the
southwest.   With the wind abeam, they stood on the rest
of the day, picking up a pilot.   The next night they doubled
Cape Look Out, a very good landmark for those going
north to keep in view, as a reminder of the stormy and
sunken Hatteras, and arrived off Beaufort harbor just as
the sun was rising the succeeding morning   By this time
the northwester was done, and both schooners entered
Beaufort, with a light southerly breeze, there being just
water enough to receive them.   This was the only place
on all that coast into which it would have answered their
purposes to go ; and it was, perhaps, the very port of all
others that was best suited to supply the present wants of
Roswell Gardiner.   Pine timber, and spars of all sorts,
abounded in that region ; and the "Banker," who acted as
pilot, told our young master that he could get the very
sticks he needed in one hour's time after entering the
haven.   This term of "Banker" applies to a scattering
population of wreckers and fishermen, who dwell on the
long, low, narrow beaches which extend along the whole
of this part of the coast, reaching from Cape Fear to near
Cape Henry, a distance of some hundred and fifty miles.
Within lie the capacious sounds already mentioned, including Albemarle and Pamlico, and which form the watery
portals to the sea-shores of all North Carolina.   Well is
the last headland of that region, but one which the schooners did not double, named Cape Fear.   It is the commencement, on that side, of the dangerous part of the coast, and
puts the mariner on his guard by its very appellation, admonishing him to be cautious and prudent.

Off the entrance of Beaufort, a very perfect and beautiful haven, if it had a greater depth of water, the schooners
hove to, in waiting for the tide to rise a little ; and Roswell Gardiner took that occasion to go on board the sister
craft, and express to Daggett a sense of the obligations he
felt for the services the other had rendered.

"Of course you will not think of going in, Captain Daggett," continued our hero, in dwelling on the subject,
"after having put yourself, already, to so much unnecessary trouble.   If I find the spars the 'Banker' talks of, I
shall be out again in eight-and-forty hours, and we may
meet, some months hence, off Cape Horn."

"I'll tell you what it is, Gar'ner" returned the Vineyard mariner, pushing the rum toward his brother master, "I'm a plain sort of a fellow, and don't make much talk when I do a thing, but I like good-fellowship. We came near going, both of us—nearer than I ever was before, and escape wrackin'; but escape we did—and when men have gone through such trials in company, I don't like the notion of casting off till I see you all a-tanto ag'in, and with as many legs and arms as I carry myself. That's just my feelin', Gar'ner, and I won't say whether it's a right feelin' or not—help yourself."

"It's a right feeling, as between you and me, Captain Daggett, as I can answer for. My heart tells me you are right, and I thank you from it, for these marks of friendship. But you must not forget there are such persons as owners in this world. I shall have trouble enough on my hands with my owner, and I do not wish you to have trouble with yours. Here is a nice little breeze to take you out to sea again; and by passing to the southward of Bermuda, you can make a short cut, and hit the trades far enough to windward to answer all your purposes."

"Thankee, thankee, Gar'ner—I knew the road, and can find the places I'm going to, though no great navigator. Now, I never took a lunar in my life, and can't do anything with a chronometer; but as for finding the way between Martha's Vineyard and Cape Horn, I'll turn my back on no shipmaster living."

"I'm afraid, Captain Daggett, that we have both of us turned our backs on our true course, when we suffered ourselves to get jammed away down here, on Hatteras. Why, I never saw the place before, and never wish to see it again! It's as much out of the track of a whaler or sealer, as Jupiter is out of the track of Mars or Venus."

"Oh, there go your lunars, about which I know nothing and care nothing. I tell you, Gar'ner, a man with a good judgment, can just as well jog about the 'arth, without any acquaintance with lunars, as he can with. Then, your sealer hasn't half as much need of your academy sort of navigation as another man. More than half of our calling is luck; and all the best sealing stations I ever heard of, have been blundered on by some chap who has lost his way. I despise lunars, if the truth must be said; yet I like to go straight to my port of destination. Take a little sugar with your rum-and-water—we Vineyard folks like sweetening."

" For which purpose, or that of going straight to your port, Captain Daggett, you've come down here, on your way to the Pacific ; or, about five hundred miles out of your way ! "

" I came here for company, Gar'ner. We hadn't much choice, you must allow, for we couldn't have weathered the shoals on the other tack. I see no great harm in our positions, if you hadn't got dismasted. That's a two or three hundred dollar job, and may make your owner grumble a little, but it's no killing matter. I'll stick by you, and you can tell the deacon as much in the letter you'll write him, when we get in."

" It seems like doing injustice to *your* owners, as well as to my own, keeping you here, Captain Daggett," returned Roswell, innocently, for he had not the smallest suspicion of the true motive of all this apparent good-fellowship, " and I really wish you would now quit me."

" I couldn't think of it, Gar'ner. 'Twould make an awful talk on the Vineyard, was I to do anything of the sort. 'Stick to your consort,' is an eleventh commandment in our island."

" Which is the reason why there are so many old maids there, I suppose, Daggett," cried Roswell Gardiner laughing. " Well, I thank you for your kindness, and will endeavor to remember it when you may have occasion for some return. But, the tide must be making, and we ought to lose no time unnecessarily. Here's a lucky voyage to us both, Captain Daggett, and a happy return to sweethearts and wives."

Daggett tossed off his glass to this toast, and the two then went on deck. Roswell Gardiner thought that a kinder ship's company never sailed together than this of the Sea Lion of Holmes' Hole ; for, notwithstanding the interest of every man on board depended on the returns of their own voyage, each and all appeared willing to stick by him and his craft so long as there was a possibility of being of any service.

Whalers and sealers do not ship their crews for wages in money, as is done with most vessels. So much depends on the exertions of the people in these voyages, that it is the practice to give every man a direct interest in the result. Consequently, all on board engage for a compensation to be derived from a division of the return cargo. The terms on which a party engages are called his " lay ;" and he gets so many parts of a hundred, according to station, experience, and qualifications. The owner is paid for his risk and expenses in the same way, the vessel and outfits usually taking about two-thirds of the whole returns, while the officers and crew get the other. These conditions vary a little, as the proceeds of whaling and sealing rise or fall in the market, and also in reference to the cost of equipments. It follows that Captain Daggett and his crew were actually putting their hands into their own pockets when they lost time in remaining with the crippled craft. This Gardiner knew, and it caused him to appreciate their kindness at a rate so much higher than he might otherwise have done.

At first sight it might seem that all this unusual kindness was superfluous and of no avail. This, however, was not really the case, since the crew of the second schooner was of much real service in forwarding the equipment of the disabled vessel. Beaufort has an excellent harbor for vessels of a light draught of water like our two sealers; but the town is insignificant, and extra laborers, especially those of an intelligence suited to such work, very difficult to be had. At the bottom, therefore, Roswell Gardiner found his friendly assistants of much real advantage, the two crews pushing the work before them with as much rapidity as suited even a seaman's impatience. Aided by the crew of his consort, Gardiner got on fast with his repairs, and on the afternoon of the second day after he had entered Beaufort, he was ready to sail once more; his schooner probably in a better state of service than the day she left Oyster Pond.

The lightning-line did not exist at the period of which we are writing. It is our good fortune to be an intimate acquaintance of the distinguished citizen who bestowed this great gift on his country—one that will transmit his name to posterity, side by side with that of Fulton. In his case, as in that of the last-named inventor, attempts have been made to rob him equally of the honors and the profits of his very ingenious invention. As respects the last, we hold that it is every hour becoming less and less possible for any American to maintain his rights against numbers. There is no question that the government of this great republic was intended to be one of well-considered and upright principles, in which certain questions are to be referred periodically to majorities, as the wisest and most natural, as well as the most just mode of disposing of them. Such a government, well administered, and with an accurate observance of its governing principles, would probably be the best that human infirmity will allow men to administer; but when the capital mistake is made of supposing that mere numbers are to control all things, regardless of those great fundamental laws that the state has adopted for its own restraint, it may be questioned if so loose, and capricious, and selfish a system is not in great danger of becoming the very worst scheme of polity that cupidity ever set in motion. The tendency—not the *spirit* of the institutions, the two things being the very antipodes of each other, though common minds are so apt to confound them—the *tendency* of the institutions of this country, in flagrant opposition to their *spirit* or *intentions*, which were devised expressly to restrain the disposition of men to innovate, is out of all question to foster this great abuse, and to place numbers above principles, even when the principles were solemnly adopted expressly to bring numbers under the control of a sound fundamental law. This influence of numbers, this dire mistake of the very nature of liberty, by placing men and their passions above those great laws of right which come direct from God himself, is increasing in force, and threatens consequences which may set at naught all the well-devised schemes of the last generation for the security of the state, and the happiness of that very people, who can never know either security or even peace, until they learn to submit themselves, without a thought of resistance, to those great rules of right which in truth form the *spirit* of their institutions, and which are only too often in opposition to their own impulses and motives.

We pretend to no knowledge on the subject of the dates of discoveries in the arts and sciences, but well do we remember the earnestness and single-minded devotion to a laudable purpose, with which our worthy friend first communicated to us his ideas on the subject of using the electric spark by way of a telegraph. It was in Paris, and during the winter of 1831–2, and the succeeding spring, a time when we were daily together; and we have a satisfaction in recording this date, that others may prove better claims if they can. Had Morse set his great invention on foot thirty years earlier, Roswell Gardiner might have communicated with his owner, and got a reply, ere he again sailed, considerable as was the distance between them. As things then were, he was fain to be content with writing a letter, which was put into the deacon's hand about a week after it was written, by his niece, on his own return from a short journey to Southold, whither he had been to settle and discharge a tardy claim against his schooner.

"Here is a letter for you, uncle," said Mary Pratt, struggling to command her feelings, though she blushed with the consciousness of her own interest in the missive. "It came from the Harbor, by some mistake ; Baiting Joe bringing it across just after you left home."

"A letter with a post-mark—'Beaufort, N. C.' Who in natur' can this letter be from ? What a postage, too, to charge on a letter ! Fifty cents ! "

"That is a proof, sir, that Beaufort must be a long way off. Besides, the letter is double. I think the handwriting is Roswell's."

Had the niece fired a six-pounder under her uncle's ears, he would scarcely have been more startled. He even turned pale, and instead of breaking the wafer as he had been about to do, he actually shrunk from performing the act, like one afraid to proceed.

"What can this mean ?" said the deacon, taking a moment to recover his voice. "Gar'ner's handwriting ! So it is, I declare. If that imprudent young man has lost my schooner, I'll never forgive him in this world, whatever a body may be *forced* to do in the next ! "

"It is not necessary to believe anything as bad as that, uncle. Letters are often written at sea, and sent in by vessels that are met. I dare say Roswell has done just this."

"Not he—not he—the careless fellow ! He has lost that schooner, and all my property is in the hands of wrackers, who are worse than so many rats in the larder. ' Beaufort, N. C.' Yes, that must be one of the Bahamas, and N. C. stands for New Providence. Ah's me ! Ah's me ! "

"But N. C. does *not* stand for New Providence—it would be N. P. in that case, uncle."

"N. C. or N. P., they sound so dreadfully alike that I don't know what to think ! Take the letter and open it. Oh ! how big it is !—there must be a protest, or some other costly thing, enclosed."

Mary did take the letter, and she opened it, though with trembling hands. The enclosure soon appeared, and the first glance of her eye told her it was a letter addressed to herself.

"What is it, Mary ? What is it, my child ? Do not

9

be afraid to tell me," said the deacon, in a low, faltering voice. "I hope I know how to meet misfortunes with Christian fortitude. Has it one of them awful-looking seals that Notary Publics use when they want money?"

Mary blushed rosy red, and she appeared very charming at that moment, though as resolute as ever to give her hand only to a youth whose "God should be her God."

"It is a letter to me, sir—nothing else, I do assure you, uncle. Roswell often writes to me, as you know; he has sent one of his letters enclosed in this to you."

"Yes, yes—I'm glad it's no worse. Well, where was his letter written? Does he mention the latitude and longitude? It will be some comfort to learn that he was well to the southward and eastward."

Mary's color disappeared, and a paleness came over her face, as she ran through the few first lines of the letter. Then she summoned all her resolution, and succeeded in telling her uncle the facts.

"A misfortune has befallen poor Roswell," she said, her voice trembling with emotion, "though it does not seem to be half as bad as it might have been. The letter is written at Beaufort, in North Carolina, where the schooner has put in to get new masts, having lost those with which she sailed in a gale of wind off Cape Hatteras."

"Hatteras!" interrupted the deacon, groaning—"what in natur' had my vessel to do down there?"

"I am sure I don't know, sir—but I had better read you the contents of Roswell's letter, and then you will hear the whole story."

Mary now proceeded to read aloud. Gardiner gave a frank, explicit account of all that had happened since he parted with his owner, concealing nothing, and not attempting even to extenuate his fault. Of the Sea Lion of Holmes' Hole he wrote at large, giving it as his opinion that Captain Daggett really possessed some clew—what, he did not know—to the existence of the sealing islands, though he rather thought that he was not very accurately informed of their precise position. As respected the key Roswell was silent, for it did not at all occur to him that Daggett knew anything of that part of his own mission. In consequence of this opinion, not the least suspicion of the motive of the Vineyard-man, in sticking by him, presented itself to Gardiner's mind; and nothing on the subject was communicated in the letter. On the contrary, our young master was quite eloquent in expressing his gratitude to

Daggett and his crew, for the assistance they had volunteered, and without which he could not have been ready to go to sea again in less than a week. As it was, the letter was partly written as the schooner repassed the bar, and was sent ashore by the pilot to be mailed. This fact was stated in full, in a postscript.

"Volunteered!" groaned the deacon aloud. "As if a man ever volunteers to work without his pay!"

"Roswell tells us that Captain Daggett did, uncle," answered Mary, "and that it is understood between them he is to make no charge for his going into Beaufort, or for anything he did while there. Vessels often help each other in this kind way, I should hope, for the sake of Christian charity, sir."

"Not without salvage, not without salvage! Charity is a good thing, and it is our duty to exercise it on all occasions; but salvage comes into charity all the same as into any other interest. This schooner will ruin me, I fear, and leave me in my old age to be supported by the town!"

"That can hardly happen, uncle, since you owe nothing for her, and have your farms, and all your other property, unencumbered. It is not easy to see how the schooner can ruin you."

"Yes, I am undone," returned the deacon, beating the floor with his foot in nervous agitation; "as much undone as ever Roswell Gar'ner's father was; and he might have been the richest man between Oyster Pond and Riverhead, had he kept out of the way of speculation. I remember him much better off than I am myself, and he died but little more than a beggar. Yes, yes; I see how it is; this schooner has undone me!"

"But Roswell sends an account of all that he has paid, and draws a bill on you for its payment. The entire amount is but one hundred and sixteen dollars and seventy-two cents."

"That's not for salvage. The next thing will be a demand for salvage in behalf of the owners and crew of the Sea Lion of Humses' Hull! I know how it will be, child! I know how it will be! Gar'ner has undone me, and I shall go down into my grave a beggar, as his father has done already."

"If such be the fact, uncle, no one but I would be the sufferer, and I will strive not to grieve over your losses. But here is a paper that Roswell has enclosed in his letter to me, by mistake no doubt. See, sir; it is an acknowledgment, signed by Captain Daggett and all his crew, admitting that they went into Beaufort with Roswell out of good feeling, and allowing that they have no claims to salvage. Here it is, sir ; you can read it for yourself."

The deacon did not only read it—he almost devoured the paper, which, as Mary suggested, had been enclosed in her letter by mistake. The relief produced by this document so far composed the uncle, that he not only read Gardiner's letter himself, with a very close attention to its contents, but he actually forgave the cost of the repairs incurred at Beaufort. While he was in the height of his joy at this change in the aspect of things, the niece stole into her own room in order to read the missive she had received by herself.

The tears that Mary Pratt profusely shed over Roswell's letter were both sweet and bitter. The manifestations of his affection for her, which were manly and frank, brought tears of tenderness from her eyes ; while the recollection of the width of the chasm that separated them had the effect to embitter these proofs of love. Most females would have lost the sense of duty which sustained our heroine in this severe trial, and, in accepting the man of their heart, would have trusted to time, and their own influence, and the mercy of Divine Providence, to bring about the changes they desired ; but Mary Pratt could not thus blind herself to her own high obligations. The tie of husband and wife she rightly regarded as the most serious of all the obligations we can assume, and she could not— *would* not plight her vows to any man whose "God was not her God."

Still there was much of sweet consolation in this little-expected letter from Roswell. He wrote, as he always did, simply and naturally, and attempted no concealments. This was just as true of his acts as the master of the schooner, as it was in his character of a suitor. To Mary he told the whole story of his weakness, acknowledging that a silly spirit of pride, which would not permit him to seem to abandon a trial of the qualities of the two schooners, had induced him to stand on to the westward longer than he should otherwise have done, and the currents had come to assist in increasing the danger. As for Daggett, he supposed him to have been similarly influenced ; though he did not withhold his expressions of gratitude for the generous manner in which that seaman had stuck to him to the last.

For weary months did Mary Pratt derive sweet consolation from her treasure of a letter. It was, perhaps, no
more than human nature, or woman's nature at least, that,
in time, she got most to regard those passages which best
answered to the longings of her own heart ; and that she
came at last to read the missive, forgetful, in a degree,
that it was written by one who had deliberately, and as a
matter of faith, adopted the idea that the Redeemer was
not, in what may be called the catholic sense of the term,
the Son of God. The papers gave an account of the arrival of the " Twin Sea Lions," as the article styled them,
in the port of Beaufort, to repair damages ; and of their
having soon sailed again in company. This paragraph she
cut out of the journal in which it met her eye, and inclos-
ing it in Roswell's last letter, there was not a day in the
succeeding year in which both were not in her hand, and
read for the hundredth time or more. These proofs of
tenderness, however, are not to be taken as evidence of
any lessening of principle, or as signs of a disposition to
let her judgment and duty submit to her affection. So
far from this her resolution grew with reflection, and her
mind became more settled in a purpose that she deemed
sacred, the longer she reflected on the subject. But her
prayers in behalf of her absent lover grew more frequent
and much more fervent.

In the meantime the Twin Lions sailed. On leaving
Beaufort they ran off the coast with a smart breeze from
southwest, making a leading wind of it. There had been
some variance of opinion between Daggett and Gardiner,
touching the course they ought to steer. The last was
for hauling up higher and passing to the southward of
Bermuda, while the first contended for standing nearly
due east and going to the northward of those islands.
Gardiner felt impatient to repair his blunder, and make
the shortest cut he could ; whereas Daggett reasoned more
coolly and took the winds into the account, keeping in
view the main results of the voyage. Perhaps the last
wished to keep his consort away from all the keys until
he was compelled to alter his course in a way that would
leave no doubt of his intentions. Of one thing the last
was now certain : he knew by a long trial that the Sea
Lion of Oyster Pond could not very easily run away from
the Sea Lion of Holmes's Hole, and he was fully resolved
that she should not escape from him in the night, or in
the squalls. As for Roswell Gardiner, not having the

smallest idea of looking for his key, until he came north, after visiting the antarctic circle, he had no notion whatever of the reason why the other stuck to him so closely ; and, least of all, why he wished to keep him clear of the West Indies, until ready to make a descent on his El Dorado.

Beaufort lies about two degrees to the northward of the four hundred rocks, islets, and small islands, which are known as the Bermudas ; an advanced naval station, that belongs to a rival commercial power, and which is occupied by that power solely as a check on this republic in the event of war. Had the views of real statesmen prevailed in America, instead of those of mere politicians, the whole energy of this republic would have been long since directed to the object of substituting our own flag for that of England in these islands. As things are, there they exist ; a station for hostile fleets, a receptacle for prizes, and a depot for the munitions of war, as if expressly designed by nature to hold the whole American coast in command. While little men with great names are wrangling about southwestern acquisitions and northeastern boundaries, that are of no real moment to the growth and power of the republic, these islands, that ought never to be out of the mind of the American statesman, have not yet entered into the account at all ; a certain proof how little the minds that do, or ought to, influence events, are really up to the work they have been delegated to perform. Military expeditions have twice been sent from this country to Canada, when both the Canadas are not of one-half the importance to the true security and independence of the country—(no nation is independent until it holds the control of all its greater interests in its own hands)—as the Bermudas. When England asked the cession of territory undoubtedly American, because it overshadowed Quebec, she should have been met with this plain proposition—" Give us the Bermudas, and we will exchange with you. You hold those islands as a check on our power, and we will hold the angle of Maine for a check on yours, unless you will consent to make a fair and mutual transfer. We will not attack you for the possession of the Bermudas, for we deem a just principle even more important than such an accession ; but when you ask us to cede, we hold out our hands to take an equivalent in return. The policy of this nation is not to be influenced by saw-logs, but by these manifest, important, and ulterior interests. If you wish Maine, give us Bermuda in exchange, or go with your wishes ungratified." Happily, among us, events are stronger than men, and the day is not distant when the mere force of circumstances will compel the small-fry of diplomacy to see what the real interests and dignity of the republic demand in reference to this great feature of its policy.

Roswell Gardiner and Daggett had several discussions touching the manner in which they ought to pass those islands. There were about four degrees to spare between the trades and the Bermudas; and the former was of opinion that they might pass through this opening, and make a straighter wake, than by going farther north. These consultations took place from quarter-deck to quarter-deck, as the two schooners ran off free, steering directly for the islands, as a sort of compromise between the two opinions. The distance from the main to the Bermudas is computed at about six hundred miles, which gave sufficient leisure for the discussion of the subject in all its bearings. The conversation was amicable, and the weather continuing mild, and the wind standing, they were renewed each afternoon, when the vessels closed, as if expressly to admit of the dialogue. In all this time, five days, altogether, it was farther ascertained that the difference in sailing between the Twin Lions, as the sailors now began to call the two schooners, was barely perceptible. If anything, it was slightly in favor of the Vineyard craft, though there yet remained many of the vicissitudes of the seas, in which to make the trial. While this uncertainty as to the course prevailed, the low land appeared directly ahead, when Daggett consented to pass it to the southward, keeping the cluster in sight, however, as they went steadily on toward the southward and eastward.

CHAPTER XI.

"With glossy skin, and dripping mane,
And reeling limbs, and reeking flank,
The wild steed's sinewy nerves still strain
Up the repelling bank."—*Mazeppa.*

ROSWELL GARDINER felt as if he could breathe more freely when they had run the Summers Group fairly out of sight, and the last hummock had sunk into the waves

of the west. He was now fairly quit of America, and
hoped to see no more of it until he made the well-known
rock that points the way into the most magnificent of all
the havens of the earth, the bay of Rio de Janeiro. Travellers dispute whether the palm ought to be given to this
port, or to those of Naples and Constantinople. Each,
certainly, has its particular claims to surpassing beauty,
which ought to be kept in view in coming to a decision.
Seen from its outside, with its minarets, and Golden Horn,
and Bosphorus, Constantinople is probably the most glorious spot on earth. Ascend its mountains and overlook
the gulfs of Salerno and Gaeta, as well as its own waters,
the *Campagna Felici*, and the memorials of the past, all seen
in the witchery of an Italian atmosphere, and the mind becomes perfectly satisfied that nothing equal is to be found
elsewhere ; but enter the bay of Rio, and take the whole
of the noble panorama in at a glance, and even the experienced traveller is staggered with the stupendous, as
well as bewitching, character of the loveliness that meets
his eye. Witchery is a charm that peculiarly belongs to
Italy, as all must feel who have ever been brought within
its influence ; but it is a witchery that is more or less shared
by all regions of low latitudes.

Our two Sea Lions met with no adventures worthy of
record until they got well to the southward of the equator.
They had been unusually successful in getting through
the calm latitudes ; and forty-six days from Montauk, they
spoke a Sag Harbor whaler, homeward bound, that had
come out from Rio only the preceding week, where she
had been to dispose of her oil. By this ship, letters were
sent home ; and as Gardiner could now tell the deacon
that he should touch at Rio even before the time first anticipated, he believed that he should set the old man's
heart at peace. A little occurrence that took place the very
day they parted with the whaler, added to the pleasure this
opportunity of communicating with the owner had afforded.
As the schooners were moving on in company, about a
cable's length asunder, Hazard saw a sudden and extraordinary movement on board the Vineyard Lion, as the men
now named that vessel, to distinguish her from her consort.

"Look out for a spout !" shouted the mate to Stimson,
who happened to be on the fore-topsail-yard at work, when
this unexpected interruption to the quiet of the passage
occurred. "There is a man overboard from the other
schooner, or they see a spout."

"A spout! a spout!" shouted Stimson, in return; "and a spalm (sperm, or spermaceti, was meant) whale in the bargain! Here he is, sir, two p'ints on our weather beam."

This was enough. If any one has had the misfortune to be in a coach drawn by four horses, when a sudden fright starts them off at speed, he can form a pretty accurate notion of the movement that now took place on board of Deacon Pratt's craft. Every one seemed to spring into activity, as if a single will directed a common set of muscles. Those who were below, literally "tumbled up," as the seamen express it, and those who were aloft, slid down to the deck like flashes of lightning. Captain Gardiner sprang out of his cabin, seemingly at a single bound; at another, he was in the whale-boat that Hazard was in the very act of lowering into the water, as the schooner rounded-to. Perceiving himself anticipated here, the mate turned to the boat on the other quarter, and was in her, and in the water, almost as soon as his commanding officer.

Although neither of the schooners was thoroughly fitted for a whaler, each had lines, lances, harpoons, etc., in readiness in their quarter-boats, prepared for any turn of luck like this which now offered. The process of paddling up to whales, which is now so common in the American ships, was then very little or not at all resorted to. It is said that the animals have got to be so shy, in consequence of being so much pursued, that the old mode of approaching them will not suffice, and that it now requires much more care and far more art to take one of these creatures, than it did thirty years since. On this part of the subject, we merely repeat what we hear, though we think we can see an advantage in the use of the paddle that is altogether independent of that of the greater quiet of that mode of forcing a boat ahead. He that paddles looks *ahead*, and the approach is more easily regulated, when the whole of the boat's crew are apprised, by means of their own senses, of the actual state of things, than when they attain their ideas of them through the orders of an officer. The last must govern in all cases, but the men are prepared for them, when they can see what is going on, and will be more likely to act with promptitude and intelligence, and will be less liable to make mistakes.

The four boats, two from each schooner, dropped into the water nearly about the same time. Daggett was at the steering-oar of one, as was Roswell at that of another. Hazard, and Macy, the chief mate of the Vineyard craft, were at the steering-oars of the two remaining boats. All pulled in the direction of the spot on the ocean where the spouts had been seen. It was the opinion of those who had been aloft, that there were several *fish;* and it was certain that they were of the most valuable species, or the spermaceti, one barrel of the oil of which was worth about as much as the oil of three of the ordinary sort, or that of the *right* whale, supposing them all to yield the same quantity in number of barrels. The nature or species of the fish was easily enough determined by the spouts; the right whale throwing up two high arched jets of water, while the spermaceti throws but a single, low, bushy one.

It was not long ere the boats of the two captains came abreast of each other, and within speaking distance. A stern rivalry was now apparent in every countenance, the men pulling might and main, and without even a smile among them all. Every face was grave, earnest, and determined; every arm strung to its utmost powers of exertion. The men rowed beautifully, being accustomed to the use of their long oars in rough water, and in ten minutes they were all fully a mile dead to windward of the two schooners.

Few things give a more exalted idea of the courage and ingenuity of the human race than to see adventurers set forth, in a mere shell, on the troubled waters of the open ocean, to contend with and capture an animal of the size of the whale. The simple circumstance that the last is in its own element, while its assailants are compelled to approach it in such light and fragile conveyances, that, to the unpractised eye, it is sufficiently difficult to manage them amid the rolling waters, without seeking so powerful an enemy to contend with, indicates the perilous nature of the contest. But, little of all this did the crews of our four boats now think. They had before them the objects, or *one* of the objects, rather, of their adventure, and so long as that was the case, no other view but that of prevailing could rise before their eyes.

"How is it, Gar'ner?" called out the Vineyard master, "shall it be shares? or does each schooner whale on her own hook?"

This was asked in a friendly way, and apparently with great indifference as to the nature of the reply, but with profound art. It was Daggett's wish to establish a sort of partnership, which, taken in connection with the good feeling created by the affair at Beaufort, would be very apt to lead on to further and more important association. Luckily for Gardiner, an idea crossed his mind, just as he was about to reply, which induced the wisest answer. It was the thought, that competition would be more likely to cause exertion than a partnership, and that the success of all would better repay them for the toils and risks, should each vessel act exclusively for itself. This is the principle that renders the present state of society more healthful and advantageous than that which the friends of the different systems of associating, that are now so much in vogue, wish to substitute in its place. Individuality is an all-important feeling in the organization of human beings into communities ; and the political economist who does not use it as his most powerful auxiliary in advancing civilization, will soon see it turn round in its tracks, and become a dead weight ; indulging its self-love, by living with the minimum of exertion, instead of pushing his private advantage, with the maximum.

"I think each vessel had better work for herself and her owners," answered Roswell Gardiner.

As the schooners were in the trades, there was a regular sea running, and one that was neither very high nor much broken. Still, the boats were lifted on it like egg-shells or bubbles, the immense power of the ocean raising the largest ships, groaning under their vast weight of ordnance, as if they were feathers. In a few minutes, Gardiner and Daggett became a little more separated, each looking eagerly for the spouts, which had not been seen by either since quitting his vessel. All this time the two mates came steadily on, until the whole of the little fleet of boats was now not less than a marine league distant from the schooners. The vessels themselves were working up to windward, to keep as near to the boats as possible, making short tacks under reduced canvas ; a shipkeeper, the cook, steward, and one or two other hands, being all who were left on board them.

We shall suppose that most of our readers are sufficiently acquainted with the general character of that class of animals to which the whale belongs, to know that all of the genus breathe the atmospheric air, which is as necessary for life to them as it is to man himself. The only difference in this respect is that the whale can go longer without renewing his respiration than all purely land-animals, though he must come up to breathe at intervals, or die. It is the exhaling of the old stock of air, when he brings the "blow-holes," as seamen call the outlets of his respiratory organs, to the surface, that forces the water upward, and forms the "spouts," which usually indicate to the whalers the position of their game. The "spouts" vary in appearance, as has been mentioned, owing to the number and situation of the orifices by which the exhausted air escapes. No sooner is the vitiated air exhaled, than the lungs receive a new supply; and the animal either remains near the surface, rolling about and sporting amid the waves, or descends again, a short distance, in quest of its food. This food, also, varies materially in the different species. The right whale is supposed to live on what may be termed marine insects, or the molluscæ of the ocean, which it is thought he obtains by running in the parts of the sea where they most abound; arresting them by the hairy fibres which grow on the laminæ of bone that, in a measure, compose his jaws, having no teeth. The spermaceti, however, is furnished with regular grinders, which he knows very well how to use, and with which he often crushes the boats of those who come against him. Thus, the whalers have but one danger to guard against, in assaulting the common animal, viz, his flukes, or tail; while the spermaceti, in addition to the last means of defence, possesses those of his teeth or jaws. As this latter animal is quite one-third head, he has no very great dissemblance to the alligator in this particular.

By means of this brief description of the physical formation and habits of the animals of which our adventurers were in pursuit, the general reader will be the better able to understand that which it is our duty now to record. After rowing the distance named, the boats became a little separated, in their search for the fish. That spouts had been seen, there was no doubt; though, since quitting the schooners, no one in the boats had got a further view of the fish,—if fish, animals with respiratory organs can be termed. A good lookout for spouts had been kept by each man at the steering-oars, but entirely without success Had not Roswell and Daggett, previously to leaving their respective vessels, seen the signs of whales with their own eyes, it is probable that they would now have both been disposed to return, calling in their mates. But, being certain that the creatures they sought were not far distant, they continued slowly to separate, each straining his eyes in quest of his game, as his boat rose on the summit of the rolling and tossing waves. Water in motion was all around them : and the schooners working slowly up against the trades, was all that rewarded their vigilant and anxious looks. Twenty times did each fancy that he saw the dark back, or head, of the object he sought ; but as often did it prove to be no more than a lipper of water, rolling up into a hummock ere it broke, or melting away again into the general mass of the unquiet ocean. When it is remembered that the surface of the sea is tossed into a thousand fantastic outlines, as its waves roll along, it can readily be imagined how such mistakes could arise.

At length Gardiner discerned that which his practised eye well knew. It was the flukes, or extremity of the tail of an enormous whale, distant from him less than a quarter of a mile, and in such a position as to place the animal at about the same breadth of water from Daggett. It would seem that both of these vigilant officers perceived their enemy at the same instant, for each boat started for it as if it had been instinct with life. The pike or the shark could not have darted toward its prey with greater promptitude, and scarcely with greater velocity than these two boats. Very soon the whole herd was seen, swimming along against the wind, an enormous bull whale leading, while half a dozen calves kept close to the sides of their dams, or sported among themselves, much as the offspring of land-animals delight in their youth and strength. Presently a mother rolled lazily over on her side, permitting its calf to suck. Others followed this example ; and then the leader of the herd ceased his passage to windward, but began to circle the spot, as if in complaisance to those considerate nurses who thus waited on the wants of their young. At this interesting moment the boats came glancing in among the herd.

Had the competition and spirit of rivalry been at a lower point among our adventurers than it actually was, greater caution might have been observed. It is just as dangerous to assault a whale that has its young to defend, as to assault most other animals. We know that the most delicate women become heroines in such straits ; and nature seems to have given to the whole sex, whether endowed with reason or only with an instinct, the same disposition to die in defence of the helpless creatures that so much depend on their care. But no one there now thought of the risk he ran, it being the Vineyard against Oyster Pond, one

Sea Lion against the other, and, in many instances, pocket against pocket.

Roswell, as if disdaining all meaner game, pulled quite through the herd, and laid the bows of his boat directly on the side of the old bull—a hundred-barrel whale at the very least. No sooner did the enormous creature feel the harpoon, than, throwing its flukes upward, it descended into the depths of the ocean, with a velocity that caused smoke to arise from the chuck through which the line passed. Ordinarily, the movement of a whale is not much faster than an active man can walk ; and, when it runs on the surface, its speed seldom exceeds that of a swift vessel under full sail ; but, when suddenly startled, with the harpoon in its blubber, the animal is capable of making a prodigious exertion. When struck, it usually "sounds," as it is termed, or runs downward, sometimes to the depth of a mile ; and it is said that instances have been known in which the fish inflicted great injury on itself, by dashing its head against rocks.

In the case before us, after running out three or four hundred fathoms of line, the "bull" to which Gardiner had "fastened," came up to the surface, "blowed," and began to move slowly toward the herd again. No sooner was the harpoon thrown, than a change took place in the disposition of the crew of the boat, which it may be well to explain. The harpoon is a barbed javelin, fastened to a staff to give it momentum. The line is attached to this weapon, the proper use of which is to "fasten" to the fish, though it sometimes happens that the animal is killed at the first blow. This is when the harpoon has been hurled by a very skilful and vigorous harpooner. Usually, this weapon penetrates some distance into the blubber in which a whale is encased, and when it is drawn back by the plunge of the fish, the barbed parts get imbedded in the tough integuments of the hide, together with the blubber, and hold. The iron of the harpoon being very soft, the shank bends under the strain of the line, leaving the staff close to the animal's body. Owing to this arrangement, the harpoon offers less resistance to the water, as the whale passes swiftly through it. No sooner did the boat-steerer, or harpooner, cast his "irons," as whalers term the harpoon, than he changed places with Roswell, who left the steering-oar, and proceeded forward to wield the lance, the weapon with which the victory is finally consummated. The men now "peaked" their oars, as it is termed ; or they placed the handles in cleats made to receive them, leaving the blades elevated in the air, so as to be quite clear of the water. This was done to get rid of the oars, in readiness for other duty, while the instruments were left in the tholes, to be resorted to in emergencies. This gives a whale-boat a peculiar appearance, with its five long oars raised in the air, at angles approaching forty-five degrees. In the meantime, as the bull approached the herd, or school,* as the whalers term it, the boat's crew began to haul in line, the boat-steerer coiling it away carefully, in a tub placed in the stern-sheets purposely to receive it. Any one can understand how important it was that this part of the duty should be well performed, since bights of line running out of a boat, dragged by a whale, would prove so many snares to the men's legs, unless previously disposed of in a place proper to let it escape without this risk For this reason it is, that the end of a line is never permitted to run out at the bow of a boat at all. It might do some injury in its passage, and an axe is always applied near the bows, when it is found necessary to cut from a whale.

It was so unusual a thing to see a fish turn toward the spot where it was struck, that Roswell did not know what to make of this manœuvre in his bull. At first he supposed the animal meant to make fight, and set upon him with its tremendous jaws ; but it seemed that caprice or alarm directed the movement ; for, after coming within a hundred yards of the boat, the creature turned and commenced sculling away to windward, with wide and nervous sweeps of its formidable flukes. It is by this process that all the fish of this genus force their way through the water, their tails being admirably adapted to the purpose. As the men had showed the utmost activity in hauling in upon the line, by the time the whale went off to windward again they had got the boat up within about four hundred feet of him.

Now commenced a tow, dead to windward, it being known that a fish, when struck, seldom runs at first in any other direction. The rate at which the whale moved was not at the height of his speed, though it exceeded six knots. Occasionally, this rate was lessened, and in several instances his speed was reduced to less than half of that just mentioned. Whenever one of the lulls occurred, the men

* We suppose this word to be a corruption of the Dutch "*schule*," which, we take it, means the same thing.

would haul upon the line, gradually getting nearer and nearer to the fish, until they were within fifty feet of his tremendous flukes. Here, a turn was taken with the line, and an opportunity to use the lance was waited for.

Whalers say that a forty-barrel bull of the spermaceti sort is much the most dangerous to deal with of all the animals of this species. The larger bulls are infinitely the most powerful, and drive these half-grown creatures away in herds by themselves, that are called "pads," a circumstance that probably renders the young bull discontented and fierce. The last is not only more active than the larger animal, but is much more disposed to make fight, commonly giving his captors the greatest trouble. This may be one of the reasons why Roswell Gardiner now found himself towing at a reasonable rate, so close upon the flukes of a hundred-barrel whale. Still, there was that in the movements of this animal, that induced our hero to be exceedingly wary. He was now two leagues from the schooners, and half that distance from the other boats, neither of which had as yet fastened to a fish. This latter circumstance was imputed to the difficulty the different officers had in making their selections,—cows, of the spermaceti breed, when they give suck, being commonly light, and yielding, comparatively, very small quantities of head-matter and oil. In selecting the bull, Roswell had shown his judgment, the male animal commonly returning to its conquerors twice the profit that is derived from the female.

The whale to which Roswell was fast, continued sculling away to windward for quite two hours, causing the men to entirely lose sight of the other boats, and bringing the topsails of the schooners themselves down to the water's edge. Fortunately, it was not yet noon, and there were no immediate apprehensions from the darkness ; nor did the bull appear to be much alarmed, though the boat was towing so close in the rear. At first, or before the irons were thrown, the utmost care had been taken not to make a noise ; but the instant the crew were "fast," whispers were changed into loud calls, and orders were passed in shouts, rather than in verbal commands. The wildest excitement prevailed among the men, strangely blended with a cool dexterity ; but it was very apparent that a high sporting fever was raging among them. Gardiner himself was much the coolest man in his own boat, as became his station and very responsible duties.

Stimson, the oldest and the best seaman in the schooner.

—he who had admonished his young commander on the subject of the gratitude due to the Deity—acted as the master's boat-steerer, having first performed the duty of harpooner. It was to him that Gardiner now addressed the remarks he made, after having been fastened to his whale fully two hours.

"This fellow is likely to give us a long drag," said the master, as he stood balancing himself on the clumsy cleats in the bows of the boat, using his lance as an adept in saltation poises his pole on the wire, the water curling fairly above the gunwale forward, with the rapid movement of the boat ; "I would haul up alongside, and give him the lance, did I not distrust them flukes. I believe he knows we are here."

"That he does—that does he, Captain Gar'ner. It's always best to be moderate and wait your time, sir. There's a jerk about that chap's flukes that I don't like myself, and it's best to see what he would be at, before we haul up any nearer. Don't you see, sir, that every minute or two he strikes down, instead of sculling off handsomely and with a wide sweep, as becomes a whale ?"

"That is just the motion I distrust, Stephen, and I shall wait a bit to see what he would be at. I hope those ship-keepers will be busy, and work the schooners well up to windward before it gets to be dark. Our man is asleep half his time, and is apt to let the vessel fall off a point or two."

"Mr. Hazard gave him caution to keep a bright look-out, sir, and I think he'll be apt to—look out, sir !—look out !"

This warning was well-timed ; for, just at that instant, the whale ceased sculling, and lifting its enormous tail high in the air, it struck five or six blows on the surface of the water, that made a noise which might have been heard half a league, besides filling the atmosphere immediately around him with spray. As the tail first appeared in the air, line was permitted to run out of the boat, increasing the distance between its bows and the flukes to quite a hundred feet. Nothing could better show the hardy characters of the whalers than the picture then presented by Roswell Gardiner and his companions. In the midst of the Atlantic, leagues from their vessel, and no other boat in sight, there they sat patiently waiting the moment when the giant of the deep should abate in his speed, or in his antics, to enable them to approach and complete their capture. Most of the men sat with their arms crossed, and bodies half turned, regarding the scene, while the two officers, the master and boat-steerers, if the latter could properly be thus designated, watched each evolution with a keenness of vigilance that let nothing like a sign or a symptom escape them.

Such was the state of things, the whale still threshing the sea with his flukes, when a cry among his men induced Roswell for a moment to look aside. There came Daggett fast to a small bull, which was running directly in the wind's eye with great speed, dragging the boat after him, which was towing astern at a distance of something like two hundred fathoms. At first, Roswell thought he should be compelled to cut from his whale, so directly toward his own boat did the other animal direct his course. But, intimidated, most probably, by the tremendous blows with which the larger bull continued to belabor the ocean, the smaller animal sheered away in time to avoid a collision, though he now began to circle the spot where his dreaded monarch lay. This change of course gave rise to a new source of apprehension. If the smaller bull should continue to encircle the larger, there was great reason to believe that the line of Daggett might get entangled with the boat of Gardiner, and produce a collision that might prove fatal to all there. In order to be ready to meet this danger, Roswell ordered his crew to be on the lookout, and to have their knives in a state for immediate use. It was not known what might have been the consequence of this circular movement as respects the two boats ; for, before they could come together, Daggett's line actually passed into the mouth of Gardiner's whale, and drawing up tight into the angle of his jaws, set the monster in motion with a momentum and power that caused the iron to draw from the smaller whale, which by this time had more than half encircled the animal. So rapid was the rate of running now, that Roswell was obliged to let out line, his whale sounding to a prodigious depth. Daggett did the same, unwilling to cut as long as he could hold on to his line.

At the expiration of five minutes the large bull came up again for breath, with both lines still fast to him ; the one in the regular way, or attached to the harpoon, and the other jammed in the jaws of the animal by means of the harpoon and staff, which formed a sort of toggle at the angle of his enormous mouth. In consequence of feeling this unusual tenant, the fish compressed its jaws together, thus rendering the fastening so much the more secure. As both boats had let run line freely while the whale was sounding, they now found themselves near a quarter of a mile astern of him, towing along, side by side, and not fifty feet asunder. If the spirit of rivalry had been aroused among the crew of these two boats before, it was now excited to a degree that menaced acts of hostility.

"You know, of course, Captain Daggett, that this is my whale," said Gardiner. "I was fast to him regularly, and was only waiting for him to become a little quiet to lance him, when your whale crossed his course, fouled your line, and has got you fast in an unaccountable way, but not according to whaling law."

"I don't know that. I fastened to a whale, Captain Gar'ner, and am fast to a whale now. It must be *proved* that I have no right to the creatur' before I give him up."

Gardiner understood the sort of man with whom he had to deal too well to waste words in idle remonstrances. Resolved to maintain his just rights at every hazard, he ordered his men to haul in upon the line, the movement of the whale becoming so slow as to admit of this measure. Daggett's crew did the same, and a warm contest existed between the two boats, as to who should now first close with the fish and kill it. This was not a moment for prudence and caution. It was "haul in—haul in, boys," in both boats, without any regard to the danger of approaching the whale. A very few minutes sufficed to bring the parties quite in a line with the flukes, Gardiner's boat coming up on the larboard or left-hand side of the animal, where its iron was fast, and Daggett's on the opposite, its line leading out of the jaws of the fish in that direction. The two masters stood erect on their respective clumsy cleats, each poising his lance, waiting only to get near enough to strike. The men were now at the oars, and without pausing for anything, both crews sprung to their ashen instruments, and drove the boats headlong upon the fish. Daggett, perhaps, was the coolest and most calculating at that moment, but Roswell was the most nervous and the boldest The boat of the last actually hit the side of the whale, as its young commander drove his lance through the blubber, into the vitals of the fish. At the same instant Daggett threw his lance with consummate skill, and went to the quick. It was now "stern all!" for

life, each boat backing off from the danger as fast as hands
could urge.   The sea was in a foam, the fish going into
his "flurry" almost as soon as struck, and both crews were
delighted to see the red of the blood mingling its deep
hues with the white of the troubled water.   Once or twice
the animal spouted, but it was a fluid dyed in his gore.
In ten minutes it turned up and was dead.

CHAPTER XII.

"God save you, sir!"
"And you, sir! you are welcome."
"Travel you far on, or are you at the furthest?"
"Sir, at the furthest for a week or two."—SHAKESPEARE.

GARDINER and Daggett met, face to face, on the carcass
of the whale.   Each struck his lance into the blubber,
steadying himself by its handle ; and each eyed the other
in a way that betokened feelings awakened by a keen desire to defend his rights.   It is a fault of American character—a fruit of the institutions, beyond a doubt—that
renders men unusually indisposed to give up.   This stub-
bornness of temperament, that so many mistake for a love
of liberty and independence, is productive of much good,
when the parties happen to be right, and of quite as much
evil, when they happen to be wrong.   It is ever the wisest,
as, indeed, it is the noblest course, to defer to that which
is just, with a perfect reliance on its being the course
pointed out by the finger of infallible wisdom and truth.
He who does this need feel no concern for his dignity, or
for his success ; being certain that it is intended that right
shall prevail in the end, as prevail it will and does.   But
both our shipmasters were too much excited to feel the
force of these truths ; and there they stood, sternly regarding each other, as if it were their purpose to commence
a new struggle for the possession of the leviathan of the
deep.

"Captain Daggett," said Roswell sharply, "you are too
old a whaler not to know whaling law.   My irons were
fast in this fish ; I never have been loose from it since it
was first struck, and my lance killed it.   Under such circumstances, sir, I am surprised that any man, who knows
the usages among whalers, should have stuck by the creature as you have done."

"It's in my natur', Gar'ner," was the answer. "I stuck by you when you was dismasted under Hatteras, and I stick by everything that I undertake. This is what I call Vineyard natur'; and I'm not about to discredit my native country."

"This is idle talk," returned Roswell, casting a severe glance at the men in the Vineyard boat, among whom a common smile arose, as if they highly approved of the reply of their own officer. "You very well know that Vineyard law cannot settle such a question, but American law. Were you man enough to take this whale from me, as I trust you are not, on our return home you could be, and would be, made to pay smartly for the act. Uncle Sam has a long arm, with which he sometimes reaches round the whole earth. Before you proceed any further in this matter, it may be well to remember that."

Daggett reflected; and it is probable that, as he cooled off from the excitement created by his late exertions, he fully recognized the justice of the other's remarks, and the injustice of his own claims. Still, it seemed to him un-American, un-Vineyard, if the reader please, to "give up;" and he clung to his error with as much pertinacity as if he had been right

"If you are fast, I am fast too. I'm not so certain of your law. When a man puts an iron into a whale, commonly it is his fish, if he can get him, and kill him. But there is a law above all whalers' law, and that is the law of Divine Providence. Providence has fastened us to this crittur', as if on purpose to give us a right in it; and I'm by no means so sure States' law won't uphold that doctrine. Then, I lost my own whale by means of this, and am entitled to some compensation for such a loss."

"You lost your own whale because he led round the head of mine, and not only drew his own iron, but came nigh causing me to cut. If any one is entitled to damage for such an act, it is I, who have been put to extra trouble in getting my fish."

"I do believe it was my lance that did the job for the fellow! I darted, and you struck; in that way I got the start of you, and may claim to have made the crittur' spout the first blood. But, hearkee, Gar'ner—there's my hand— we've been friends so far, and I want to hold out friends. I will make you a proposal, therefore. Join stocks from this moment, and whale, and seal, and do all things else in common. When we make a final stowage for the return passage, we can make a final division, and each man take his share of the common adventure."

To do Roswell justice, he saw through the artifice of this proposition, the instant it was uttered. It had the effect, notwithstanding, a good deal to mollify his feelings, since it induced him to believe that Daggett was manœuvring to get at his great secret, rather than to assail his rights.

"You are part owner of your schooner, Captain Daggett,' our hero answered, "while I have no other interest in mine than my lay, as her master. You may have authority to make such a bargain, but I have none. It is my duty to fill the craft as fast and as full as I can, and carry her back safely to Deacon Pratt ; but, I dare say, your Vineyard people will let you cruise about the earth at your pleasure, trusting to Providence for a profit. I cannot accept your offer."

"This is answering like a man, Gar'ner, and I like you all the better for it. Forty or fifty barrels of ile sha'n't break friendship between us. I helped you into port at Beaufort, and gave up the salvage ; and now I'll help tow your whale alongside, and see you fairly through this business too. Perhaps I shall have all the better luck for being a little generous."

There was prudence, as well as art, in this decision of Daggett's. Notwithstanding his ingenious pretensions to a claim in the whale, he knew perfectly well that no law would sustain it ; and that, in addition to the chances of being beaten on the spot, which were at least equal, he would certainly be beaten in the courts at home, should he really attempt to carry out his declared design. Then, he really deferred to the expectation that his future good fortune might be influenced by his present forbearance. Superstition forms a material part of a sailor's nature, if, indeed, it do not that of every man engaged in hazardous and uncertain adventures. How far his hopes were justified in this last respect, will appear in the contents of a communication that Deacon Pratt received from the master of his schooner, and to which we will now refer, as the clearest and briefest mode of continuing the narrative.

The Sea Lion left Oyster Pond late in September. It was the third day of March in the succeeding year, that Mary was standing at the window, gazing with melancholy interest at that point in the adjacent waters where last she had seen, nearly six months before, the vessel of Roswell disappear behind the woods of the island that bears his family name. There had been a long easterly gale, but the weather had changed ; the south wind blew softly, and all the indications of an early spring were visible. For the first time in three months, she had raised the sash of that window ; and the air that entered was bland, and savored of the approaching season.

"I dare say, uncle"—the deacon was writing near a very low wood-fire, which was scarcely more than embers —"I dare say, uncle," said the sweet voice of Mary, which was a little tremulous with feeling, "that the ocean is calm enough to-day. It is very silly in us to tremble, when there is a storm, for those who must now be so many, many thousand miles away. What is the distance between the antarctic seas and Oyster Pond, I wonder?"

"You ought to be able to calculate that yourself, gal, or what is the use to pay for your schooling?"

"I should not know how to set about it, uncle," returned the gentle Mary, "though I should be very glad to know."

"How many miles are there in a degree of latitude, child? You know that, I believe."

"More than sixty-nine, sir."

"Well, in what latitude is Oyster Pond?"

"I have heard Roswell say that we were a little higher, as he calls it, than forty-one."

"Well, 41 times 69"—figuring as he spoke—"make 2,829 ; say we are 3,000 miles from the equator, the nearest way we can get there. Then the antarctic circle commences in 23° 30′ south, which deducted from 90 degrees, leave just 66° 30′ between the equator and the nearest spot within the sea you have mentioned. Now 66° 30′ give about 4,589 statute miles more, in a straight line, allowing only 69 to a degree. The two sums, added together, make 7,589 miles, or rather more. But the road is not straight by any means, as shipmasters tell me ; and I suppose Gar'ner must have gone, at the very least, 8,000 miles to reach his latitude, to say nothing of a considerable distance of longitude to travel over, to the southward of Cape Horn."

"It is a terrible distance to have a friend from us !" ejaculated Mary, though in a low, dejected tone.

"It is a terrible distance for a man to trust his property away from him, gal ; and I do not sleep a-nights for thinking of it, when I remember where my own schooner may be all this time !"

"Ah, here is Baiting Joe, and with a letter in his hand, uncle. I do declare !"

It might be a secret hope that impelled Mary, for away she bounded like a young fawn, running to meet the old fisherman at the door. No sooner did her eyes fall on the superscription, than the large package was pressed to her heart, and she seemed, for an instant, lost in thanksgiving. That no one might unnecessarily be a witness of what passed between her uncle and herself, Joe was directed to the kitchen, where a good meal, a glass of rum and water, and the quarter of a dollar that Mary gave him, as she showed the way, satisfied him with the results of his trouble.

"Here it is, uncle," cried the nearly breathless girl, re-entering the "keeping-room," and unconsciously holding the letter still pressed to her heart,—"a letter—a letter from Roswell, in his own precious hand."

A flood of tears gave some relief to feelings that had so long been pent, and eased a heart that had been compressed nearly to breaking. At any other time, and at this un-equivocal evidence of the hold the young man had on the affections of his niece, Deacon Pratt would have remon-strated with her on the folly of refusing to become "Ros-well Gar'ner's" wife; but the sight of the letter drove all other thoughts from his head, concentrating his whole be-ing in the fate of the schooner.

"Look, and see if it has the antarctic post-mark on it, Mary," said the deacon, in a tremulous voice.

This request was not made so much in ignorance as in trepidation. The deacon very well knew that the islands the Sea Lion was to visit were uninhabited, and were des-titute of post-offices; but his ideas were confused, and apprehension rendered him silly.

"Uncle," exclaimed the niece, wiping the tears from a face that was now rosy with blushes at her own weakness, "surely, Roswell can find no post-office where he is!"

"But the letter must have some post-mark, child. Bait-ing Joe has not brought it himself into the country."

"It is post-marked 'New York,' sir, and nothing else. Yes, here is 'Forwarded by Cane, Spriggs, & Button, Rio de Janeiro.' It must have been put into a post-office there"

"Rio!—Here is more salvage, gal—more salvage com-ing to afflict me!"

"But you had no salvage to pay, uncle, on the other occasion; perhaps there will be none to pay on this. Had I not better open the letter at once, and see what has hap-pened?"

"Yes, open it, child," answered the deacon, in a voice so feeble as to be scarcely audible—"open it at once, as you say, and let me know my fate. Anything is better than this torment!"

Mary did not wait for a second permission, but instantly broke the seal. It might have been the result of education, or there may be such a thing as female instinct in these matters; but certain it is, that the girl turned toward the window, as she tore the paper asunder, and slipped the letter that bore her own name into a fold of her dress, so dexterously, that one far more keen-sighted than her uncle would not have detected the act. No sooner was her own letter thus secured, than the niece offered the principal epistle to her uncle.

"Read it yourself, Mary," said the last, in his querulous tones. "My eyes are so dim, that I could not see to read it."

"'Rio de Janeiro, Province of Brazil, South America, Nov. 14th, 1819,'" commenced the niece.

"Rio de Janeiro!" interrupted the uncle. "Why, that is round Cape Horn, isn't it, Mary?"

"Certainly not, sir. Brazil is on the east side of the Andes, and Rio de Janeiro is its capital. The king of Portugal lives there now, and has lived there as long as I can remember."

"Yes, yes; I had forgotten. The Brazil Banks, where our whalers go, are in the Atlantic. But what can have taken Gar'ner into Rio, unless it be to spend more money!"

"By reading the letter, sir, we shall soon know. I see there is something about spermaceti oil here."

"Ile? And spalm ile, do you say!" exclaimed the deacon, brightening up at once—"Read on, Mary, my good gal—read the letter as fast as you can—read it at a trot."

"'Deacon Israel Pratt—Dear sir,'" continued Mary, in obedience to this command, "'the two schooners sailed from Beaufort, North Carolina, as stated already, per mail, in a letter written at that port, and which has doubtless come to hand. We had fine weather, and a tolerable run of it, until we reached the calm latitudes, where we were detained by the usual changes for about a week. On the 18th Oct. the pleasant cry of 'there she spouts' was heard aboard here, and we found ourselves in the neighborhood of whales. Both schooners lowered their boats, and I was soon fast to a fine bull, who gave us a long tow before the lance was put into him, and he was made to spout blood.

Captain Daggett set up some claims to this fish, in consequence of his line's getting foul of the creature's jaws, but
he changed his mind in good season, and clapped on to
help tow the whale down to the vessel. His irons drew
from a young bull, and a good deal of dissatisfaction existed among the other crew, until, fortunately, the school
of young bulls came round quite near us, when Captain
Daggett and his people succeeded in securing no less than
three of the fish, and Mr. Hazard got a very fine one for us.

"'I am happy to say that we had very pleasant weather
to cut in, and secured every gallon of the oil of both our
whales, as did Captain Daggett all of his. Our largest
bull made one hundred and nineteen barrels, of which
forty-three barrels was head-matter. I never saw better
case and junk in a whale in my life. The smallest bull
turned out well, too, making fifty-eight barrels, of which
twenty-one was head. Daggett got one hundred and
thirty-three barrels from his three fish, a very fair proportion of head, though not as large as our own. Having this
oil on board, we came in here after a pleasant run ; and I
have shipped, as per invoice inclosed, one hundred and
seventy-seven barrels of spermaceti oil, viz., sixty-four barrels of head, and rest in body-oil, to your order, care of
Fish & Grinnell, New York, by the brig Jason, Captain
Williams, who will sail for home about the 20th proximo,
and to whom I trust this letter——'"

"Stop, Mary, my dear—this news is overpowering—it is
almost too good to be true," interrupted the deacon, nearly
as much unmanned by this intelligence of his good fortune
as he had previously been by his apprehensions. "Yes, it
does seem too good to be true ; read it again, child ; yes,
read every syllable of it again!"

Mary complied, delighted enough to hear all she could
of Roswell's success.

"Why, uncle," said the deeply-interested girl, "all this
oil is spermaceti! It is worth a great deal more than so
much of that which comes of the right whale."

"More ! Ay, nearly as three for one. Hunt me up the
last Spectator, girl—hunt me up the last Spectator, and let
me see at once at what they quote spalm."

Mary soon found the journal, and handed it to her uncle.

"Yes, here it is, and quoted $1.12½ per gallon, as I live !
That's nine shillings a gallon, Mary—just calculate on that
bit of paper—thirty times one hundred and seventy-seven,
Mary ; how much is that, child ?"

"I make it 5,310, uncle—yes, that is right. But what are the 30 times for, sir?"

"Gallons, gal, gallons. Each barrel has 30 gallons in it, if not more. There ought to be 32 by rights, but this is a cheating age. Now multiply 5,310 by 9, and see what that comes to."

"Just 47,790, sir, as near as I can get it."

"Yes, that's the shillings. Now divide 47,790 by 8, my dear. Be actyve, Mary, be actyve."

"It leaves 5,973, with a remainder of 6, sir. I believe I'm right."

"I dare say you are, child; yes, I dare say you are. This is the dollars. A body may call them $6,000, as the barrels will a little overrun the 30 gallons. My share of this will be two-thirds, and that will net the handsome sum of, say $4,000!"

The deacon rubbed his hands with delight, and having found his voice again, his niece was astonished at hearing him utter what he had to say, with a sort of glee that sounded in her ears as very unnatural, coming from him. So it was, however, and she dutifully endeavored not to think of it.

"Four thousand dollars, Mary, will quite cover the first cost of the schooner; that is, without including outfit and spare rigging, of which her master took about twice as much as was necessary. He's a capital fellow, is that young Gar'ner, and will make an excellent husband, as I've always told you, child. A little wasteful, perhaps, but an excellent youth at the bottom. I dare say he lost his spars off Cape Hatteras in trying to outsail that Daggett; but I overlook all that now. He's a capital youth to work upon a whale or a sea-elephant! There isn't his equal, as I'll engage, in all Ameriky, if you'll only let him know where to find the creatur's. I knew his character before I engaged him; for no man but a real skinner shall ever command a craft of mine."

"Roswell *is* a good fellow," answered Mary, with emphasis, the tears filling her eyes as she listened to these eulogiums of her uncle on the youth she loved with all of a woman's tenderness, at the very moment she scrupled to place her happiness on one whose "God was not her God." "No one knows him better than I, uncle, and no one respects him more. But had I not better read the rest of his letter?—there is a good deal more of it."

"Go on, child, go on—but read the part over again

where he speaks of the quantity of the ile he has shipped to Fish & Grinnell."

Mary did as requested, when she proceeded to read aloud the rest of the communication.

"I have been much at a loss how to act in regard to Captain Daggett," said Roswell, in his letter. "He stood by me so manfully and generously off Cape Hatteras, that I did not like to part company in the night, or in a squall, which would have seemed ungrateful, as well as wearing a sort of runaway look. I am afraid he has some knowledge of the existence of our islands, though I doubt whether he has their latitude and longitude exactly. Something there is of this nature on board the other schooner, her people often dropping hints to my officers and men, when they have been gamming. I have sometimes fancied Daggett sticks so close to us, that he may get the advantage of our reckoning to help him to what he wants to find. He is no great navigator anywhere, running more by signs and currents, in my judgment, than by the use of his instruments. Still, he could find his way to any part of the world."

"Stop there, Mary ; stop a little, and let me have time to consider. Isn't it awful, child ?"

The niece changed color, and seemed really frightened, so catching was the deacon's distress, though she scarce knew what was the matter.

"What is awful, uncle ?" at length she asked, anxious to know the worst.

"This covetousness in them Vineyarders! I consider it both awful and wicked. I must get the Rev. Mr. Whittle to preach against the sin of covetousness ; it does gain so much ground in Ameriky ! The whole Church should lift its voice against it, or it will shortly lift its voice against the Church. To think of them Daggetts fitting out a schooner to follow my craft about the 'arth in this unheard-of manner ; just as if she was a pilot-boat, and young Gar'ner a pilot ! I do hope the fellows will make a wrack of it, among the ice of the antarctic seas ! That would be a fit punishment for their impudence and covetousness."

"I suppose, sir, they think that they have the same right to sail on the ocean that others have. Seals and whales are the gifts of God, and one person has no more right to them than another."

"You forget, Mary, that one man may have a secret that another doesn't know. In that case he ought not to go prying about like an old woman in a village neighborhood.

Read on, child, read on, and let me know the worst at once."

"I shall sail to-morrow, having finished all my business here, and hope to be off Cape Horn in twenty days, if not sooner. In what manner I am to get rid of Daggett, I do not yet know. He outsails me a little on all tacks, unless it be in very heavy weather, when I have a trifling advantage over him. It will be in my power to quit him any dark night ; but if I let him go ahead, and he should really have any right notions about the position of the islands, he might get there first, and make havoc among the seals."

"Awful, awful !" interrupted the deacon, again ; "that would be the worst of all ! I won't allow it ; I forbid it— it shall not be ! "

"Alas ! uncle, poor Roswell is too far from us now to hear these words. No doubt the matter is long since decided, and he has acted according to the best of his judgment."

"It is terrible to have one's property so far away ! Government ought to have steamboats, or packets of some sort, running between New York and Cape Horn, to carry orders back and forth. But we shall never have things right, Mary, so long as the democrats are uppermost."

By this remark, which savors very strongly of a species of censure that is much in fashion in the coteries of that Great Emporium, which it is the taste and pleasure of its people to term a *commercial* emporium, especially among elderly ladies, the reader will at once perceive that the deacon was a federalist, which was somewhat of a novelty in Suffolk thirty years since. Had he lived down to our own times, the old man would probably have made all the gyrations in politics that have distinguished the school to which he would have belonged, and, without his own knowledge, most probably, would have been as near an example of perpetual motion as the world will ever see, through his devotion to what are now called "whig principles." We are no great politician, but time has given us the means of comparing ; and we often smile when we hear the disciples of Hamilton, and of Adams, and of all that high-toned school, declaiming against the use of the veto, and talking of the "one man power," and of Congress leading the government ! The deacon was very apt to throw the opprobrium of even a bad season on the administration, and the reader has seen what he thought of the subject of running packets between New York and Cape Horn.

"There ought to be a large navy, Mary—a monstrous navy, so that the vessels might be kept carrying letters about, and serving the public. But we shall never have things right until Rufus King, or some man like him, gets in. If Gar'ner lets that Daggett get the start of him, he never need come home again. The islands are as much mine as if I had bought them ; and I'm not sure an action wouldn't lie for seals taken on them without my consent. Yes, yes ; we want a monstrous navy to convoy sealers, and carry letters about, and keep some folks at home, while it lets other folks go about their lawful business."

"Of what islands are you speaking, uncle ? Surely the sealing islands, where Roswell has gone, are public and uninhabited, and no one has a better right there than another ! "

The deacon perceived that he had gone too far in his tribulation, and began to have a faint notion that he was making a fool of himself. He asked his niece, in a very faint voice, therefore, to hand him the letter, the remainder of which he would endeavor to read himself. Although every word that Roswell Gardiner wrote was very precious to Mary, the gentle girl had a still unopened epistle to herself to peruse, and glad enough was she to make the exchange. Handing the deacon his letter, therefore, she withdrew at once to her private room, in order to read her own.

"Dearest Mary," said Roswell Gardiner, in this epistle, "your uncle will tell you what has brought us into this port, and all things connected with the schooner. I have sent home more than $4,000 worth of oil, and I hope my owner will forgive the accident off Currituck, on account of this run of good luck. In my opinion, we shall yet make a voyage, and that part of my fortune will be secure. Would that I could feel as sure of finding you more disposed to be kind to me on my return ! I read in your Bible every day, Mary, and I often pray to God to enlighten my mind, if my views have been wrong. As yet, I cannot flatter myself with any change, for my old opinions appear rather to be more firmly rooted than they were before I sailed." Here poor Mary heaved a heavy sigh, and wiped the tears from her eyes. She was pained to a degree she could hardly believe possible, though she did full credit to Roswell's frankness. Like all devout persons, her faith in the efficacy of sacred writ was strong ; and she so much the more lamented her suitor's continued blindness, because it remained after light had shone upon it. "Still, Mary," the letter added, "as I have every human inducement to endeavor to be right, I shall not throw aside the book, by any means. In that I fully believe; our difference being in what the volume teaches. Pray for me, sweetest girl—but I know you do, and will continue to do, as long as I am absent."

"Yes, indeed, Roswell," murmured Mary—"as long as you and I live!"

"Next to this one great concern of my life, comes that which this man Daggett gives me," the letter went on to say. "I hardly know what to do under all the circumstances. Keep in his company much longer I cannot, without violating my duty to the deacon. Yet it is not easy, in any sense, to get rid of him. He has stood by me so manfully on all occasions, and seems so much disposed to make good-fellowship of the voyage, that, did it depend on myself only, I should at once make a bargain with him to seal in company and to divide the spoils. But this is now impossible, and I must quit him in some way or other. He outsails me in most weathers, and it is a thing easier said than done. What will make it more difficult is the growing shortness of the nights. The days lengthen fast now, and as we go south they will become so much longer that, by the time when it will be indispensable to separate, it will be nearly all day. The thing must be done, however, and I trust to luck to be able to do it as it ought to be effected.

"And now, dearest, dearest Mary——" But why should we lift the veil from the feelings of this young man, who concluded his letter by pouring out his whole heart in a few sincere and manly sentences. Mary wept over them most of that day, perusing and reperusing them, until her eyes would scarce perform their proper office.

A few days later the deacon was made a very happy man by the receipt of a letter from Fish and Grinnell, notifying him of the arrival of his oil, accompanied by a most gratifying account of the state of the market, and asking for instructions. The oil was disposed of, and the deacon pocketed his portion of the proceeds as soon as possible; eagerly looking for a new and profitable investment for the avails. Great was the reputation Roswell Gardiner made by this capture of the two spermaceti whales, and by sending the proceeds to so good a market. In commerce, as in war, success is all in all, though in both success is nearly as often the result of unforeseen circumstances as of cal-

culation and wisdom. It is true, there is a sort of trade,
and a sort of war, in which prudence and care may effect
a great deal, yet are both often outstripped by the random
exertions and adventures of those who calculate almost as
wildly as they act. Audacity, as the French term it, is a
great quality in war, and often achieves more than the
most calculated wisdom—nay, it becomes wisdom in that
sort of struggle ; and we are far from being sure that audacity is not sometimes as potent in trade. At all events,
it was esteemed a bold, as well as a prosperous exploit, for
a little schooner like the Sea Lion of Oyster Pond to take
a hundred-barrel whale, and to send home its "ile," as the
deacon always pronounced the word, in common with most
others in old Suffolk.

Long and anxious months, with one exception, succeeded this bright spot of sunshine in Mary Pratt's solicitude
in behalf of the absent Roswell. She knew there was but
little chance of hearing from him again until he returned
north. The exception was a short letter that the deacon
received, dated two weeks later than that written from Rio,
in latitude forty-one, or just as far south of the equator as
Oyster Pond was north of it, and nearly fourteen hundred
miles to the southward of Rio. This letter was written in
great haste, to send home by a Pacific trader who was ac-
cidentally met nearer the coast than was usual for such
vessels to be. It stated that all was well ; that the schooner of Daggett was still in company; and that Gardiner
intended to get "shut" of her, as the deacon expressed it,
on the very first occasion.

After the receipt of this letter, the third written by Roswell Gardiner since he left home, a long and blank interval of silence succeeded. Then it was that months passed
away in an anxious and dark uncertainty. Spring followed
winter, summer succeeded to spring, and autumn came to
reap the fruits of all the previous seasons, without bringing
any further tidings of the adventurers. Then winter made
its second appearance since the Sea Lion had sailed, filling the minds of the mariners' friends with sad forebodings
as they listened to the moanings of the gales that accompanied that bleak and stormy quarter of the year. Deep
and painful were the anticipations of the deacon, in whom
failing health and a near approach to the "last of earth,"
came to increase the gloom. As for Mary, youth and
health sustained her ; but her very soul was heavy, as she
pondered on so long and uncertain an absence.

CHAPTER XIII.

" Safely in harbor
Is the king's ship , in the deep nook, where once
Thou calledst me up at midnight to fetch dew
From the still vex'd Bermoothes, there she's hid."—*Tempest.*

THE letter of Roswell Gardiner last received, bore the
date of December 10th, 1819, or just a fortnight after he
had sailed from Rio de Janeiro. We shall next present
the schooner of Deacon Pratt to the reader on the 18th
of that month, or three weeks and one day after she had
sailed from the capital of Brazil. Early in the morning
of the day last mentioned, the Sea Lion of Oyster Pond
was visible standing to the northward, with the wind
light, but freshening, from the westward, and in smooth
water. Land was not only in sight, but was quite near,
less than a league distant. Toward this land the head of
the schooner had been laid, and she was approaching it at
the rate of some four or five knots. The land was broken,
high, of a most sterile aspect, where it was actually to
be seen, and nearly all covered with a light but melting
snow, though the season was advanced to the middle of
the first month in summer. The weather was not very
cold, however, and there was a feeling about it that promised it would become still milder. The aspect of the
neighboring land, so barren, rugged, and inhospitable,
chilled the feelings, and gave to the scene a sombre hue,
which the weather itself might not have imparted. Directly ahead of the schooner rose a sort of pyramid of
broken rocks, which, occupying a small island, stood iso-
lated in a measure, and some distance in advance of other
and equally rugged ranges of mountains, which belonged
also to islands detached from the mainland thousands of
years before, under some violent convulsions of nature.

It was quite apparent that all on board the schooner regarded that ragged pyramid with lively interest. Most of
the crew were collected on the forecastle, including the
officers, and all eyes were fastened on the ragged pyramid
which they were diagonally approaching. The principal
spokesman was Stimson, the oldest mariner on board, and
one who had oftener visited those seas than any other of
the crew.

11

"You know the spot, do you, Stephen?" demanded Roswell Gardiner, with interest.

"Yes, sir, there's no mistake. That's the Horn. Eleven times have I doubled it, and this is the third time that I've been so close in as to get a fair sight of it. Once I went inside, as I've told you, sir."

"I have doubled it six times myself," said Gardiner, "but never saw it before. Most navigators give it a wide berth. 'Tis said to be the stormiest spot on the known earth!"

"That's a mistake, you may depend on't, sir. The sow-westers blow great guns hereabouts, it is true enough; and when they do, sich a sea comes tumbling in on that rock as man never seed anywhere else, perhaps; but, on the whull, I'd rather be close in here, than two hundred miles further to the southward. With the wind at sow-west and heavy, a better slant might be made from the southern position; but here I know where I am, and I'd go in and anchor, and wait for the gale to blow itself out."

"Talking of seas, Captain Gar'ner," observed Hazard, "don't you think, sir, we begin to feel the swell of the Pacific? Smooth as the surface of the water is, here is a ground-swell rolling in that must be twelve or fifteen feet in height."

"There's no doubt of that. We have felt the swell of the Pacific these two hours; no man can mistake *that*. The Atlantic has no such waves. This is an ocean in reality, and this is its stormiest part. The wind freshens and hauls, and I'm afraid we are about to be caught close in here with a regular sow-west gale."

"Let it come, sir, let it come," put in Stimson, again; "if it does, we've only to run in and anchor. I can stand pilot, and I promise to carry the schooner where twenty sow-westers will do her no harm. What I've seen done once, I know can be done again. The time will come when the Horn will be a reg'lar harbor."

Roswell left the forecastle and walked aft, pondering on what had just been said. His situation was delicate, and demanded decision as well as prudence. The manner in which Daggett had stuck by him ever since the two vessels took their departure from Block Island, is known to the reader. The Sea Lions had sailed from Rio in company, and they had actually made Staten Land together, the day preceding that on which we now bring the Oyster

Pond craft once more upon the scene, and had closed so near as to admit of a conversation between the two masters. It would seem that Daggett was exceedingly averse to passing through the Straits of Le Maire. An uncle of his had been wrecked there, and had reported the passage as the most dangerous one he had ever encountered. It has its difficulties, no doubt, in certain states of the wind and tide ; but Roswell had received good accounts of the place from Stimson, who had been through several times. The wind was rather scant to go through, and the weather threatened to be thick. As Daggett urged his reasons for keeping off and passing outside of Staten Land, a circuit of considerable extent, besides bringing a vessel far to leeward with the prevalent winds of that region, which usually blow from northwest round to southwest, Roswell was reflecting on the opportunity the circumstances afforded of giving his consort the slip. After discussing the matter for some time, he desired Daggett to lead on and he would follow. This was done, though neither schooner was kept off until Roswell got a good view of Cape St. Diego, on Tierra del Fuego, thereby enabling him to judge of the positions of the principal landmarks. Without committing himself by any promise, therefore, he told Daggett to lead on, and for some time he followed, the course being one that did not take him much out of the way. The weather was misty, and at times the wind blew in squalls. The last increased as the schooners drew nearer to Staten Land. Daggett, being about half a mile ahead, felt the full power of one particular squall that came out of the ravines with greater force than common, and he kept away to increase his distance from the land. At the same time, the mist shut in the vessels from each other. It was also past sunset, and a dark and dreary night was approaching. This latter fact had been one of Daggett's arguments for going outside. Profiting by all these circumstances, Roswell tacked, and stood over toward Tierra del Fuego. He knew from the smoothness of the water that an ebb-tide was running, and trusted to its force to carry him through the straits. He saw no more of the Sea Lion of the Vineyard. She continued shut in by the mist until night closed around both vessels. When he got about mid-channel, Roswell tacked again. By this time the current had sucked him fairly into the passage, and no sooner did he go about than his movement to the southward was very rapid. The squalls gave some trouble, but on the

whole, he did very well. Next morning he was off Cape
Horn, as described. By this expression, it is generally understood that a vessel is somewhere near the longitude of
that world-renowned cape, but not necessarily in sight of
it. Few navigators actually see the extremity of the
American continent, though they double the cape, it being
usually deemed the safest to pass well to the southward.
Such was Daggett's position ; who, in consequence of having gone outside of Staten Land, was now necessarily a
long distance to leeward, and who could not hope to beat
up abreast of the Hermits, even did the wind and sea favor
him, in less than twenty-four hours. A great advantage
was obtained by coming through the Straits of Le Maire,
and Roswell felt very certain that he should not see his
late consort again that day, even did he heave-to for him.
But our hero had no idea of doing anything of the sort.
Having shaken off his leech, he had no wish to suffer it
to fasten to him again. It was solely with the intention
of making sure of this object that he thought of making a
harbor.

In order that the reader may better understand those
incidents of our narrative which we are about to relate, it
may be well to say a word of the geographical features of
the region to which he has been transported, in fiction, if
not in fact. At the southern extremity of the American
continent is a cluster of islands, which are dark, sterile,
rocky, and most of the year covered with snow. Ever-
greens relieve the aspect of sterility, in places that are a
little sheltered, and there is a meagre vegetation, in spots,
that serves to sustain animal life. The first strait which
separates this cluster of islands from the main, is that of Ma-
gellan, through which vessels occasionally pass, in preference to going farther south. Then comes Tierra del Fuego,
which is much the largest of all the islands. To the southward of Tierra del Fuego lies a cluster of many small islands, which bear different names; though the group farthest
south of all, and which it is usual to consider as the southern termination of our noble continent, but which is not on
a continent at all, is known by the appropriate appellation
of the Hermits. If solitude, and desolation, and want, and a
contemplation of some of the sublimest features of this earth,
can render a spot fit for a hermitage, these islands are very
judiciously named. The one that is farthest south contains
the cape itself, which is marked by the ragged pyramid of
rock already mentioned ; placed there by nature, a never-

tiring sentinel of the war of the elements. Behind this cluster of the Hermits it was that Stimson advised his officer to take refuge against the approaching gale, of which the signs were now becoming obvious and certain. Roswell's motive, however, for listening to such advice, was less to find a shelter for his schooner than to get rid of Daggett. For the gale he cared but little, since he was a long way from the ice, and could stretch off the land to the southward into a waste of waters that seems interminable. There are islands to the southward of Cape Horn, and a good many of them too, though none very near. It is now known, also, by means of the toils and courage of various seamen, including those of the persevering and laborious Wilkes, ever the most industrious and the least rewarded of all the navigators who have ever worked for the human race in this dangerous and exhausting occupation, that a continent is there also ; but, at the period of which we are writing, the existence of the Shetlands and Palmer's Land was the extent of the later discoveries in that part of the ocean. After pacing the quarter-deck a few minutes, when he quitted the forecastle as mentioned, Roswell Gardiner again went forward among the men.

"You are quite sure that this high peak is the Horn, Stimson ?" he observed, inquiringly.

"Sartain of it, sir. There's no mistaking sich a place, which, once seen, is never forgotten."

"It agrees with the charts and our reckoning, and I may say it agrees with our eyes also. Here is the Pacific Ocean plain enough, Mr. Hazard."

"So I think, sir. We are at the end of Ameriky, if it *has* an end anywhere. This heavy long swell is an old acquaintance, though I never was in close enough to see the land, hereabouts, before."

"It is fortunate we have one trusty hand on board who can stand pilot. Stimson, I intend to go in and anchor, and I shall trust to you to carry me into a sung berth."

"I'll do it, Captain Gar'ner, if the weather will permit it," returned the seaman, with an unpretending sort of confidence that spoke well for his ability.

Preparations were now commenced in earnest, to come to. It was time that some steady course should be adopted, as the wind was getting up, and the schooner was rapidly approaching the land. In half an hour the Sea Lion was bending to a little gale, with her canvas reduced to close-reefed mainsail and foresail, and the bonnet off her jib.

The sea was fast getting up, though it came in long, and mountain-like. Roswell dreaded the mist. Could he pass through the narrow channels that Stimson had described to him, with a clear sky, one half of his causes of anxiety would be removed. But the wind was not a clear one, and he felt that no time was to be lost.

It required great nerve to approach a coast like that of Cape Horn in such weather. As the schooner got nearer to the real cape, the sight of the seas tumbling in and breaking on its ragged rock, and the hollow roaring sound they made, actually became terrific. To add to the awe inspired in the breast of even the most callous-minded man on board, came a doubt whether the schooner could weather a certain point of rock, the western extremity of the island, after she had got so far into a bight as to render wearing questionable, if not impossible. Every one now looked grave and anxious. Should the schooner go ashore in such a place, a single minute would suffice to break her to pieces, and not a soul could expect to be saved. Roswell was exceedingly anxious, though he remained cool.

" The tides and eddies about these rocks, and in so high a latitude, sweep a vessel like chips," he said to his chief mate. "We have been set in here by an eddy, and a terrible place it is."

"All depends on our gear's holding on, sir," was the answer, "with a little on Providence. Just watch the point ahead, Captain Gar'ner; though we are not actually to leeward of it, see with what a drift we have drawn upon it ! The manner in which these seas roll in from the sowwest is terrific ! No craft can go to windward against them."

This remark of Hazard's was very just. The seas that came down upon the cape resembled a rolling prairie in their outline. A single wave would extend a quarter of a mile from trough to trough, and as it passed beneath the schooner, lifting her high in the air, it really seemed as if the glancing water would sweep her away in its force. But human art had found the means to counteract even this imposing display of the power of nature. The little schooner rode over the billows like a duck, and when she sank between two of them, it was merely to rise again on a new summit, and breast the gale gallantly. It was the current that menaced the greatest danger ; for that, unseen except in its fruits, was clearly setting the little craft to leeward, and bodily toward the rocks. By this time our adventurers were so near to the land that they almost gave up hope itself. Cape Hatteras, and its much-talked-of danger, seemed a place of refuge compared to that in which our navigators now found themselves. Could the deepest bellowings of ten thousand bulls be united in a common roar, the noise would not have equalled that of the hollow sound which issued from a sea as it went into some cavern of the rocks. Then, the spray filled the air like driving rain, and there were minutes when the cape, though so frightfully near, was hid from view by the vapor.

At this precise moment, the Sea Lion was less than a quarter of a mile to windward of the point she was struggling to weather, and toward which she was driving under a treble impetus ; that of the wind, acting on her sails, and pressing her ahead at the rate of fully five knots, for the craft was kept a rap full ; that of the eddy, or current, and that of the rolling waters. No man spoke, for each person felt that the crisis was one in which silence was a sort of homage to the Deity. Some prayed privately, and all gazed on the low rocky point that it was indispensable to pass, to avoid destruction. There was one favorable circumstance ; the water was known to be deep, quite close to the iron-bound coast, and it was seldom that any danger existed that it was not visible to the eye. This Roswell knew from Stimson's accounts, as well as from those of other mariners, and he saw that the fact was of the last importance to him. Should he be able to weather the point ahead, that which terminated at the mouth of the passage that led within the Hermits, it was now certain it could be done only by going fearfully near the rocks.

Roswell Gardiner took his station between the knight-heads, beckoning to Stimson to come near him. At the same time, Hazard himself went to the helm.

"Do you remember this place ?" asked the young master of the old seaman.

"This is the spot, sir ; and if we can round the rocky point ahead, I will take you to a safe anchorage. Our drift is awful, or we are in an eddy tide here, sir !"

"It is the eddy," answered Roswell, calmly, "though our drift is not trifling. This is getting frightfully near to that point !"

"Hold on, sir—it's our only chance ;—hold on, and we may rub and go."

"If we *rub*, we are lost; that is certain enough. Should we get by *this* first point, there is another a short distance beyond it, which must certainly fetch us up, I fear. See—it opens more, as we draw ahead."

Stimson saw the new danger, and fully appreciated it. He did not speak, however; for, to own the truth, he now abandoned all hope, and, being a piously-inclined person, he was privately addressing himself to God. Every man on board was fully aware of the character of this new danger, and all seemed to forget that of the nearest point of rock, toward which they were now wading with portentous speed. That point *might* be passed; there was a little hope there; but as to the point a quarter of a mile beyond, with the leeward set of the schooner, the most ignorant hand on board saw how unlikely it was that they should get by it.

An imposing silence prevailed in the schooner, as she came abreast of the first rock. It was about fifty fathoms under the lee bow, and, as to *that* spot, all depended on the distance outward that the dangers thrust themselves. This it was impossible to see amid the chaos of waters produced by the collision between the waves and the land. Roswell fastened his eyes on objects ahead, to note the rate of his leeward set, and, with a seaman's quickness, he noted the first change.

"She feels the under-tow, Stephen," he said, in a voice so compressed as to seem to come out of the depths of his chest, "and is breasted up to windward!"

"What means that sudden luff, sir? Mr. Hazard must keep a good full, or we shall have no chance."

Gardiner looked aft, and saw that the mate was bearing the helm well up, as if he met with much resistance. The truth then flashed upon him, and he shouted out—

"All's well, boys! God be praised, we have caught the ebb-tide, under our lee bow!"

These few words explained the reason of the change. Instead of setting to leeward, the schooner was now meeting a powerful tide of some four or five knots, which hawsed her up to windward with irresistible force. As if conscious of the danger she was in, the tight little craft receded from the rocks as she shot ahead, and rounded the second point, which, a minute before, had appeared to be placed there purposely to destroy her. It was handsomely doubled, at the safe distance of a hundred fathoms. Roswell believed he might now beat his schooner off the land far enough to double the cape altogether, could he but keep her in that current. It doubtless expended itself, however, a short distance in the offing, as its waters diffused themselves on the breast of the ocean ; and it was this diffusion of the element that produced the eddy which had proved so nearly fatal.

In ten minutes after striking the tide, the schooner opened the passage fairly, and was kept away to enter it. Notwithstanding it blew so heavily, the rate of sailing, by the land, did not exceed five knots. This was owing to the great strength of the tide, which sometimes rises and falls thirty feet, in high latitudes and narrow waters. Stimson now showed he was a man to be relied on. Conning the craft intelligently, he took her in behind the island on which the cape stands, luffed her up into a tiny cove, and made a cast of the lead. There were fifty fathoms of water, with a bottom of mud. With the certainty that there was enough of the element to keep him clear of the ground at low water, and that his anchors would hold, Roswell made a flying moor, and veered out enough cable to render his vessel secure.

Here, then, was the Sea Lion of Oyster Pond, that craft which the reader had seen lying at Deacon Pratt's wharf, only three short months before, safely anchored in a nook of the rocks behind Cape Horn. No navigator but a sealer would have dreamed of carrying his vessel into such a place, but it is a part of their calling to poke about in channels and passages where no one else has ever been. It was in this way that Stimson had learned to know where to find his present anchorage. The berth of the schooner was perfectly snug, and entirely land-locked. The tremendous swell that was rolling in on the outside, caused the waters to rise and fall a little within the passage, but there was no strain upon the cables in consequence. Neither did the rapid tides affect the craft, which lay in an eddy that merely kept her steady. The gale came howling over the Hermits, but was so much broken by the rocks as to do little more than whistle through the cordage and spars aloft.

Three days, and as many nights, did the gale from the south-west continue. The fourth day there was a change, the wind coming from the eastward. Roswell would now have gone out, had it not been for the apprehension of falling in with Daggett again. Having at length gotten rid of that pertinacious companion, it would have been an act of great weakness to throw himself blindly in his way once more. It was possible that Daggett might not suppose he had been left intentionally, in which case he would be very apt to look for his lost consort in the vicinity of the cape. As for the gale, it might, or it might not, have blown him to leeward. A good deal would depend on the currents, and his distance to the southward. Near the land, Gardiner believed the currents favored a vessel doubling it, going west; and if Daggett was also aware of this fact, it might induce him to keep as near the spot as possible.

Time was very precious to our sealers, the season being so short in the high latitudes. Still, they were a little in advance of their calculations, having got off the Horn fully ten days sooner than they had hoped to be there. Nearly the whole summer was before them, and there was the possibility of their even being too soon for the loosening of the ice farther south The wind was the strongest inducement to go out, for the point to which our adventurers were bound lay a considerable distance to the westward, and fair breezes were not to be neglected. Under all the circumstances, however, it was decided to remain within the passage one day longer, and this so much the more, because Hazard had discovered some signs of sea-elephants frequenting an island at no great distance. The boats were lowered accordingly, and the mate went in one direction, while the master pulled up to the rocks, and landed on the Hermit, or the island which should bear that name *par excellence*, being that in which the group terminates.

Taking Stimson with him, to carry a glass, and armed with an old lance as a pike-pole, to aid his efforts, Roswell Gardiner now commenced the ascent of the pyramid already mentioned. It was ragged, and offered a thousand obstacles, but none that vigor and resolution could not overcome. After a few minutes of violent exertion, and by helping each other in difficult places, both Roswell and Stimson succeeded in placing themselves on the summit of the elevation, which was an irregular peak. The height was considerable, and gave an extended view of the adjacent islands, as well as of the gloomy and menacing ocean to the southward. The earth, probably. does not contain a more remarkable sentinel than this pyramid on which our hero had now taken his station. There it stood, actually the Ultima Thule of this vast continent, or, what was much the same, so closely united to it as to seem a part of our own moiety of the globe, looking out on the broad expanse of waters. The eye saw, to the right, the Pacific ; in front was the Southern, or Antarctic Ocean ; and to the left was the great Atlantic. For several minutes, both Roswell and Stephen sat mute, gazing on this grand spectacle. By turning their faces north, they beheld the highlands of Tierra del Fuego, of which many of the highest peaks were covered with snow. The pyramid on which they were, however, was no longer white with the congealed rain, but stood, stern and imposing, in its native brown. The outlines of all the rocks, and the shores of the different islands, had an appearance of volcanic origin, though the rocks themselves told a somewhat different story. The last were principally of trap formation. Cape pigeons, gulls, petrels, and albatross were wheeling about in the air, while the rollers that still came in on this noble sea-wall were really terrific. Distant thunder wants the hollow, bellowing sound that these waves made when brought in contact with the shores. Roswell fancied that it was like a groan of the mighty Pacific, at finding its progress suddenly checked. The spray continued to fly, and, much of the time, the air below his elevated seat was filled with vapor.

As soon as our young master had taken in the grandest features of this magnificent view, his eyes sought the Sea Lion of Martha's Vineyard. There she was, sure enough, at a distance of only a couple of leagues, and apparently standing directly for the Cape. Could it be possible that Daggett suspected his manœuvre, and was coming in search of him, at the precise spot in which he had taken shelter ? As respects the vessel, there was no question as to her character. From the elevation at which he was placed, Roswell, aided by the glass, had no difficulty in making her out, and in recognizing her rig, form, and character. Stimson also examined her, and knew her to be the schooner. On that vast and desolate sea she resembled a speck, but the art of man had enabled those she held to guide her safely through the tempest, and bring her up to her goal, in a time that really seemed miraculous for the circumstances.

"If we had thought of it, Captain Gar'ner," said Stephen, "we might have brought up an ensign, and set it on these rocks, by way of letting the Vineyarders know where we are to be found. But we can always go out and meet them, should this wind stand."

"Which is just what I have no intention of doing, Stephen. I came in here on purpose to get rid of that schooner."

"You surprise me, sir! A consort is no bad thing, when a craft is a sealin' in a high latitude. The ice makes such ticklish times, that, for me, I'm always glad to know there is such a chance for taking a fellow off, should there happen to be a wrack."

"All that is very true, but there are reasons which may tell against it. I have heard of some islands where seals abound, and a consort is not quite so necessary to take them, as when one is wrecked."

"That alters the case, Captain Gar'ner. Nobody is obliged to tell of his sealing station. I was aboard one of the very first craft that found out that the South Shetlands was a famous place for seals, and no one among us thought it necessary to tell it to the world. Some men are weak enough to put sich discoveries in the newspapers ; but, for my part, I think it quite enough to put them in the log."

"That schooner must have the current with her, she comes down so fast. She'll be abreast of the Horn in half an hour longer, Stephen. We will wait, and see what she would be at."

Gardiner's prediction was true. In half an hour the Sea Lion of Holmes' Hole glided past the rocky pyramid of the Horn, distant from it less than a mile. Had it been the object of her commander to pass into the Pacific, he might have done so with great apparent ease. Even with a southwest wind, that which blows fully half the time in those seas, it would have been in his power to lay past the islands, and soon get before it. A northeast course, with a little offing, will clear the islands, and when a vessel gets as far north as the main land, it would take her off the coast.

But Daggett had no intention of doing anything of the sort. He was looking for his consort, which he had hoped to find somewhere near the cape. Disappointed in this expectation, after standing far enough west to make certain nothing was in sight in that quarter, he hauled up on an easy bowline, and stood to the southward. Roswell was right glad to see this, inasmuch as it denoted ignorance of the position of the islands he sought. They lay much farther to the westward ; and no sooner was he sure of the course steered by the other schooner, than he hastened down to the boat, in order to get his own vessel under way, to profit by the breeze.

Two hours later the Sea Lion of Oyster Pond glanced through the passage which led into the ocean, on an ebb-tide. By that time, the other vessel had disappeared in the southern board ; and Gardiner came out upon the open waters again, boldly, and certain of his course. All sail was set, and the little craft slipped away from the land with the ease of an aquatic bird that is plying its web-feet. Studding-sails were set, and the pyramid of the Horn soon began to lower in the distance, as the schooner receded. When night closed over the rolling waters, it was no longer visible, the vessel having fairly entered the Antarctic Ocean, if anything north of the circle can properly so be termed.

CHAPTER XIV.

" All gone ! 'tis ours the goodly land——
Look round—the heritage behold !
Go forth—upon the mountain stand ;
Then, if you can, be cold."—SPRAGUE.

IT was an enterprising and manly thing for a little vessel like the Sea Lion to steer with an undeviating course into the mysterious depths of the antarctic circle—mysterious, far more in that day, than at the present hour. But the American sealer rarely hesitates. He has very little science, few charts, and those oftener old than new, knows little of what is going on among the savans of the earth, though his ear is ever open to the lore of men like himself, and he has his mind stored with pictures of islands and continents that would seem to have been formed for no other purpose than to meet the wants of the race of animals it is his business to pursue and to capture. Cape Horn and its vicinity have so long been frequented by this class of men, that they are at home among their islands, rocks, currents, and sterility ; but to the southward of the Horn itself, all seemed a waste. At the time of which we are writing, much less was known of the antarctic regions than is known to-day ; and even now our knowledge is limited to a few dreary outlines, in which barrenness and ice compete for the mastery. Wilkes, and his competitors, have told us that a vast frozen continent exists in that quarter of the globe ; but even their daring and perseverance have not been able to determine more than the general fact.

We should be giving an exaggerated and false idea of Roswell Gardiner's character, did we say that he steered into that great void of the southern ocean in a total indifference to his destination and objects. Very much the reverse was his state of mind, as he saw the highland of the cape sink, as it might be foot by foot, into the ocean, and then lost sight of it altogether. Although the weather was fine for the region, it was dark and menacing. Such, indeed, is usually the case in that portion of this globe, which appears to be the favorite region of the storms. Although the wind was no more than a good breeze, and the ocean was but little disturbed, there were those symptoms in the atmosphere and in the long ground-swells that came rolling in from the southwest, that taught the mariner the cold lessons of caution. We believe that heavier gales of wind at sea are encountered in the warm than in the cold months; but there is something so genial in the air of the ocean during summer, and something so chilling and repulsive in the rival season, that most of us fancy that the currents of air correspond in strength with the fall of the mercury. Roswell knew better than this, it is true; but he also fully understood where he was, and what he was about. As a sealer, he had several times penetrated as far south as the Ne Plus Ultra of Cook; but it had ever before been in subordinate situations. This was the first time in which he had had the responsibility of command thrown on himself, and it was no more than natural that he should feel the weight of this new burden. So long as the Sea Lion of the Vineyard was in sight, she had presented a centre of interest and concern. To get rid of her had been his first care, and almost absorbing object; but, now that she seemed to be finally thrown out of his wake, there remained the momentous and closely approaching difficulties of the main adventure directly before his eyes. Roswell, therefore, was thoughtful and grave, his countenance offering no bad reflection of the sober features of the atmosphere and the ocean.

Although the season was that of summer, and the weather was such as is deemed propitious in the neighborhood of Cape Horn, a feeling of uncertainty prevailed over every other sensation. To the southward a cold mistiness veiled the view, and every mile the schooner advanced appeared like penetrating deeper and deeper into regions that nature had hitherto withheld from the investigation of the mariner. Ice, and its dangers, were known to exist a few degrees farther in that direction; but islands also had been discovered, and turned to good account by the enterprise of the sealers.

It was truly a great thing for the Sea Lion of Oyster Pond to have thrown off her namesake of the Vineyard. It is true both vessels were still in the same sea, with a possibility of again meeting; but Roswell Gardiner was steering onward toward a haven designated in degrees and minutes, while the other craft was most probably left to wander in uncertainty in that remote and stormy ocean. Our hero thought there was now very little likelihood of his again falling in with his late consort, and this so much the more, because the islands he sought were not laid down in the vicinity of any other known land, and were consequently out of the usual track of the sealers. This last circumstance was fully appreciated by our young navigator, and gave him confidence of possessing its treasures to himself, could he only find the place where nature had hid them.

When the sun went down in that vast waste of water which lies to the southward of this continent, the little Sea Lion had fairly lost sight of land, and was riding over the long southwestern ground-swell like a gull that holds its way steadily toward its nest. For many hours her course had not varied half a point, being as near as possible to south-southwest, which kept her a little off the wind. No sooner, however, did night come to shut in the view, than Roswell Gardiner went aft to the man at the helm, and ordered him to steer to the southward, as near as the breeze would conveniently allow. This was a material change in the direction of the vessel, and, should the present breeze stand, would probably place her, by the return of light, a good distance to the eastward of the point she would otherwise have reached. Hitherto it had been Roswell's aim to drop his consort; but, now it was dark, and so much time had already passed and been improved since the other schooner was last seen, he believed he might venture to steer in the precise direction he desired to go. The season is so short in those seas, that every hour is precious, and no more variation from a real object could be permitted than circumstances imperiously required. It was now generally understood that the craft was making the best of her way toward her destined sealing-ground.

Independently of the discoveries of the regular explorers, a great deal of information has been obtained from the sealers themselves, within the present century, touching the antarctic seas. It is thought that many a headland, and various islands, that have contributed their shares in procuring the *accolades* for different European navigators, were known to the adventurers from Stonington and other by-ports of this country, long before science ever laid its eyes upon them, or monarchs their swords on the shoulders of their secondary discoverers.

That divers islands existed in this quarter of the ocean was a fact recognized in geography long before the Sea Lion was thought of ; probably before her young master was actually born ; but the knowledge generally possessed on the subject was meagre and unsatisfactory. In particular cases, nevertheless, this remark would not apply, there being at that moment on board our little schooner several mariners who had often visited the South Shetlands, New Georgia, Palmer's Land, and other known places in those seas. Not one of them all, however, had ever heard of any island directly south of the present position of the schooner.

No material change occurred during the night, or in the course of the succeeding day, the little Sea Lion industriously holding her way toward the south pole ; making very regularly her six knots each hour. By the time she was thirty six hours from the Horn, Gardiner believed himself to be fully three degrees to the southward of it, and consequently some distance within the parallel of sixty degrees south. Palmer's Land, with its neighboring islands, would have been near, had not the original course carried the schooner so far to the westward. As it was, no one could say what lay before them.

The third day out the wind hauled, and it blew heavily from the northeast. This gave the adventurers a great run. The blink of ice was shortly seen, and soon after ice itself, drifting about in bergs. The floating hills were grand objects to the eye, rolling and wallowing in the seas ; but they were much worn and melted by the wash of the ocean, and comparatively of greatly diminished size. It was now absolutely necessary to lose most of the hours of darkness, it being much too dangerous to run in the night. The great barrier of ice was known to be close at hand ; and Cook's "Ne Plus Ultra," at that time the great boundary of antarctic navigation, was near the parallel of latitude to which the schooner had reached. The weather, however, continued very favorable, and after the blow from the northeast the wind came from the south, chill, and attended with flurries of snow, but sufficiently steady and not so fresh as to compel our adventurers to carry very short sail. The smoothness of the water would of itself have announced the vicinity of ice : not only did Gardiner's calculations tell him as much as this, but his eyes confirmed their results. In the course of the fifth day out, on several occasions when the weather cleared a little, glimpses were had of the ice in long mountainous walls, resembling many of the ridges of the Alps, though moving heavily under the heaving and setting of the restless waters. Dense fogs from time to time clouded the whole view, and the schooner was compelled more than once that day to heave-to, in order to avoid running on the sunken masses of ice, or fields, of which many of vast size now began to make their appearance.

Notwithstanding the dangers that surrounded our adventurers, they were none of them so insensible to the sublime powers of nature as to withhold their admiration from the many glorious objects which that lone and wild scene presented. The icebergs were of all the hues of the rainbow, as the sunlight gilded their summits or sides, or they were left shaded by the interposition of dark and murky clouds. There were instances when certain of the huge frozen masses even appeared to be quite black, in particular positions and under peculiar lights, while others at the same instant were gorgeous in their gleams of emerald and gold !

The aquatic birds also had now become numerous again. Penguins were swimming about, filling the air with their discordant cries, while there was literally no end of the cape-pigeons and petrels. Albatrosses, too, helped to make up the picture of animated nature, while whales were often heard blowing in the adjacent waters. Gardiner saw many signs of the proximity of land, and began to hope he should yet actually discover the islands laid down on his chart, as their position had been given by Daggett.

In that high latitude a degree of longitude is necessarily much shorter than when nearer to the middle of our orb. On the equator a degree of longitude measures, as is known to most boarding-school young ladies, just sixty geographical, or sixty-nine and a half English statute miles. But, as is not known to most boarding-school young ladies, or is understood by very few of them in-

deed, even when known, in the sixty-second degree of latitude, a degree of longitude measures but little more than
thirty-two of those very miles. The solution of this seeming contradiction is so very simple that it may assist a certain class of our readers if we explain it, by telling them
that it arises solely from the fact that these degrees of
longitude, which are placed sixty geographical miles asunder at the centre or middle of the earth, converge toward
the poles, where they all meet in a point. According to
the best observations Roswell Gardiner could obtain, he
was just one of these short degrees of longitude, or two-
and-thirty miles, to the westward of the parallel where he
wished to be, when the wind came from the southward.
The change was favorable, as it emboldened him to run
nearer than he otherwise might have felt disposed to do,
to the great barrier of ice which now formed a sort of
weather-shore. Fortunately, the loose bergs and sunken
masses had drifted off so far to the northward, that once
within them the schooner had pretty plain sailing; and
Roswell, to lose none of the precious time of the season,
ventured to run, though under very short canvas, the
whole of the short night that succeeded. It is a great
assistance to the navigation of those seas that, during the
summer months, there is scarcely any night at all, giving
the adventurer sufficient light by which to thread his way
among the difficulties of his pathless journey.

When the sun reappeared, on the morning of the sixth
day after he had left the Horn, Roswell Gardiner believed
himself to be far enough west for his purposes. It now
remained to get a whole degree farther to the south, which
was a vast distance in those seas and in that direction, and
would carry him a long way to the southward of the " Ne
Plus Ultra." If there was any truth in Daggett, however,
that mariner had been there ; and the instructions of the
owner rendered it incumbent on our young man to attempt
to follow him. More than once, that morning, did our
hero regret he had not entered into terms with the Vineyard men, that the effort might have been made in company. There was something so portentous in a lone
vessel's venturing within the ice, in so remote a region,
that, to say the truth, Roswell hesitated. But pride of
profession, ambition, love of Mary, dread of the deacon,
native resolution, and the hardihood produced by experience in dangers often encountered and escaped, nerved
him to the undertaking. It must be attempted, or the

voyage would be lost; and our young mariner now set
about his task with a stern determination to achieve it.

By this time the schooner had luffed up within a cable's
length of the ice, along the margin of which she was running under easy sail. Gardiner believed himself to be
quite as far to the westward as was necessary, and his present object was to find an opening, by means of which he
could enter among the floating chaos that was spread, far
and wide, to windward. As the breeze was driving the
drifting masses to the northward, they became loosened
and more separated every moment ; and glad enough was
Gardiner to discover, at length, a clear spot that seemed
to favor his views. Without an instant's delay, the sheets
were flattened in, a pull was taken on the braces, and away
went the little Sea Lion into a passage that had a hundred-
fold more real causes of terror than the Scylla and Char-
ybdis of old.

One effect of the vicinity of ice, in extensive fields, is to
produce comparatively still water. It must blow a gale,
and that over a considerable extent of open sea, to produce
much commotion among the fields and bergs, though that
heaving and setting, which has been likened to the respiration of some monster, and which seamen call the "ground-
swell," is never entirely wanting among the waters of an
ocean. On the present occasion our adventurers were
favored in this respect, their craft gliding forward unim-
peded by anything like opposing billows. At the end of
four hours, the schooner, tacking and wearing when necessary, had worked her way to the southward and westward,
according to her master's reckoning, some five-and-twenty
miles. It was then noon, and the atmosphere being unusually clear, though never without fog, Gardiner went
aloft, to take a look for himself at the condition of things
around him.

To the northward, and along the very passage by which
the vessel had sailed, the ice was closing, and it was far
easier to go on than to return. To the eastward, and
toward the southeast in particular, however, did Roswell
Gardiner turn his longing eyes. Somewhere in that quarter of the ocean, and distant now less than ten leagues, did
he expect to find the islands of which he was in quest, if
indeed they had any existence at all. In that direction
there were many passages open among the ice, the latter
being generally higher than in the particular place to
which the vessel had reached. Once or twice, Roswell

mistook the summits of some of these bergs for real mountains, when, owing to the manner in which the light fell
upon them, or rather did not fall upon them directly, they
appeared dark and earthy.   Each time, however, the sun's
rays soon came to undeceive him ; and that which had so
lately been black and frowning, was, as by the touch of
magic, suddenly illuminated, and became bright and gorgeous, throwing out its emerald hues, or perhaps a virgin
white, that filled the beholder with delight, even amid the
terrors and dangers by which, in very truth, he was surrounded.   The glorious Alps themselves, those wonders
of the earth, could scarcely compete in scenery with the
views that nature lavished, in that remote sea, on a seeming void.   But the might and honor of God were there, as
well as beneath the equator.

For one whole hour did Roswell Gardiner remain in
the cross-trees, having hailed the deck, and caused the
schooner's head to be turned to the southeast, pressing
her through the openings as near the wind as she could
go.   The atmosphere was never without fog, though the
vapor drifted about, leaving large vacancies that were
totally clear.   One spot, in particular, seemed to be a
favorite resting-place for these low clouds, which just
there appeared to light upon the face of the ocean itself.
A wide field of ice, or, it were better to say, a broad belt
of bergs, lay between this stationary cloud and the schooner,
though the existence of the vapor early caught Roswell's
attention ; and during the hour he was aloft, conning the
craft through a very intricate and ticklish channel, not a
minute passed that the young man did not turn a look toward that veiled spot.   He was in the act of placing a
foot on the ratlin below him, to descend to the deck, when
he half-unconsciously turned to take a last glance at this
distant and seemingly immovable object.   Just then, the
vapor, which had kept rolling and moving, like a fluid in
ebullition, while it still clung together, suddenly opened,
and the bald head of a real mountain, a thousand feet high,
came unexpectedly into the view ! There could be no mistake ; all was too plain to admit of a doubt.   There, beyond all question, was land ; and it was doubtless the most
western of the islands described by the dying seaman.
Everything corroborated this conclusion. The latitude and
longitude were right, or nearly so, and the other circumstances went to confirm the conjecture, or conclusion.
Daggett had said that one island, high, mountainous, rag-

ged, and bleak, but of some size, lay the most westerly in the group, while several others were within a few miles of it. The last were lower, much smaller, and little more than naked rocks. One of these last, however, he insisted on it, was a volcano in activity, and that at intervals it emitted flames as well as a fierce heat. By his account, however, the party to which he belonged had never actually visited that volcanic caldron, being satisfied with admiring its terrors from a distance.

As to the existence of the land, Roswell got several pretty distinct and certain views, leaving no doubt of its character and position. There is a theory which tells us that the orb of day is surrounded by a luminous vapor, the source of heat and light, and that this vapor, being in constant motion, occasionally leaves the mass of the planet itself to be seen, forming what it is usual to term the "spots on the sun." Resembling this theory, the fogs of the antarctic seas rolled about the mountain now seen, withdrawing the curtain at times, and permitting a view of the striking and majestic object within. Well did that lone and nearly barren mass of earth and rock merit these appellations! The elevation has already been given ; and a rock that is nearly perpendicular, rising out of the ocean for a thousand feet, is ever imposing and grand. This was rendered so much the more so by its loneliness, its stable and stern position amid floating and moving mountains of ice, its brown sides and bold summit, the latter then recently whitened with a fall of pure snow, and its frowning and fixed aspect amid a scene that might otherwise be said to be ever in motion.

Roswell Gardiner's heart beat with delight when assured of success in discovering this, the first great goal of his destination. To reach it was now his all-absorbing desire. By this time the wind had got round to the southwest, and was blowing quite fresh, bringing him well to windward of the mountain, but causing the icebergs to drift in toward the land, and placing an impassable barrier along its western shore. Our young man, however, remembered that Daggett had given the anchorage as on the northeastern side of the island, where, according to his statements, a little haven would be found, in which a dozen craft might lie in security. To this quarter of the island Gardiner consequently endeavored to get.

There was no opening to the northward, but a pretty good channel was before the schooner to the southward of the group.   In this direction, then, the Sea Lion was steered, and by eight bells (four in the afternoon) the southern point of the largest island was doubled. The rest of the group were made, and to the infinite delight of all on board her, abundance of clear water was found between the main island and its smaller neighbors. The bergs had grounded, apparently, as they drew near the group, leaving this large bay entirely free from ice, with the exception of a few small masses that were floating through it.   These bodies, whether field or berg, were easily avoided ; and away the schooner went, with flowing sheets, into the large basin formed by the different members of the group. To render "assurance doubly sure," as to the information of Daggett, the smoke of a volcano arose from a rock to the eastward, that appeared to be some three or four miles in circumference, and which stood on the eastern side of the great basin, or some four leagues from Sealer's Land, as Daggett had at once named the principal island.   This was, in fact, about the breadth of the main basin, which had two principal passages into it, the one from the south and the other from the northeast.

Once within the islands, and reasonably clear of all ice, it was an easy thing for the schooner to run across the basin, or great bay, and reach the northeastern extremity of Sealer's Land.   As the light would continue some hours longer, there being very little night in that high latitude in December, the month that corresponds to our June, Roswell caused a boat to be lowered and manned, when he pulled at once toward the spot where it struck him the haven must be found, if there were any such place at all. Everything turned out as it had been described by Daggett, and great was our young man's satisfaction when he rowed into a cove that was little more than two hundred yards in diameter, and which was so completely landlocked as not to feel the influence of any sea outside.   In general, the great difficulty is to land on any of the antarctic rocks, the breakers and surf opposing it ; but in this spot the smallest boat could be laid with its bow on a beach of shingle, without the slightest risk of its being injured. The lead also announced good anchorage in about eight fathoms of water.   In a word, this little haven was one of those small basins that so often occur in mountainous islands, where fragments of rock appear to have fallen from the principal mass as it was forced upward out of the ocean, as if purposely intended to meet the wants of mariners.

Nor was the outer bay, or the large basin formed by the entire group, by any means devoid of advantages to the navigator. From north to south this outer bay was at least six leagues in length, while its breadth could not much have fallen short of four. Of course it was much more exposed to the winds and waves than the little harbor proper, though Roswell was struck with the great advantages it offered in several essential particulars. It was almost clear of ice, while so much was floating about outside of the circle of islands; thus leaving a free navigation in it for even the smallest boat. This was mainly owing to the fact that the largest island had two long crescent-shaped capes, the one at its northeastern and the other at its southeastern extremity, giving to its whole eastern side the shape of a new moon. The harbor just described was to the southward of, or within, the northeastern cape, which our young master at once named Cape Hazard, in honor of his chief mate's vigilance; that officer having been the first to point out the facilities probably offered by the formation of the land for an anchorage.

Though rocky and broken, it was by no means difficult to ascend the rugged banks on the northern side of the harbor, and Gardiner went up it, attended by Stimson, who of late had much attached himself to the person of his commander. The height of this barrier above the waves of the ocean was but a little less than a hundred feet, and when the summit was reached, a common exclamation of surprise, not to say delight, broke from the lips of both. Hitherto not a seal of any sort had been seen, and Gardiner had felt some misgivings touching the benefits that were to be derived from so much hardship, exposure, and enterprise. All doubts, however, vanished, the instant he got a sight of the northern shore of the island. This shore, a reach of several miles in extent, was fairly alive with the monsters of which he was in search. They lay in thousands on the low rocks that lined that entire side of the island, basking in the sun of the antarctic seas. There they were, sure enough! Sea lions, sea elephants, huge, clumsy, fierce-looking and revolting creatures, belonging properly to neither sea nor land. These animals were constantly going and coming in crowds, some waddling to the margin of the rocks and tumbling into the ocean in search of food, while others scrambled out of the water, and got upon shelves and other convenient places to repose and enjoy the light of day. There was very little contention or fighting among these revolting-looking creatures, though nearly every known species of the larger seals was among them.

"There is famous picking for us, master Stephen," said Roswell to his companion, fairly rubbing his hands in delight. "One month's smart work will fill the schooner, and we can be off before the equinox. Does it not seem to you that yonder are the bones of sea lions, or of seals of some sort, lying hereaway, as if men had been at work on the creatures?"

"No doubt on't at all, Captain Gar'ner; as much out of the way as this island is—and I never heard of the place afore, old a sealer as I am—but, as much out of the way as it is, we are not the first to find it. Somebody has been here, and that within a year or two; and he has picked up a cargo, too, depend on't."

As all this merely corresponded with Daggett's account of the place, Roswell felt no surprise; on the contrary, he saw in it a confirmation of all that Daggett had stated, and as furnishing so much the more reason to hope for a successful termination to the voyage in all its parts. While on the rocks, Roswell took such a survey of the localities as might enable him to issue his orders hereafter with discretion and intelligence. The schooner was already making short tacks to get close in with the island, in obedience to a signal to that effect; and the second mate had pulled out to the entrance of the little haven, with a view to act as pilot. Before the captain had descended from the summit of the northern barrier, the vessel came in under her jib, the wind being nearly aft, and she dropped two anchors in suitable spots, making another flying moor of it.

General joy now illuminated every face. It was, in itself, a great point gained to get the schooner into a perfectly safe haven, where her people could take their natural rest at night, or during their watches below, without feeling any apprehension of being crushed in the ice; but here was not only security, but the source of that wealth of which they were in quest, and which had induced them all to encounter so many privations and so much danger. The crew landed to a man, each individual ascending to the summit of the barrier, to feast his eyes on the spectacle that lay spread in such affluent abundance along the low rocks of the northern side of the island.

As there were yet several hours of light remaining, Roswell, still attended by Stimson, each armed with a

sealing-spear or lance, not only as a weapon of defence,
but as a leaping-staff, set out to climb as high up the central acclivity of the island as circumstances would allow
him to go. He was deceived in the distances, however,
and soon found that an entire day would be necessary to
achieve such an enterprise, could it be performed at all;
but he did succeed in reaching a low spur of the central
mountain that commanded a wide and noble view of all
that lay to the north and east of it. From this height,
which must have been a few hundred feet above the
level of the ocean, our adventurers got a still better view
of the whole north coast, or of what might have been
called the sealing quarter of the island. They also got a
tolerably accurate idea of the general formation of that
lone fragment of rock and earth, as well as of the islets
and islands that lay in its vicinity. The outline of the
first was that of a rude, and of course an irregular triangle,
the three principal points of which were the two low capes
already mentioned, and a third that lay to the northward
and westward. The whole of the western or southwestern
shore seemed to be a nearly perpendicular wall of rock,
that, in the main, rose some two or three hundred feet
above the ocean. Against this side of the island, in particular, the waves of the ocean were sullenly beating, while
the ice drove up "home," as sailors express it; showing
a vast depth of water. On the two other sides it was different. The winds prevailed most from the southwest,
which rendered the perpendicular face of the island its
weather wall; while the two other sides of the triangle
were more favored by position. The north side, of course,
lay most exposed to the sun, everything of this nature
being reversed in the southern hemisphere from what we
have it in the northern; while the eastern, or northeastern
side, to be precisely accurate, was protected by the group
of islands that lay in its front. Such was the general
character of Sealer's Land, so far as the hurried observations of its present master enabled him to ascertain. The
near approach of night induced him now to hasten to get
off of the somewhat dangerous acclivities to which he had
climbed, and to rejoin his people and his schooner.

CHAPTER XV.

" Ye dart upon the deep, and straight is heard
   A wilder roar ; and men grow pale, and pray :
Ye fling its waters round you, as a bird
   Flings o'er his shivering plumes the fountain's spray.
See ! to the breaking mast the sailor clings !
Ye scoop the ocean to its briny springs,
And take the mountain billows on your wings,
   And pile the wreck of navies round the bay."
              —BRYANT'S WINDS.

No unnecessary delay was permitted to interfere with the one great purpose of the sealers. The season was so short, and the difficulties and dangers of entering among and of quitting the ice were so very serious, that every soul belonging to the schooner felt the importance of activity and industry. The very day that succeeded the vessel's arrival, not only was great progress made in the preliminary arrangements, but a goodly number of fur-seals, of excellent quality, were actually killed and secured. Two noble sea elephants were also lanced, animals that measured near thirty feet in length, each of which yielded a very ample return for the risk and trouble of taking it, in oil. The skins of the fur seals, however, were Roswell's principal object ; and glad enough was he to find the creature that pays this tribute to the wants and luxuries of man, in numbers sufficient to promise him a speedy return to the northward. While the slaughter, and skinning, and curing, and trying out, were all in active operation, our young man paid some attention to certain minor arrangements, which had a direct bearing on the comforts of his people, as well as the getting in of cargo.

An old storehouse, of respectable size, had stood on the deacon's wharf, while the schooner was fitting out, but it had been taken to pieces, in order to make room for a more eligible substitute. The materials of this building Roswell Gardiner had persuaded his owner to send on board, and they had all been received and stowed away, a part below and a part on deck, as a provison for the possible wants of the people. As it was necessary to clear the decks and break out the hold, all these materials, consisting principally of the timbers of the frame, the siding, and a quantity of planks and boards, were now floated ashore in the cove, and hauled up on the rocks. Roswell took a leisure moment to select a place for the site of his building, which he intended to erect at once, in order to save the time that would otherwise be lost in pulling between the schooner and the shore.

It was not difficult to find the sort of spot that was desirable for the dwelling. That chosen by Gardiner was a shelf of rock of sufficient extent, that lay perfectly exposed to the north and northeast, or to the sunny side of the island, while it was sheltered from the south and southwest by masses of rock, that formed a complete protection against the colder winds of the region. These walls of stone, however, were not sufficiently near to permit any snows they might collect to impend over the building, but enough space was left between them and the house, to admit of a capacious yard, in which might be placed any articles that were necessary to the ordinary work, or to the wants of the sealers.

Had it been advisable to set all hands at the business of slaughtering, Roswell Gardiner certainly would not have lost the time he did, in the erection of his house But our master was a judicious and wary commander at his calling. The seals were now perfectly tame, and nothing was easier than to kill them in scores. The great difficulty was in removing the spoils across the rocks, as it was sometimes necessary to do so for a distance of several miles. Means were found, in the end, to use the boats on this service, though even then, at midsummer, the northern shore of the island was frequently so closely beset by the ice as completely to block up the passage. This, too, occurred at times when the larger bay was nearly free, and the cove, which went by the name of the "Deacon's Bight" among the men, was entirely so. In order to prevent a premature panic among the victims of this intended foray, then, Gardiner allowed no one to go out to "kill" but the experienced hands, and no more to be slain each day than could be skinned or cut up at that particular time. In consequence of this prudent caution, the work soon got into a regular train ; and it was early found that more was done in this mode, than could have been effected by a less guarded assault on the seals.

As for the materials of the building, they were hauled up the rocks without much difficulty. The frame was of some size, as is the case generally with most old constructions in America ; but being of pine, thoroughly seasoned, the sills

and plates were not so heavy but that they might be readily
enough handled by the non-sealing portion of the crew.
Robert Smith, the landsman, was a carpenter by trade, and
it fell to his lot to put together again the materials of the
old warehouse.   Had there not been such a mechanic
among the crew, however, a dozen Americans could, at any
time, construct a house, the " rough and ready " habits of
the people usually teaching them, in a rude way, a good
deal of a great many other arts, besides this of the carpenter.   Mott had served a part of his time with a blacksmith,
and he now set up his forge.   When the frame was ready,
all hands assembled to assist in raising it ; and, by the end
of the first week, the building was actually inclosed, the
labor amounting to no more than putting each portion in
its place and securing it there, the saw being scarcely used
during the whole process.   This building had two apart-
ments, one of which Gardiner appropriated to the uses of
a sitting-room, and the other to that of a dormitory.   Rough
bunks were constructed, and the mattresses of the men
were all brought ashore and put in the house.   It was intended that everybody should sleep in the building, as it
would save a great deal of going to and fro, as well as a
great deal of time.   The cargo was to be collected on a
shelf of rock, that lay about twenty feet below that on which
the building stood ; by following which, it was possible to
turn the highest point of the pass, that which formed the
southern protection of the building, and come out on the
side of the cove at another shelf, that was not more than
fifty feet above the level of the vessel's decks.   Down this
last declivity, Roswell proposed to lower his casks by means
of a projecting derrick, the rock being sufficiently precipi-
tous to admit of this arrangement, while his spare spars
furnished him with the necessary means.   Thus was every
preparation made with judgment and foresight.

In this manner did the first ten days pass, every man
and boy being as busy as bees.   To own the truth, no attention was paid to the Sabbath, which would seem to have
been left behind them by the people, among the descendants of those Puritans who were so rigid in their observance
of that festival.   At the end of the time just mentioned, a
great deal had been done.   The house, such as it was, was
completed.   To be sure, it was nothing but an old storehouse revamped, but it was found to be of infinite service,
and greatly did all hands felicitate themselves at having
brought its materials along with them.   Even those who

had most complained of the labor of getting the timbers
on board, had the most often cursed them for being in the
way during the passage, and had continued the loudest to
deride the idea of "sealers turning carpenters," were
shortly willing to allow that the possession of this dwelling was of the greatest value to them, and that, so far from
the extra work's causing them to fall behind in their main
operations, the comfort they found, in having a home like
this to go to, after a long day's toil, refreshed them to a
degree which enabled every man to return to his labor
with a zeal and an energy that might otherwise have been
wanting. Although it was in the warmest season of the
year, and the nights could scarcely be called nights at all,
yet the sun never got very low without leaving a chilliness
in the air that would have rendered sleeping without a
cover and a protection from the winds not only excessively
uncomfortable, but somewhat dangerous. Indeed, it was
often found necessary to light a fire in the old warehouse.
This was done by means of a capacious box-stove, that was
almost as old as the building itself, and which had also
been brought along as an article of great necessity in that
climate. Fuel could not be wanting, so long as the
"scraps" from the try-works abounded, and there were
many more of these than were needed to "try out" the
sea elephant oil. The schooner, however, had a very ample
supply of wood to burn, that being an article which abounded on Shelter Island, and which the deacon had consented
to lay in, in some abundance. Gardiner got this concession
out of the miserly temperament of the old man, by persuading him that a sealer could not work to any advantage
unless he had the means of occasionally warming himself.
The miserly propensities of the deacon were not so engrossing that he did not comprehend the wisdom of making
sufficient outlay to secure the execution of his main object ;
and among other things of this nature, the schooner had
sailed with a very large supply of wood, as has just been
stated. Wood and onions, indeed, were more abundant
in her than any other stores.

The arrangements described were completed by the end
of the first fortnight, during which period the business of
sealing was also carried on with great industry and success. So very tame were the victims, and so totally unconscious of the danger they incurred from the presence of
man, that the crew moved round among them, seemingly
but very little observed, and not at all molested. The

utmost care was taken to give no unnecessary alarm; and when an animal was lanced, it was done in such a quiet way as to produce as little commotion as possible. By the end of the time named, however, the sealing had got so advanced as to require the aid of all hands in securing the spoils. To work, then, everybody went, with a hearty good-will; and the shelf of rock just below the house was soon well garnished with casks and skins. Had the labor been limited to the mere killing, and skinning, and curing, and barrelling of oil, it would have been comparatively quite light; but the necessity of transporting the fruits of all this skill and luck considerable distances, in some cases several miles, and this over broken rocks, formed the great obstacle to immediate success. It was the opinion of Ros-well Gardiner, that he could have filled his schooner in a month, were it possible to place her directly alongside of the rocks frequented by the seals, and prevent all this toil in transporting. This, however, was impossible, the waves and the ice rendering it certain destruction to lay a craft anywhere along the northern shore of the island. The boats might be, and occasionally they were used, bringing loads of skin and oil round the cape, quite into the cove. These little cargoes were immediately transferred to the hold of the schooner, a ground tier of large casks having been left in her purposely to receive the oil, which was emptied into them by means of a hose. By the end of the third week, this ground tier was filled, and the craft be-came stiff, and was in good ballast trim, although the spare water was now entirely pumped out of her.

All this time the weather was very fair for so high a latitude, and every way propitious. The twenty-third day after the schooner got in, Roswell was standing on a spur of the hill, at no great distance from the house, overlook-ing the long reach of rocky coast over which the "sea-elephants," and "lions," and "dogs," and "bears," were waddling in as much seeming security as the hour when he first saw them. The sun was just rising, and the seals were clambering up out of the water to enjoy its warm rays, as they placed themselves in positions favorable to such a purpose.

"That is a pleasant sight to a true sealer, Captain Gar'-ner," observed Stimson, who as usual had kept near his officer, "and one that I can say I never before saw equalled. I've been in this business now some five-and-twenty years, and never before have I met with so safe a harbor for a craft, and so large herds that have not been stirred up and got to be skeary."

"We have certainly been very fortunate thus far, Stephen, and I am now in hopes we may fill up and be off in good season to get clear of the ice," returned Roswell. "Our luck has been surprising, all things considered."

"You call it luck, Captain Gar'ner; but in my creed, there is truer and a better word for it, sir."

"Ay, I know well enough what you mean, Stephen; though I cannot fancy that Providence cares much whether we shall take a hundred seals to-day, or none at all."

"Such is not my idee, sir; and I'm not ashamed to own it. In my humble way of thinking, Captain Gar'ner, the finger of Divine Providence is in all that comes to pass; if not straight ahead like, as a body would receive a fall, still, by sartain laws that bring about everything that is to happen, just as it does happen. I believe now, sir, that Providence does not intend we shall take any seals at all to-day, sir."

"Why not, Stimson? It is the very finest day we have had since we have been on the island."

"That's true enough; and it is this glorious sunny day, glorious and sunny for sich a high latitude, that makes me feel and think that this day was not intended for work, You probably forget it is the Sabbath, Captain Gar'ner!"

"Sure enough; I had forgotten that, Stephen; but we sealers seldom lie by for such a reason."

"So much the worse for us sealers, then, sir. This is my seventeenth v'y'ge into these seas, sir, and I will say that more of them have been made with officers and crews that did *not* keep the Sabbath, than with officers and crews that did. Still, I have observed one thing, sir, that the man who takes his rest one day in seven, and freshens his mind, as it might be, with thinking of other matters than his every-day consarns, comes to his task with so much better will, when he *does* set about it, as to turn off greater profit than if he worked night and day, Sundays and all."

Roswell Gardiner had no great reverence for the Christian Sabbath, and this more because it was so *called*, than for any sufficient reason in itself. Pride of reason rendered him jealous of everything like a concession to the faith of those who believed in the Son of God; and he was very apt to dissent from all admission that had even the most remote bearing on its truth. Still, as a kind-hearted commander, as well as a judicious reasoner on the economy of his fellow-creatures, he fully felt the policy of granting relax-

ation to labor. Nor was he indisposed to believe in the
care of a Divine Providence, or in its justice, though less
believing in this respect than the illiterate but earnest-
minded seaman who stood at his side. He knew very well
that "all work, and no play, makes Jack a dull boy ;" and
he understood well enough that it was good for a man, at
stated seasons, to raise his mind from the cares and business of this world, to muse on those of the world that is to
come. Though inclined to Deism, Roswell worshipped in
his heart the Creator of all he saw and understood, as well
as much that he could neither scan nor comprehend.

"This is not the seaman's usual way of thinking," returned our hero, after regarding his companion for a moment, a little intently. "With us, there is very little Sabbath in blue water."

"Too little, sir ; much too little. Depend on't, Captain
Gar'ner, God is on the face of the waters as well as on the
hill-tops. His Spirit is everywhere ; and it must grieve it
to see human beings, that have been created in his image,
so bent on gain as to set apart no time even for rest ; much
less for his worship and praise !"

"I am not certain you are wrong, Stimson, and I feel
much more sure that you are right as a political economist
than in your religion. There *should* be seasons of rest and
reflection—yet I greatly dislike losing a day as fine as this."

"'The better the day, the better the deed,' sir. No time
is lost to him who stops in his work to think a little of his
God. Our crew is used to having a Sabbath ; and though
we work on lays, there is not a hand aboard us, Captain
Gar'ner, who would not be glad to hear the word pass
among 'em which should say this is the Lord's day, and
you've to knock off your labor."

"As I believe you understand the people, Stephen, and
we have had a busy time of it since we got in, I'll take you
at your word, and give the order. Go and tell Mr. Hazard
there'll be no duty carried on to-day beyond what is indispensable. It is Sunday, and we'll make it a day of rest."

Truth compels us to say that Roswell was quite as much
influenced in giving this order, by recollecting the pleasure it would give Mary, as by any higher consideration.

Glad enough was Stimson to hear this order, and away
he hastened to find the mate, that it might at once be communicated to the men. Although this well-disposed seaman a little overrated the motives of a portion of the crew at
least, he was right enough as to the manner in which they

would receive the new regulation. Rest and relaxation had become, in a measure, necessary to them ; and leisure was also needed to enable the people to clean themselves ; the business in which they had been engaged being one that accumulates oily substances, and requiring occasional purifications of the body in order to preserve the health. The scurvy, that great curse of long voyages, is as much owing to neglect of cleanliness as to diet.

No sooner was it known that this day was to be treated as the Sabbath, than soap, razors, scissors, and all the usual appliances of the sailor's toilet, were drawn out of bags and chests, and paraded about on the rocks. An hour passed in scrubbing, shaving, cutting hair, holding garments up to the light to look for holes and ascertain their condition, and rummaging among " properties," as the player would term the different wardrobes that were thus brought into view. The mates came out of the *mêlée* "shaven and shorn," as well as neatly attired ; and there was not a man on the island who did not look like a different being from what he had appeared an hour before, in consequence, of this pause in the regular business of sealing, and the promised holiday. A strict order was given that no one should go among the seals, as it was feared that some indiscretion or other might have a tendency to create an alarm. In all other respects the island was placed at the disposal of the men, if anything could be made of such a lone spot, a speck on the surface of the antarctic seas, and nearly encircled by mountains of floating ice.

As for Roswell himself, after reading a chapter or two in Mary Pratt's Bible, he determined to make another effort to ascend to the summit of the sterile rocks which capped the pile that rose vertically in the centre of the island. The day was nearly all before him ; and, summoning Stimson as a companion, for he had taken a great fancy to this man, away he went, young, active, and full of buoyancy. Almost at the same instant, Hazard, the chief mate, pulled out of the cove in one of the whale-boats, manned by volunteers, and provided with sails, with an intention to cross the Great Bay, and get a nearer view of the volcanic hill, out of which smoke was constantly pouring, and occasionally flames. The second mate and one or two of the hands remained near the house, to keep a lookout on the vessel and other property.

The season had now advanced to the first day of Jan-

uary, a month that in the southern hemisphere corresponds
with our own July. As Roswell picked his way among
the broken rocks that covered the ascent to what might
be termed the table-land of the island, if indeed any portion of so ragged a bit of this earth could properly be so
named, his thoughts recurred to this question of the season, and to the probability of his getting a cargo before it
would be absolutely necessary to go to the northward.
On the whole, he fancied his chances good ; and such he
found to be Stimson's opinion, when this experienced
sealer was questioned on the subject.

"We've begun right in all respects but one, Captain
Gar'ner," said Stephen, as he closed his remarks on the
subject ; "and even in that matter in which we made a
small mistake at the outset, we are improving, and I hope
will come out right in the end. I said a *small* mistake,
but in this I'm wrong, as it was a *great* mistake."

"And what was it, Stephen ? Make no bones of telling
me of any blunder I may have committed, according to
your views of duty. You are so much older than myself,
that I'll stand it."

"Why, sir, it's not in seamanship, or in sealing ; if it was,
I'd hold my tongue ; but it's in not keeping the Lord's
day from the hour when we lifted our anchor in that bay
that bears the name of your family, Captain Gar'ner ; and
which ought to be, and I make no doubt *is*, dear to you on
that account, if for no other reason. I rather think, from
what they tell me, that the old Lord Gar'ner of all had
much preaching of the word, and much praying to the
Lord in the old times, when he lived there."

"There never was any *Lord* Gardiner among us," returned Roswell modestly, "though it was a fashion among
the eastenders to give that title to the owner of the island.
My ancestor who first got the place was Lyon Gardiner,
an engineer in the service of the colony of Connecticut."

"Well, whether he was a lion or a lamb, I'll answer for
it the Lord was not forgotten on that island, Captain
Gar'ner, and he shouldn't be on this. No man ever lost
anything in this world, or in that which is to come a'ter it,
by remembering once in seven days to call on his Creator
to help him on in his path. I've heard it said, sir, that
you're a little partic'lar like in your ideas of religion, and
that you do not altogether hold to the doctrines that are
preached up and down the land."

Roswell felt his cheeks warm at this remark, and he

thought of Mary, and of her meek reliance on that Saviour whom, in the pride of his youth, strength, and, as he fancied, of his reason also, he doubted about, as being the Son of God. The picture thus presented to his mind had its pleasant and its unpleasant features. Strange as it may seem, it is certain that the young man would have loved, would have respected Mary less than he now did, could he imagine that *she* entertained the same notions on this very subject as those he entertained himself! Few men relish infidelity in a woman, whose proper sphere would seem to be in believing and in worshipping, and not in cavilling, or in splitting straws on matters of faith. Perhaps it is that we are apt to associate laxity of morals with laxity of belief, and have a general distaste for releasing the other sex from any, even the smallest of the restraints that the dogmas of the church impose ; but we hold it to be without dispute that, with very few exceptions, every man would prefer that the woman in whom he feels an interest should err on the side of bigotry rather than on that of what is called liberalism in points of religious belief. Thus it is with most of us, and thus was it with Roswell Gardiner. He could not wonder at Mary's rigid notions, considering her education ; and, on the whole, he rather liked her the better for them, at the very moment that he felt they might endanger his own happiness. If women thoroughly understood how much of their real power and influence with men arises from their seeming dependence, there would be very little tolerance in their own circles for those among them who are for proclaiming their independence and their right to equality in all things.

While our young mariner and his companion were working their way up to the table-land, which lay fully three hundred feet above the level of the sea, there was little opportunity for further discourse, so rough was the way, and so difficult the ascent. At the summit, however, there was a short pause, ere the two undertook the mountain proper, and they came to a halt to take a look at the aspect of things around them. There was the boat, a mere white speck on the water, flying away with a fresh northerly breeze toward the volcano, while the smoke from the latter made a conspicuous and not very distant landmark. Nearer at home, all appeared unusually plain for a region in which fogs were apt to prevail. The cove lay almost beneath them, and the schooner, just then, struck the imagination of her commander, as a fearfully small craft to come so far from home and to penetrate so deep among the mazes of the ice. It was that ice itself, however, that attracted most of Roswell's attention. Far as the eye could reach, north, south, east, and west, the ocean was brilliant and chill with the vast floating masses. The effect on the air was always perceptible in that region, "killing the summer," as the sealers expressed it ; but it seemed to be doubly so at the elevation to which the two adventurers had attained. Still, the panorama was magnificent. The only part of the ocean that did not seem to be alive with icebergs, if one may use such an expression, was the space within the group, and that was as clear as an estuary in a mild climate. It really appeared as if nature had tabooed that privileged spot, in order that the communication between the different islands should remain open. Of course, the presence of so many obstacles to the billows without, and indeed even to the rake of the winds, produced smooth water within, the slow, breath-like heaving and setting of the ceaseless ground-swell, being the only perceptible motion to the water inside.

"'Tis a very remarkable view, Stephen," said Roswell Gardiner, "but there will be one much finer, if we can work our way up that cone of a mountain, and stand on its naked cap. I wish I had brought an old ensign and a small spar along to set up the gridiron in honor of the States. We're beginning to put out our feelers, old Stimson, and shall have 'em on far better bits of territory than this, before the earth has gone round in its track another hundred years."

"Well, to my notion, Captain Gar'ner," answered the seaman, following his officer toward the base of the cone, "Uncle Sam has got more land now than he knows what to do with. If a body could discover a bit of ocean, or a largish sort of a sea, there might be some use in it. Whales are getting to be skeary, and are mostly driven off their old grounds ; and as for the seals, you must bury yourself, craft and all, up to the truck in ice, to get a smile from one of their good-lookin' count'nances, as I always say."

"I'm afraid, Stephen, it is all over with the discovery of more seas. Even the moon, they now say, is altogether without water, having not so much as a lake or a large pond to take a duck in."

"Without water, sir !" exclaimed Stimson, quite aghast. "If 'tis so, sir, it *must* be right, since the same hand that made the moon made this 'arth and all it contains. But what *can* they do for seafaring folks in the moon, if what you tell me, Captain Gar'ner, is the truth?"

"They must do without them. I fancy oil and skins are not very much in demand among the moonites, Stephen. What's that, off here to the eastward, eh? East-and-by-north-half-east, or so?"

"I see what you mean, sir. It does look wonderfully like a sail, and a sail pretty well surrounded by ice too!"

There was no mistake in the matter. The white canvas of a vessel was plainly visible, over a vast breadth of field-ice, a little to the northward of the island that lay directly opposite the cove. Although the sails of this stranger were spread, it was plain enough he was closely beset, if not actually jammed. From the first instant he saw the strange craft, Roswell had not a doubt of her character. He felt convinced it was his late consort, the Sea Lion of the Vineyard, which had found her way to the group by means of some hint that had fallen into Daggett's hands, if not by a positive nautical instinct. So great had been his own success, however, and so certain did he now feel of filling up in due season, that he cared much less for this invasion on his privacy than he would have done a fort-night earlier. On the contrary, it might be a good thing to have a consort in the event of any accident occurring to his own vessel. From the moment, then, that Gardiner felt certain of the character of the strange sail, his policy was settled in his own mind. It was to receive his old ac-quaintance with good-will, and to help fill him up, too, as soon as he had secured his own cargo, in order that they might sail for home in company. By his aid and advice the other schooner might save a week in time at that most important season of the year; and by the experience and exertions of his people, a whole month in filling up might readily be gained.

All thoughts of climbing the peak were at once aban-doned; and, in fifteen minutes after the sail was seen, Roswell and Stephen both came panting down to the house; so much easier is it to descend in this world than to mount. A swivel was instantly loaded and fired as a signal; and, in half an hour, a boat was manned and ready. Roswell took command himself, leaving his second mate to look after the schooner. Stimson went with his captain, and less than one hour after he had first seen the strange sail, our hero was actually pulling out of the cove, with a

view to go to her assistance. Roswell Gardiner was as
good-hearted a fellow as ever lived. He had a sufficient
regard for his own interests, as well as for those of others
intrusted to his care ; but, these main points looked after,
he would cheerfully have worked a month to relieve the
Vineyard men from the peril that so plainly beset them.
Setting his sails the instant the boat was clear of the rocks,
away he went, then, as fast as ash and canvas could carry
him, which was at a rate but little short of eight knots in
the hour.

As he was thus flying toward his object, our young mariner formed a theory in his own mind, touching the drift of
the ice in the adjacent seas. It was simply this. He had
sounded in entering the great bay, and had ascertained
that comparatively shallow water existed between the
southeastern extremity of Sealer's Land and the nearest
island opposite. It was deep enough to admit the largest
vessel that ever floated, and a great deal more than this ;
but it was not deep enough to permit an iceberg to pass.
The tides, too, ran in races among the islands, which prevented the accumulation of ice at the southern entrance,
while the outer currents seemed to set everything past
the group, to allow of the floating mountains to collect to
the eastward, where they appeared to be thronged. It
was on the western verge of this wilderness of icebergs
and ice fields that the strange sail had been seen working
her way toward the group, which must be plainly in view
from her decks, as her distance from the nearest of the
islands certainly did not exceed two leagues.

It required more than two hours for the whale-boat of
Roswell to cross the bay, and reach the margin of that
vast field of ice which was prevented from drifting into
the open space only by encountering the stable rocks of the
first of the group. Every eye was now turned in quest of
an opening, by means of which it might be possible to get
further to the eastward. One, at length, was discovered,
and into it Gardiner dashed, ordering his boat's crew to
stretch themselves out at their oars, though every man
with him thought they were plunging into possible destruction. On the boat went, however, now sheering to
starboard, now to port, to avoid projecting spurs of ice,
until she had ploughed her way through a fearfully narrow,
and a deviating passage, that sometimes barely permitted
them to go through, until a spot was reached where the
two fields which formed this strait actually came in close,

crushing contact with each other. Roswell took a look
before and behind him, saw that his boat was safe, owing
to the formation of the two outlines of the respective
fields, when he sprang upon the ice itself, bidding the
boat-steerer to wait for him. A shout broke out of the
lips of the young captain the instant he was erect on the
ice. There lay the schooner, the Martha's Vineyard craft,
within half a mile of him, in plain sight, and in as plain
jeopardy. She was jammed, with every prospect, as Roswell thought, of being crushed, ere she could get free
from the danger.

CHAPTER XVI.

" A sculler's notch in the stern he made,
    An oar he shaped of the battle blade;
    Then sprung to his seat with a lightsome leap,
    And launched afar on the calm, blue deep."
                                —*The Culprit Fay.*

ROSWELL was hardly on the ice before a sound of a most
portentous sort reached his ear. He knew at once that the
field had been rent in twain by outward pressure, and that
some new change was to occur that might release or might
destroy the schooner. He was on the point of springing
forward in order to join Daggett, when a call from the boat
arrested his steps.

"These here fields are coming together, Captain Gar'ner,
and our boat will soon be crushed unless we get it out of
the water."

Sure enough, a single glance behind him sufficed to assure the young master of the truth of this statement. The
field he was on was slowly swinging, bringing its western
margin in closer contact with the eastern edge of the floe
that lay within it. The movement could be seen merely
by the closing of the channel through which the boat had
come, and by the cracking and crushing of the ice on the
edges of the two fields. So tremendous was the pressure,
however, that cakes as large as a small house were broken
off, and forced upward on the surface of the field, or ground
into small fragments, as it might be under the vice of a
power hitherto unknown to the spectators. Slow as was
the movement of the floe, it was too fast to allow of delay;
and, finding a suitable place, the boat was hauled up, and
put in security on the floe that lay nearest the schooner.

"This may give us a long drag to get back into the water, Stimson, and a night out of our bunks," said Roswell, looking about him, as soon as the task was achieved.

"I do not know that, sir," was the answer. "It seems to me that the floe has parted alongside of them rocks, and if so-be that should turn out to be the case, the whull on us, schooner, boat, and all hands, may drift into the bay ; for that there is a current setting from this quarter up toward our island, I'm sartain of, by the feel of my oar, as we come along."

"It may be so ; the currents run all manner of ways, and field ice may pass the shoals, though a berg never can. I do not remember, nevertheless, to have ever seen even a floe within the group—nothing beyond large cakes that have got adrift by some means or other."

"I have, sir, though only once. A few days a'ter we got in, when I was ship-keeper, and all hands was down under the rocks of the north eend, a field come in at the northern entrance of the bay, and went out at the southern. It might have been a league athwart it, and it drifted, as a body might say, as if it had some one aboard to give it the right sheer. Touch it did at the south cape, but just winding as handy as a craft could have done it, in a good tide's way, out to sea it went ag'in, bound to the south pole for-ti-'now."

"Well, this is good news, and may be the means of saving the Vineyard craft in the end. We do seem to be setting bodily into the bay, and if we can only get clear of that island, I do not see what is to hinder it. Here is a famous fellow of a mountain to the northward, coming down before the wind, as one might say, and giving us a cant into the passage. I should think that chap must produce some sort of a change, whether it be for better or worse."

"Ay, ay, sir," put in Thompson, who acted as a boat-steerer at need, "he may do just that, but it is all he can do. Mr. Green and I sounded out from the cove for a league or more, a few days since, and we found less than twenty fathoms, as far as we went. That chap up to the nor'ard there draws something like a hundred fathoms, if he draws an inch. He shows more above water than a first-rate's truck."

"That does he, and a good deal to spare. Thompson, do you and Todd remain here, and look after the boat, while the rest of us will shape our course for the schooner.

She seems to be in a wicked berth, and 'twill be no more than neighborly to try to get her out of it."

Truly enough might Roswell call the berth of the Sea Lion of the Vineyard by any expressive name that implied danger. When the party reached her, they found the situation of that vessel to be as follows: She had been endeavoring to work her way through a passage between two large fields, when she found the ice closing, and that she was in great danger of being "nipped." Daggett was a man of fertile resources, and great decision of character. Perceiving that escape was impossible, all means of getting clear being rendered useless by the floes seen touching, both before and behind him, he set about adopting the means most likely to save his vessel. Selecting a spot where a curve, in the margin of the field to leeward, promised temporary security, at least, he got his vessel into it, anchored fast to the floe. Then he commenced cutting away the ice, by means of axes first, and of saws afterward, in the hope that he might make such a cavity as, by its size and shape, would receive the schooner's hull, and prevent her destruction. For several hours had he and his people been at this work, when, to their joy, as well as to their great astonishment, they were suddenly joined by Roswell and his party. The fact was, that so intently had every one of the Vineyard men's faculties been absorbed by their own danger, and so much was each individual occupied by his own duty, that not a man among them had seen the boat, or even any of the crew, until Gardiner called out to Daggett as he approached, announcing his presence by his voice.

"This is good fortune, truly, Captain Gar'ner," said Daggett, shaking his brother master cordially by the hand; "good fortune, do I call it! I was satisfied that I should fall in with you somewhere about this group of islands, for they lie just about where my late uncle had given us reason to suppose some good sealing-ground might be met with; but I did not hope to see you this morning. You observe our position, Captain Gar'ner; there is every prospect of a most awful nip!"

"There is, indeed, though I see you have been making some provision for it. What luck have you had in digging a slip to let the schooner into?"

"Well, we might have had worse, though better would have been more agreeable. It's plain sailing, so long as we can work above water, and you see we've cleared a fine berth for the craft, down to the water's edge ; but, below that, 'tis blind work and slow. The field is some thirty feet thick, and sawing through it is out of the question. The most we can do is to get off pieces diagonally   I am not without hopes that we have done enough of this to make a wedge on which the schooner will rise, if pressed hard on her off-side. I have heard of such things, Captain Gar'ner, though I cannot say I ever saw it."

"It's a ticklish business to trust to such a protector; still a great deal must be gained by cutting away so much of this upper ice, and it is possible your schooner may be lifted, as you seem to expect. Has anything been done to strengthen the craft inboard ?"

"Not as yet ; though I've thought of that, too. But what is the stoutest ship that ever floated against the pressure of such an enormous field of ice? Had we not better keep cutting away ?"

"You can continue to work the saw and the axes, but I will give an eye to strengthening the craft inboard. Just point out the spars and plank you can spare, and we'll see what can be done. At any rate, my lads, you can now work with the certainty that your lives are safe. My schooner lies about six leagues from you, as safely moored as if she lay in a dock. Come, Captain Daggett, let me see your spare spars and plank."

Great encouragement it certainly was to these mariners, so far from home, and in their imminently perilous condition, to know that a countryman and a friend was so near them to afford shelter and protection. The American sailor is not a cheering animal, like his English relative, but he quite as clearly understands what ought to be received with congratulation, as those who are apt to make more noise. The Vineyard men, in particular, were habitually quiet and thoughtful, there being but one seaman in the craft who did not husband his lay and look forward to meet the wants of a future day. This is the result of education, men usually becoming quiet as they gain ideas, and feel that the tongue has been given to us in order to communicate them to our fellows. Still the joy at receiving this unlooked-for assistance was great among the Vineyard men, and each party went to work with activity and zeal.

The task of Roswell Gardiner was inboard, while that of Daggett and his men continued to be on the ice. The latter resumed the labor of cutting and sawing the field, and of getting up fenders, or skids, to protect the inner side of their vessel from the effects of a "nip." As for Gardiner, he set about his self-assumed duty with great readiness and intelligence. His business was to strengthen the craft by getting supports up in her hold. This was done without much difficulty, all the upper part of the hold being clear and easily come at. Spars were cut to the proper length, plank were placed in the broadest part of the vessel, opposite to each other, and the spars were wedged in carefully, extending from side to side, so as to form a great additional support to the regular construction of the schooner. In little more than an hour, Roswell had his task accomplished, while Daggett did not see that he could achieve much more himself. They met on the ice to consult and to survey the condition of things around them.

The outer field had been steadily encroaching upon the inner, breaking the edges of both, until the points of junction were to be traced by a long line of fragments forced upward, and piled high in the air. Open spaces, however, still existed, owing to irregularities in the outlines of the two floes ; and Daggett hoped that the little bay into which he had got his schooner might not be entirely closed, ere a shift of wind, or a change in the tides, might carry away the causes of the tremendous pressure that menaced his security. It is not easy for those who are accustomed to look at natural objects in their more familiar aspects, fully to appreciate the vast momentum of the weight that was now drifting slowly down upon the schooner. The only ray of hope was to be found in the deficiency in one of the two great requisites of such a force. Momentum being *weight* multiplied into *velocity*, there were some glimpses visible, of a nature to produce a slight degree of expectation that the last might yet be resisted The movement was slow, but it was absolutely grand, by its steadiness and power. Any one who has ever stood on a lake or river shore, and beheld the undeviating force with which a small cake of ice crumbles and advances before a breeze, or in a current, may form some idea of the majesty of the movement of a field of ice leagues in diameter, and which was borne upon by a gale of the ocean, as well as by currents, and by the weight of drifting icebergs from without. It is true that the impetus came principally from a great distance, and could scarcely be detected or observed by those around the schooner ; still, these last were fully aware of the whole character of the danger, which each minute appeared to render more and more imminent and imposing. The two fields were obviously closing still, and that with a resistless power that boded destruction to the unfortunate vessel. The open water near her was already narrowed to a space that half an hour might suffice to close entirely.

"Have you set that nearest island by compass, Daggett?" asked Roswell Gardiner, as soon as he had taken a good look around him. "To me it seems that it bears more to the eastward than it did an hour since. If this should be true, our inner field here must have a very considerable westerly set."

"In which case we may still hope to drift clear," returned Daggett, springing on board the schooner, and running aft to the binnacle, Roswell keeping close at his side. "By George! it is as you say; the bearings of that island are altered at least two points!"

"In which case our drift has exceeded a league—Ha! what noise is that? Can it be an eruption of the volcano?"

Daggett, at first, was inclined to believe it was a sound produced by some of the internal convulsions of the earth, which within, as if in mockery of the chill scene that prevailed without, was a raging volcano, the fierce heats of which found vent at the natural chimneys produced by its own efforts. This opinion, however, did not last long, and he gave expression to his new thoughts in his answer.

"'Tis the ice," he said. "I do believe the pressure has caused the fields to part on the rocks of that island. If so, our leeward floe may float away, as fast as the weather field approaches."

"Hardly," said Roswell, gazing intently toward the nearest island; "hardly; for the most weatherly of the two will necessarily get the force of the wind and the impetus of those bergs first, and make the fastest drift. It may lessen the violence of the nip, but I do not think it will avert it altogether."

This opinion of Gardiner's fully described all that subsequently occurred. The outer floe continued its inroads on the inner, breaking up the margins of both, until the channel was so nearly closed as to bring the field from which the danger was most apprehended in absolute contact with the side of the schooner. When the margin of the outer floe first touched the bilge of the schooner, it was at the precise spot where the vessel had just been fortified within. Fenders had also been provided without, and there was just a quarter of a minute, during which the two captains hoped that these united means of defence might enable the craft to withstand the pressure. This delusion lasted but a moment, however, the cracking of timbers letting it be plainly seen that the force was too great to be resisted. For another quarter of a minute, the two masters held their breath, expecting to see the deck rise beneath their feet, as the ice rose along the points of contact between the floes. Such, in all probability, would have been the result, had not the pressure brought about another change, that was quite as much within the influence of the laws of mechanical forces, though not so much expected. Owing to the wedge-like form of the vessel's bottom, as well as to the circumstance that the ice of the outer floe had a similar shape, projecting beneath the schooner's keel, the craft was lifted bodily, with an upward jerk, as if she were suddenly released from some imprisoning power. Released she was, indeed, and that most opportunely, for another half minute would have seen her ribs broken in, and the schooner a mangled wreck. As she now rose, Roswell gave vent to his delight in a loud cry, and all hands felt that the occurrence might possibly save them. The surge upward was fearful, and several of the men were thrown off their feet; but it effectually released the schooner from the nip, laying her gradually up in the sort of dock that her people had been so many hours preparing for her reception. There she lay, inclining a little, partly on her bilge, or sewed, as seamen term it, when a vessel gets a list from touching the ground and being left by the tide, neither quite upright, nor absolutely on her beam-ends.

No sooner was the vessel thus docked, than all apprehension of receiving further injury from the outer floe ceased. It might force the schooner altogether on the inner field, driving the vessel before it, as an avalanche of mud in the Alps is known to force cottages and hamlets in its front; but it could no longer "nip" it. It did not appear probable to the two masters, however, that the vessel would be forced from its present berth, the rending and cracking of the ice sensibly diminishing, as the two floes came closer and closer together. Nor was this all; it was soon very obvious that the inner field was drifting, with an increased motion, into the bay, while the larger, or outer floe, seemed to hang, from some cause or other. Of the fact there was soon no doubt, the fissure beginning to open, as slowly and steadily as it had closed, but noiselessly, and without any rending of the ice.

"We shall get you clear, Daggett! we shall get you clear!" cried Roswell, with hearty good-will, forgetting, in that moment of generous effort, all feelings of competition and rivalry. "I know what you are after, my good fellow—have understood it from the first. Yonder high land is the spot you seek; and along the north shore of that island are elephants, lions, dogs, bears, and other animals, to fill up all the craft that ever came out of the Vineyard!"

"This is hearty, Gar'ner," returned the other, giving his brother master a most cordial shake of the hand, "and it's just what I like. Sealing is a sociable business, and a craft should never come alone into these high latitudes. Accidents will happen to the most prudent man living, as you see by what has just befallen me; for, to own the truth, we've had a narrow chance of it!"

The reader will remember that all which Daggett now said, was uttered by a man who saw his vessel lying on the ice, with a list that rendered it somewhat difficult to move about on her deck, and still in circumstances that would have caused half the navigators of this world to despair. Such was not the fact with Daggett, however. Seven thousand miles from home, alone, in an unknown sea, and uncertain of ever finding the place he sought, this man had picked his way among mountains and fields of ice, with perhaps less hesitation and reluctance than a dandy would encounter the perils of a crossing, when the streets were a little moistened by rain. Even then, with his vessel literally shelved on the ice, certain that she had been violently nipped, he was congratulating himself on reaching a sealing ground from which he could never return without encountering all the same dangers over again. As for Roswell, he laughed a little at the other's opinion of the sealing business, for he was morally certain the Vineyard man would have kept the secret, had it been in his possession alone.

"Well, well, we'll forget the past," he said, "all but what we've done to help one another. You stood by me off Hatteras, and I've been of some service to you here. You know how it is in our calling, Daggett; first come, first served. I got here first, and have had the cream of the business for this season; though I do not by any means wish to be understood as saying that you are too late."

" I hope not, Gar'ner. 'Twould be vexatious to have all
this risk and trouble for nothing. How much ile have you
stowed ? "

"All my ground tier, and a few riders. It is with the
skins that we are doing the best business."

Daggett's eyes fairly snapped at this announcement,
which aroused all his professional ambition, to say nothing
of that propensity to the "root of all evil," which had
become pretty thoroughly incorporated with his moral
being, by dint of example, theory, and association. We
have frequently had occasion to remark how much more
"enjoyable," for the intellectual and independent, is a
country on the decline, than a country on the advance.
The one is accumulating that wealth which the other has
already possessed and improved ; and men cease to dwell
so much on riches in their inmost souls, when the means
of obtaining them would seem to have got beyond their
reach. This is one of the secrets of the universal popular
ity of Italy with the idle and educated ; though the climate.
and the monuments, and the recollections, out of doubt
contribute largely to its charms. Nevertheless, man, as a
rule, is far more removed from the money-getting mania
in Italy than in almost any other portion of the Christian
world ; and this merely because the time of her wealth
and power has gone by, leaving in its train a thousand
fruits that would seem to be the most savory, as the stem
on which they grew would appear to be approaching its
decay. Neither on Martha's Vineyard, however, nor in
any part of the Great Republic, indeed, has this waning
season yet commenced, and the heart of man is still en
grossed with those desires that are to produce the mean
which are to lay the foundations for the enjoyment o
generations to come.

"That's luck, indeed, for a craft so early in the season,
returned Daggett, when his eyes had done snapping. "Ar
the critturs getting to be wild and skeary ? "

"Not more so than the day we began upon them.
have taken the greatest care to send none but my mos
experienced hands out to kill and skin, and their order
have been rigid to give as little alarm as possible. If yo
wish to fill up, I would advise you to take the same pre
cautions, for the heel of the season is beginning to sho'
itself."

" I will winter here, but I get a full craft," said Dagget
with a resolute manner, if not absolutely serious in wha

he said.   "Trouble enough have I had to find the group,
and we Vineyard men don't relish the idee of being outdone."

"You would be done up, my fine fellow," answered Roswell, laughing, "did you attempt to pass a winter here.
The Sea Lion of Humses' Hull would not herself keep you
in fuel, and you would have to raft it off next summer on
your casks, or remain here forever."

"I suppose a body might expect to see you back again,
another season," observed Daggett, glancing meaningly
toward his companion, as if he had seriously revolved so
desperate a plan in his mind.   "'Tisn't often that a sealer
lets a station like that you've described drop out of his
recollection in a single v'y'ge."

"I may be back or I may not," said Roswell, just then
remembering Mary, and wondering if she would continue
to keep him any longer in suspense, should he return successful from his present adventure: "that will depend on
others more than on myself.   I wish, however, now we are
both here, and there can no longer be any 'hide and go
seek' between us, that you would tell me how you came to
know anything about this cluster of islands, or of the seals
then and there to be found?"

"You forget my uncle, who died on Oyster Pond, and
whose effects I crossed over to claim?"

"I remember him very well—saw him often while living,
and helped to bury him when dead."

"Well, our information came from him.   He threw out
several hints consarning sealing grounds aboard the brig in
which he came home; and you needn't be told, Gar'ner,
that a hint of that kind is sartain to find its way through
all the ports down east.   But hearing that there was new
sealing ground wasn't knowing where to find it.   I should
have been at a loss, wasn't it for the spot on my uncle's
chart that had been rubbed over lately, as I concluded, to
get rid of some of his notes.   You know, as well as I do,
that the spot was in this very latitude and longitude, and
so I came here to look for the much-desired land."

"And you have undertaken such an outfit, and come
this long distance into an icy sea, on information as slight
as this!" exclaimed Roswell, astonished at this proof of
sagacity and enterprise, even in men who are renowned for
scenting dollars from pole to pole.

"On this, with a few hints picked up, here and there,
among some of the old gentleman's papers.   He was fond

of scribbling, and I have got a sort of a chart that he scratched on a leaf of his Bible, that was made to represent this very group, as I can now see."

"Then you could have had no occasion for the printed chart, with the mark of obliteration on it, and did not come here on that authority after all"

"There you're wrong, Captain Gar'ner. The chart of the group had no latitude or longitude, but just placed each island with its bearings and distances from the other islands. It was no help in finding the place, which might be in one hemisphere as well as the other."

"It was, then, the mark of the obliteration——"

"*Marks*, if you please, Captain Gar'ner," interrupted the other, significantly. "My uncle talked a good deal aboard of that brig about other matters besides sealing. We think several matters have been obliterated from the old chart, and we intend to look 'em all up. It's our right, you know, seeing that the old man was Vineyard-born, and we are his nearest of kin."

"Certainly," rejoined Roswell, laughing again, but somewhat more faintly than before. "Every man for himself in this world is a good maxim ; it being pretty certain if we do not take care of ourselves, no one will take care of us."

"Yes, sir," said Stimson, who was standing near; "there is One to care for every hair of our heads, however forgetful and careless we may be ourselves. Wasn't it for this, Captain Gar'ner, there's many a craft that comes into these seas that would never find its way out of 'em ; and many a bold sailor, with a heart boiling over with fun and frolic, that would be frozen to an ice-cicle every year!"

Gardiner felt the justice of this remark, and easily pardoned its familiarity for its truth. In these sealers the discipline is by no means of that distant and military or naval character that is found in even an ordinary merchantman. As every seaman has an interest in the result of the voyage, some excuse was made for this departure from the more general usage; and this familiarity itself never exceeded the bounds that were necessary to the observance of duty.

"Ay. ay," returned Roswell, smiling, "in one sense you are right enough ; but Captain Daggett and myself were speaking of human affairs, as human affairs are carried on. Is not this inner field drifting fast away from the outer, Daggett ? If so, we shall go directly into the bay !"

It was as Gardiner thought. By some means that were

14

not apparent, the floes were now actually separating, and at a rate of movement which much exceeded that of their junction. All idea of further danger from the outer field disappeared, as a matter of course.

"It's so, Captain Gar'ner," said Stimson, respectfully, but with point ; "and who and what brought it about for our safety and the preservation of this craft ? I just ventur' to ask that question; sir."

"It may be the hand of Providence, my good fellow ; for I very frankly own I can see no direct physical cause. Nevertheless, I fancy it would be found that the tides or currents have something to do with it, if the truth could be come at."

"Well, sir, and who causes the tides and currents to run, this-a-way and that-a-way ? "

"There you have me, Stephen ; for I never could get hold of the clew to their movements at all," answered Roswell, laughing. "There is a reason for it all, I dare say, if one could only find it out. Captain Daggett, it is high time to look after the safety of your schooner. She ought to be in the cove before night sets in, since the ice has found its way into the bay."

This appeal produced a general movement. By this time the two fields were a hundred fathoms asunder ; the smaller, or that on which the vessel lay, drifting quite fast into the bay, under the joint influences of wind and current ; while the larger floe had clearly been arrested by the islands. This smaller field was much lessened in surface, in consequence of having been broken at the rocks, though the fragment that was thus cut off was more than a league in diameter, and of a thickness that exceeded many yards.

As for the Sea Lion of the Vineyard, she was literally shelved, as has been said. So irresistible had been the momentum of the great floe, that it lifted her out of the water as two or three hands would run up a bark canoe on a gravelly beach. This lifting process had, very fortunately for the craft, been effected by an application of force from below, in a wedge-like manner, and by bringing the strongest defences of the vessel to meet the power. Consequently, no essential injury had been done the vessel in thus laying her on her screw-dock.

"If a body could get the craft *off* as easily as she was got *on*," observed Daggett, as he and Roswell Gardiner stood looking at the schooner's situation, "it would be but a light job. But, as it is, she lies on ice at least twenty feet thick, and ice that seems as solid as flint ! "

"We know it is not quite as hard as that, Daggett," was Roswell's reply ; "for our saws and axes make great havoc in it, when we can fairly get at it."

"If one *could* get fairly at it ! But here you see, Gar'ner, everything is under water, and an axe is next to useless. Nor can the saws be used with much advantage on ice so thick."

"There is no help for it but hard work and great perseverance. I would advise that a saw be set at work at each end of the schooner, allowing a little room in case of accidents, and that we weaken the foundation by two deep cuts. The weight of the vessel will help us, and in time she will settle back into her 'native element,' as the newspapers have it."

There was, indeed, no other process that promised success, and the advice of Gardiner was followed In the course of the next two hours deep cuts were made with the saws, which were pushed so low as to reach quite to the bottom of the cake. This could be done only by what the sailors called "jury-handles," or spars secured to the plates. The water offered the principal obstacle, for that lay on the shelf at least five feet deep. Perseverance and ingenuity, however, finally achieved their aim. A cracking was heard, the schooner slowly righted, and settled off into the sea again, as easily and harmlessly as if scientifically launched. The fenders protected her sides and copper, though the movement was little more than slowly sinking on the fragment of the cake, which, by means of the cuts, had been gradually so much reduced as to be unable to uphold so great a weight. It was merely reversing the process of breaking the camel's back, by laying the last feather on his load.

This happy conclusion to several hours of severe toil, occurred just as the field had drifted abreast of the cove, and was about the centre of the bay. Hazard came up also at that point, on his return from the volcano, altering his course a little to speak the strangers. The report of the mate concerning his discoveries was simple and brief. There was a volcano, and one in activity ; but it had nothing remarkable about it. No seal were seen, and there was little to reward one for crossing the bay. Sterility, and a chill grandeur, were the characteristics of all that region ; and these were not wanting to any part of the

group. Just as the sun was setting, Gardiner piloted his
companion into the cove ; and the two Sea Lions were
moored amicably side by side, and that too at a spot
where thousands of the real animals were to be found
within a league.

CHAPTER XVII.

"The morning air blows fresh on him ;
   The waves dance gladly in his sight ;
The sea-birds call, and wheel, and skim—
   O blessed morning light !"—DANA.

THE very day succeeding the arrival of the Sea Lion of
the Vineyard, even while his mate was clearing the vessel,
Daggett had a gang on the north shore, killing and skinning. As Roswell's rules were rigidly observed, no other
change was produced by this accession to the force of the
sealers, than additional slaughter. Many more seals were
killed, certainly, but all was done so quietly that no great
alarm was awakened among the doomed animals themselves. One great advantage was obtained by the arrival
of the new party that occasioned a good deal of mirth at
first, but which, in the end, was found to be of great importance to the progress of the work. Daggett had taken
to pieces and brought with him the running part of a common country wagon, which was soon found of vast service
in transporting the skins and blubber across the rocks.
The wheels were separated, leaving them in pairs, and
each axle was loaded with a freight that a dozen men
would hardly have carried, whereas two or three hands
would drag in the load, with an occasional lift from other
gangs, to get them up a height, or over a cleft. This portion of the operation was found to work admirably, owing
in a great measure to the smooth surfaces of the rocks ;
and unquestionably, these wheels advanced the business
of the season at least a fortnight ;—Gardiner thought a
month. It rendered the crews better natured, too, much
diminishing their toil, and sending them to their bunks at
night in a far better condition for rest than they otherwise could have been.

Just one month, or four weeks to a day, after the second
schooner got in, it being Sunday of course, Gardiner and
Daggett met on the platform of a perfectly even rock that

lay stretched for two hundred yards directly beneath the house. It was in the early morning. Notwithstanding there was a strong disposition to work night and day on the part of the new-comers, Roswell's rule of keeping the Sabbath as a day of rest had prevailed, and the business of washing, scrubbing, and shaving had just commenced. As for the two masters, they required fewer ablutions than their men, had risen earlier, and were already dressed for the day.

"To-morrow will be the first day of February," said Daggett, when the salutations of the morning were passed, "and I was calculating my chances of getting full this season. You will be full this week, I conclude, Gar'ner?"

"We hope to be so, by the middle of it," was the answer. "I think the seal are getting to be much shyer than they were, and I am afraid we shall demonstrate that the more haste is the worse speed.'"

"What is that to you?" returned Daggett, quickly. "Of course you will sail for home as soon as you can get off."

Gardiner did not like the "of course," which was indirectly saying what the other would do himself under similar circumstances. Still, it caused no difference in his own decision, which had been made up under the influence of much reflection and of a great deal of good feeling.

"I shall do no such thing, Captain Daggett," was the answer. "I do not fancy the idea of leaving a fellow-creature, a countryman—nay, I might say, a neighbor, on this lone spot, with the uncertainty of his ever getting out of it. If you can come to some understanding with my officers and crew, I will keep the schooner here until we are both full, and ready to sail in company."

"In which case you would nat'rally ask a lay for yourself?"

"Naturally, perhaps, I might," returned Roswell, smiling, "though positively, I shall not. Not one of us in the cabin will look for any other advantage than your good company. I have talked this matter over with my mates, and they say that the advantage of having a consort in getting through the ice is sufficient to justify us in holding on two or three weeks longer. With the men, it will be a little different, perhaps; and they will require some pay. The poor fellows live by their hands, and what their hands do they will expect to be compensated for."

"They shall have good lays, depend on it. As for your-

self, Captain Gar'ner, I trust my owners will not forget to
do what is right, if we ever get home, and meet with luck
in the market."

"Never fear for me, Daggett.   I look for my reward in
the bright eyes and pleasant smiles of as excellent a girl as
Long Island can produce.   Mary never fails to reward me
in that way whenever I do right. It *is* right to stand by you
just now—to do as I would be done by ; and I'll do it. Set
the thing down as decided, but make your bargain with my
men. And now, Daggett, what say you to climbing yonder
mountain to-day, by way of getting a good survey of our
territories, as well as to take a look at the state of the
ice ?"

Daggett assented very cheerfully, his mind being greatly
relieved by this assurance of standing by him, on the part
of Roswell ; for he had been undecided whether to remain
after the departure of the other schooner or not.   All was
now clear to him, however, and the two masters made their
preparations to ascend the mountain as soon as they had
breakfasted.   Stimson was summoned to be of the party,
his officer having got to be accustomed to, and desirous of
his company.

For the first two hours after quitting the house, Gardiner, Daggett, and the boat-steerer were busily employed in
working their way across the broken surface of the island,
to the base of the cone-line pinnacle that formed the apex
of all.   There they rested and took a little refreshment,
conversing the while on the state of the ice in the offing,
so far as the last could be seen from their present elevation.

"We shall have a sharp hill to climb, should we succeed
in getting up here," observed Roswell, "though the rocks
appear to be quite clear of snow just now."

"Just now, or never.   This is the antarctic dog-days,
Gar'ner," answered Daggett, laughing, "and we must make
the most of them.   A man can move about without his
pea-jacket at noonday, and that is something gained ; for,
I have heard of ice making in the bays, even at midsummer."

"We are not in a high enough latitude for that, thank
heaven, though pretty well south too. This is our harvest-
time, sure enough, and we had better look to it."

As Gardiner said this, the eyes of all three were turned
on the sterile scene around them.   The island was not absolutely destitute of vegetation, as is the case a few de-

grees further south ; but it might be said to be nearly so.
A few stunted plants were to be seen in the fissures of the
rocks, and a little soil had been made, seemingly by the
crumbling of the stones, in which a wiry grass occasionally
showed itself. As for the mountain, however, it was
mostly bare ; and when our party began to climb, the ascent was not only difficult, but in places dangerous. Roswell had foreseen this, and he had made a provision
accordingly. In addition to his lance, used as a leaping-
staff and walking-pike, each man had a small coil of
ratlin-stuff thrown over his shoulder, in order to help him
in difficult places, or enable him to help his companions.
It was in the descent chiefly that these ropes were expected to be of service, though their utility was made apparent ere the three reached the summit. The ascent of a
mountain a thousand feet in height is no great exploit
under ordinary circumstances. Even when there are pre-
cipitous cliffs, gorges, ravines, and broken masses, youth,
activity, and courage will commonly overcome all the difficulties, placing the foot of man on eminences that nature
would appear to have intended solely for the dominion of
the goat. Thus did it turn out with the three sealers, all
of whom stood on the bald cap of that mountain, after a
vigorous and somewhat hazardous ascent, that occupied
rather more than an hour. They had greatly aided each
other in achieving their purpose, to be sure ; and the
ratlin-stuff was found of use on more than one occasion.

An extraordinary, and, considering the accessories, a
most brilliant view, rewarded the adventurers. But, after
a few minutes passed in pure admiration of what they beheld, the minds of all three adverted to the parts which
gave such unusual splendor to the panorama. Icebergs
were visible on all sides of them, the great bay excepted ;
and the group was surrounded by them, in a way that
would seem to proclaim a blockade. At that season, the
south winds prevailed, though changes were frequent and
sudden, and the vast frozen fleet was drifting north. Gardiner saw that the passage by which he had brought in
his schooner was now completely closed, and that the
only means of exit from the bay was by its northern outlet. The great depth of the bergs still prevented their
coming within the cluster of islands, while their number
and size completely stopped the floes from passing.

To the northward, the sea was much more open. Gardiner and Daggett both thought, as they gazed in that di-

rection, that it would be easy enough to take a vessel through the difficulties of the navigation, and that a good run of eight-and-forty hours would carry her quite beyond the crowded ice. This sight awakened some regrets in the two masters, that they were not then in a condition to depart.

"I am almost sorry that we have made a holiday of the Sunday," said Daggett, seating himself on a point of rock, to get a little rest after so fatiguing an ascent. "Every minute of time is precious to men in our situation."

"Every minute of time is precious to all men, Captain Daggett, in another and a still more important sense, if they did but know it," put in Stimson, with a zealous freedom, and a Christian's earnestness.

"I understand you, Stephen, and will not gainsay it. But a sealin' v'y'ge is no place, after all, for a man to give himself up to Sabbaths and religion."

"All places are good, sir, and all hours Sabbaths, when the heart is in the true state. God is on this naked rock, as he is on the Vineyard; and a thought, or a syllable, in his praise, on this mountain, are as pleasant to him as them that arise from churches and priests."

"I believe it is, at least, a mistake in policy to give the men no day of rest," said Roswell, quietly. "Though not prepared to carry matters as far as my friend Stephen here, I agree with him entirely in *that*."

"And not in believing, sir, that the Spirit of God is on this island?"

"In that too, certainly. Neither Captain Daggett nor myself will be disposed to dispute either of these two propositions, I think, when we come to reflect on them. A day of rest would seem to be appointed by nature; and I make no doubt we have filled up all the sooner for having observed one. Seamen have so many calls on their time which cannot be neglected, that it is unwise in them to increase the number unnecessarily."

"This is not the spirit, Captain Gar'ner, I'm sorry to say, in which we should keep our day of rest, though it is well that we keep it at all. I'm no stickler for houses and congregations, though they are good enough in their times and seasons; for every man has a tabernacle in his own heart, if he's disposed to worship."

"And if any place on earth can particularly incline one to worship God, surely it must be some such spot as this!" exclaimed Roswell, with a degree of fervor it was not usual for him to exhibit. "Never in my life have my eyes seen a sight as remarkable and as glorious as this!"

Well might our young mariner thus exclaim. The day was fine for the region, but marked by the caprice and changeful light of high latitudes. There was mist in places, and flurries of snow were to be seen to the southward, while the ocean to the northward of the group was glittering under the brightness of an unclouded sun. It was the mixed character of this scene that rendered it so peculiar, while its grandeur, sublimity, and even beauty, were found in its vastness, its noble though wild accessories, its frozen and floating mountains, glowing in prismatic light, and the play of summer on the features of an antarctic view.

"'Tis a remarkable spot, as no one can deny," answered Daggett; "but I like its abundance of seal the most of all. I cannot say I have much taste for sights, unless they bring the promise of good profit with them. We Vine-yarders live in a small way, and are not rich enough to take delight in landscapes."

"Serve God, and reverence his holy name," said Stimson, earnestly, "and all places will be good to look upon. I have been on the Vineyard in my time, and have never found any difference as to the spot, so long as the heart is right."

"A poor man must work," answered Daggett, dropping his eyes from the more distant and gorgeous views of the drifting ice-mountains, to the rocky shore, that was still frequented by thousands of seals, some of the largest of which might be seen, even from that elevation, waddling about; "ay, a poor man must work, Sundays or no Sundays; and he who would make his hay, must do it while the sun shines. I like meetin'-goin' at the right place, and sealin' when sealin' ought to be done. This day is lost, I fear, and I hope we shall not have reason to regret it."

Stimson did not abandon what he conceived to be his duty, but answered this cold, worldly spirit in the best manner his uncultivated speech enabled him to do. But his words were thrown away on Daggett. The lust of gold was strong within him; and while that has full dominion over the heart, it is vain to expect that any purely spiritual fruits will ripen there. Daggett was an instance of what, we fear, many thousands resembling him might be found, up and down the land, of a man energetic by temperament, industrious by habit, and even moderate in his views, but whose whole existence is concentrated in the accumulation of property. Born poor, and in a state of society in which no one other generally recognized mode of distinction is so universally acknowledged as that of the possession of money, it is not surprising that a man of his native disposition should early bend all his faculties to this one great object. He was not a miser, like Deacon Pratt, for he could spend freely, on occasion, and perfectly understood the necessity of making liberal outfits to insure ample returns; but he lived for little else than for gain. What such a man might have become, under more favorable auspices, and with different desires instilled into his youthful mind, it is not easy to say; it is only certain that, as he was, the steel-trap is not quicker to spring at the touch, than he was to arouse all his manifold energies at the hopes or promise of profit. As his whole life had been passed in one calling, it was but natural that his thoughts should most easily revert to the returns that calling had so often given. He never dreamed of speculations, knew nothing of stocks, had no concerns with manufactures in cotton or wool, nor had any other notion of wealth than the possession of a good farm on the Vineyard, a reasonable amount of money "at use," certain interests in coasters, whalers, and sealers, and a sufficiency of household effects, and this in a very modest way, to make himself and family comfortable. Notwithstanding this seeming moderation, Daggett was an intensely covetous man; but his wishes were limited by his habits.

While one of the masters of the sealing crafts was drawing these pictures, in his imagination, of wealth after his manner, very different were the thoughts of the other. Roswell's fancy carried him far across that blue and sparkling ocean, northward, to Oyster Pond, and Deacon Pratt's homestead, and to Mary. He saw the last in her single-hearted simplicity, her maiden modesty, her youthful beauty,—nay, even in her unyielding piety; for, singular as it may seem, Gardiner valued his mistress so much the more for that very faith to which, in his own person, he laid no claim. Irreligious he was not, himself, though skeptical on the one great tenet of Christianity. But, in Mary, it struck him it was right that she should believe that which she had been so sedulously taught; for he did not at all fancy those inquiring minds, in the other sex, that lead their possessors in quest of novelties and paradoxes. In this humor, then, the reader will not be surprised to hear that he imagined the deacon's niece in her most pleasing attributes, and bedecked her with all those charms that render maidens pleasant to youthful lovers. Had Mary been less devout, less fixed in her belief that Jesus was the Son of God; strange as it may seem, the skeptical young man would have loved her less.

And what was that rugged, uncultivated seaman, who stood near the two officers, thinking of all this time? Did he, too, bend his thoughts on love, and profit, and the pleasures of this world? Of love, most truly, was his heart full to overflowing; but it was the love of God, with that affection for all his creatures, that benevolence and faith, which glow as warmly in the hearts of the humblest and least educated, as in those of the great and learned. His mind was turned toward his Creator, and it converted the extraordinary view that lay before his sight into a vast, magnificent, gorgeous, though wild temple, for his worship and honor. It might be well for all of us occasionally to pause in our eager pursuit of worldly objects, and look around on the world itself, considering it as but a particle in the illimitable fields of creation,—one among the many thousands of other known worlds, that have been set in their places in honor of the hand that made them. These brief but vivid glances at the immensity of the moral space which separates man from his Deity, have very healthful effects in inculcating that humility which is the stepping-stone of faith and love.

After passing an hour on the bald cap of the mountain, sometimes conversing, at others ruminating on the scene, a change in the weather induced our party to move. There had been flurries of snow visible all the morning, but it was in the distance, and among the glittering bergs. Once the volcano had thus been shut in from view; but now a driving cloud passed over the mountain itself, which was quickly as white as the pure element could make it. So heavy was the fall of snow, that it was soon impossible to see a dozen yards, and of course the whole of the plain of the island was concealed. At this most inauspicious moment, our adventurers undertook their descent.

It is always much less dangerous to mount an acclivity than to go down it. The upper progress is easily enough arrested, while that in the other direction is frequently too rapid to be under perfect command. Roswell felt the truth of this, and would have proposed a delay until the atmosphere became clear again, but it struck him that this was not likely to occur very soon. He followed

Daggett, therefore, though reluctantly, and with due caution. Stimson brought up the rear.

For the first ten minutes our adventurers got along without any great difficulty. They found the precise point at which they had reached the summit of the mountain, and began to descend. It was soon apparent that great caution must be used, the snow rendering the footing slippery. Daggett, however, was a bold and hot-blooded man when in motion, and he preceded the party some little distance, calling out to those behind him to come on without fear. This the last did, though it was with a good deal more caution than was observed by their leader. At length all three reached a spot where it seemed they could not overcome the difficulties. Beneath them was the smooth face of a rock already covered with snow, while they could not see far enough in advance to ascertain in what this inclined plane terminated. Daggett, however, insisted that he knew the spot; that they had passed up it. There was a broad shelf a short distance below them, and once on that shelf, it would be necessary to make a considerable circuit in order to reach a certain ravine down which the path would be reasonably easy. All remembered the shelf and the ravine; the question was merely whether the first lay beneath them, and as near as Daggett supposed. A mistaken confidence beset the last, and he carried this feeling so far as to decline taking the end of a line which Roswell threw to him, but seated himself on the snow and slid downward, passing almost immediately out of sight.

"What has become of him?" demanded Roswell, endeavoring to pierce the air by straining his eyeballs. "He is not to be seen!"

"Hold on to the line, sir, and give me the other end of it; I will go and see," answered Stimson.

It being obviously the most hazardous to remain to the last, and descend without the support of one above him, Roswell acquiesced in this proposal, lowering the boat-steerer down the rock, until he too was hid from his sight. But, though out of sight in that dense snow-storm, Stimson was not so distant as to be beyond the reach of the voice.

"Go more to the right, sir," called out the seaman, "and steady me with the line along with you."

This was done, the walking being sufficiently secure at the elevation where Roswell was. Presently, Stimson shook the line, and called out again.

"That will do, Captain Gar'ner," he said. "I am on the shelf *now*, and have pretty good footing. Lay the line down on the snow, sir, and slide as slowly as you can; mind and keep close at its side. I'll stand by to fetch you up."

Gardiner understood all this perfectly, and did as he was desired to do. By keeping near the line he reached the shelf precisely at the spot where Stimson was ready to meet him; the latter arresting his downward movement by throwing the weight of his own body forward to meet his officer. By such a precaution Roswell was stopped in time, else would he have gone over the shelf, and down a declivity that was so nearly perpendicular as to offer no means of arresting the movement.

"And what has become of Captain Daggett?" demanded Gardiner, as soon as on his feet again.

"I fear he has shot off the rock, sir," was the answer. "At the place where I reached this shelf, it was so narrow I could with great difficulty walk—could not, indeed, had not the line been there to steady me; and, judging from the marks in the snow, the poor man has gone down helpless!"

This was appalling intelligence to receive at such a time, and in such a place. But Roswell was not unmanned by it; on the contrary, he acted coolly, and with great judgment. Making a coil of the ratlin-stuff, he threw the line down until certain it reached bottom, at the distance of about six fathoms. Then he caused Stimson to brace himself firmly, holding on to the line, aided by a turn round a rise in the rock, and he boldly lowered himself down the precipice, reaching its base at about the distance he had calculated so to do.

It still snowed violently, the flakes being large, and eddying round the angles of the rocks in flurries so violent as, at moments, to confound all the senses of the young man. He was resolute, however, and bent on an object of humanity, as well as of good fellowship. Living or dead, Daggett must be somewhere on his present level; and he began to grope his way among the fragments of rock, eager and solicitous. The roaring of the wind almost prevented his hearing other sounds; though once or twice he heard, or fancied that he heard, the shouts of Stimson from above. Suddenly the wind ceased, the snow lessened in quantity, soon clearing away altogether; and the rays of the sun—and this in the dog-days of that region, be it re-

membered—fell bright and genial on the glittering scene.
At the next instant, the eyes of Roswell fell on the object of his search.

Dagget had been carried over the narrow shelf on which
Stimson landed, in consequence of his having no support,
or any means of arresting his momentum.   He did thrust
forward his lance, or leaping-staff , but its point met nothing but air.   The fall, however, was by no means perpendicular, several projections of the rocks helping to lessen
it ; though it is probable that the life of the unfortunate
sealer was saved altogether by means of the lance.   This
was beneath him as he made his final descent, and he slid
along it the whole length, canting him into a spot where
was the only piece of stinted vegetation that was to be
seen for a considerable distance.   In consequence of coming down on a tolerably thick bunch of furze, the fall was
essentially broken.

When Roswell reached his unfortunate companion, the
latter was perfectly sensible and quite cool.

" God be thanked that you have found me, Gar'ner," he
said ; "at one time I had given it up "

" Thank God, also, that you are living, my friend," answered the other.   " I expected only to find your body ;
but you do not seem to be much hurt."

" More than appears, Gar'ner ; more than appears. My
left leg is broken, certainly ; and one of my shoulders
pains me a good deal, though it is neither out of joint or
broken.   This is a sad business for a sealing v'y'ge !"

"Give yourself no concern about your craft, Daggett—
I will look to her and to your voyage."

"Will you stand by the schooner, Gar'ner ?—Promise
me that, and my mind will be at peace."

"I do promise.   The two vessels shall stick together, at
all events until we are clear of the ice."

"Ay, but that won't do.   *My* Sea Lion must be filled up
as well as your own.   Promise me *that*."

"It shall be done, God willing.   But here comes Stimson ; the first thing will be to get you out of this spot."

Daggett was obviously relieved by Roswell's pledges ; for
amid the anguish and apprehensions of his unexpected
state, his thoughts had most keenly adverted to his vessel
and her fortunes   Now that his mind was somewhat relieved on this score, the pains of his body became more
sensibly felt   The situation of our party was sufficiently
embarrassing.   The leg of Daggett was certainly broken, a

little distance above his ankle ; and various bruises in other places, gave notice of the existence of other injuries. To do anything with the poor man, lying where he was, was out of the question, however ; and the first thing was to remove the sufferer to a more eligible position. Fortunately it was no great distance to the foot of the mountain, and a low, level piece of rock was accessible, by means of care and steady feet. Daggett was raised between Roswell and Stimson in a sitting attitude, and supporting himself by putting an arm around the neck of each. The legs hung down, the broken as well as the sound limb. To this accidental circumstance the sufferer was indebted to a piece of incidental surgery that proved of infinite service to him. While dangling in this manner the bone got into its place, and Daggett instantly became aware of that important fact, which was immediately communicated to Roswell. Of course the future mode of proceeding was regulated by this agreeable piece of information.

Sailors are often required to act as physicians, surgeons, and priests. It is not often that they excel in either capacity ; but in consequence of the many things they are called to turn their hands to, it does generally happen that they get to possess a certain amount of address that renders them far more dexterous, in nearly everything they undertake, than the generality of those who are equally strangers to the particular act that is thus to be exercised. Roswell had set one or two limbs already, and had a tolerable notion of the manner of treating the case. Daggett was now seated on a rock at the base of the mountain, with his legs still hanging down, and his back supported by another rock. No sooner was he thus placed than Stimson was despatched, post-haste, for assistance. His instructions were full, and the honest fellow set off at a rate that promised as early relief as the circumstances would at all allow.

As for our hero, he set about his most important office the instant Stimson left him. Daggett aided with his counsel, and a little by his personal exertions ; for a seaman does not lie down passively, when anything can be done, even in his own case

Baring the limb, Roswell soon satisfied himself that the bone had worked itself into place. Bandages were instantly applied to keep it there while splints were making. It was, perhaps, a little characteristic that Daggett took out his knife and aided in shaving down these splints to

the necessary form and thickness. They were made out
of the staff of the broken lance, and were soon completed.
Roswell manifested a good deal of dexterity and judgment
in applying the splints. The handkerchiefs were used to
relieve the pressure in places, and rope-yarns from the
ratlin-stuff furnished the means of securing everything in
its place. In half an hour, Roswell had his job completed,
and that before there was much swelling to interfere with
him. As soon as the broken limb was thus attended to,
it was carefully raised and laid upon the rock along with
its fellow, a horizontal position being deemed better than
one that was perpendicular.

Not less than four painful hours now passed ere the gang
of hands from the vessels reached the base of the mountain. It came prepared, however, to transport the sufferer
on a handbarrow that had been used in conveying the
skins of seal across the rocks. On this barrow Daggett
was now carefully placed, when four men lifted him up
and walked away with him for a few hundred yards. These
were then relieved by four more ; and in this manner was
the whole distance to the house passed over. The patient
was put in his bunk, and some attention was bestowed on
his bruises and other injuries.

Glad enough was the sufferer to find himself beneath a
roof, and in a room that had its comforts ; or what were
deemed comforts on a sealing voyage. As the men were
in the dormitory very little of the time except at night, he
was enabled to sleep ; and Roswell had hopes, as he now
told Stimson, that a month or six weeks would set the patient on his feet again.

"He has been a fortunate fellow, Stephen, that it was no
worse," added Roswell on that occasion. "But for the
luck which turned the lance-pole beneath him, every bone
he has would have been broken."

"What you call *luck*, Captain Gar'ner, I call *Providence*,"
was Stephen's answer. "The great book tells us that not
a sparrow shall fall without the eye of Divine Providence
being on it."

CHAPTER XVIII.

" Now far he sweeps, where scarce a summer smiles,
  On Behring's rocks, or Greenland's naked isles ;
  Cold on his midnight watch the breezes blow,
  From wastes that slumber in eternal snow,
  And waft across the waves' tumultuous roar,
  The wolf's long howl from Oonalaska's shore."—CAMPBELL.

ROSWELL GARDINER set about his duties the succeeding day with a shade of deep reflection on his brow. A crisis had, indeed, come in his affairs, and it behooved him to look well to his proceedings. Daggett's presence on the island was no longer of any moment to himself or his owner, but there remained the secret of the key, and of the buried treasure. Should the two schooners keep together, how was he to acquit himself in that part of his duty, without admitting of a partnership, against which he knew that every fibre in the deacon's system, whether physical or moral, would revolt. Still, his word was pledged, and he had no choice but to remain and help fill up the rival Sea Lion, and trust to his own address in getting rid of her again, as the two vessels proceeded north.

The chief mate of Daggett's craft, though a good sealer, was an impetuous and reckless man, and had more than once found fault with the great precautions used, by the orders of Roswell. Macy, as this officer was called, was for making a regular onslaught upon the animals, slaying as many as they could at once, and then take up the business of curing and trying-out as a regular job. He had seen such things done with success, and he believed it was the most secure mode of getting along. "Some of these fine mornings," as he expressed it, "Captain Gar'-ner would turn out and find that his herd was off—gone to pasture in some other field." This was a view of the matter with which Roswell did not at all agree. His forbearing and cautious policy had produced excellent results so far, and he hoped it would continue so to do until both schooners were full. On the morning when the men next went forth, he as leader of both crews, therefore, our young master renewed his admonitions, pointing out to the new-comers, in particular, the great necessity there was of using forbearance, and not to alarm the seals more than the work indispensably required. The usual number of

15

"Ay, ay's, sir!" were given in reply, and the gangs went along the rocks, seemingly in a good humor to obey these injunctions.

Circumstances, however, were by no means favorable to giving Roswell the same influence over the Vineyard-men as he possessed over his own crew. He was a young commander, and this was his first voyage in that capacity, as all well knew; then there had been rivalry and competi-tion between the two crafts, which was a feeling not so easi-ly removed; next, Macy felt and even intimated, that he was the lawful commander of his own schooner, in cases in which Daggett was disabled, and that the latter had no power to transfer him and his people to the authority of any other individual. All these points were discussed that day, with some freedom, particularly among the Vineyard-men, and especially the last.

Wisely has it been said that "the king's name is a tower of strength." They who have the law on their side carry with them a weight of authority that it is not easy to shake by means of pure reasoning on right or wrong. Men are much inclined to defer to those who are thus armed, legal control being ordinarily quite as effective in achieving a victory as having one's "quarrel just." In a certain sense, authority indeed becomes justice, and we look to its prop-er exercise as one of the surest means of asserting what "is right between man and man."

"The *commodore* says that the critturs are to be treated delicately," said Macy, laughing, as he lanced his first seal that morning, a young one of the fur species; "so take up the pet, lads, and lay it in its cradle, while I go to look for its mamma."

A shout of merriment succeeded this sally, and the men were only so much the more disposed to be rebellious and turbulent, in consequence of hearing so much freedom of remark in their officer.

"The child's in its cradle, Mr. Macy," returned Jenkins, who was a wag as well as the mate. "In my judgment, the best mode of rocking it to sleep will be by knocking over all these grim chaps that are so plenty in our neigh-borhood"

"Let 'em have it!" cried Macy, making an onset on an elephant, as he issued the order. In an instant the rocks at that point of the island were a scene of excitement and confusion. Hazard, who was near at hand, succeeded in restraining his own people, but it really seemed as if the

Vineyard-men were mad. A great many seals were killed, it is true ; but twenty were frightened to take refuge in the ocean where one was slain. All animals have their alarm cries, or, if not absolutely cries, signals that are understood by themselves. Occasionally, one sees a herd, or a flock, take to its heels, or to its wings, without any apparent cause, but in obedience to some warning that is familiar to their instincts. Thus must it have been with the seals ; for the rock was soon deserted, even at the distance of a league from the scene of slaughter, leaving Hazard and his gang literally with nothing to do, unless, indeed, they returned to complete some stowage that remained to be done on board their own craft.

"I suppose you know, Mr. Macy, all this is contrary to orders," said Hazard, as he was leading his own gang back toward the cove. "You see I am obliged to go in and report."

"Report and welcome," was the answer. "I have no commander but Captain Daggett ;—and, by the way, if you see him, Hazard, just tell him we have made a glorious morning's work of it."

"Ay, ay ; you will have your hands full enough to-day, Macy ; but how will it be to-morrow ?"

"Why, just as it has been to-day. The devils must come up to blow, and we're sartin of 'em, somewhere along the shore. This day's work is worth any two that I've seen since I came upon the island."

"Very true ; but what will to-morrow's work be worth ? I will tell Captain Daggett what you wish me to say, however, and we will hear his opinion on the subject. In my judgment, he means to command his craft till she gets back to the hole, legs or no legs."

Hazard went his way, shaking his head ominously as he proceeded. Nor was he much mistaken in what he expected from Daggett's anger. That experienced sealer sent for his mate, and soon gave him to understand that he was yet his commander. Loose and neighborly as is usually the discipline of one of these partnership vessels, there is commonly a man on board who is every way competent to assert the authority given him by the laws, as well as by his contract. Macy was sent for, rebuked, and menaced with degradation from his station, should he again presume to violate his orders. As commonly happens in cases of this nature, regrets were expressed by the offender, and future obedience promised.

But the mischief was done. Sealing was no longer the regular, systematic pursuit it had been on that island, but had become precarious and changeful. At times the men met with good success; then days would occur in which not a single creature of any of the different species would be taken. The Vineyard schooner was not more than half full, and the season was fast drawing to a close. Roswell was quite ready to sail, and he began to chafe a little under the extra hazards that were thus imposed on himself and his people.

In the meantime, or fully three weeks after the occurrence of the accident to Daggett, the injuries received by the wounded man were fast healing. The bones had knit, and the leg promised in another month to become tolerably sound, if not as strong as it had been before the hurt. All the bruises were well, and the captain of the Vineyard craft was just beginning to move about a little on crutches; a prodigious relief to one of his habits, after the confinement to the house. By dint of great care, he could work his way down on the shelf that stretched, like a terrace, for two hundred yards beneath the dwelling. Here he met Roswell, on the morning of the Sabbath, just three weeks after their unfortunate visit to the mountain. Each took his seat on a low point of rock, and they began to converse on their respective prospects, and on the condition of their vessels and crews. Stephen was near his officer, as usual.

"I believe Stimson was right in urging me to give the men their Sabbaths," observed Gardiner, glancing round at the different groups, in which men were washing, shaving, and otherwise getting rid of the impurities created by another week of toil. "They begin anew, after a little rest, with a better will and steadier hands."

"Yes, the Sabbath *is* a great privilege, especially to such as are on shore," returned Daggett. "At sea I make no great account of it; a craft must jog along, high days or holidays."

"Depend on it, the same account is kept of the day, Captain Daggett, in the great log-book above, whether a man is on or off soundings," put in Stephen, who was privileged ever to deliver his sentiments on such subjects. "The Lord is God on the sea, as on the land."

There was a pause; for the solemn manner and undoubted sincerity of the speaker produced an impression on his companions, little given as they were to thinking deeply on things of that nature. Then Roswell renewed the discourse, turning it on a matter that had been seriously uppermost in his mind for several days.

" I wish to converse with you, Captain Daggett, about our prospects and chances," he said. " My schooner is full, as you know. We could do no more, if we stayed here another season. You are about half full, with a greatly diminished chance of filling up this summer. Mr. Macy's attack on the seals has put you back a month, at least, and every day we shall find the animals less easy to take. The equinox is not very far off, and then, you know, we shall get less and less sun—so little as to be of no great use to us. We want daylight to get through the ice, and we shall have a long hundred leagues of it between us and clear water, even were we to get under way to-morrow. Remember what a serious thing it would be to get caught up here, in so high a latitude, after the sun has left us ! "

" I understand you, Gar'ner," answered the other quietly, though his manner denoted a sort of compelled resignation, rather than any cordial acquiescence in that which he believed his brother master intended to propose. " You're master of your own vessel ; and I dare say Deacon Pratt would be much rejoiced to see you coming in between Shelter Island and Oyster Pond. I'm but a cripple, or I think the Vineyard craft wouldn't be many days' run astarn ! "

Roswell was provoked ; but his pride was touched also. Biting his lip, he was silent for a moment, when he spoke very much to the point, but generously, and like a man.

" I'll tell you what it is, Daggett," said our hero, " good-fellowship is good-fellowship, and the flag is the flag. It is the duty of all us Yankee seamen to stand by the stripes ; and I hope I'm as ready as another to do what I ought to do in such a matter ; but my owner is a close calculator, and I am much inclined to think that he will care less for this sort of feeling than you and I. The deacon was never in blue water."

" So I suppose. He has a charming daughter, I believe, Gar'ner ? "

" You mean his niece, I suppose," answered Roswell, coloring. " The deacon never had any child himself, I believe—at least he has none living. Mary Pratt is his niece."

" It's all the same—niece or daughter, she's comely, and

will be rich, I hear.   *Well*, I am *poor*, and what is more, a *cripple !*"

Roswell could have knocked his companion down, for he perfectly understood the character of the allusion ; but he had sufficient self-command to forbear saying anything that might betray how much he felt.

It is always easier to work upon the sensitiveness of a spirited and generous-minded man than to influence him by force or apprehensions.   Roswell had never liked the idea of leaving Daggett behind him, at that season, and in that latitude ; and he relished it still less, now that he saw a false reason might be attributed to his conduct.

"You certainly do not dream of wintering here, Captain Daggett ?" he said, after a pause.

"Not if I can help it.   But the schooner can never go back to the Vineyard without a full hold.   The very women would make the island too hot for us in such a case.   Do your duty by Deacon Pratt, Gar'ner, and leave me here to get along as well as I can.   I shall be able to walk a little in a fortnight ; and in a month I hope to be well enough to get out among the people, and regulate their sealing a little myself.   Mr. Macy will be more moderate with my eye on him."

"A month !   He who stays here another month may almost make up his mind to stay eight more of them ; if, indeed, he ever get away from the group at all !"

"A late start is better than a half-empty vessel.   When you get in to Oyster Pond, Gar'ner, I hope you will send a line across to the Vineyard, and tell 'em all about us."

Another long and brooding pause succeeded, during which Roswell's mind was made up.

"I will do this with you, Daggett," he said, speaking like one who had fully decided on his course.   "Twenty days longer will I remain here, and help to make out your cargo ; after which I sail, whether you get another skin or a thousand.   This will be remaining as long as any prudent man ought to stay in so high a latitude."

"Give me your hand, Gar'ner.   I knew you had the clear stuff in you, and that it would make itself seen at the proper moment.   I trust that Providence will favor us— it's really a pity to lose as fine a day as this ; especially as the critturs are coming up on the rocks to bask something like old times."

"You'll gain no great help from that Providence you just spoke of, Captain Daggett, by forgetting to keep 'holy the Sabbath,' " said Stimson, earnestly. " Try forbearance a little, and find the good that will come of it."

" He is right," said Roswell, " as I know from having done as he advises. Well, our bargain is made. For twenty days longer I stay here, helping you to fill up. That will bring us close upon the equinox, when I shall get to the northward as fast as I can. In that time, too, I think you will be able to return to duty."

This, then, was the settled arrangement. Roswell felt that he conceded more than he ought to do ; but the feeling of good-fellowship was active within him, and he was strongly averse to doing anything that might wear the appearance of abandoning a companion in his difficulties. All this time our hero was fully aware that he was becoming a competitor ; and he was not without his suspicions that Daggett wished to keep him within his view until the visit had been paid to the Kev. Nevertheless, Roswell's mind was made up. He would remain the twenty days, and do all he could in that time to help along the voyage of the Vineyarders.

The sealing was now continued with more order and method than had been observed under Macy's control. The old caution was respected, and the work prospered in proportion. Each night, on his return to the house, Gardiner had a good report to make ; and that peculiar snapping of the eye, that denoted Daggett's interest in his calling, was to be again traced in the expression of the Vineyarder's features ; a certain proof that he was fast falling into his old train of thought and feeling. Daggett was never happier than when listening to some account of the manner in which an old elephant or lion had been taken, or a number of fur-seals had been made to pay their tribute to the enterprise and address of his people.

As for Roswell, though he complied with his promise, and carried on the duty with industry and success, his eye was constantly turned on those signs that denote the advance of the seasons. Now he scanned the ocean to the northward, and noted the diminished number as well as lessened size of the floating bergs ; proofs that the summer and the waves had been at work on their sides. Next, his look was on the sun, which was making his daily course lower and lower each time that he appeared, settling rapidly away toward the north, as if in haste to quit a hemisphere that was so little congenial to his character. The nights, always cool in that region, began to menace frost ;

and the signs of the decline of the year that come so much later in more temperate climates began to make themselves apparent here. It is true, that of vegetation there was so little, and that little so meagre and of so hardy a nature, that in this respect the progress of the seasons was not to be particularly noted; but in all others Roswell saw with growing uneasiness that the latest hour of his departure was fast drawing near.

The sealing went on the while, and with reasonable returns, though the golden days of the business had been seriously interrupted by Macy's indiscretion and disobedience. The men worked hard, for they too foresaw the approach of the long night of the antarctic circle, and all the risk of remaining too long As we have had frequent occasion to use the term "antarctic," it may be well here to say a few words in explanation It is not our wish to be understood that these sealers had penetrated literally within that belt of eternal snows and ice, but approximatively. Few navigators, so far as our knowledge extends, have absolutely gone so far south as this. Wilkes did it, it is true; and others among the late explorers have been equally enterprising and successful The group visited by Gardiner on this occasion was quite near to this imaginary line; but we do not feel at liberty precisely to give its latitude and longitude. To this hour it remains a species of private property; and in this age of anti-rentism and other audacious innovations on long-received and venerable rules of conduct, we do not choose to be parties to any inroads on the rights of individuals when invaded by the cupidity and ruthless power of numbers Those who wish to imitate Roswell must find the islands by bold adventure, as he reached them; for we are tongue-tied on the subject. It is enough, therefore, that we say the group is *near* the antarctic circle; whether a little north or a little south of it is a matter of no moment. As those seas have a general character, we shall continue to call them the antarctic seas; with the understanding that, included in the term, are the nearest waters without as well as within the circle.

Glad enough was Roswell Gardiner when his twenty days were up. March was now far advanced, and the approach of the long nights was near. The Vineyard craft was not full, nor was Daggett yet able to walk without a crutch; but orders were issued by Gardiner, on the evening of the last day, for his own crew to "knock off sealing," and to prepare to get under way for home

"Your mind is made up, Gar'ner," said Daggett, in a deprecating sort of way, as if he still had latent hopes or persuading his brother-master to remain a little longer. "Another week would almost fill us up."

"Not another day," was the answer. "I have stayed too long already, and shall be off in the morning. If you will take my advice, Captain Daggett, you will do the same thing. Winter comes in this latitude very much as spring appears in our own ; or, with a hop, skip, and a jump. I have no fancy to be groping about among the ice after the nights get to be longer than the days !"

"All true enough, Gar'ner ; all quite true—but it has such a look to take a craft home, and she not full !"

"You have a great abundance of provisions ; stop and whale awhile on the False Banks, as you go north. I would much rather stick by you there a whole month than remain here another day."

"You make me narvous talking of the group in this way ! I'm sartain that this bay must remain clear of ice several weeks longer."

"Perhaps it may ; it is more likely to be so than to freeze up. But this will not lengthen the days and carry us safe through the fields and bergs that we know are drifting about out here to the northward. There's a hundred leagues of ocean thereaway, Daggett, that I care for more just now than for all the seal that are left on these islands. But, talking is useless ; I go to-morrow ; if you are wise, you will sail in company."

This settled the matter. Daggett well knew it would be useless to remain without the aid of Roswell's counsel, and that of his crew's hands ; for Macy was not to be trusted any more as the leader of a gang of sealers. The man had got to be provoked and reckless, and had called down upon himself latterly more than one rebuke. It was necessary, therefore, that one of the Sea Lions should accompany the other. The necessary orders were issued accordingly, and "hey for home !" were the words that now cheerfully passed from mouth to mouth. That pleasant idea of "home," in which is concentrated all that is blessed in this life, the pale of the Christian duties and charities excepted, brings to each mind its particular forms of happiness and good. The weather-beaten seaman, the foot-worn soldier, the weary traveller, the adventurer in whatever lands interest or pleasure may lead, equally feels a throb in his heart as he hears the welcome sounds of " hey for home." Never were craft prepared for sea with greater rapidity than was the case now with our two Sea Lions. It is true that the Oyster-Ponders were nearly ready, and had been so for a fortnight; but a good deal remained to be done among the Vineyarders. The last set themselves to their task with a hearty good-will, however, and with corresponding results.

"We will leave the house standing for them that come after us," said Roswell, when the last article belonging to his schooner was taken out of it. "The deacon has crammed us so full of wood that I shall be tempted to throw half of it overboard, now we have so much cargo. Let all stand, Hazard, bunks, planks, and all; for really we have no room for the materials. Even this wood," pointing to a pile of several cords that had been landed already to make room for skins and casks that had been brought out in shocks, "must go to the next comer. Perhaps it may be one of ourselves; for we sailors never know what port will next fetch us up."

"I hope it will be old Sag, sir," answered Hazard, cheerfully; "for, though no great matter of a seaport, it is near every man's home, and may be called a sort of door-way to go in and out of the country through."

"A side-door, at the best," answered Roswell. "With you, I trust it will be the next haven that we enter; though I shall take the schooner at once in behind Shelter Island, and tie her up to the deacon's wharf."

What images of the past and future did these few jocular words awaken in the mind of our young sealer! He fancied that he saw Mary standing in the porch of her uncle's habitation, a witness of the approach of the schooner, looking wistfully at the still indistinct images of those who were to be seen on her decks. Mary had often done this in her dreams; again and again had she beheld the white sails of the Sea Lion driving across Gardiner's Bay, and entering Peconic; and often had she thus gazed in the weather-worn countenance of him who occupied so much of her thoughts—so many of her prayers—picturing through the mysterious images of sleep the object she so well loved when waking.

And where was Mary Pratt at that day and hour when Roswell was thus issuing his last orders at Sealer's Land; and what was her occupation, and what her thoughts? The difference in longitude between the group and Montauk was so trifling that the hour might be almost called identical. Literally so, it was not; but mainly so, it was. There were not the five degrees in difference that make the twenty minutes in time. More than this we are not permitted to say on this subject; and this is quite enough to give the navigator a pretty near notion of the position of the group. As a degree of longitude measures less than twenty-eight statute miles at the polar circles, this is coming within a day's run of the spot, so far as longitude is concerned; and nearer than that we do not intend to carry the over-anxious reader, let his curiosity be as lively as it may.

And where, then, was Mary Pratt? Safe, well, and reasonably happy, in the house of her uncle, where she had passed most of her time since infancy. The female friends of mariners have always fruitful sources of uneasiness in the pursuit itself; but Mary had no other cause for concern of this nature than what was inseparable from so long a voyage, and the sea into which Roswell had gone. She well knew that the time was arrived when he was expected to be on his way home; and as hope is an active and beguiling feeling, she already fancied him to be much advanced on his return. But a dialogue which took place that very day—nay, that very hour—between her and the deacon will best explain her views and opinions, and expectations.

"It's very extr'or'nary, Mary," commenced the uncle, "that Gar'ner doesn't write! If he only know'd how a man feels when his property is ten thousand miles off, I'm sartain he would write, and not leave me with so many misgivings in the matter."

"By whom is he to write, uncle?" answered the more considerate and reasonable niece. "There are no post-offices in the antarctic seas, nor any travellers to bring letters by private hands."

"But he *did* write once; and plaguy good news was it that he sent us in that letter!"

"He did write from Rio, for there he had the means. By my calculations, Roswell has left his sealing-ground some three or four weeks, and must now be as many thousand miles on his way home"

"D'ye think so, gal—dy'e think so?" exclaimed the deacon, his eyes fairly twinkling with pleasure. "That would be good news; and if he doesn't stop too long by the way, we might look for him home in less than ninety days from this moment!"

Mary smiled pensively, and a richer color stole into her cheeks slowly, but distinctly.

"I do not think, uncle, that Roswell Gardiner will be very likely to stop on his way to us here, on Oyster Pond," was the answer she made.

"I should be sorry to think that. The best part of his v'y'ge may be made in the West Ingees, and I hope he is not a man to overlook his instructions."

"Will Roswell be obliged to stop in the West Indies, uncle!"

"Sartain—if he obeys his orders ; and I think the young man will do *that*. But the business there will not detain him long"—Mary's countenance brightened again at this remark—"and, should you be right, we may still look for him in the next ninety days."

Mary remained silent for a short time, but her charming face was illuminated by an expression of heartfelt happiness, which, however, the next remark of her uncle's had an obvious tendency to disturb.

"Should Gar'ner come home successful, Mary," inquired the deacon ; "successful in all things—successful in sealing, and successful in that other matter—the West Ingee business, I mean—but successful in all, as I daily pray he may be,—I want to know if you would then have him ; always supposing that he got back himself unchanged?"

"Unchanged, I shall never be his wife," answered Mary tremulously, but firmly.

The deacon looked at her in surprise ; for he had never comprehended but one reason why the orphan and penniless Mary should refuse so pertinaciously to become the wife of Roswell Gardiner ; and that was his own want of means. Now the deacon loved Mary more than he was aware of himself, but he had never actually made up his mind to leave her the heiress of his estate. The idea of parting with property at all was too painful for him to think of making a will ; and without such an instrument there were others who would have come in for a part of the assets, "share and share alike," as the legal men express it. Of all this was the deacon fully aware, and it occasionally troubled him ; more of late than formerly, since he felt in his system the unerring signs of decay. Once had he got so far as to write on a page of foolscap, " In the name of God, Amen ;" but the effort proved too great for him, and he abandoned the undertaking   Still Deacon Pratt loved his niece, and was well inclined to see her be-

come the wife of " young Gar'ner," more especially should
the last return successful.

" Unchanged !" repeated the uncle, slowly ; "you ṣar-
tainly would not wish to marry him, Mary, if he was
changed !"

" I do not mean changed in the sense you are thinking
of, uncle. But we will not talk of this now. Why should
Roswell stop in the West Indies at all ? It is not usual for
our vessels to stop there."

" No, it is not. If Gar'ner stop at all it will be on a
very *unusual* business, and one that may make all our fortunes—your'n, as well as his'n and mine, Mary."

" I hope that sealers never meddle with the transportation of slaves, uncle !" the girl exclaimed, with a face filled
with apprehension. " I would rather live and die poor
than have anything to do with them !"

" I see no such great harm in the trade, gal ; but such is
not Roswell's ar'nd in the West Ingees It's a great secret,
the reason of his call there ; and I will venture to foretell
that, should he make it, and should it turn out successful,
you will marry him, gal."

Mary made no reply. Well was she assured that Roswell
had an advocate in her own heart that was pleading for
him, night and day ; but firm was her determination not to
unite herself with one, however dear to her, who set up his
own feeble understanding of the nature of the mediation
between God and man in opposition to the plainest language of revelation, as well as to the prevalent belief of the
church since the ages that immediately succeeded the
Christian era.

CHAPTER XIX.

"Poor child of danger, nursling of the storm,
    Sad are the woes that wreck thy manly form !
    Rocks, waves, and winds the shatter'd bark delay ;
    Thy heart is sad, thy home is far away."—CAMPBELL.

IT was about midday when the two Sea Lions opened
their canvas, at the same moment, and prepared to quit
Sealer's Land. All hands were on board, every article was
shipped for which there was room, and nothing remained
that denoted the former presence of man on that dreary
island but the deserted house and three or four piles of

cord-wood, that had grown on Shelter Island and Martha's Vineyard, and which was now abandoned on the rocks of the antarctic circle. As the topsails were sheeted home, and the heavy fore-and-aft mainsails were hoisted, the songs of the men sounded cheerful and animating. "Home" was in every tone, each movement, all the orders. Daggett was on deck, in full command, though still careful of his limb, while Roswell appeared to be everywhere. Mary Pratt was before his mind's eye all that morning; nor did he even once think how pleasant it would be to meet her uncle, with a "There, deacon, is your schooner, with a good cargo of elephant oil, well chucked off with fur-seal skins."

The Oyster Pond craft was the first clear of the ground. The breeze was little felt in that cove, where usually it did not seem to blow at all, but there was wind enough to serve to cast the schooner, and she went slowly out of the rocky basin under her mainsail, foretopsail, and jib. The wind was at southwest—the nor-wester of that hemisphere —and it was fresh and howling enough on the other side of the island. After Roswell had made a stretch out into the bay of about a mile, he laid his foretopsail flat aback, hauled over his jib-sheet, and put his helm hard down, in waiting for the other schooner to come out and join him. In a quarter of an hour Daggett got within hail.

"Well," called out the last, "you see I was right, Gar'ner; wind enough out here, and more, still further from the land. We have only to push in among them bergs while it is light, pick out a clear spot, and heave-to during the night. It will hardly do for us to travel among so much ice in the dark."

"I wish we had got out earlier, that we might have made a run of it by daylight," answered Roswell. "Ten hours of such a wind, in my judgment, would carry us well toward clear water."

"The delay could not be helped. I had so many traps ashore, it took time to gather them together. Come, fill away, and let us be moving. Now we are under way, I'm in as great haste as you are yourself."

Roswell complied, and away the two schooners went, keeping quite near to each other, having smooth water, and still something of a moderated gale, in consequence of the proximity and weatherly position of the island. The course was toward a spot to leeward, where the largest opening appeared in the ice, and where it was hoped a passage to the northward would be found. The further the two vessels got from the land, the more they felt the power of the wind, and the greater was their rate of running. Daggett soon found that he could spare his consort a good deal of canvas, a consequence of his not being full, and he took in his topsail; though, running nearly before the wind, his spar would have stood even a more severe strain.

As the oldest mariner, it had been agreed between the two masters that Daggett should lead the way. This he did for an hour, when both vessels were fairly out of the great bay, clear of the group altogether, and running off northeasterly, at a rate of nearly ten knots in the hour. The sea got up as they receded from the land, and everything indicated a gale, though one of no great violence. Night was approaching, and an Alpine-like range of icebergs was glowing, to the northward, under the oblique rays of the setting sun. For a considerable space around the vessels, the water was clear, not even a cake of any sort being to be seen; and the question arose in Daggett's mind, whether he ought to stand on, or to heave-to and pass the night well to windward of the bergs. Time was precious, the wind was fair, the heavens clear, and the moon would make its appearance about nine, and might be expected to remain above the horizon until the return of day. This was one side of the picture. The other presented less agreeable points. The climate was so fickle, that the clearness of the skies was not to be depended on, especially with a strong southwest wind—a little gale, in fact; and a change in this particular might be produced at any moment. Then it was certain that floes, and fragments of bergs, would be found near, if not absolutely among the sublime mountain-like piles that were floating about, in a species of grand fleet, some twenty miles to leeward. Both of our masters, indeed all on board of each schooner, very well understood that the magnificent array of icy islands which lay before them was owing to the currents, for which it is not always easy to account. The clear space was to be attributed to the same cause, though there was little doubt that the wind, which had now been to the southward fully eight-and-forty hours, had contributed to drive the icy fleet to the northward. As a consequence of these facts, the field-ice must be in the vicinity of the bergs, and the embarrassment from that source was known always to be very great.

It required a good deal of nerve for a mariner to run in among dangers of the character just described, as the sun was setting. Nevertheless, Daggett did it; and Roswell Gardiner followed the movement, at the distance of about a cable's length. To prevent separation, each schooner showed a light at the lower yard-arm, just as the day was giving out its last glimmerings. As yet, however, no difficulty was encountered; the Alpine-looking range being yet quite two hours' run still to leeward. Those two hours must be passed in darkness; and Daggett shortened sail in order not to reach the ice before the moon rose. He had endeavored to profit by the light as long as it remained, to find a place at which he might venture to enter among the bergs, but he had met with no great success. The opening first seen now appeared to be closed, either by means of the drift or by means of the change in the position of the vessels; and he no longer thought of *that.* Fortune must be trusted to, in some measure; and on he went, Roswell always closely following.

The early hours of that eventful night were intensely dark. Nevertheless, Daggett stood down toward the icy range, using no other precautions than shortening sail and keeping a sharp look-out. Every five minutes the call from the quarter-deck of each schooner to "keep a bright look-out" was heard, unless, indeed, Daggett or Roswell was on his own forecastle, thus occupied in person. No one on board of either vessel thought of sleep. The watch had been called, as is usual at sea, and one-half of the crew was at liberty to go below and turn in. What was more, those small fore-and-aft rigged craft were readily enough handled by a single watch; and this so much the more easily, now that their topsails were in. Still, not a man left the deck. Anxiety was too prevalent for this, the least experienced hand in either crew being well aware that the next four-and-twenty hours would in all human probability be decisive of the fate of the voyage.

Both Daggett and Gardiner grew more and more uneasy as the time for the moon to rise drew near without the orb of night making its appearance. A few clouds were driving athwart the heavens, though the stars twinkled as usual, in their diminutive but sublime splendor. It was not so dark that objects could not be seen at a considerable distance; and the people of the schooners had no difficulty in very distinctly tracing, and that not very far ahead, the broken outlines of the chain of floating mountains.

No Alpine pile, in very fact, could present a more regular
or better defined range, and in some respects more fantastic outlines. When the bergs first break away from their
native moorings, their forms are ordinarily somewhat regular; the summits commonly resembling tableland. This
regularity of shape, however, is soon lost under the rays
of the summer sun, the wash of the ocean, and most of all
by the wear of the torrents that gush out of their own
frozen bosoms. A distinguished navigator of our own
time has compared the appearance of these bergs, after
their regularity of shape is lost and they begin to assume
the fantastic outlines that uniformly succeed, to that of a
deserted town, built of the purest alabaster, with its edi-
fices crumbling under the seasons, and its countless un-
peopled streets, avenues, and alleys. All who have seen
the sight unite in describing it as one of the most remarkable that comes from the lavish hand of nature.

About nine o'clock on the memorable night in question
there was a good deal of fog driving over the ocean to increase the obscurity. This rendered Daggett doubly cautious, and he actually hauled up close to the wind, heading
off well to the westward, in order to avoid running in
among the bergs in greater uncertainty than the circumstances would seem to require. Of course Roswell followed the movement; and, when the moon first diffused
its mild rays on the extraordinary scene, the two schooners were pitching into a heavy sea, within less than a mile
of the weather-line of the range of bergs. It was soon apparent that floes or field-ice accompanied the floating mountains, and extended so far to the southward of them as to
be already within an inconvenient, if not hazardous, proximity to the two vessels. These floes, however, unlike those
previously encountered, were much broken by the undulations of the waves, and seldom exceeded a quarter of a
mile in diameter; while thousands of them were no larger
than the ordinary drift ice of our own principal rivers in
the time of a freshet. Their vicinity to the track of the
schooners, indeed, was first ascertained by the noise they
produced in grinding against each other, which soon made
itself audible even above the roaring of the gale.

Both of our masters now began to be exceedingly uncomfortable. It was soon quite apparent that Daggett
had been too bold, and had led down toward the ice without sufficient caution and foresight. As the moon rose
higher and higher the difficulties and dangers to leeward

16

became at each minute more and more apparent. Nothing could have been more magnificent than the scene which lay before the eyes of the mariners, or would have produced a deeper feeling of delight, had it not been for the lively consciousness of the risk the two schooners and all who were in them unavoidably ran by being so near and to windward of such an ice coast, if one may use the expression as relates to floating bodies. By that light it was very easy to imagine Wilkes' picture of a ruined town of alabaster. There were arches of all sizes and orders; pinnacles without number; towers, and even statues and columns. To these were to be added long lines of perpendicular walls, that it was easy enough to liken to fortresses, dungeons, and temples. In a word, even the Alps, with all their peculiar grandeur, and certainly on a scale so vastly more enlarged, possess no one aspect that is so remarkable for its resemblance to the labors of man, composed of a material of the most beautiful transparency, and, considered as the results of human ingenuity, on a scale so gigantic. The glaciers have often been likened, and not unjustly, to a frozen sea; but here were congealed mountains seemingly hewed into all the forms of art, not by the chisel it is true, but by the action of the unerring laws which produced them.

Perhaps Roswell Gardiner was the only individual in those two vessels that night who was fully alive to all the extraordinary magnificence of its unusual pictures. Stephen may, in some degree, have been an exception to the rule; though he saw the hand of God in nearly all things. "It's wonderful to look at, Captain Gar'ner, isn't it?" said this worthy seaman, about the time the light of the moon began to tell on the view; "wonderful, truly, did we not know who made it all!" These few and simple words had a cheering influence on Roswell, and served to increase his confidence in eventual success. God did produce all things, either directly or indirectly; this even his skeptical notions could allow; and that which came from divine wisdom must be intended for good. He would take courage, and for once in his life trust to Providence. The most resolute man by nature feels his courage augmented by such a resolution.

The gales of the antarctic sea are said to be short, though violent. They seldom last six-and-thirty hours, and for about a third of that time they blow with their greatest violence. As a matter of course, the danger amid the ice

is much increased by a tempest ; though a good working
breeze, or small gale of wind, perhaps, adds to a vessel's
security, by rendering it easier to handle her, and to avoid
floes and bergs. If the ice is sufficient to make a lee,
smooth water is sometimes a consequence ; though it oftener happens that the turbulence produced in clear water
is partially communicated over a vast surface, causing the
fields and mountains to grind against each other under the
resistless power of the waves. On the present occasion,
however, the schooners were still in open water, where the
wind had a long and unobstructed rake, and a sea had got
up that caused both of the little craft to bury nearly to
their gunwales What rendered their situation still more unpleasant was the fact that all the water which came aboard
of them now soon froze. To this, however, the men were accustomed, it frequently happening that the moisture deposited on the rigging and spars by the fogs froze during
the nights of the autumn. Indeed, it has been thought by
some speculators on the subject, that the bergs themselves
are formed in part by a similar process, though snows undoubtedly are the principal element in their composition.
This it is which gives the berg its stratified appearance, no
geological formation being more apparent or regular in
this particular than most of those floating mountains.

About ten, the moon was well above the horizon ; the
fog had been precipitated in dew upon the ice, where it
congealed, and helped to arrest the progress of dissolution ; while the ocean became luminous for the hour, and
objects comparatively distinct. Then it was that the seamen first got a clear insight into the awkwardness of their
situation. The bold are apt to be reckless in the dark ;
but when danger is visible, their movements become more
wary and better calculated than those of the timid. When
Daggett got this first good look at the enormous masses
of the field-ice, that, stirred by the unquiet ocean, were
grinding each other, and raising an unceasing, rushing
sound, like that the surf produces on a beach, though far
louder, and with a hardness in it that denoted the collision
of substances harder than water, he almost instinctively
ordered every sheet to be flattened down, and the schooner's head brought as near the wind as her construction
permitted Roswell observed the change in his consort's
line of sailing, slight as it was, and imitated the manœuvre.
The sea was too heavy to dream of tacking, and there was
not room to wear. So close, indeed, were some of the

cakes, those that might be called the stragglers of the grand array, that repeatedly each vessel brushed along so near them as actually to receive slight shocks from collisions with projecting portions. It was obvious that the vessels were setting down upon the ice, and that Daggett did not haul his wind a moment too soon.

The half-hour that succeeded was one of engrossing interest. It settled the point whether the schooners could or could not eat their way into the wind sufficiently to weather the danger. Fragment after fragment was passed; blow after blow was received; until suddenly the field-ice appeared directly in front. It was in vast quantities, extending to the southward far as the eye could reach. There remained no alternative but to attempt to wear. Without waiting longer than to assure himself of the facts, Daggett ordered his helm put up and the main gaff lowered. At that moment both the schooners were under their jibs and foresails, each without its bonnet, and double-reefed mainsails. This was not canvas very favorable for wearing, there being too much after-sail; but the sheets were attended to, and both vessels were soon driving dead to leeward, amid the foam of a large wave; the next instant ice was heard grinding along their sides.

It was not possible to haul up on the other tack ere the schooners would be surrounded by the floes; and seeing a comparatively open passage a short distance ahead, Daggett stood in boldly, followed closely by Roswell In ten minutes they were fully a mile within the field, rendering all attempts to get out of it to windward so hopeless as to be almost desperate. The manœuvre of Daggett was begun under circumstances that scarcely admitted of any alternative, though it might be questioned if it were not the best expedient that offered. Now that the schooners were so far within the field-ice the water was much less broken, though the undulations of the restless ocean were still considerable, and the grinding of ice occasioned by them was really terrific. So loud was the noise produced by these constant and violent collisions, indeed, that the roaring of the wind was barely audible, and that only at intervals. The sound was rushing, like that of an incessant avalanche, attended by cracking noises that resembled the rending of a glacier.

The schooners now took in their foresails, for the double purpose of diminishing their velocity and of being in a better condition to change their course, in order to avoid dangers ahead. These changes of course were necessarily frequent; but, by dint of boldness, perseverance, and skill, Daggett worked his way into the comparatively open passage already mentioned. It was a sort of river amid the floes, caused doubtless by some of the inexplicable currents, and was fully a quarter of a mile in width, straight as an air-line, and of considerable length; though how long could not be seen by moonlight. It led, moreover, directly down toward the bergs, then distant less than a mile. Without stopping to ascertain more, Daggett stood on, Roswell keeping close on his quarter. In ten minutes they drew quite near to that wild and magnificent ruined city of alabaster that was floating about in the antarctic sea!

Notwithstanding the imminent peril that now most seriously menaced the two schooners, it was not possible to approach that scene of natural grandeur without feelings of awe that were allied quite as much to admiration as to dread. Apprehensions certainly weighed on every heart; but curiosity, wonder, even delight, were all mingled in the breasts of the crews. As the vessels came driving down into the midst of the bergs, everything contributed to render the movements imposing in all senses, appalling in one. There lay the vast maze of floating mountains, generally of a spectral white at that hour, though many of the masses emitted hues more pleasing, while some were black as night. The passages between the bergs, or, what might be termed the streets and lanes of this mysterious-looking, fantastical, yet sublime city of the ocean, were numerous, and of every variety. Some were broad, straight avenues, a league in length; others winding and narrow; while a good many were little more than fissures, that might be fancied lanes.

The schooners had not run a league within the bergs before they felt much less of the power of the gale; and the heaving and setting of the seas were sensibly diminished. What was, perhaps, not to be expected, the field-ice had disappeared entirely within the passages of the bergs, and the only difficulty in navigating was to keep in such channels as had outlets, and which did not appear to be closing. The rate of sailing of the two schooners was now greatly lessened, the mountains usually intercepting the wind, though it was occasionally heard howling and scuffling in the ravines, as if in a hurry to escape and pass on to the more open seas. The grinding of the ice, too, came down in the currents of air, furnishing fearful evidence of dangers that were not yet distant. As the water was now sufficiently smooth, and the wind, except at the mouths of particular ravines, was light, there was nothing to prevent the schooners from approaching each other. This was done, and the two masters held a discourse together on the subject of their present situation.

"You're a bold fellow, Daggett, and one I should not like to follow in a voyage round the world," commenced Roswell. "Here we are, in the midst of some hundreds of icebergs; a glorious sight to behold, I must confess—but are we ever to get out again?"

"It is much better to be here, Gar'ner," returned the other, "than to be among the floes. I'm always afraid of my starn and my rudder when among the field-ice; whereas there is no danger hereabouts that cannot be seen before a vessel is on it. Give me my eyes, and I feel that I have a chance."

"There is some truth in that; but I wish these channels were a good deal wider than they are. A man may *feel* a berg as well as see it. Were two of these fellows to take it into their heads to close upon us, our little craft would be crushed like nuts in the crackers!"

"We must keep a good look-out for that. Here seems to be a long bit of open passage ahead of us, and it leads as near north as we can wish to run If we can only get to the other end of it, I shall feel as if half our passage back to Ameriky was made."

The citizen of the United States calls his country "America," *par excellence,* never using the addition of "North," as is practised by most European people. Daggett meant "home," therefore, by his "Ameriky," in which he saw no other than the east end of Long Island, Gardiner's Island, and Martha's Vineyard. Roswell understood him, of course; so no breath was lost.

"In my judgment," returned Gardiner, "we shall not get clear of this ice for a thousand miles. Not that I expect to be in a wilderness of it, as we are to-night; but, after such a summer, you may rely on it, Daggett, that the ice will get as far north as $45°$, if not a few degrees further."

"It is possible; I have seen it in $42°$ myself; and in $40°$ to the nor'ard of the equator. If it get as far as $50°$, however, in this part of the world, it will do pretty well. That will be play to what we have just here——In the name of Divine Providence. what is that. Gar'ner?"

Not a voice was heard in either vessel ; scarcely a breath was drawn. A heavy groaning sound had been instantly succeeded by such a plunge into the water as might, be imagined to succeed the fall of a fragment from another planet. Then all the bergs near by began to rock as if agitated by an earthquake. This part of the picture was both grand and frightful. Many of those masses rose above the sea more than two hundred feet perpendicularly, and showed wall-like surfaces of half a league in length. At the point where the schooners happened to be just at that moment, the ice-islands were not so large, but quite as high, and consequently were more easily agitated. While the whole panorama was bowing and rocking, pinnacles, arches, walls, and all seeming about to totter from their bases, there came a wave sweeping down the passage that lifted them high in the air, some fifty feet at least, and bore them along like pieces of cork fully a hundred yards. Other waves succeeded, though of less height and force ; when gradually the water regained its former and more natural movement, and subsided.

"This has been an earthquake!" exclaimed Daggett. "That volcano has been pent up, and the gas is stirring up the rocks beneath the sea."

"No, sir," answered Stimson, from the forecastle of his own schooner, "it's not that, Captain Daggett. One of them bergs has turned over, like a whale wallowing, and it has set all the others a-rocking."

This was the true explanation ; one that did not occur to the less experienced sealers. It is a danger, however, of no rare occurrence in the ice, and one that ever needs to be looked to. The bergs, when they first break loose from their native moorings, which is done by the agency of frosts, as well as by the action of the seasons in the warm months, are usually tabular, and of regular outlines ; but this shape is soon lost by the action of the waves on ice of very different degrees of consistency ; some being composed of frozen snow, some of the moisture precipitated from the atmosphere in the shape of fogs, and some of pure frozen water. The first melts soonest ; and a berg that drifts for any length of time with one particular face exposed to the sun's rays, soon loses its equilibrium, and is canted with an inclination to the horizon. Finally the centre of gravity gets outside of the base, when the still monstrous mass rolls over in the ocean, coming literally bottom upward. There are all degrees and varieties of

these ice-slips, if one may so term them, and they bring in
their train the many different commotions that such accidents would naturally produce. That which had just
alarmed and astonished our navigators was of the following character. A mass of ice that was about a quarter of
a mile in length, and of fully half that breadth, which
floated quite two hundred feet above the surface of the
water, and twice that thickness beneath it, was the cause
of the disturbance. It had preserved its outlines unusually
well, and stood upright to the last moment; though, owing
to numerous strata of snow-ice, its base had melted much
more on one of its sides than on the other. When the
precise moment arrived that would have carried a perpendicular line from the centre of gravity without this base,
the monster turned leisurely in its lair, producing some
such effect as would have been wrought by the falling of
a portion of a Swiss mountain into a lake ; a sort of accident of which there have been many and remarkable instances.

Stimson's explanation, while it raised the curtain from
all that was mysterious, did not serve very much to quiet
apprehensions. If one berg had performed such an evolution, it was reasonable to suppose that others might do
the same thing ; and the commotion made by this, which
was at a distance, gave some insight into what might be
expected from a similar change in another nearer by. Both
Daggett and Gardiner were of opinion that the fall of a
berg of equal size within a cable's length of the schooners
might seriously endanger the vessels by dashing them
against some wall of ice, if in no other manner. It was
too late, however, to retreat, and the vessels stood on
gallantly.

The passage between the bergs now became quite
straight, reasonably broad, and was so situated as regarded
the gale as to receive a full current of its force. It
was computed that the schooners ran quite three marine
leagues in the hour that succeeded the overturning of the
berg. There were moments when the wind blew furiously ;
and, taking all the accessories of that remarkable view into
the account, the scene resembled one that the imagination
might present to the mind in its highest flights, but which
few could ever hope to see with their proper eyes. The
moonlight, the crowd of icebergs of all shapes and dimensions, seeming to flit past by the rapid movements of the
vessels ; the variety of hues, from spectral white to tints of

orange and emerald, pale at that hour, yet distinct ; streets
and lanes that were scarce opened ere they were passed ;
together with all the fantastic images that such objects
conjured to the thoughts, contributed to make that hour
much the most wonderful that Roswell Gardiner had ever
passed. To add to the excitement, a couple of whales
came blowing up the passage, coming within a hundred
yards of the schooners. They were fin-backs, which are
rarely if ever taken, and were suffered to pass unharmed.
To capture a whale, however, amid so many bergs, would
be next to impossible, unless the animal were killed by the
blow of the harpoon, without requiring the keener thrust
of the lance.

At the end of the hour mentioned, the Sea Lion of the
Vineyard rapidly changed her course, hauling up by a
sudden movement to the westward The passage before
her was closed, and there remained but one visible outlet,
toward which the schooner slowly made her way, having
got rather too much to leeward of it, in consequence of
not earlier seeing the necessity for the change of course in
that dim and deceptive light. Roswell, being to windward, had less difficulty, but, notwithstanding, he kept his
station on his consort's quarter, declining to lead The
passage into which Daggett barely succeeded in carrying
his schooner was fearfully narrow, and appeared to be fast
closing ; though it was much wider further ahead, could
the schooners but get through the first dangerous strait.
Roswell remonstrated ere the leading vessel entered, and
pointed out to Daggett the fact that the bergs were evidently closing, each instant increasing their movement,
most probably through the force of attraction. It is known
that ships are thus brought in contact in calms, and it is
thought a similar influence is exercised on the icebergs.
At all events, the wind, the current, or attraction, was fast
closing the passage through which the schooners had now
to go.

Scarcely was Daggett within the channel, when an enormous mass fell from the summit of one of the bergs, literally
closing the passage in his wake, while it compelled Gardiner to put his helm down, and to tack ship, standing off
from the tottering berg. The scene that followed was
frightful ! The cries on board the leading craft denoted
her peril, but it was not possible for Roswell to penetrate
to her with his vessel. All he could do was to heave-to
his own schooner, lower a boat, and pull back toward the

point of danger. This he did at once, manfully, but with
an anxious mind and throbbing heart. He actually urged
his boat into the chasm beneath an arch in the fallen fragment, and made his way to the very side of Daggett's
vessel. The last was nipped again, and that badly, but was
not absolutely lost. The falling fragment from the berg
alone prevented her, and all in her, from being ground
into powder. This block, of enormous size, kept the two
bergs asunder ; and now that they could not absolutely
come together, they began slowly to turn in the current,
gradually opening and separating, at the very point where
they had so lately seemed attracted to a closer union. In
an hour the way was clear, and the boats towed the
schooner stern foremost into the broader passage.

CHAPTER XX.

"A voice upon the prairies,
    A cry of woman's woe,
That mingleth with the autumn blast
    All fitfully and low."—MRS. SIGOURNEY.

THE accident to the Sea Lion of the Vineyard occurred
very near the close of the month of March, which, in the
southern hemisphere, corresponds to our month of September. This was somewhat late for a vessel to remain in
so high a latitude, though it was not absolutely dangerous
to be found there several weeks longer. We have given a
glance at Mary Pratt and her uncle about this time ; but
it has now become expedient to carry the reader forward
for a considerable period, and take another look at our
heroine and her miserly uncle some seven months later.
In that interval a great change had come over the deacon
and his niece, and hope had nearly deserted all those who
had friends on board the Sea Lion of Oyster Pond, as the
following explanation will show was reasonable and to be
expected.

When Captain Gardiner sailed it was understood that
his absence would not extend beyond a single season. All
who had friends and connections on board his schooner
had been assured of this, and great was the anxiety, and
deep the disappointment, when the first of our own summer months failed to bring back the adventurers. As

week succeeded week and the vessel did not return, the concern increased, until hope began to be lost in apprehension. Deacon Pratt groaned in spirit over his loss, finding little consolation in the gains secured by means of the oil sent home, as is apt to be the case with the avaricious when their hearts are once set on gain. As for Mary, the load on *her* heart increased in weight, as it might be, day by day, until those smiles, which had caused her sweet countenance to be radiant with innocent joy, entirely disappeared, and she was seen to smile no more. Still complaints never passed her lips. She prayed much, and found all her relief in such pursuits as comported with her feelings, but she seldom spoke of her grief; never, except at weak moments, when her querulous kinsman introduced the subject in his frequent lamentations over his losses.

The month of November is apt to be stormy on the Atlantic coasts of the republic. It is true that the heaviest gales do not then occur, but the weather is generally stern and wintry, and the winds are apt to be high and boisterous At a place like Oyster Pond the gales from the ocean are felt with almost as much power as on board a vessel at sea ; and Mary became keenly sensible of the change from the bland breezes of summer to the sterner blasts of autumn. As for the deacon, his health was actually giving way before anxiety, until the result was getting to be a matter of doubt. Premature old age appeared to have settled on him, and his niece had privately consulted Dr. Sage on his case. The excellent girl was grieved to find that the mind of her uncle grew more worldly, his desires for wealth more grasping, as he was losing his hold on life, and was approaching nearer to that hour when time is succeeded by eternity. All this while, however, Deacon Pratt "kept about," as he expressed it himself, and struggled to look after his interests, as had been his practice through life. He collected his debts, foreclosed his mortgages when necessary, drove tight bargains for his wood and other salable articles, and neglected nothing that he thought would tend to increase his gains Still his heart was with his schooner, for he had expected much from that adventure, and the disappointment was in proportion to the former hopes.

One day near the close of November the deacon and his niece were alone together in the "keeping-room"—as it was, if it be not still, the custom among persons of New

England origin to call the ordinary sitting-apartment—
he bolstered up in an easy chair, on account of increasing
infirmities, and she plying the needle in her customary
way. The chairs of both were so placed that it was easy
for either to look out upon that bay, now of a wintry aspect,
where Roswell had at last anchored previously to sailing.

"What a pleasant sight it would be, uncle," Mary, almost unconsciously to herself, remarked, as, with tearful
eyes, she sat gazing intently on the water, "could we only
awake and find the Sea Lion at anchor under the point of
Gardiner's Island! I often fancy that such *may* be—nay,
must be the case yet; but it never comes to pass! I would
not tell you yesterday, for you did not seem to be as well
as common, but I have got an answer, by Baiting Joe, to
my letter sent across to the Vineyard."

The deacon started and half turned his body toward his
niece, on whose face his own sunken eyes were now fastened with almost ferocious interest. It was the love of
Mammon stirring within him the lingering remains of
covetousness. He thought of his property, while Mary
thought of those whose lives had been endangered, if not
lost, by the unhappy adventure. The latter understood
the look, however, so far as to answer its inquiry in her
usual gentle, feminine voice.

"I am sorry to say, sir, that no news has been heard
from Captain Daggett or any of his people," was the sad
reply to this silent interrogatory. "No one on the island
has heard a word from the Vineyard vessel since the day
before she sailed from Rio. There is the same uneasiness
felt among Captain Daggett's friends, as we feel for poor
Roswell. They think, however, that the two vessels have
kept together, and believe that the same fate has befallen
both."

"Heaven forbid!" exclaimed the deacon as sharply as
wasting lungs would allow; "heaven forbid! If Gar'ner
has let that Daggett keep in his company an hour longer
than was necessary, he has deserved to meet with shipwreck, though the loss always falls heaviest on the
owners."

"Surely, uncle, it is more cheering to think that the two
schooners are together in those dangerous seas, than to
imagine one, alone, left to meet the risks, without a companion!"

"You talk idly, gal—as women always talk. If you
know'd all, you wouldn't think of such a thing."

"So you have said often, uncle, and I fear there is some mystery preying all this time on your spirits. Why not relieve your mind, by telling your troubles to me? I am your child in affection, if not by birth."

"Your're a good gal, Mary," answered the deacon, a good deal softened by the plaintive tones of one of the gentlest voices that ever fell on human ear; "an excellent creatur' at the bottom—but of course you know nothing of the sealing business, and next to nothing about taking care of property."

"I hope you do not think me wasteful, sir? That is a character I should not like to possess."

"No, not wasteful ; on the contrary, curful (so the deacon pronounced the word) and considerate enough, as to *keeping*, but awfully indifferent as to *getting*. Had I been as indifferent as you are yourself, your futur' days would not be so comfortable and happy as they are now likely to be, a'ter my departure—if depart I *must*."

"My future life happy and comfortable!" *thought* Mary ; then she struggled to be satisfied with her lot, and contented with the decrees of Providence. "It is but a few hours that we live in this state of trials, compared to the endless existence that is to succeed it."

"I wish I knew all about this voyage of Roswell's," she added, aloud ; for she was perfectly certain that there was something to be told that, as yet, the deacon had concealed from her. "It might relieve your mind, and lighten your spirits of a burden, to make me a confidant."

The deacon mused in silence for more than five minutes. Seldom had his thoughts gone over so wide a reach of interests and events in so short a space of time ; but the conclusion was clear and decided.

"You ought to know all, Mary, and you shall know all," he answered, in the manner of a man who had made up his mind beyond appeal. "Gar'ner has gone a'ter seal to some islands that the Daggett who died here, about a year and a half ago, told me of ; islands of which nobody know'd anything, according to his account, but himself. His shipmates, that saw the place when he saw it, were all dead, afore he let me into the secret."

"I have long suspected something of the sort, sir, and have also supposed that the people on Martha's Vineyard had got some news of this place, by the manner in which Captain Daggett has acted."

"Isn't it wonderful, gal? Islands, they tell me, where a

schooner can fill up with ile and skins in the shortest season
in which the sun ever shone upon an antarctic summer !
Wonderful ! wonderful ! "

"Very extraordinary, perhaps ; but we should remember, uncle, at how much risk the young men of the country
go on these distant voyages, and how dearly their profits
are sometimes bought."

"Bought ! If the schooner would only come back, I
should think nothing of all that It's the cost of the vessel
and outfit, Mary, that weighs so much on *my* spirits. Well,
Gar'ner's first business is with them islands, which are at
an awful distance for one to trust his property ; but, 'nothing ventured, nothing got,' they say. By my calculations,
the schooner has had to go a good five hundred miles
among the ice to get to the spot ; not such ice as a body
falls in with, in going and coming between England and
Ameriky, as we read of in the papers, but ice that covers
the sea as we sometimes see it piled up in Gar'ner's Bay,
only a hundred times higher, and deeper, and broader, and
colder ! It's desperate *cold* ice, the sealers all tell me, that
of the antarctic seas. Some on 'em think it's colder down
south than it is the other way, up toward Greenland and
Iceland itself.   It's extr'or'nary, Mary, that the weather
should grow cold as a body journeys south ; but so it is, by
all accounts. I never could understand it, and it isn't so
in Ameriky, I'm sartin. I suppose it must come of their
turning the months round, and having their winter in the
midst of the dog-days. I never could understand it, though
Gar'ner has tried, more than once, to reason me into it. I
believe, but I don't understand."

"It is all told in my geography here," answered Mary,
mechanically taking down the book, for her thoughts were
far away in those icy seas that her uncle had been so
graphically describing. "I dare say we can find it all explained in the elementary parts of this book."

"They *do* make their geographies useful, nowadays,"
said the deacon, with rather more animation than he had
shown before that morning. "They've got 'em to be now
almost as useful as almanacs. Read what it says about the
seasons, child."

"It says, sir, that the changes in the seasons are owing
to 'the inclination of the earth's axis to the plane of its
orbit.' I do not exactly understand what that means, uncle."

"No ; it's not as clear as it might be. The declination—"

"*In*clination, sir, is what is printed here."

"Ay, inclination. I do not see why anyone should have much inclination for winter, but so it must be, I suppose. The ''arth's orbit has an inclination toward changes,' you say."

"The changes in the seasons, sir, are owing to 'the inclination of the earth's axis to the plane of its orbit.' It does not say that the orbit has an inclination in any particular way."

Thus was it with Mary Pratt, and thus was it with her uncle, the deacon. One of the plainest problems in natural philosophy was Hebrew to both, simply because the capacity that Providence had so freely bestowed on each had never been turned to the consideration of such useful studies. But, while the mind of Mary Pratt was thus obscured on this simple, and, to such as choose to give it an hour of reflection, perfectly intelligible proposition, it was radiant as the day on another mystery, and one that has confounded thousands of the learned, as well as of the unlearned. To her intellect nothing was clearer, no moral truth more vivid, no physical fact more certain, than the incarnation of the Son of God. She had the "evidence of things not seen," in the fulness of Divine grace; and was profound on this, the greatest concern of human life, while unable even to comprehend how the "inclination of the earth's axis to the plane of its orbit" could be the cause of the change of the seasons. And was it thus with her uncle?—he who was a pillar of the "meeting," whose name was often in men's mouths as a "shining light," and who had got to be identified with religion in his own neighborhood to a degree that caused most persons to think of Deacon Pratt when they should be thinking of the Saviour? We are afraid he knew as little of one of these propositions as of the other.

"It's very extr'or'nary," resumed the deacon, after ruminating on the matter for a few moments, "but I suppose it *is* so. Wasn't it for this 'inclination' to cold weather, our vessels might go and seal under as pleasant skies as we have here in June. But, Mary, I suppose that wasn't to be, or it would be."

"There would have been no seals, most likely, uncle, if there was no ice. They tell me that such creatures love the cold, and the ice, and the frozen oceans. Too much warm weather would not suit them"

"But, Mary, it might suit other folks! Gar'ner's whole ar'nd isn't among the ice, or a'ter them seals."

"I do not know that I understand you, sir.   Surely Roswell has gone on a sealing voyage."

"Sartain ; there's no mistake about *that*.   But there may be many stopping-places in so long a road."

"Do you mean, sir, that he is to use any of these stopping-places, as you call them ?" asked Mary, cagerly, half-breathless with her anxiety to hear all.   "You said something about the West Indies once."

"Harkee, Mary—just look out into the entry and see if the kitchen door is shut.   And now come nearer to me, child, so that there may be no need of bawling what I've got to say all over Oyster Pond. There, sit down, my dear, and don't look so eager, as if you wanted to eat me, or my mind may misgive me, and then I couldn't tell you, a'ter all. Perhaps it would be best, if I was to keep my own secret."

"Not if it has anything to with Roswell, dear uncle ; not if it has anything to do with him !   You have often advised me to marry him, and I ought to know all about the man you wish me to marry."

"Yes, Gar'ner will make a right good husband for any young woman, and I *do* advise you to have him.   You are my brother's da'ghter, Mary, and I give you this advice, which I should give you all the same, had you been my own child, instead of his'n "

"Yes, sir, I know that.   But what about Roswell, and his having to stop, on his way home ?"

"Why, you must know, Mary, that this v'y'ge came altogether out of that seaman who died among us, last year. I was kind to him, as you may remember, and helped him to many little odd comforts "—odd enough were they, of a verity—"and he was grateful.   Of all virtues, give me gratitude, say I !   It is the noblest, as it is the most oncommon of all our good qualities.   How little have I met with in my day !   Of all the presents I have made, and gifts bestowed, and good acts done, not one in ten has ever met with any gratitude."

Mary sighed : for well did she know how little he had given, of his abundance, to relieve the wants of his fellow-creatures.   She sighed, too, with a sort of mild impatience, that the information she sought with so much eagerness was so long and needlessly delayed.   But the deacon had made up his mind to tell her all.

"Yes, Gar'ner has got something to do, beside sealing," he resumed of himself, when his regret at the prevalence of ingratitude among men had exhausted itself   "Suthin'"

—for this was the way he pronounced that word—"that is of more importance than the schooner's hold full of ile. Ile is ile, I know, child ; but gold is gold. What do you think of *that ?* "

" Is Roswell, then, to stop at Rio again, in order to sell his oil, and send the receipts home in gold ? "

" Better than that—much better than that, if he gets back at all." Mary felt a chill at her heart. " Yes, that is the p'int—if he gets back at all. If Gar'ner ever does come home, child, I shall expect to see him return with a considerable sized keg—almost a barrel, by all accounts— filled with gold ! "

The deacon stared about him as he made this announcement, like a man who was afraid that he was telling too much. Nevertheless, it was to his own niece, his brother's daughter, that he had confided thus much of his great secret—and reflection reassured him.

" How is Roswell to get all this gold, uncle, unless he sells his cargo ? " Mary asked, with obvious solicitude.

" That's another p'int. I'll tell you all about it, gal, and you'll see the importance of keeping the secret. This Daggett—not the one who is out in another schooner, another Sea Lion, as it might be, but his uncle, who died down here at the Widow White's—well, *that* Daggett told more than the latitude and longitude of the sealing islands—he told me of a buried treasure ! "

" Buried treasure !—Buried by whom, and consisting of what, uncle ? "

" Buried by seamen who make free with the goods of others on the high seas, ag'in the time when they might come back and dig it up, and carry it away to be used. Consisting of what, indeed ! Consisting principally, accordin' to Daggett's account, of heavy doubloons ; though there was a lot of old English guineas among 'em. Yes, I remember that he spoke of them guineas—three thousand and odd, and nearly as many doubloons ! "

" Was Daggett, then, a pirate, sir ?—for they who make free with the goods of others on the high seas are neither more nor less than pirates."

" No ; not he, himself. He got this secret from one who *was* a pirate, however, and who was a prisoner in a jail where he was himself confined for smuggling. Yes; that man told him all about the buried treasure, in return for some acts of kindness shown him by Daggett. It's well to be kind sometimes, Mary."

17

"It is well to be kind always, sir; even when it is misunderstood, and the kindness is abused. What was the redemption but kindness and love, and god-like compassion on those who neither understood it nor felt it? But money collected and buried by pirates can never become *yours*, uncle; nor can it ever become the property of Roswell Gardiner."

"Whose is it, then, gal?" demanded the deacon, sharply. "Gar'ner had some such silly notion in his head when I first told him of this treasure; but I soon brought *him* to hear reason."

"I think Roswell must always have seen that a treasure obtained by robbery can never justly belong to any but its rightful owner."

"And who is this rightful owner, pray? or *owners*, I might say; for the gold was picked up, here and there, out of all question, from many hands. Now, supposing Gar'ner gets this treasure, as I still hope he may, though he is an awful time about it—but suppose he gets it, how is he to find the rightful owners? There it is, a bag of doubloons, say—all looking just alike, with the head of a king, a Don Somebody, and the date, and the Latin and Greek —now who can say that 'this is my doubloon; I lost it at such a time—it was taken from me by such a pirate, in such a sea; and I was whipped till I told the thieves where I had hid the gold?' No, no, Mary; depend on't, no action of 'plevy would lie ag'in a single one of all them pieces. They are lost, one and all, to their former owners, and will belong to the man that succeeds in getting hold on 'em ag'in; who will become a rightful owner in his turn. All property comes from law; and if the law won't 'plevy money got in this way, nobody can maintain a claim to it."

"I should be very, very sorry, my dear uncle, to have Roswell enrich himself in this way."

"You talk like a silly young woman, and one that doesn't know her own rights. We had no hand in robbing the folks of their gold. They lost it years ago, and maybe dead—probably are, or they would make some stir about it—or have forgotten it, and couldn't for their lives tell a single one of the coins they once had in their possession; and don't know whether what they lost was thrown into the sea, or buried in the sand on a key. Mary, child, you must never mention anything I tell you on this subject!"

"You need fear nothing, sir, from me. But I do most earnestly hope Roswell will have nothing to do with any such ill-gotten wealth. He is too noble-hearted and generous to get rich in this way."

"Well, well, say no more about it, child ; you're romantic and notional. Just pour out my drops ; for all this talking makes me breathe thick. I'm not what I was, Mary, and cannot last long ; but was it the last breath I drew, I would stand to it, that treasure desarted and found in this way belongs to the last holder. I go by the law, however ; let Gar'ner only find it—well, well, I'll say no more about it now ; for it distresses you, and that I don't like to see. Go and hunt up the Spectator, child, and look for the whaling news—perhaps there may be suthin' about the sealers too."

Mary did not require to be told twice to do as her uncle requested. The paper was soon found, and the column that contained the marine intelligence consulted. The niece read a long account of whalers spoken, with so many hundred or so many thousand barrels of oil on board, but could discover no allusion to any sealer. At length she turned her eyes into the body of the journal, which being semi-weekly, or tri-weekly, was crowded with matter, and started at seeing a paragraph to the following effect :

"By the arrival of the Twin Sisters at Stonington, we learn that the ice has been found farther north in the southern hemisphere this season, than it has been known to be for many years. The sealers have had a great deal of difficulty in making their way through it ; and even vessels bound round the Cape of Good Hope have been much embarrassed by its presence."

"That's it !—Yes, Mary, that's just it !" exclaimed the deacon. "It's that awful ice. If 'twasn't for the ice, sealin' would be as pleasant a calling as preachin' the gospel ! It is possible that this ice has turned Gar'ner back, when he has been on his way home, and that he has been waiting for a better time to come north. There's one good p'int in this news—they tell me that when the ice is seen drifting about in low latitudes, it's a sign there's less of it in the higher."

"The Cape of Good Hope is certainly, in one sense, in a low latitude, uncle ; if I remember right, it is not as far south as we are north ; and, as you say, it *is* a good sign if the ice has come anywhere near it."

"I don't say it has, child ; I don't say it has. But it may have come to the northward of Cape Horn, and that

will be a great matter; for all the ice that is drifting about
there comes from the polar seas, and is so much taken out
of Gar'ner's track."

"Still he must come *through* it to get home," returned
Mary, in her sweet, melancholy tones.   "Ah! why cannot
men be content with the blessings that Providence places
within our immediate reach, that they must make distant
voyages to accumulate others!"

"You like your tea, I fancy, Mary Pratt—and the sugar
in it, and your silks and ribbons that I've seen you wear;
how are you to get such matters if there's to be no going
on v'y'ges?   Tea and sugar, and silks and satins don't grow
along with the clams on ' Yster Pond ' "—for so the deacon
uniformly pronounced the word "oyster."

Mary acknowledged the truth of what was said, but
changed the subject.   The journal contained no more that
related to sealing or sealers, and it was soon laid aside.

"It may be that Gar'ner is digging for the buried treasure all this time," the deacon at length resumed.   "That
may be the reason he is so late.   If so, he has nothing to
dread from ice."

"I understand you, sir, that this money is supposed to
be buried on a key—in the West Indies, of course."

"Don't speak so loud, Mary—there's no need of letting
all 'Yster Pond know where the treasure is.   It may be in
the West Ingees, or it may not; there's keys all over the
'arth, I take it."

"Do you not think, uncle, that Roswell would write, if
detained long among those keys?"

"You wouldn't hear to post-offices in the antarctic ocean,
and now you want to put them on the sand-keys of the
West Ingees! Woman's always a sailin' ag'in wind and tide."

"I do not think so, sir, in this case at least.   There
must be many vessels passing among the keys of the
West Indies, and nothing seems to me to be easier than
to send letters by them.   I am quite sure Roswell would
write, if in a part of the world where he thought what
he wrote would reach us."

"Not he—not he—Gar'ner's not the man I take him for,
if he let any one know what he is about in them keys, until he had done up all his business there. No, no, Mary.
We shall never hear from him in that quarter of the world.
It may be that Gar'ner is a-digging about, and has difficulty
in finding the place; for Daggett's account had some weak
spots in it."

Mary made no reply, though she thought it very little likely that Roswell would pass months in the West Indies employed in such a pursuit, without finding the means of letting her know where he was, and what he was about. The intercourse between these young people was somewhat peculiar, and ever had been. In listening to the suit of Roswell, Mary had yielded to her heart ; in hesitating about accepting him, she deferred to her principle. Usually, a mother—not a managing, match-making, interested parent, but a prudent, feminine, well-principled mother—is of the last importance to the character and well-being of a young woman. It sometimes happens, however, that a female who has no parent of her own sex, and who is early made to be dependent on herself, if the bias of her mind is good, becomes as careful and prudent of herself and her conduct, as the advice and solicitude of the most tender mother could make her. Such had been the case with Mary Pratt. Perfectly conscious of her own deserted situation, high principled, and early awake to the defects in her uncle's character, she had laid down severe rules for the government of her own conduct ; and from these rules she never departed. Thus it was that she permitted Roswell to write, though she never answered his letters. She permitted him to write, because she had promised not to shut her ears to his suit, so long as he practised toward her his native and manly candor ; concealing none of his opinions, and confessing his deficiency on the one great point that formed the only obstacle to their union.

A young woman who has no mother, if she escapes the ills attendant on the privation while her character is forming, is very apt to acquire qualities that are of great use in her future life. She learns to rely on herself, gets accustomed to think and act like an accountable being, and is far more likely to become a reasoning and useful head of a family, than if brought up in dependence, and under the control of even the best maternal government. In a word, the bias of the mind is sooner obtained in such circumstances than when others do so much of the thinking ; whether that bias be in a right or a wrong direction. But Mary Pratt had early taken the true direction in all that relates to opinion and character, and had never been wanting to herself in any of the distinctive and discreet deportment of her sex.

Our heroine hardly knew whether or not to seek for consolation in her uncle's suggestion of Roswell being de-

tained among the keys, in order to look for the hidden
treasure. The more she reflected on this subject, the
more did it embarrass her. Few persons who knew of
the existence of such a deposit would hesitate about taking possession of it; and, once reclaimed, in what way
were the best intentions to be satisfied with the disposition of the gold? To find the owners would probably be
impossible; and a question in casuistry remained. Mary
pondered much on this subject, and came to the conclusion that, were she the person to whom such a treasure
were committed, she would set aside a certain period for
advertising; and failing to discover those who had the best
claim to the money, that she would appropriate every dollar to a charity.

Alas! Little did Mary understand the world. The fact
that money was thus advertised would probably have
brought forward a multitude of dishonest pretenders to
having been robbed by pirates; and scarce a doubloon
would have found its way into the pocket of its right owner, even had she yielded all to the statements of such claim-
ants.

All this, however, did not bring back the missing Roswell. Another winter was fast approaching, with its chilling storms and gales, to awaken apprehensions by keeping
the turbulence of the ocean, as it might be, constantly before the senses. Not a week now passed that the deacon
did not get a letter from some wife, or parent, or sister, or
perhaps from one who hesitated to avow her relations to
the absent mariner; all inquiring after the fate of those
who had sailed in the Sea Lion of Oyster Pond, under the
orders of Captain Roswell Gardiner.

Even those of the Vineyard sent across questions, and
betrayed anxiety and dread, in the very manner of putting
their interrogatories. Each day did the deacon's apprehensions increase, until it was obvious to all around him
that this cause, united to others that were more purely
physical, perhaps, was seriously undermining his health,
and menacing his existence. It is a sad commentary on
the greediness for gain manifested by this person, that
ere the adventure he had undertaken on the strength of
Daggett's reluctant communications was brought to any apparent result, he himself was nearly in the condition of that
diseased seaman, with as little prospect of being benefited
by his secrets as was the man himself who first communicated their existence. Mary saw all this clearly, and

mourned almost as much over the blindness and world-
liness of her uncle as she did over the now nearly assured
fate of him whom she had so profoundly loved in her
heart's core.

Day by day did time roll on, without bringing any tidings of either of the Sea Lions. The deacon grew weak
fast, until he seldom left his room, and still more rarely the
house. It was now that he was induced to make his will,
and this by an agency so singular as to deserve being
mentioned. The Rev. Mr. Whittle broached the subject
one day, not with any interested motive of course, but
simply because the "meeting-house" wanted some material repairs, and there was a debt on the congregation that
it might be a pleasure to one who had long stood in the
relation to it that Deacon Pratt filled, to pay off, when he
no longer had any occasion for the money for himself.
It is probable the deacon at length felt the justice of this
remark ; for he sent to Riverhead for a lawyer, and made
a will that would have stood even the petulant and envious
justice of the present day ; a justice that inclines to divide
a man's estate infinitesimally, lest some heir become a little richer than his neighbors. After all, no small portion
of that which struts about under the aspects of right, and
liberty, and benevolence, is in truth derived from some of
the most sneaking propensities of human nature !

CHAPTER XXI.

"I, too, have seen thee on thy surging path,
    When the night-tempest met thee ; thou didst dash
Thy white arms high in heaven, as if in wrath,
    Threatening the angry sky ; thy waves did lash
    The laboring vessel, and with deadening crash
Rush madly forth to scourge its groaning sides ;
    Onward thy billows came, to meet and clash
    In a wild warfare, till the lifted tides
Mingled their yesty tops, where the dark storm-cloud rides."
                                          —PERCIVAL.

THE first movement of the mariner, when his vessel has
been brought in collision with any hard substance, is to
sound the pumps. This very necessary duty was in the
act of performance by Daggett, in person, even while the
boats of Roswell Gardiner were towing his strained and

roughly-treated craft into the open water. The result of this examination was waited for by all on board, including Roswell, with the deepest anxiety. The last held the lantern by which the height of the water in the well was to be ascertained; the light of the moon scarce sufficing for such a purpose. Daggett stood on the top of the pump himself, while Gardiner and Macy were at its side. At length the sounding-rod came up, and its lower end was held out, in order to ascertain how high up it was wet.

"Well, what do you make of it, Gar'ner?" Daggett demanded, a little impatiently. "Water there must be; for no craft that floats could have stood such a squeeze, and not have her sides open."

"There must be near three feet of water in your hold," answered Roswell, shaking his head. "If this goes on, Captain Daggett, it will be hard work to keep your schooner afloat!"

"Afloat she shall be, while a pump-break can work. Here, rig this larboard-pump at once, and get it in motion."

"It is possible that your seams opened under the nip, and have closed again, as soon as the schooner got free. In such a case, ten minutes at the pump will let us know it."

Although there is no duty to which seamen are so averse as pumping—none, perhaps, that is actually so exhausting and laborious—it often happens that they have recourse to it with eagerness, as the only available means of saving their lives. Such was now the case, the harsh but familiar strokes of the pump-break being audible amid the more solemn and grand sounds of the grating of icebergs, the rushing of floes, and the occasional scuffling and howling of the winds. The last appeared to have changed in their direction, however; a circumstance that was soon noted, there being much less of biting cold in the blasts than had been felt in the earlier hours of the night.

"I do believe that the wind has got round here to the northeast," said Roswell, as he paced the quarter-deck with Daggett, still holding in his hand the well wiped and dried sounding-rod, in readiness for another trial. "That last puff was right in our teeth!"

"Not in our teeth, Gar'ner; no, not in *my* teeth," answered Daggett, "whatever it may be in *your'n*. I shall try to get back to the island, where I shall endeavor to beach the schooner, and get a look at her leaks. This is the *most* I can hope for. It would never do to think of carrying a craft, after such a nip, as far as Rio, pumping every foot of the way ! "

"That will cause a great delay, Captain Daggett," said Roswell, doubtingly. "We are now well in among the first great body of the ice ; it may be as easy to work our way to the northward of it, as to get back into clear water to the southward."

"I dare say it would ; but back I go. I do not ask you to accompany us, Gar'ner ; by no means. A'ter the handsome manner in which you've waited for us so long, I couldn't think of such a thing ! If the wind has r'ally got round to northeast, and I begin to think it has, I shall get the schooner into the cove in four-and-twenty hours ; and there's as pretty a spot to beach her, just under the shelf where we kept our spare casks, as a body can wish. In a fortnight we'll have her leaks all stopped, and be jogging along in your wake. You'll tell the folks on Oyster Pond that we're a-coming, and they'll be sure to send the news across to the Vineyard."

This was touching Roswell on a point of honor, and Daggett knew it very well. Generous and determined, the young man was much more easily influenced by a silent and indirect appeal to his liberal qualities, than he could possibly have been by any other consideration. The idea of deserting a companion in distress, in a sea like that in which he was, caused him to shrink from what, under other circumstances, he would regard as an imperative duty. The deacon, and still more, Mary, called him north ; but the necessities of the Vineyarders would seem to chain him to their fate.

"Let us see what the pump tells us now," cried Roswell, impatiently. "Perhaps the report may make matters better than we have dared to hope for. If the pump gains on the leak, all may yet be well."

"It's encouraging and hearty to hear you say this ; but no one who was *in* that nip, as a body might say, can ever expect the schooner to make a run of two thousand miles without repairs. To my eye, Gar'ner, these bergs are separating, leaving us a clearer passage back to the open water."

"I do believe you are right ; but it seems a sad loss of time, and a great risk, to go through these mountains again," returned Roswell. "The wind has shifted ; and the nearest bergs, from some cause or other, are slowly opening ; but recollect what a mass of floe-ice there is outside. Let us sound again."

The process was renewed this time much easier than before, the boxes being already removed. The result was soon known.

"Well, what news, Gar'ner?" demanded Daggett, leaning down, in a vain endeavor to perceive the almost imperceptible marks that distinguished the wet part of the rod from that which was dry. "Do we gain on the leak, or does the leak gain on us? God send it may be the first!"

"God has so sent it, sir," answered Stimson, reverently; for he was holding the lantern, having remained on board the damaged vessel by the order of his officer. "It is He alone, Captain Daggett, who could do this much to seamen in distress."

"Then to God be thanks, as is due! If we can but keep the leak under, the schooner may yet be saved."

"I think it may be done, Daggett," added Roswell. "That one pump has brought the water down more than two inches; and, in my judgment, the two together would clear her entirely."

"We'll pump her till she sucks!" cried Daggett. "Rig the other pump, men, and go to the work heartily."

This was done, though not until Roswell ordered fully half of his own crew to come to the assistance of his consort. By this time the two vessels had filled away, made more sail, and were running off before the new wind, retracing their steps, so far as one might judge of the position of the great passage. Daggett's vessel led, and Hazard followed; Roswell still remaining on board the injured craft. Thus passed the next few hours. The pumps soon sucked, and it was satisfactorily ascertained that the schooner could be freed from the water by working at them about one-fourth of the time. This was a bad leak, and one that would have caused any crew to become exhausted in the course of a few days. As Roswell ascertained the facts more clearly, he became better satisfied with a decision that, in a degree, had been forced on him. He was passively content to return with Daggett, convinced that taking the injured vessel to Rio was out of the question, until some attention had been paid to her damages.

Fortune—or as Stimson would say, Providence—favored our mariners greatly in the remainder of their run among the bergs. There were several avalanches of snow quite near to them, and one more berg performed a revolution at no great distance; but no injury was sustained by either vessel. As the schooners got once more near to the field-ice, Roswell went on board his own craft; and all the boats, which had been towing in the open passage, were run up and secured. Gardiner now led, leaving his consort to follow as closely in his wake as she could keep.

Much greater difficulty, and dangers indeed, were encountered among the broken and grating floes, than had been expected, or previously met with. Notwithstanding fenders were got out on all sides, many a rude shock was sustained, and the copper suffered in several places. Once or twice Roswell apprehended that the schooners would be crushed by the pressure on their sides. The hazards were in some measure increased by the bold manner in which our navigators felt themselves called on to push ahead; for time was very precious in every sense, not only on account of the waning season, but actually on account of the fatigue undergone by men who were compelled to toil at the pumps one minute in every four.

At the return of day, now getting to be later than it had been during the early months of their visit to these seas, our adventurers found themselves in the centre of vast fields of floating ice, driving away from the bergs, which, influenced by under-currents, were still floating north, while the floes drove to the southward. It was very desirable to get clear of all this cake-ice, though the grinding among it was by no means so formidable as when the seas were running high and the whole of the frozen expanse was in violent commotion. Motion, however, soon became nearly impossible, except as the schooners drifted in the midst of the mass, which was floating south at the rate of about two knots.

Thus passed an entire day and night. So compact was the ice around them that the mariners passed from one vessel to the other on it, with the utmost confidence. No apprehension was felt so long as the wind stood in its present quarter, the fleet of bergs actually forming as good a lee as if they had been so much land. On the morning of the second day, all this suddenly changed. The ice began to open; why, was matter of conjecture, though it was attributed to a variance between the wind and the currents. This, in some measure, liberated the schooners, and they began to move independently of the floes. About noon, the smoke of the volcano became once more visible; and before the sun went down the cap of the highest elevation in the group was seen, amid flurries of snow.

Every one was glad to see these familiar landmarks;

dreary and remote from the haunts of men as they were
known to be ; for there was a promise in them of a temporary termination of their labors. Incessant pumping—
one minute in four being thus employed on board the
Vineyard craft—was producing its customary effect ; and
the men looked jaded and exhausted. No one who has
not stood at a pump-break on board a vessel, can form any
notion of the nature of the toil, or of the extreme dislike
with which seamen regard it. The tread-mill, as we conceive—for our experience extends to the first, though not
to the last of these occupations—is the nearest approach
to the pain of such toil, though the convict does not work
for his life.

On the morning of the fourth day our mariners found
themselves in the great bay, in clear water, about a league
from the cove, and nearly dead to windward of their
port. The helms were put up, and the schooners were
soon within the well-known shelter. As they ran in,
Roswell gazed around him, in regret, awe, and admiration. He could not but regret being compelled to lose
so much precious time, at that particular season. Short as
had been his absence from the group, sensible changes in
the aspect of things had already occurred. Every sign of
summer—and they had ever been few and meagre—was
now lost ; a chill and dreary autumn having succeeded.
As a matter of course, nothing was altered about the dwelling ; the piles of wood and other objects placed there by
the hands of man, remaining just as they had been left ;
but even these looked less cheering, more unavailable, than
when last seen. To the surprise of all, not a seal was visible. From some cause unknown to the men, all of these
animals had disappeared, thereby defeating one of Daggett's secret calculations ; this provident master having
determined, in his own mind, to profit by his accident and
seize the occasion to fill up. Some said that the creatures
had gone north to winter ; others asserted that they had
been alarmed and had taken refuge on one of the other
islands ; but all agreed in saying that they were gone.

It is known that a seal will occasionally wander a great
distance from what may be considered his native waters ;
but we are not at all aware that they are to be considered as
migratory animals. The larger species usually take a
wide range of climate to dwell in, and even the little fur-
seal sometimes gets astray, and is found on coasts that do
not usually come within his haunts. As respects the ani-

mals that so lately abounded on Sealer's Land, we shall
hazard no theory, our business being principally with facts;
but a conversation that took place between the two chief
mates on this occasion may possibly assist some inquiring
mind in its speculations.

"Well, Macy," said Hazard, pointing along the deserted
rocks, "what do you think of *that* ? Not an animal to be
seen, where there were lately thousands ! "

"What do I think of it ? Why, I think they are off, and
I've know'd such things to happen afore."—The sealers of
1819 were not very particular about their English, even
among their officers.—"Any man who watches for signs
and symptoms may know how to take this."

"I should like to hear it explained ; to me it is quite
new."

"The seals are off, and that is a sign *we* should be off
too. There's my explanation, and you may make what
you please of it. Natur' gives sich hints, and no prudent
seaman ought to overlook 'em. I say, that when the seal
go, the sealers should go likewise."

"And you set this down as a hint from natur', as you
call it ?"

"I do ; and a useful hint it is. If we was in sailing
trim, I'd ha'nt the old man, but I'd get him off this blessed
night. Now, mark my words, Hazard—no good will come
of that nip, and of this return into port ag'in ; and of all
this veering and hauling upon cargo."

The other mate laughed ; but a call from his commanding officer put a stop to the dialogue. Hazard was wanted
to help secure the schooner of Daggett in the berth in
which she was now placed. The tides do not appear to
rise and fall in very high latitudes, by any means, as much
as they do in about 50°. In the antarctic sea they are reported to be of medium elevation and force. This fact
our navigators had noted ; and Daggett had, at once, carried his schooner on the only thing like a beach that was
to be found on any part of that wild coast. His craft was
snug within the cove and quite handy for discharging and
taking in. Beach, in a proper sense, it was not ; being,
with a very trifling exception, nothing but a shelf of rock
that was a little inclined, and which admitted of a vessel's
being placed upon it, as on the floor of a dock.

Into this berth Daggett took his schooner, while the
other vessel anchored. There was nearly a whole day before them, and all the men were at once set to work to

discharge the cargo of the injured vessel. To get rid of the pumps, they would cheerfully have worked the twenty-four hours without intermission. As fast as the vessel was lightened she was hove further and further on the rock, until she was got so high as to be perfectly safe from sinking, or from injuring anything on board her; when the pumps were abandoned. Before night came, however, the schooner was so secured by means of shores, and purchases aloft that were carried out to the rocks, as to stand perfectly upright on her keel. She was thus protected when the tide left her. At low water it was found that she wanted eight feet of being high and dry, having already been lightened four feet. A good deal of cargo was still in, on this the first night after her return.

The crew of Daggett's vessel carried their mattresses ashore, took possession of the bunks, lighted a fire in the stove, and made their preparations to get the caboose ashore next day, and do their cooking in the house, as had been practised previously to quitting the island. Roswell, and all his people, remained on board their own vessel.

The succeeding day the injured schooner was cleared of everything, even to her spars, the lower masts and bowsprit excepted. Two large sealing crews made quick work with so small a craft. Empty casks were got under her, and at the top of the tide she was floated quite up to the small beach that was composed of the *débris* of rock, already mentioned. As the water left her, she fell over a little, of course; and at half-tide her keel lay high and dry.

The prying eyes of all hands were now busy looking out for the leaks. As might have been expected, none were found near the garboard streak, a fact that was clearly enough proved by a quantity of the water remaining in the vessel after she lay, entirely bare, nearly on her bilge.

"Her seams have opened a few streaks below the bends," said Roswell, as he and Daggett went under the vessel's bottom, looking out for injuries; "and you had better set about getting off the copper at once. Has there been an examination made inside?"

None had yet been made, and our two masters clambered up to the main hatch, and got as good a look at the state of things in the hold, as could be thus obtained. So tremendous had been the pressure, that three of the deck beams were broken. They would have been driven quite clear of their fastenings, had not the wall of ice at each end prevented the possibility of such a thing. As it was, the top-timbers had slightly given way, and the seams must have been opened just below the water-line. When the tide came in again, the schooner righted of course ; and the opportunity was taken to pump her dry. There was then no leak ; another proof that the defective places must be sought above the present water-line.

With the knowledge thus obtained, the copper was removed, and several of the seams examined. The condition of the pitch and oakum pointed out the precise spots that needed attention, and the calking-irons were immediately set at work. In about a week the job was completed, as was fancied, the copper replaced, and the schooner was got afloat again. Great was the anxiety to learn the effect of what had been done, and quite as great the disappointment, when it was found that there was still a serious leak, that admitted too much water to think of going to sea until it was stopped. A little head-work, however, and that on the part of Roswell, speedily gave a direction to the search that was immediately set on foot.

"This leak is not as low down as the vessel's bilge," he said ; "for the water did not run out of her, nor into her, until we got her afloat. It is somewhere, then, between her light-water load-line and her bilge. Now we have had all the copper off, and the seams examined in the wake of this section of the vessel's bottom, from the fore-chains to the main ; and, in my judgment, it will be found that something is wrong about her stem, or her stern-post. Perhaps one of her wood ends has started. Such a thing might very well have happened under so close a squeeze."

"In which case we shall have to lay the craft ashore again, and go to work anew," answered Daggett. "I see how it is ; you do not like the delay, and are thinking of Deacon Pratt and Oyster Pond. I do not blame you, Gar'-ner ; and shall never whisper a syllable ag'in you, or your people, if you sail for home this very a'ternoon, leaving me and mine to look out for ourselves. You've stood by us nobly thus far ; and I am too thankful for what you have done already, to ask for more."

Was Daggett sincere in these professions ? To a certain point he was ; while he was only artful on others. He wished to appear just and magnanimous ; while, in secret, it was his aim to work on the better feelings, as well as on the pride of Gardiner, and thus secure his services in getting his own schooner ready, as well as keep him in sight until a certain key had been examined, in the proceeds of which he conceived he had a share, as well as in those of Sealer's Land. Strange as it may seem, even in the strait in which he was now placed, with so desperate a prospect of ever getting his vessel home again, this man clung like a leech to the remotest chance of obtaining property. There is a bull-dog tenacity on this subject among a certain portion of the great American family—the god-like Anglo-Saxon—that certainly leads to great results in one respect; but which it is often painful to regard, and never agreeable to any but themselves, to be subject to. Of this school was Daggett, whom no dangers, no toil, no thoughts of a future, could divert from a purpose that was colored by gold. We do not mean to say that other nations are not just as mercenary; many are more so; those in particular that have long been corrupted by vicious governments. You may buy half a dozen Frenchmen, for instance, more easily than one Yankee; but let the last actually get his teeth into a dollar, and the muzzle of the ox fares worse in the jaws of the bull-dog.

Roswell was deeply reluctant to protract his stay in the group; but professional pride would have prevented him from deserting a consort under such circumstances, had not a better feeling inclined him to remain and assist Daggett. It is true the last had, in a manner, thrust himself on him, and the connection had been strangely continued down to that moment; but this he viewed as a dispensation of Providence, to which he was bound to submit. The result was a declaration of a design to stand by his companion as long as there was any hope of getting the injured craft home.

This decision pointed at once to the delay of another week. No time was lost in vain regrets, however; but all hands went to work to get the schooner into shallow water again, and to look further for the principal leak. Accurate trimming and pumping showed that a good deal of the water was already stopped out; but too much still entered to render it prudent to think of sailing until the injury was repaired. This time the schooner was not suffered to lie on her bilge at all. She was taken into water just deep enough to permit her to stand upright, sustained by shores, while the tide left two or three streaks dry forward; it being the intention to wind her, should the examination forward not be successful.

On stripping off the copper, it was found that a wood-end had indeed started, the inner edge of the plank having got as far from its bed as where the outer had been originally placed. This opened a crack through which a small stream of water must constantly pour, each hour rendering the leak more dangerous by loosening the oakum, and raising the plank from its curvature. Once discovered, however, nothing was easier than to repair the damage. It remained merely to butt-bolt anew the wood-end, drive a few spikes, calk, and replace the copper. Roswell, who was getting each moment more and more impatient to sail, was much vexed at a delay that really seemed unavoidable, as it arose from the particular position of the leak. Placed as it was, in a manner, between wind and water, it was not possible to work at it more than an hour each tide ; and the staging permitted but two hands to be busy at the same time. As a consequence of these embarrassments, no less than six tides came in and went out, before the stem was pronounced tight again. The schooner was then pumped out, and the vessel was once more taken into deep water. This time it was found that the patience and industry of our sealers were rewarded with success ; no leak of any account existing.

"She's as tight as a bottle with a sealed cork, Gar'ner," cried Daggett, a few hours after his craft was at her anchor, meeting his brother-master at his own gangway, and shaking hands with him cordially. "I owe much of this to you, as all on the Vineyard shall know, if we ever get home ag'in."

"I am rejoiced that it turns out so, Captain Daggett," was Roswell's reply ; "for to own the truth to you, the fortnight we have lost, or shall lose, before we get you stowed and ready to sail again, has made a great change in our weather. The days are shortening with frightful rapidity, and the great bay was actually covered with a skim of ice this very morning. The wind has sent in a sea that has broken it up ; but look about you, in the cove here—a boy might walk on that ice near the rocks."

"There'll be none of it left by night, and the two crews will fill me up in twenty-four hours. Keep a good heart, Gar'ner ; I'll take you clear of the bergs in the course of a week."

"I have less fear of the bergs now than of the new ice and the floes. The islands must have got pretty well to the northward by this time ; but each night gets colder,

18

and the fields seem to be setting back toward the group, instead of away from it."

Daggett cheered his companion by a good deal of confident talk ; but Roswell was heartily rejoiced when, at the end of four-and-twenty hours more, the Vineyard craft was pronounced entirely ready. It was near the close of the day, and Gardiner was for sailing, or moving at once : but Daggett offered several very reasonable objections. In the first place, there was no wind ; and Roswell's proposition to tow the schooners out into the middle of the bay, was met by the objection that the people had been hard at work for several days, and that they needed some rest. All that could be gained by moving the schooners then, was to get them outside of the skim of ice that now regularly formed every still night near the land, but which was as regularly broken and dispersed by the waves, as soon as the wind returned. Roswell, however, did not like the appearance of things ; and he determined to take his own craft outside, let Daggett do as he might. After discussing the matter in vain, therefore, and finding that the people of the other schooner had eaten their suppers and turned in, he called all hands, and made a short address to his own crew, leaving it to their discretion whether to man the boats or not. As Roswell had pointed out the perfect absence of wind, the smoothness of the water, and the appearances of a severe frost, or cold, for frost there was now, almost at mid-day, the men came reluctantly over to his view of the matter, and consented to work instead of sleeping. The toil, however, could be much lessened, by dividing the crew into the customary watches. All that Roswell aimed at was to get his schooner about a league from the cove, which would be taking her without a line drawn from cape to cape, the greatest danger of new ice being within the curvature of the crescent. This he thought might easily be done in the course of a few hours ; and should there come any wind, much sooner. On explaining this to the crew, the men were satisfied.

Roswell Gardiner felt as if a load were taken off his spirits, when his schooner was clear of the ground, and his mainsail was hoisted. A boat was got ahead, and the craft was slowly towed out of the cove, the canvas doing neither good nor harm. As the vessel passed that of Daggett, the last was on deck, the only person visible in the Vineyard craft. He wished his brother-master a good night, promising to be out as soon as there was any light next morning.

It would not be easy to imagine a more dreary scene than that in which Deacon Pratt's schooner moved out into the waters that separated the different islands of this remote and sterile group. Roswell could just discern the frowning mass of rocks that crowned the centre of Sealer's Land; and that was soon lost in the increasing obscurity. The cold was getting to be severe, and the men soon complained that ice was forming on the blades of their oars. Then it was that a thought occurred to our young mariner, which had hitherto escaped him. Of what use would it be for his vessel to be beyond the ice, if that of Daggett should be shut in the succeeding day? So sensible did he become to the importance of this idea, that he called in his boat, and pulled back into the cove, in order to make one more effort to persuade Daggett to follow him out.

Gardiner found all of the Vineyarders turned in, even to their officers. The fatigue they had lately undergone, united to the cold, rendered the berths very agreeable; and even Daggett begged his visitor would excuse him for not rising to receive his guest. Argument with a man thus circumstanced, and so disposed, was absolutely useless. After remaining a short time with Daggett, Roswell returned to his own schooner. As he pulled back, he ascertained that ice was fast making; and the boat actually cut its way through a thin skim, ere it reached the vessel.

Our hero was now greatly concerned lest he should be frozen in himself, ere he could get into the more open water of the bay. Fortunately a light air sprung up from the northward, and trimming his sails, Gardiner succeeded in carrying his craft to a point where the undulations of the ground-swell gave the assurance of her being outside the segment of the crescent. Then he brailed his foresail, hauled the jib-sheet over, lowered his gaff, and put his helm hard down. After this, all the men were permitted to seek their berths; the officers looking out for the craft in turns.

It wanted but an hour of day, when the second mate gave Roswell a call, according to orders. The young master found no wind, but an intensely cold morning, on going on deck. Ice had formed on every part of the rigging and sides of the schooner where water had touched them; though the stillness of the night, by preventing the spray from flying, was much in favor of the navigators in this respect. On thrusting a boat-hook down, Roswell ascertained that the bay around him had a skim of ice nearly an inch in thickness. This caused him great uneasiness ; and he waited with the greatest anxiety for the return of light, in order to observe the condition of Daggett.

Sure enough, when the day came out distinctly, it was seen that ice of sufficient thickness to bear men on it, covered the entire surface within the crescent. Daggett and his people were already at work on it, using the saw. They must have taken the alarm before the return of day ; for the schooner was not only free from the ground, but had been brought fully a cable's length without the cove. Gardiner watched the movements of Daggett and his crew with a glass for a short time, when he ordered all hands called. The cook was already in the galley, and a warm breakfast was soon prepared. After eating this, the two whale-boats were lowered, and Roswell and Hazard both rowed as far as the ice would permit them, when they walked the rest of the way to the imprisoned craft, taking with them most of their hands, together with the saw.

It was perhaps fortunate for Daggett that it soon began to blow fresh from the northward, sending into the bay a considerable sea, which soon broke up the ice, and enabled the Vineyard craft to force her way through the fragments, and join her consort about noon.

Glad enough was Roswell to regain his own vessel ; and he made sail on a wind, determined to beat out of the narrow waters at every hazard, the experience of that night having told him that they had remained in the cove too long. Daggett followed willingly, but not like a man who had escaped by the skin of his teeth, from wintering near the antarctic circle.

CHAPTER XXII.

"Beside the Moldau's rushing stream,
   With the wan moon overhead,
   There stood, as in an awful dream,
   The army of the dead."—LONGFELLOW.

MOST of our readers will understand what was meant by Mary Pratt's "inclination of the earth's axis to the plane of its orbit ;" but as there may be a few who do not, and as the consequences of this great physical fact are materially connected with the succeeding events of the narrative, we propose to give such a homely explanation of the phenomenon as we humbly trust will render it clear to the most clouded mind. The orbit of the earth is the path which it follows in space in its annual revolution around the sun. To a planet there is no up or down, except as ascent and descent are estimated from and toward itself. In all other respects it floats in vacuum, or what is so nearly so as to be thus termed. Now let the uninstructed reader imagine a large circular table, with a light on its surface, and near to its centre. The light shall represent the sun, the outer edge of the circle of the table the earth's orbit, and its surface the plane of that orbit. In nature there is no such thing as a plane at all, the space within the orbit being vacant; but the surface of the table gives a distinct notion of the general position of the earth as it travels around the sun. It is scarcely necessary to say that the axis of the earth is an imaginary line drawn through the planet, from one pole to the other; the name being derived from the supposition that our daily revolution is made on this axis.

Now the first thing that the student is to fix in his mind, in order to comprehend the phenomenon of the seasons, is the leading fact that the earth does not change its attitude in space, if we may so express it, when it changes its position. If the axis were *perpendicular* to the plane of the orbit, this circumstance would not affect the temperature, as the simplest experiment will show. Putting the equator of a globe on the outer edge of the table, and holding it perfectly *upright*, causing it to turn on its axis as it passes round the circle, it would be found that the light from the centre of the table would illumine just one-half of the globe, at all times and in all positions, cutting the two poles. Did this movement correspond with that of nature, the days and nights would be always of the same length, and there would be no changes of the seasons, the warmest weather being nearest to the equator, and the cold increasing as the poles were approached. Nowhere, however, would the cold be so intense as it now is, nor would the heat be so great as at present, except at or quite near to the equator. The first fact would be owing to the regular return of the sun, once in twenty-four hours; the last to the oblique manner in which its rays struck this orb, in all places but near its centre.

But the globe ought not to be made to move around the table with its axis perpendicular to its surface, or to the

"plane of the earth's orbit."   In point of fact, the earth is
inclined to this plane, and the globe should be placed at a
corresponding inclination.   Let the globe be brought to
the edge of the table, at its south side, and with its upper
or north pole inclining to the sun, and then commence the
circuit, taking care always to keep this north pole of the
globe pointing in the same direction, or to keep the globe
itself in what we have termed a fixed attitude.   As one
half of the globe must always be in light, and the other
half in darkness, this inclination from the perpendicular
will bring the circle of light some distance beyond the
north pole, when the globe is due-south from the light, and
will leave an equal space around the opposite pole without
any light at all, or any light directly received.   Now it is
that what we have termed the *fixed attitude* of the globe be-
gins to tell.   If the north pole inclined toward the orbit
facing the rim of the table, the light would still cut the
poles, the days and nights would still be equal, and there
would be no changes in the seasons, though there would
be a rival revolution of the globe by causing it to turn
once a year, shifting the poles end for end.   The inclination being to the surface of the table, or to the *plane* of the
orbit, the phenomena that are known to exist are a consequence.   Thus it is that the change in the seasons is as
much owing to the fixed attitude of the earth in space, as
we have chosen to term its polar directions, as to the inclination of its axis.   Neither would produce the phenomena without the assistance of the other, as our experiment
with the table will show.

Place, then, the globe at the south side of the rim of the
table, with its axis inclining toward its surface, and its
poles always pointing in the same general direction, not
following the circuit of the orbit, and set it in motion
toward the east, revolving rapidly on its axis as it moves.
While directly south of the light, it would be found that
the north pole would be illuminated, while no revolution
on the axis would bring the south pole within the circle
of the light.   This is when a line drawn from the axis of
the globe would cut the lamp, were the inclination brought
as low as the surface of the table.   Next set the globe in
motion, following the rim of the table, and proceeding to
the east or right hand, keeping its axis always looking in
the same general direction, or in an attitude that would
be parallel to a north and south line drawn through the
sun, were the inclination as low as the surface of the

table. This movement would be, in one sense, sideways, the circle of light gradually lessening around the north pole, and extending toward the south, as the globe proceeded east and north, diminishing the length of the days in the northern hemisphere, and increasing them in the southern. When at east, the most direct rays of the light would fall on the equator, and the light would cut the two poles, rendering the days and nights equal. As the globe moved north, the circle of light would be found to increase around the *south* pole, while none at all touched the *north*. When on the north side of the table, the *northern* pole of the globe would incline so far from the sun as to leave a space around it in shadow that would be of precisely the same size as had been the space of light when it was placed on the opposite side of the table. Going round the circle west, the same phenomena would be seen, until coming directly south of the lamp, the north pole would again come into light altogether, and the south equally into shadow.

Owing to this very simple but very wonderful provision of divine power and wisdom, this earth enjoys the relief of the changes in the seasons, as well as the variations in the length of the days. For one half the year, or from equinox to equinox, from the time when the globe is at a due-west point of the table until it reaches the east, the north pole would always receive the light, in a circle around it, that would gradually increase and diminish ; and for the other half, the same would be true of the other hemisphere. Of course there is a precise point on the earth where this polar illumination ceases. The shape of the illuminated part is circular ; and placing the point of a pencil on the globe at the extremest spot on the circle, holding it there while the globe is turned on its axis, the lines made would just include the portions of the earth around the globe that thus receives the rays of the sun at midsummer. These lines compose what are termed the arctic and antarctic circles, with the last of which our legend has now a most serious connection. After all, we are by no means certain that we have made our meaning as obvious as we could wish, it being very difficult to explain phenomena of this nature clearly, without actually experimenting.

It is usual to say that there are six months day and six months night in the polar basins. This is true, literally, at the poles only ; but, approximately, it is true as a whole. We apprehend that few persons—none, perhaps, but those

who are in habits of study—form correct notions of the
extent of what may be termed the icy seas. As the polar
circles are in 23° 28″, a line drawn through the south pole,
for instance, commencing on one side of the earth at the
antarctic circle, and extending to the other, would traverse
a distance materially exceeding that between New York
and Lisbon.   This would make those frozen regions cover
a portion of this globe that is almost as large as the whole
of the Atlantic Ocean, as far south as the equator. Any
one can imagine what must be the influence of frost over
so vast a surface, in reproducing itself, since the presence
of icebergs is thought to affect our climate, when many of
them drift far south in summer.   As power produces
power, riches wealth, so does cold produce cold.   Fill, then,
in a certain degree, a space as large as the North Atlantic
Ocean with ice in all its varieties, fixed, mountain and
field, berg and floe, and one may get a tolerably accurate
notion of the severity of its winters, when the sun is
scarce seen above the horizon at all, and then only to shed
its rays so obliquely as to be little better than a chill-look-
ing orb of light, placed in the heavens simply to divide
the day from the night.

This, then, was the region that Roswell Gardiner was so
very anxious to leave ; the winter he so much dreaded.
Mary Pratt was before him, to say nothing of his duty to
the deacon ; while behind him was the vast polar ocean
just described, about to be veiled in the freezing obscurity
of its long and gloomy twilight, if not of absolute night.
No wonder, therefore, that when he trimmed his sails that
evening, to beat out of the great bay, it was done with the
earnestness with which we all perform duties of the highest
import, when they are known to affect our well-being,
visibly and directly.

"Keep her a good full, Mr. Hazard," said Roswell, as he
was leaving the deck, to take the first sleep in which he
had indulged for four-and-twenty hours ; "and let her go
through the water. We are behind our time, and must
keep in motion. Give me a call if anything like ice appears in a serious way."

Hazard "ay-ay'd" this order, as usual, buttoned his pea-
jacket tighter than ever, and saw his young superior—the
transcendental delicacy of the day is causing the difference in rank to be termed "*senior* and *junior*"—but Hazard
saw *his* superior go below with a feeling allied to envy, so
heavy were his eyelids with the want of rest.   Stimson

was in the first-mate's watch, and the latter approached that old sea-dog with a wish to keep himself awake by conversing.

"You seem as wide awake, king Stephen," the mate remarked, "as if you never felt drowsy!"

"This is not a part of the world for hammocks and berths, Mr. Hazard," was the reply. "I can get along, and must get along, with a quarter part of the sleep in these seas as would sarve me in a low latitude."

"And I feel as if I wanted all I can get. Them fellows look up well into our wake, Stephen."

"They do, indeed, sir, and they ought to do it; for we have been longer than is for our good in their'n."

"Well, now we have got a fresh start, I hope we may make a clear run of it. I saw no ice worth speaking of to the nor'ard here, before we made sail."

"Because you see'd none, Mr. Hazard, is no proof there is none. Floe-ice can't be seen at any great distance, though its blink may. But it seems to me, it's all blink in these here seas!"

"There you're quite right, Stephen; for turn which way you will, the horizon has a show of that sort——"

"Starboard!" called out the lookout forward—"keep her away—keep her away—there is ice ahead."

"Ice in here!" exclaimed Hazard, springing forward—"That is more than we bargained for! Where away is your ice, Smith?"

"Off here, sir, on our weather bow—and a mortal big field of it—jist sich a chap as nipped the Vineyard Lion, when she first came in to join us. Sich a fellow as that would take the sap out of our bends, as a squeezer takes the juice from a lemon!"

Smith was a carpenter by trade, which was probably the reason why he introduced this figure. Hazard saw the ice with regret, for he had hoped to work the schooner fairly out to sea in his watch; but the field was getting down through the passage in a way that threatened to cut off the exit of the two schooners from the bay. Daggett kept close in his wake, a proof that this experienced navigator in such waters saw no means to turn farther to windward. As the wind was now abeam, both vessels drove rapidly ahead; and in half an hour the northern point of the land they had so lately left came into view close aboard of them. Just then the moon rose, and objects became more clearly visible.

Hazard hailed the Vineyard Lion and demanded what was to be done. It was possible, by hauling close on a wind, to pass the cape a short distance to windward of it, and seemingly thus clear the floe. Unless this were done both vessels would be compelled to wear, and run for the southern passage, which would carry them many miles to leeward, and might place them a long distance on the wrong side of the group.

"Is Captain Gar'ner on deck?" asked Daggett, who had now drawn close up on the lee-quarter of his consort, Hazard having brailed his foresail and laid his topsail sharp aback, to enable him to do so—"If he isn't, I'd advise you to give him a call at once."

This was done immediately; and while it was doing the Vineyard Lion swept past the Oyster Pond schooner. Roswell announced his presence on deck just as the other vessel cleared his bows.

"There's no time to consult, Gar'ner," answered Daggett. "There's our road before us. Go through it we must, or stay where we are until that field-ice gives us a jam down yonder in the crescent. I will lead, and you can follow as soon as your eyes are open."

One glance let Roswell into the secret of his situation. He liked it little, but he did not hesitate.

"Fill the topsail and haul aft the foresheet," were the quiet orders that proclaimed what he intended to do.

Both vessels stood on. By some secret process every man on board the two craft became aware of what was going on, and appeared on deck. All hands were not called, nor was there any particular noise to attract attention; but the word had been whispered below that there was a great risk to run. A risk it was, of a verity! It was necessary to stand close along that iron-bound coast where the seals had so lately resorted, for a distance of several miles. The wind would not admit of the schooners steering much more than a cable's length from the rocks for quite a league; after which the shore trended to the southward, and a little sea-room would be gained. But on those rocks the waves were then beating heavily, and their bellowings as they rolled into the cavities were at almost all times terrific. There was some relief, however, in the knowledge obtained of the shore, by having frequently passed up and down it in the boats. It was known that the water was deep close to the visible rocks, and that there was no danger so long as a vessel could keep off them.

No one spoke. Every eye was strained to discern objects ahead, or was looking astern to trace the expected collision between the ice-floe and the low promontory of the cape. The ear soon gave notice that this meeting had already taken place; for the frightful sound that attended the cracking and rending of the field might have been heard fully a league. Now it was that each schooner did her best. Yards were braced up, sheets flattened, and the helm tended. The close proximity of the rocks on the one side, and the secret presentiment of there being more field-ice on the other, kept every one wide awake. The two masters, in particular, were all eyes and ears. It was getting to be very cold; and the sort of shelter aloft that goes by the quaint name of "crow's-nest," had been fitted up in each vessel. A mate was now sent into each, to ascertain what might be discovered to windward. Almost at the same instant these young seamen hailed their respective decks, and gave notice that a wide field was coming in upon them, and must eventually crush them unless avoided. This startling intelligence reached the two commanders in the very same moment. The emergency demanded decision, and each man acted for himself. Roswell ordered his helm put *down*, and his schooner *tacked*. The water was not rough enough to prevent the success of the manœuvre. On the other hand, Daggett kept a rap full, and *stood on*. Roswell manifested the most judgment and seamanship. He was now far enough from the cape to beat to windward; and, by going nearer to the enemy, he might always run along its southern boundary, profit by any opening, and would be by as much as he could thus gain to windward of the coast. Daggett had one advantage. By standing on, in the event of a return becoming necessary, he would gain in time. In ten minutes the two schooners were a mile asunder. We shall first follow that of Roswell Gardiner's in his attempt to escape.

The first floe, which was ripping and tearing one of its angles into fragments, as it came grinding down on the cape, soon compelled the vessel to tack. Making short reaches, Roswell ere long found himself fully a mile to windward of the rocks, and sufficiently near to the new floe to discern its shape, drift, and general character. Its eastern end had lodged upon the field that first came in, and was adding to the vast momentum with which that enormous floe was pressing down upon the cape. Large as was the first visitor to the bay, this was of at least twice if not of thrice its dimensions. What gave Roswell the most concern was the great distance that this field extended to the westward. He went up into the crow's-nest himself, and aided by the light of a most brilliant moon, and a sky without a cloud, he could perceive the blink of ice in that direction, as he fancied, for fully two leagues. What was unusual, perhaps, at that early season of the year, these floes did not consist of a vast collection of numberless cakes of ice ; but the whole field, so far as could then be ascertained, was firm and united. The nights were now so cold that ice made fast wherever there was water ; and it occurred to our young master that, possibly, fragments that had once been separated and broken by the waves, might have become reunited by the agency of the frost. Roswell descended from the crow's-nest half chilled by a cutting wind, though it blew from a warm quarter. Summoning his mates, he asked their advice.

"It seems to me, Captain Gar'ner," Hazard replied, "there's very little choice. Here we are, so far as I can make it out, embayed, and we have only to box about until daylight comes, when some chance may turn up to help us. If so, we must turn it to account; if not, we must make up our minds to winter here."

This was coolly and calmly said ; though it was clear enough that Hazard was quite in earnest.

"You forget there may be an open passage to the westward, Mr. Hazard," Roswell rejoined, "and that we may yet pass out to sea by it. Captain Daggett is already out of sight in the western board, and we may do well to stand on after him."

"Ay, ay, sir—I know all that, Captain Gar'ner, and it may be as you say ; but when I was aloft, half an hour since, if there wasn't the blink of ice in that direction, quite round to the back of the island, there wasn't the blink of ice nowhere hereabouts. I'm used to the sight of it, and can't well be mistaken."

"There is always ice on that side of the land, Hazard, and you may have seen the blink of the bergs which have hugged the cliffs in that quarter all summer. Still that is not proving we shall find no outlet. This craft can go through a very small passage, and we must take care and find one in proper time. Wintering here is out of the question. A *hundred* reasons tell us not to think of such a thing, besides the interests of our owners. We are walking along this floe pretty fast, though I think the vessel is too much by the head; don't it strike you so, Hazard?"

"Lord, sir, it's nothing but the ice that has made, and is making for'ard! Before we got so near the field as to find a better lee, the little lipper that came athwart our bows froze almost as soon as it wet us. I do suppose, sir, there are now several tons of ice on our bows, counting from channel to channel, forward."

On an examination this proved to be true, and the knowledge of the circumstance did not at all contribute to Gardiner's feeling of security. He saw there was no time to be lost, and he crowded sail with a view of forcing the vessel past the dangers if possible, and of getting her into a milder climate. But even a fast-sailing schooner will scarcely equal our wishes under such circumstances. There was no doubt that the Sea Lion's speed was getting to be affected by the manner in which her bows were weighed down by ice, in addition to the discomfort produced by cold, damp, and the presence of a slippery substance on the deck and rigging. Fortunately there was not much spray flying, or matters would have been much worse. As it was, they were bad enough, and very ominous of future evil.

While the Sea Lion of Oyster Pond was running along the margin of the ice in the manner just described, and after the blink to the westward had changed to a visible field, making it very uncertain whether any egress was to be found in that quarter or not, an opening suddenly appeared trending to the northward, and sufficiently wide, as Roswell thought, to enable him to beat through it. Putting his helm down, his schooner came heavily round, and was filled on a course that soon carried her half a mile into this passage. At first, everything seemed propitious, the channel rather opening than otherwise, while the course was such—north-northwest—as enabled the vessel to make very long legs on one tack, and that the best. After going about four or five times, however, all these flattering symptoms suddenly changed, by the passage terminating in a *cul de sac*. Almost at the same instant the ice closed rapidly in the schooner's wake. An effort was made to run back, but it failed in consequence of an enormous floe's turning on its centre having met resistance from a field closer in, that was, in its turn, stopped by the rocks. Roswell saw at once that nothing could be done at the moment. He took in all his canvas, as well as the frozen

cloth could be handled, got out ice-anchors and hauled
his vessel into a species of cove where there would be the
least danger of a nip, should the fields continue to close.

All this time Daggett was as busy as a bee. He rounded
the headland, and flattered himself that he was about to
slip past all the rocks and get out into open water, when
the vast fields of which the blink had been seen even by
those in the other vessels, suddenly stretched themselves
across his course in a way that set at defiance all attempts
to go any further in that direction. Daggett wore round
and endeavored to return. This was by no means so easy
as it was to go down before the wind, and his bows were
also much encumbered with ice ; more so, indeed, than
those of the other schooner. Once or twice his craft
missed stays in consequence of getting so much by the
head, and it was deemed necessary to heave-to and take
to the axes. A great deal of extra and cumbrous weight
was gotten rid of, but an hour of most precious time was
lost.

By the time Daggett was ready to make sail again, he
found his return round the headland was entirely cut off,
by the field's having come in absolute contact with the
rocks.

It was now midnight, and the men on board both vessels
required rest. A watch was set in each, and most of the
people were permitted to turn in. Of course, proper
look-outs were had, but the light of the moon was not
sufficiently distinct to render it safe to make any final
efforts under its favor. No great alarm was felt, there
being nothing unusual in the vessel's being embayed in
the ice ; and so long as she was not nipped or pressed
upon by actual contact, the position was thought safe
rather than the reverse. It was desirable, moreover, for
the schooners to communicate with each other ; for some
advantage might be known to one of the masters that was
concealed by distance from his companion. Without concert, therefore, Roswell and Daggett came to the same
general conclusions, and waited patiently.

The day came at last, cold and dreary, though not altogether without the relief of an air that blew from regions
far warmer than the ocean over which it was now travelling.
Then the two schooners became visible from each other,
and Roswell saw the jeopardy of Daggett, and Daggett saw
the jeopardy of Roswell. The vessels were little more
than a mile apart, but the situation of the Vineyard Lion

was much the most critical. She had made fast to the floe, but her support itself was in a steady and most imposing motion. As soon as Roswell saw the manner in which his consort was surrounded, and the very threatening aspect of the danger that pressed upon him, his first impulse was to hasten to him, with a party of his own people, to offer any assistance he could give. After looking at the ice immediately around his own craft, where all seemed to be right, he called over the names of six of his men, ordered them to eat a warm breakfast, and to prepare to accompany him.

In twenty minutes, Roswell was leading his little party across the ice, each man carrying an axe, or some other implement that it was supposed might be of use. It was by no means difficult to proceed; for the surface of the floe, one seemingly more than a league in extent, was quite smooth, and the snow on it was crusted to a strength that would have borne a team.

"The water between the ice and the rocks is a much narrower strip than I had thought," said Roswell, to his constant attendant Stimson. "Here it does not appear to be a hundred yards in width."

"Nor is it, sir—whew—this trotting in so cold a climate makes a man puff like a whale blowing—but, Captain Gar'-ner, that schooner will be cut in two before we can get to her. Look, sir; the floe has reached the rocks already, quite near her, and it does not stop the drift at all, seemingly."

Roswell made no reply; the state of the Vineyard Lion did appear to be much more critical than he had previously imagined. Until he came nearer to the land, he had formed no notion of the steady power with which the field was setting down on the rocks on which the broken fragments were now creeping like creatures endowed with life. Occasionally, there would be loud disruptions, and the movement of the floe would become more rapid; then, again, a sort of pause would succeed, and for a moment the approaching party felt a gleam of hope. But all expectations of this sort were doomed to be disappointed.

"Look, sir," exclaimed Stimson—"she went down afore it twenty fathoms at that one set. She must be awful near the rocks, sir."

All the men now stopped. They knew they were powerless; and intense anxiety rendered them averse to move. Attention appeared to interfere with their walking on the

ice ; and each held his breath in expectation. They saw
that the schooner, then less than a cable's length from
them, was close to the rocks ; and the next shock, if anything like the last, must overwhelm her. To their astonishment, instead of being nipped, the schooner rose by a
stately movement that was not without grandeur, upheld
by broken cakes that had got beneath her bottom, and
fairly reached the shelf of rocks almost unharmed. Not
a man had left her ; but there she was, placed on the
shore, some twenty feet above the surface of the sea, on
rocks worn smooth by the action of the waves ! Had the
season been propitious, and did the injury stop here, it
might have been possible to get the craft into the water
again, and still carry her to America.

But the floe was not yet arrested. Cake succeeded cake,
one riding over another, until a wall of ice rose along the
shore, that Roswell and his companions, with all their
activity and courage, had great difficulty in crossing.
They succeeded in getting over it, however ; but when
they reached the unfortunate schooner, she was literally
buried. The masts were broken, the sails torn, rigging
scattered, and sides stove. The Sea Lion of Martha's Vineyard was a worthless wreck—worthless as to all purposes
but that of being converted into materials for a smaller
craft, or to be used as fuel.

All this had been done in ten minutes ! Then it was
that the vast superiority of nature over the resources of
man made itself apparent. The people of the two vessels
stood aghast with this sad picture of their own insignificance before their eyes. The crew of the wreck, it is true,
had escaped without difficulty ; the movement having
been as slow and steady as it was irresistible. But there
they were, in the clothes they had on, with all their effects
buried under piles of ice that were already thirty or forty
feet in height.

"She looks as if she was built there, Gar'ner !" Daggett
coolly observed, as he stood regarding the scene with eyes
as intently riveted on the wreck as human organs were
ever fixed on any object. "Had a man told me this *could*
happen, I would not have believed him !"

"Had she been a three-decker, this ice would have
treated her in the same way. There is a force in such a
field that walls of stone could not withstand."

"Captain Gar'ner—Captain Gar'ner," called out Stimson, hastily ; "we'd better go back, sir ; our own craft is

in danger. She is drifting fast in toward the cape, and
may reach it afore we can get to her !"

Sure enough, it was so. In one of the changes that are
so unaccountable among the ice, the floe had taken a sudden and powerful direction toward the entrance of the
Great Bay. It was probably owing to the circumstance
that the inner field had forced its way past the cape, and
made room for its neighbor to follow. A few of Daggett's people, with Daggett himself, remained to see what
might yet be saved from the wreck ; but all the rest of the
men started for the cape, toward which the Oyster Pond
craft was now directly setting. The distance was less than
a league ; and, as yet, there was not much snow on the
rocks. By taking an upper shelf, it was possible to make
pretty good progress ; and such was the manner of Roswell's present march.

It was an extraordinary sight to see the coast along
which our party was hastening, just at that moment. As
the cakes of ice were broken from the field, they were
driven upward by the vast pressure from without, and the
whole line of the shore seemed as if alive with creatures
that were issuing from the ocean to clamber on the rocks.
Roswell had often seen that very coast peopled with seals,
as it now appeared to be in activity with fragments of ice,
that were writhing, and turning, and rising, one upon
another, as if possessed of the vital principle.

In half an hour Roswell and his party reached the
house. The schooner was then less than half a mile from
the spot, still setting in, along with the outer field, but not
nipped. So far from being in danger of such a calamity,
the little basin in which she lay had expanded, instead of
closing ; and it would have been possible to handle a
quick-working craft in it, under her canvas. An exit, however, was quite out of the question ; there being no sign
of any passage to or from that icy dock. There the craft
still lay, anchored to the weather-floe, while the portion of
her crew which remained on board was as anxiously watching the coast as those who were on the coast watched her.
At first, Roswell gave his schooner up ; but on closer examination found reason to hope that she might pass the
rocks, and enter the inner, rather than the Great Bay.

19

CHAPTER XXIII.

" To prayer ;—for the glorious sun is gone,
    And the gathering darkness of night comes on ;
    Like a curtain from God's kind hand it flows,
    To shade the couch where his children repose.
    Then kneel, while the watching stars are bright,
    And give your last thoughts to the guardian of night."—WARE.

DESOLATE, indeed, and nearly devoid of hope, had the situation of our sealers now become. It was midday, and it was freezing everywhere in the shade. A bright genial sun was shedding its glorious rays on the icy panorama ; but it was so obliquely as to be of hardly any use in dispelling the frosts. Far as the eye could see, even from the elevation of the cape, there was nothing but ice, with the exception of that part of the Great Bay into which the floe had not yet penetrated. To the southward there stood clustering around the passage a line of gigantic bergs, placed like sentinels, as if purposely to stop all egress in that direction. The water had lost its motion in the shift of wind, and new ice had formed over the whole bay, as was evident by a white sparkling line that preceded the irresistible march of the floe.

As Roswell gazed on this scene, serious doubts darkened his mind as to his escaping from this frozen chain until the return of another summer. It is true that a south wind might possibly produce a change, and carry away the blockading mass ; but every moment rendered this so much the less probable. Winter, or what would be deemed winter in most regions, was already setting in ; and should the ice really become stationary in and around the group, all hope of its moving must vanish for the next eight months.

Daggett reached the house about an hour before sunset. He had succeeded in cutting a passage through the ice as far as the cabin-door of his unfortunate schooner, when there was no difficulty in descending into the interior parts of the vessel. The whole party came in staggering under heavy loads. Pretty much as a matter of course, each man brought his own effects. Clothes, tobacco, rum, small-stores, bedding, quadrants, and similar property, was that first attended to. At that moment, little was thought of the skins and oil. The cargo was neglected, while the minor articles had been eagerly sought.

Roswell was on board his own schooner, now again in dangerous proximity to the cape. She was steadily setting in when Daggett rejoined him. The crew of the lost vessel remained in the house, where they lighted a fire and deposited their goods, returning to the wreck for another load, taking the double sets of wheels along with them. When the two masters met they conferred together earnestly, receiving into their councils such of the officers as were on board. The security of the remaining vessel was now all-important; and it was not to be concealed that she was in imminent jeopardy. The course taken by the floe was directly toward the most rugged part of Cape Hazard; and the rate of the movement such as to threaten a very speedy termination of the matter. There was one circumstance, however, and only that one, which offered a single chance to escape. The opening around the schooner still existed in part, about half of it having been lost in the collision with the outermost point of the rocks. It was this species of vacuum that, by removing all resistance at that particular spot, indeed, which had given the field its most dangerous cant, turning the movement of the vessel toward the rocks. The chance, therefore, existed in the possibility—and it was little more than a bare possibility—of moving the schooner in that small area of open water, and of taking her far enough south to clear the most southern extremity of the wall of stone that protected the cove. As yet, this open water did not extend far enough to admit of the schooner's being taken to the point in question; but it was slowly tending in that direction, and did not the basin close altogether ere that desirable object was achieved, the vessel might yet be saved. In order, however, to do this, it would be necessary to cut a sort of dock or slip in the ice of the cove, into which the craft might shoot, as a place of refuge. Once within the cove, fairly behind the point of the rocks, there would be perfect safety; if suffered to drift to the southward of that shelter, this schooner would probably be lost like her consort, and very much in the same manner.

Gardiner now sent a gang of hands to the desired point, armed with saws, and the slip was commenced. The ice in the cove was still only two or three inches thick, and the work went bravely on. Instead of satisfying himself with cutting a passage merely behind the point of rock, Hazard opened one quite up into the cove, to the precise place where the schooner had so long been at anchor.

Just as the sun was setting, the crisis arrived. So heavy had been the movement toward the rock, that Roswell saw he could delay no longer. Were he to continue where he was, a projection on the cape would prevent his passage to the entrance of the cove ; he would be shut in, and he might be certain that the Sea Lion would be crushed if the floe pressed home upon the shore. The ice-anchors were cut out accordingly, the jib was hoisted, and the schooner wore short round on her heel. The space between the floe and the projection in the rocks just named did not now exceed a hundred feet ; and it was lessening fast. Much more room existed on each side of this particular excrescence in the rugged coast, the space north being still considerable, while that to the southward might be a hundred yards in width ; the former of these areas being owing to the form of the basin, and the latter to the shape of the shore.

In the first of the basins named the schooner wore short round on her heel, her foresail being set to help her. A breathless moment passed as she ran down toward the narrow strait. It was quickly reached, and that none too soon ; the opening now not exceeding sixty feet. The yards of the vessel almost brushed the rocks in passing ; but she went clear. As soon as in the lower basin, as one might call it, the jib and foresail were taken in, and the head of the mainsail was got on the craft. This helped her to luff up toward the slip, which she reached under sufficient headway fairly to enter it. Lines were thrown to the people on the ice, who soon hauled the schooner up to the head of her frozen dock. Three cheers broke spontaneously out of the throats of the men, as they thus achieved the step which assured them of the safety of the vessel so far as the ice was concerned ! In this way do we estimate our advantages and disadvantages by comparison. In the abstract, the situation of the sealers was still sufficiently painful ; though compared with what it would have been with the other schooner wrecked, it was security itself.

By this time it was quite dark ; and a day of excitement and fatigue required a night of rest. After supping, the men turned in ; the Vineyarders mostly in the house, where they occupied their old bunks. When the moon rose, the party from the wreck arrived with their carts well loaded, and themselves half frozen, notwithstanding their toil. In a short time all were buried in sleep.

When Roswell Gardiner came on deck next morning

his first glance told him how little was the chance of his party's returning north that season. The strange floe had driven into the Great Bay, completely covering its surface, lining the shores far and near with broken and glittering cakes of ice; and, as it were, hermetically sealing the place against all egress. New ice, an inch or two thick, or even six or eight inches thick, might have been sawed through, and a passage cut even for a league, should it be necessary. Such things were sometimes done, and great as would have been the toil, our sealers would have attempted it, in preference to running the risk of passing a winter in that region. But almost desperate as would have been even that source of refuge, the party was completely cut off from its possession. To think of sawing through ice as thick as that of the floe, for any material distance, would be like a project to tunnel the Alps.

Melancholy was the meeting between Roswell and Daggett that morning. The former was too manly and generous to indulge in reproaches, else might he well have told the last that all this was owing to him. There is a singular propensity in us all to throw the burden of our own blunders on the shoulders of other folk. Roswell had a little of this weakness, overlooking the fact that he was his own master; and as he had come to the group by himself, he ought to have left it in the same manner, as soon as his own particular task was accomplished. But Roswell did not see this quite as distinctly as he saw the fact that Daggett's detentions and indirect appeals to his better feelings had involved him in all these difficulties. Still, while thus he felt, he made no complaint.

All hope of getting north that season now depended on the field-ice drifting away from the Great Bay before it got fairly frozen in. So jammed and crammed with it did every part of the bay appear to be, however, that little could be expected from that source of relief. This Daggett admitted in the conversation he held with Roswell, as soon as the latter joined him on the rocky terrace beneath the house.

"The wisest thing we can do, then," replied our hero, "will be to make as early preparations as possible to meet the winter. If we are to remain here, a day gained now will be worth a week a month hence. If we should happily escape, the labor thus expended will not kill us."

"Quite true—very much as you say, certainly," answered Daggett, musing. "I was thinking as you came ashore,

Gar'ner, if a lucky turn might not be made in this wise :
I have a good many skins in the wreck, you see, and you
have a good deal of ile in your hold—now, by starting
some of that ile, and pumping it out, and shooking the
casks, room might be made aboard of you for all my skins.
I think we could run all of the last over on them wheels in
the course of a week."

"Captain Daggett, it is by yielding so much to your skins
that we have got into all this trouble."

"Skins, measure for measure, in the way of tonnage,
will bring a great deal more than ile."

Roswell smiled, and muttered something to himself, a
little bitterly. He was thinking of the grievous disappointment and prolonged anxiety that, it pained him to
believe, Mary would feel at his failure to return home at
the appointed time ; though it would probably have pained
him more to believe she would not thus be disappointed
and anxious. Here his displeasure, or its manifestation,
ceased ; and the young man turned his thoughts on the
present necessities of his situation.

Daggett appearing very earnest on the subject of removing his skins before the snows came to impede the path,
Roswell could urge no objections that would be likely to
prevail ; but his acquiescence was obtained by means of a
hint from Stimson, who by this time had gained his officer's ear.

"Let him do it, Captain Gar'ner," said the boat-steerer,
in an aside, speaking respectfully, but earnestly "He'll
never stow 'em in our hold, this season at least ; but they'll
make excellent filling-in for the sides of this hut."

"You think then, Stephen, that we are likely to pass the
winter here ?"

"We are in the hands of Divine Providence, sir, which
will do with us as seems the best in the eyes of never-fail-
ing wisdom. At all events, Captain Gar'ner, I think 'twill
be safest to act at once as if we had the winter afore us.
In my judgment, this house might be made a good deal
more comfortable for us all, in such a case, than our craft ;
for we should not only have more room, but might have
as many fires as we want, and more than we can find fuel
for."

"Ay, there's the difficulty, Stephen. Where are we to
find wood, throughout a polar winter, for even one fire ?"

"We must be saving, sir, and thoughtful, and keep ourselves warm as much as we can by exercise. I have had a

taste of this once, in a small way, already ; and know what ought to be done, in many partic'lars. In the first place, the men must keep themselves as clean as water will make them—dirt is a great helper of cold—and the water must be just as frosty as human natur' can bear it. This will set everything into actyve movement inside, and bring out warmth from the heart, as it might be. That's my principle of keeping warm, Captain Gar'ner."

"I dare say it may be a pretty good one, Stephen," answered Roswell, "and we'll bear it in mind. As for stoves we are well enough off, for there is one in the house, and a good large one it is ; then, there is a stove in each cabin, and there are the two cabooses. If we had fuel for them all, I should feel no concern on the score of warmth."

"Ther's the wrack, sir. By cutting her up at once we should get wood enough, in my judgment, to see it out."

Roswell made no reply ; but he looked intently at the boat-steerer for half a minute. The idea was new to him ; and the more he thought on the subject, the greater was the confidence it gave him in the result. Daggett, he well knew, would not consent to the mutilation of his schooner, wreck as it was, so long as the most remote hope existed of getting her again into the water. The tenacity with which this man clung to property was like that which is imputed to the life of the cat ; and it was idle to expect any concessions from him on a subject like that. Nevertheless, necessity is a hard master ; and if the question were narrowed down to one of burning the materials of a vessel that was in the water, and in good condition, and of burning those of one that was out of the water, with holes cut through her bottom in several places, and otherwise so situated as to render repairs extremely difficult, if not impossible, even Daggett would be compelled to submit to circumstances.

It was accordingly suggested to the people of the Vineyard Lion that they could do no better than to begin at once to remove everything they could come at, and which could be transported from the wreck to the house. As there was little to do on board the vessel afloat, her crew cheerfully offered to assist in this labor. The days were shortening sensibly and fast, and no time was to be lost, the distance being so great as to make two trips a day a matter of great labor. No sooner was the plan adopted, therefore, than steps were taken to set about its execution.

It is unnecessary for us to dwell minutely on everything that occurred during the succeeding week or ten days. The wind shifted to southwest the very day that the Sea Lion got back into her little harbor ; and this seemed to put a sudden check on the pressure of the vast floe. Nevertheless, there was no counter-movement, the ice remaining in the Great Bay seemingly as firmly fastened as if it had originally been made there. Notwithstanding this shift of the wind to a cold point of the compass, the thermometer rose, and it thawed freely about the middle of the day, in all places to which the rays of the sun had access. This enabled the men to work with more comfort than they could have done in the excessively severe weather, as it was found that respiration became difficult when it was so very cold.

Access was now obtained to the wreck by cutting a regular passage to the main hatch through the ice. The schooner stood nearly upright, sustained by fragments of the floe ; and there were extensive caverns all around her, produced by the random manner in which the cakes had come up out of their proper element like so many living things. Among these caverns one might have wandered for miles without once coming out into the open air, though they were cold and cheerless, and had little to attract the adventurer after the novelty was abated.

In rising from the water the schooner had been roughly treated, but once sustained by the ice her transit had been easy and tolerably safe. Several large cakes lay on or over her, sustained more by other cakes that rested on the rocks than by the timbers of the vessel herself. These cakes formed a sort of roof, and, as they did not drip, they served to make a shelter against the wind ; for, at the point where the wreck lay, the southwest gales came howling round the base of the mountain, piercing the marrow itself in the bones. At the hut it was very different. There the heights made a lee that extended all over the cape, and for some distance to the westward ; while the whole power the sun possessed in that high latitude was cast, very obliquely it is true, but clearly, and without any other drawback than its position in the ecliptic, fairly on the terrace, the hut above, and the rocks around it. On the natural terrace, indeed, it was still pleasant to walk and work, and even to sit for a few hours in the middle of the day ; for winter was not yet come in earnest in that frozen world.

One of Roswell's first objects was to transport most of the eatables from the wreck ; for he foresaw the need there would be for everything of the sort. Neither vessel had laid in a stock of provisions for a longer period than about twelve months, of which nearly half were now gone. This allowance applied to salted meats and bread, which are usually regarded as the base of a ship's stores. There were several barrels of flour, a few potatoes, a large quantity of onions, a few barrels of corn-meal, or "injin," as it is usually termed in American parlance, an entire barrel of pickled cucumbers, another about half full of cabbage preserved in the same way, and an entire barrel of molasses. In addition, there was a cask of whiskey, a little wine and brandy to be used medicinally, sugar, brown, whitey-brown, and browny-white, and a pretty fair allowance of tea and coffee ; the former being a Hyson-skin, and the latter San Domingo of no very high quality. Most of these articles were transported from the wreck to the house in the course of the few days that succeeded, though Daggett insisted on a certain portion of the supplies being left in his stranded craft. Not until this was done would Roswell listen to any proposal of Daggett's to transfer the skins. Twice during these few days, indeed, did the Vineyard master come to a pause in his proceedings, as the weather grew milder, and gleams of a hope of being able to get away that season crossed his mind. On the last of these occasions of misgivings, Roswell was compelled to lead his brother master up on the plain of the island, to an elevation of some three hundred feet above the level of the ocean, and more than half that distance higher than the house, and point out to him a panorama of field-ice that the eye could not command. Until that vast plain opened, or became riven by the joint action of the agitated ocean and the warmth of a sun from which the rays did not glance away from the frozen surface, like light obliquely received and as obliquely reflected from a mirror, it was useless to think of releasing even the uninjured vessel ; much less that which lay riven and crushed on the rocks.

"Were every cake of this ice melted into water, Daggett," Roswell continued, "it would not float off your schooner. The best supplied ship-yard in America could hardly furnish the materials for ways to launch her ; and I never knew of a vessel's being dropped into the water some twenty feet nearly perpendicular."

"I don't know that," answered Daggett, stoutly. "See

what they're doing nowadays, and think nothing of it. I have seen a whole row of brick houses turned round by the use of jack-screws; and one building actually taken down a hill much higher than the distance you name. Commodore Rodgers has just hauled a heavy frigate out of the water, and means to put her back again, when he has done with her. What has been done once can be done twice. I do not like giving up 'till I'm forced to it."

"That is plain enough, Captain Daggett," returned Roswell, smiling. "That you are game, no one can deny; but it will all come to nothing. Neither Commodore Rodgers nor Commodore anybody else could put your craft into the water again without something to do it with"

"You think it would be asking too much to take your schooner, and go across to the main next season a'ter timber to make ways?" put in Daggett, inquiringly. "She stands up like a church, and nothing would be easier than to lay down ways under her bottom."

"Or more difficult than to make them of any use, after you had put them there. No, no, my good sir, you must think no more of this; though it may be possible to make a cover for the cargo, and return and recover it all, by freighting a craft from Rio, on our way north."

Daggett gave a quick, inquisitive glance at his companion, and Roswell's color mounted to his cheeks; for, while he really thought the plan just mentioned quite feasible, he was conscious of foreseeing that it might be made the means of throwing off his troublesome companion, as he himself drew near to the West Indies and their keys.

This terminated the discussion for the time. Both of the masters busied themselves in carrying on the duty which had now fallen into a regular train. As much of the interest of what is to be related will depend on what was done in these few days, it may be well to be a little more explicit in stating the particulars.

The reader will understand that the house, of which so much had already been made by our mariners, was nothing but a shell. It had a close roof, one that effectually turned water, and its siding, though rough, was tight and rather thicker than is usual; being made of common inch boards, roughly planed, and originally painted red. There were four very tolerable windows, and a decent substantial floor of planed plank. All this had been well put together, rather more attention than is often bestowed on such structures having been paid by the carpenter to the cracks and joints on account of the known sharpness of the climate, even in the warm months. Still, all this made a mere shell. The marrow-freezing winds which would soon come—had indeed come—might be arrested by such a covering, it is true ; but the little needle-like particles of the frost would penetrate such a shelter, as their counterparts of steel pierce cloth. It was a matter of life and death, therefore, to devise means to exclude the cold, in order that the vital heat might be kept in circulation during the tremendous season that was known to be approaching.

Stimson had much to say on the subject of the arrangements taken. He was the oldest man in the two crews, and the most experienced sealer. It happened that he had once passed a winter at Orange Harbor, in the immediate vicinity of Cape Horn. It is true that it is an inhabited country, if the poor degraded creatures who dwell there can be termed inhabitants ; and has its trees and vegetation, such as they are. The difference between Orange Harbor and Sealer's Land, in this respect, must be something like that which all the travelling world knows to exist between a winter's residence at the Hospital of the Great St. Bernard, and a winter's residence at one of the villages a few leagues lower down the mountain. At Sealer's Land, if there was literally no vegetation, there was. so little as scarcely to deserve the name. Of fuel there was none, with the exception of that which had been brought there. Nevertheless, the experience of a winter passed in such a place as Orange Harbor must count for a great deal. Cape Horn is in nearly 56°, and Sealer's Land —we may as well admit this much—is by no means 10° to the southward of that. There must be a certain general resemblance in the climates of the two places ; and he who had gone through a winter at one of them must have had a very tolerable foretaste of what was to be suffered at the other. This particular experience, therefore, added to his general knowledge, as well as to his character, contributed largely to Stephen's influence in the consultations that took place between the two masters, at which he was usually present.

"It's useless to be playing off in an affair like this, Captain Gar'ner," said Stephen, on one occasion. "Away from this spot all the navies of the 'arth could not now carry us, until God's sun comes back in his course to drive the winter afore it. I have my misgivin's, gentlemen, touching this great floe that has got jammed in among these islands, whether it will ever move ag'in ; for I don't think its coming in here is a common matter."

"In which case, what would become of us, Stephen?"

"Why, sir, we should be at God's mercy then, jist as we be now ; or would be, was we on the east eend itself. I won't say that two resolute and strong arms might not cut a way through for one little craft like our'n, if they had summer fully afore 'em, and know'd they was a-workin' toward a fri'nd instead of toward an inimy. There's a great deal in the last ; every man is encouraged when he thinks he's nearer to the eend of his journey a'ter a hard day's work, than he was when he set out in the mornin'. But to undertake sich an expedition at this season would be sartain destruction. No, sir ; all we can do now is to lay up for the winter, and that with great care and prudence. We must turn ourselves into so many ants, and show their forethought and care."

"What would you recommend as our first step, Stimson?" asked Daggett, who had been an attentive listener.

"I would advise, sir, to begin hardening the men as soon as I could. We have too much fire in the stove, both for our stock of wood and for the good of the people. Make the men sleep under fewer clothes, and don't let any on 'em hang about the galley fire, as some on 'em love to do, even now, most desperately. Them 'ere men will be good for nothin' ten weeks hence, unless they're taken off the fires, as a body would take off a pot or a kettle, and are set out to harden."

"This is a process that may be easier advised than performed, perhaps," Roswell quietly observed.

"Don't you believe that, Captain Gar'ner. I've known the most shiverin', smoke-dried hands in a large crew hardened and brought to an edge, a'ter a little trouble, as a body would temper an axe with steel. The first thing to be done is to make 'em scrub one another every mornin' in cold water. This gives a life to the skin that acts much the same as a suit of clothes. Yes, gentlemen ; put a fellow in a tub for a minute or two of a mornin', and you may do almost anything you please with him all day a'terward. One pail of water is as good as a pea-jacket. And above all things, keep the stoves clear. The cooks should be told not to drive their fires so hard ; and we can do without the stove in the sleeping-room a great deal better now than most on us think. It will help to save much wood, if we begin at once to calk and thicken our siding, and make the house warmer. Was the hut in a good state, we might do without any other fire than that in the caboose for two months yet."

Such was the general character of Stephen's counsel, and very good advice it was. Not only did Roswell adopt the scrubbing process, which enabled him to throw aside a great many clothes in the course of a week, but he kept aloof from the fires, to harden, as Stimson had called it. That which was thus enforced by example was additionally enjoined by precept. Several large, hulking, idle fellows, who greatly loved the fire, were driven away from it by shame; and the heat was allowed to diffuse itself more equally through the building.

Any one who has ever had occasion to be a witness of the effect of the water-cure process in enabling even delicate women to resist cold and damp, may form some notion of the great improvement that was made among our sealers, by adopting and rigidly adhering to Stimson's cold-water and no-fire system. Those who had shivered at the very thoughts of ice-water, soon dabbled in it like young ducks; and there was scarcely an hour in the day when the half-hogshead, that was used as a bath, had not its tenant. This tub was placed on the ice of the cove, with a tent over it; and a well was made through which the water was drawn. Of course, the axe was in great request, a new hole being required each morning, and sometimes two or three times in the course of the day. The effect of these ablutions was very soon apparent. The men began to throw aside their pea-jackets, and worked in their ordinary clothing, which was warm and suited to a high latitude, with a spirit and vigor at which they were themselves surprised. The fire in the caboose sufficed as yet; and, at evening, the pea-jacket, with the shelter of the building, the crowded rooms, and the warm meals, for a long time enabled them to get on without consuming anything in the largest stove. Stimson's plans for the protection of the hut, moreover, soon began to tell. The skins, sails, and much of the rigging were brought over from the wreck; by means of the carts, so long as there was no snow, and by means of sledges when the snow fell and rendered wheeling difficult. Luckily, the position of the road along the rocks caused the upper snow to melt a little at noon-day, while it froze again, firmer and firmer, each night. The crust soon

bore, and it was found that the sledges furnished even better means of transportation than the wheels.

There was a little controversy about the use of the skins,
Daggett continuing to regard them as cargo. Necessity
and numbers prevailed in the end, and the whole building
was lined with them, four or five deep, by placing them
inside of beckets made of the smaller rigging. By stuffing
these skins compactly, within ropes so placed as to keep
all snug, a very material defence against the entrance of
cold was interposed. But this was not all. Inside of the
skins Stimson got up hangings of canvas, using the sails
of the wreck for that purpose. It was not necessary to
cut these sails—Daggett would not have suffered it—but
they were suspended, and cramped into openings, and
otherwise so arranged as completely to conceal and shelter
every side, as well as the ceilings of both rooms. Portions
were fitted with such address as to fall before the windows,
to which they formed very warm if not very ornamental
curtains. Stephen, however, induced Roswell to order
outside shutters to be made and hung ; maintaining that
one such shutter would soon count as a dozen cords of wood.

Much of the wood, too, was brought over from the
wreck ; and that which had been carelessly abandoned on
the rocks was all collected and piled carefully and conveniently near the outer door of the hut ; which door, by the
way, looked inward, or toward the rocks in the rear of
the building, where it opened on a sort of yard, that Roswell hoped to be able to keep clear of ice and snow
throughout the winter. He might as well have expected
to melt the glaciers of Grindewald by lighting a fire on
the meadows at their base !

Stephen had another project to protect the house, and to
give facilities for moving outside, when the winter should
be at the hardest. In his experience at Orange Harbor, he
had found that great inconvenience was sustained in consequence of the snow's melting around the building he inhabited, which came from the warmth of the fire within.
To avoid this, a very serious evil, he had spare sails of
heavy canvas laid across the roof of the warehouse, a building of no great height, and secured them to the rocks
below by means of anchors, kedges, and various other de-
vices ; in some instances, by lashings to projections in the
cliffs. Spare spars, leaning from the roof, supported this
tent-like covering, and props beneath sustained the spars.
This arrangement was made on only two sides of the build-

ing—one end, and the side which looked to the north ; materials failing before the whole place was surrounded. The necessity for admitting light, too, admonished the sealers of the inexpediency of thus shrouding all their windows. The bottom of this tent was only ten feet from the side of the house, which gave it greater security than if it had been more horizontal, while it made a species of verandah in which exercise could be taken with greater freedom than in the rooms. Everything was done to strengthen the building in all its parts that the ingenuity of seamen could suggest ; and particularly to prevent the tent-verandah from caving in.

Stephen intimated that their situation possessed one great advantage, as well as disadvantage. In consequence of standing on a shelf with a lower terrace so close as to be within the cast of a shovel, the snow might be thrown below, and the hut relieved. The melted snow, too, would be apt to take the same direction, under the law that governs the course of all fluids. The disadvantage was in the barrier of rock behind the hut, which, while it served admirably to break the piercing south winds, would very naturally tend to make high snow-banks in drifting storms.

CHAPTER XXIV.

"My foot on the iceberg has lighted,
 When hoarse the wild winds veer about
My eye, when the bark is benighted,
 Sees the lamp of the lighthouse go out.
 I'm the sea-bird, sea-bird, sea-bird,
 Lone looker on despair ;
 The sea-bird, sea-bird, sea-bird,
 The only witness there."—BRAINARD.

Two months passed rapidly away in the excitement and novelty of the situation and pursuits of the men. In that time, all was done that the season would allow ; the house being considered as complete, and far from uncomfortable. The days had rapidly lessened in length, and the nights increased proportionably, until the sun was visible only for a few hours at a time, and then merely passing low along the northern horizon. The cold increased in proportion, though the weather varied almost as much in that high latitude as it does in our own. It had ceased to thaw much, however; and the mean of the thermometer was not many degrees above zero. Notwithstanding this low range of the mercury, the men found that they were fast getting acclimated, and that they could endure a much greater intensity of cold than they had previously supposed possible. As yet, there had been nothing to surprise natives of New York and New England, there rarely occurring a winter in which weather quite as cold as any they had yet experienced in the antarctic sea, does not set in, and last for some little time. Even while writing this very chapter of our legend, here in the mountains of Otsego, one of these Siberian visits has been paid to our valley. For the last three days the thermometer has ranged, at sunrise, between 17° and 22° below zero; though there is every appearance of a thaw, and we may have the mercury up to 40° above in the course of the next twenty-four hours. Men accustomed to such transitions, and such extreme cold, are not easily laid up or intimidated.

A great deal of snow fell about this particular portion of the year; more, indeed, than at a later period. This snow produced the greatest inconvenience; for it soon became so deep as to form high banks around the house, and to fill all the customary haunts of the men. Still, there were places that were in a great measure exempt from this white mantle. The terrace immediately below the hut, which has so often been mentioned, was one of these bare spots. It was so placed as to be swept by both the east and the west winds, which generally cleared it of everything like snow, as fast as it fell; and this more effectually than could be done by a thousand brooms. The level of rock usually travelled in going to or from the wreck was another of these clear places. It was a sort of shelf, too narrow to admit of the snow's banking, and too much raked by the winds that commonly accompanied snow, to suffer the last to lodge to any great depth. Snow there was, with a hard crust, as has already been mentioned; but it was not snow ten or fifteen feet deep, as occurred in many other places. There were several points, however, where banks had formed, even on this ledge, through which the men were compelled to cut their way by the use of shovels, an occupation that gave them exercise, and contributed to keep them in health, if it was of no other service. It was found that the human frame could not endure one-half the toil, in that low state of the mercury, that it could bear in one a few degrees higher.

Daggett had not, by any means, abandoned his craft as much as he had permitted her to be dismantled. Every day or two he had some new expedient for getting the schooner off in the spring; though all who heard them were perfectly convinced of their impracticableness. This feeling induced him to cause his own men to keep open the communication; and scarce a day passed in which he did not visit the poor unfortunate craft. Nor was the place without an interest of a very peculiar sort. It has been said that the fragments of ice, some of which were more than a hundred feet in diameter, and all of which were eight or ten feet in thickness, had been left on their edges, inclining in a way to form caverns that extended a great distance. Now it happened that just around the wreck the cakes were so distributed as to intercept the first snows which filled the outer passages, got to be hardened, and, covered anew by fresh storms, thus interposed an effectual barrier to the admission of any more of the frozen element within the ice. The effect was to form a vast range of natural galleries amid the cakes, that were quite clear of any snow but that which had adhered to their surfaces, and which offered little or no impediment to motion—nay, which rather aided it, by rendering the walking less slippery. As the deck of the schooner had been cleared, leaving an easy access to all its entrances, cabin, hold, and forecastle, this put the Vineyard Lion under cover, while it admitted of all her accommodations being used. A portion of her wood had been left in her, it will be remembered, as well as her caboose. The last was got into the cabin, and Daggett, attended by two or three of his hands, would pass a good deal of his time there. One reason given for this distribution of the forces, was the greater room it allowed those who remained at the hut for motion. The deck of this vessel being quite clear, it offered a very favorable spot for exercise ; better, in fact, than the terrace beneath the hut, being quite sheltered from the winds, and much warmer than it had been originally, or ever since the heavy fall of snows commenced. Daggett paced his quarter-deck hour after hour, almost deluding himself with the expectation of sailing for home as soon as the return of summer would permit him to depart.

Around the hut the snow early made vast embankments. Every one accustomed to the action of this particular condition of one of the great elements, will understand that a bend in the rocks outward, or a curve inward, must neces-

sarily affect the manner in which these banks were formed.
The wind did not, by any means, blow from any one point
of the compass ; though the southwestern cliffs might be
almost termed the weather-side of the island, so much
more frequently did the gales come from that quarter than
from any other. The cape where the cove lay, and where
the house had been set up, being at the northeastern point,
and much protected by the high table-land in its rear, it
occupied the warmest situation in the whole region. The
winds that swept most of the north shore, but which, owing to a curvature in its formation, did not often blow home
to the hut, even when they whistled along the terrace only
a hundred feet beneath, and more salient, were ordinarily
from the southwest outside ; though they got a more westerly inclination by following the land under the cliffs.

A bank of snow may be either a cause of destruction or
a source of comfort. Of course, a certain degree of cold
must exist wherever snow is to be found ; but unless in
absolute contact with the human body, it does not usually
affect the system beyond a certain point. On the other
hand, it often breaks the wind, and it has been known to
form a covering to flocks, houses, etc., that has contributed
essentially to their warmth. We incline to the opinion
that if one slept in a cavern formed in the snow, provided
he could keep himself dry, and did not come in absolute
contact with the element, he would not find his quarters
very uncomfortable, so long as he had sufficient clothing
to confine the animal warmth near his person. Now our
sealers enjoyed some such advantage as this ; though not
literally in the same degree. Their house was not covered
with snow, though a vast bank was already formed quite
near it, and a good deal had begun to pile against the tent.
Singular as it may seem, on the east end of the building,
and on the south front, which looked in toward the cliff
next the cove, there was scarcely any snow at all. This
was in part owing to the constant use of the shovel and
broom, but more so to the currents of air, which usually
carried everything of so light a nature as a flake to more
quiet spots, before it was suffered to settle on the ground.

Roswell early found, what his experience as an American might have taught him, that the *melting* of the snow,
in consequence of the warmth of the fires, caused much
more inconvenience than the snow itself. The latter, when
dry, was easily got along with ; but, when melted in the
day, and converted into icicles at night, it became a most

unpleasant and not altogether a safe neighbor ; inasmuch as there was really danger from the sort of damp atmosphere it produced.

The greatest ground of Roswell Gardiner's apprehensions, however, was for the supply of fuel. Much of that brought from home had been fairly used in the caboose, and in the stove originally set up in the hut. Large as that stock had been, a very sensible inroad had been made upon it ; and, according to a calculation he had made, the wood regularly laid in would not hold out much more than half the time that it would be indispensable to remain on the island. This was a grave circumstance, and one that demanded very serious consideration. Without fuel it would be impossible to survive ; no hardening process being sufficient to fortify the human frame to a degree that would resist the influence of an antarctic winter.

From the moment it was probable the party would be obliged to pass the winter at Sealer's Land, therefore, Roswell had kept a vigilant eye on the wood. Stimson had more than once spoken to him on the subject, and with great prudence.

"Warmth must be kept among us," said the old boat-steerer, "or there will be no hope for the stoutest man in either crew. We've a pretty good stock of coffee, and that is better, any day, than all the rum and whiskey that was ever distilled. Good hot coffee of a morning will put life into us the coldest day that ever come out of either pole ; and they do say the south is colder than the north, though I never could understand why it should be so."

"You surely understand the reason why it grows warmer as we approach the equator, and colder as we go from it, whether we go north or south ?"

Stimson assented ; though had the truth been said, he would have been obliged to confess that he knew no more than the facts.

"All sailors know sich things, Captain Gar'ner ; though they know it with very different degrees of exper'ence. But few get as far south as I have been to pass a winter. A good pot of hot coffee of a morning will go as far as a second pee-jacket, if a man has to go out into the open air when the weather is at the hardest."

"Luckily, our small stores are quite abundant, and we are better off for coffee and sugar than for anything else. I laid in of both liberally when we were at Rio."

"Yes, Rio is a good place for the articles. But coffee

must be *hot* to do a fellow much good in one of these high-latitude winters ; and to be hot there must be fuel to heat it."

"I am afraid the wood will not hold out much more than half the time we shall be here. Fortunately, we had a large supply ; but the other schooner was by no means as well furnished with fuel as she ought to have been for such a voyage."

"Well, sir, I suppose you know what must be done next in such a case. Without *warm* food, men can no more live through one of these winters, than they can live without food at all. If the Vineyard craft has no proper fuel aboard her, we must make fuel of her."

Roswell regarded Stephen with fixed attention for some time. The idea was presented to his mind for the second time, and he greatly liked it.

"That might do," he said ; "though it will not be an easy matter to make Captain Daggett consent to such a thing "

"Let him go two or three mornings without his warm meal and hot coffee," answered Stimson, shaking his head, "and he will be glad enough to come into the scheme. A man soon gets willing to set fire to anything that will burn in such a climate. A notion has been floating about in my mind, Captain Gar'ner, that I've several times thought I would mention to you. D'ye think, sir, any benefit could be made of that volcano over the bay, should the worst get to the worst with us ?"

"I have thought of the same thing, Stephen ; though I fear in vain. I suppose no useful heat can be given out there, until one gets too near the bad air to breathe it. What you say about breaking up the other schooner, however, is worthy of consideration ; and I will speak to Captain Daggett about it."

Roswell was as good as his word ; and the Vineyard mariner met the proposal as one repels an injury. Never were our two masters so near a serious misunderstanding, as when Roswell suggested to Daggett the expediency of breaking up the wreck, now that the weather was endurable, and the men could work with reasonable comfort and tolerable advantage.

"The man who puts an axe or a saw into that unfortunate craft," said Daggett, firmly, "I shall regard as an enemy. It is a hard enough bed that she lies on, without having her ribs and sides torn to pieces by hands."

This was the strange spirit in which Daggett continued to look at the condition of the wreck. It was true that the ice prevented his actually seeing the impossibility of his ever getting his schooner into the water again ; but no man at all acquainted with mechanics, and who knew the paucity of means that existed on the island, could for a moment entertain the idle expectation that seemed to have got into the Vineyard-master's mind, unless subject to a species of one-idea infatuation. This infatuation, however, existed not only in Daggett's mind, but in some degree in those of his men. It is said that "in a multitude of counsellors there is wisdom ;" and the axiom comes from an authority too venerable to be disputed. But it might almost with equal justice be said that "in a multitude of counsellors there is folly ;" for men are quite as apt to sustain each other in the wrong as in the right. The individual who would hesitate about advancing his fallacies and mistakes with a single voice, does not scruple to proclaim them on the hilltops, when he finds other tongues to repeat his errors. Divine wisdom, foreseeing this consequence of human weakness, has provided a church-catholic, and proceeding directly from its Great Head on earth, as the repository of those principles, facts, and laws, that it has deemed essential to the furtherance of its own scheme of moral government on earth ; and yet we see audacious imitators starting up on every side, presuming in their ignorance, longing in their ambition, and envious in these longings, who do not scruple to shout out upon the housetops crudities over which knowledge wonders as it smiles, and humility weeps as it wonders. Such is man, when sustained by his fellows, in every interest of life ; from religion, the highest of all, down to the most insignificant of his temporal concerns.

In this spirit did Daggett and his crew now feel and act. Roswell had early seen, with regret, that something like a feeling of party was getting up among the Vineyarders, who had all along regarded the better fortune of their neighbors with an ill-concealed jealousy. Ever since the shipwreck, however, this rivalry had taken a new and even less pleasant aspect. It was slightly hostile, and remarks had been occasionally made that sounded equivocally ; as if the Vineyarders had an intention of separating from the other crew, and of living by themselves. It is probable, however, that all this was the fruit of disappointment ; and that, at the bottom, nothing very serious was in contemplation. Daggett had permitted his people to aid in transporting most of the stores to the house ; though a considerable supply had been left in the wreck. This last arrangement was made seemingly without any hostile design, but rather in furtherance of a plan to pass as much time as circumstances would allow on board the stranded vessel. There was, in truth, a certain convenience in this scheme that commended it to the good sense of all. So long as any portion of the Vineyarders could be made comfortable in the wreck it was best they should remain there ; for it saved the labor of transporting all the provisions, and made more room to circulate in and about the house. The necessity of putting so many casks, barrels, and boxes within doors, had materially circumscribed the limits ; and space was a great desideratum for several reasons, health in particular.

Roswell was glad, therefore, when any of the Vineyarders expressed a wish to go to the wreck and to pass a few days there. With a view to encourage this disposition, as well as to ascertain how those fared who chose that abode, he paid Daggett a visit, and passed a night or two himself in the cabin of the craft. This experiment told him that it was very possible to exist there when the thermometer stood at zero ; but how it would do when ranging a great deal lower he had his doubts. The cabin was small, and a very moderate fire in the caboose served to keep it reasonably warm ; though Daggett, at all times a reasonable and reasoning man, when the "root of all evil" did not sorely beset him, came fully into his own views as to the necessity of husbanding the fuel and of hardening the men. None of that close stewing over stoves, which is so common in America, and which causes one-half of the winter diseases of the climate, was tolerated in either gang. Daggett saw the prudence of Roswell's, or rather of Stimson's system, and fell into it freely and with hearty goodwill. It was during Gardiner's visit to the wreck that our two masters talked over their plans for the winter, while taking their exercise on the schooner's deck, each well muffled up to prevent the frost from taking hold of the more exposed parts. Every one had a seal-skin cap, made in a way to protect the ears and most of the face ; and our two masters were thus provided, in common with their men.

"I suppose that we are to consider this as pleasant winter weather," Roswell remarked, "the thermometer being down only at zero. Stimson tells me that even at Orange Harbor, the season he was there, they paid out mercury until it all got into the ball. A month or two hence we may look out for the season of frosts, as the Injuns call it. You will hardly think of staying out here when the really hard weather sets in."

"I do not believe we shall feel the cold much more than we do now. This daily washing is a capital stove; for I find all hands say that, when it is once over, they feel like new men. As for me, I shall stick by my craft while there is a timber left in her to float!"

Roswell thought how absurd it was to cling thus to a useless mass of wood, and iron, and copper; but he said nothing on that subject.

"I am now sorry that we took over to the house so many of our supplies," Daggett continued, after a short pause. "I am afraid that many of them will have to be brought back again."

"That would hardly quit cost, Daggett; it would be better to come over and pass the heel of the winter with us, when the supplies get to be short here. As we eat, we make room in the hut, you know; and you will be so much the more comfortable. An empty pork-barrel was broken up for the caboose yesterday morning."

"We shall see—we shall see, Gar'ner. My men have got a notion that your people intend to break up this schooner for fuel, should they not keep an anchor-watch aboard her."

"Anchor-watch!" repeated Roswell, smiling. "It is well named—if there ever was an anchor-watch, you keep it here; for no ground tackle will ever hold like this."

"We still think the schooner may be got off," Daggett said, regarding his companion inquiringly.

While the Vineyard-man had a certain distrust of his brother-master, he had also a high respect for his fair-dealing propensities, and a strong disposition to put confidence in his good faith. The look that he now gave was if possible, to read the real opinion of the other, in a countenance that seldom deceived.

"I shall be grateful to God, Captain Daggett," returned Roswell, after a short pause, "if we get through the long winter of this latitude, without burning too much of *both* craft, than will be for our good. Surely it were better to begin on that which is in the least serviceable condition?"

"I have thought this matter over, Gar'ner, with all my

mind—have dreamt of it—slept on it—had it before me at all hours and in all weathers ; and, look at it as I will, it is full of difficulties. Will you agree to take in a half-cargo of my skins and iles next season, and make in all respects a joint v'y'ge of it, from home, home ag'in, if we'll consent to let this craft be burned ? "

"It exceeds my power to make any such bargain. I have an owner who looks sharply after his property, and my crew are upon lays, like the people of all sealers. You ask too much ; and you forget that, should I assume the same power over my own craft, as you still claim in this wreck, you might never find the means of getting away from the group at all. We are not obliged to receive you on board our schooner."

"I know you think, Gar'ner, that it will be impossible for us ever to get our craft off ; but you overlook one thing that we may do—what is there to prevent our breaking her up, and of using the materials to make a smaller vessel ; one of sixty tons say—in which we might get home, besides taking most of our skins ? "

"I will not say *that* will be impossible ; but I do say it will be very difficult. It would be wiser for you, in my judgment, to leave your cargo in the house, under the keeping of a few hands if you see fit, and go off with me. I will land you at Rio, where you can almost always find some small American craft to come south in and pick up your leavings. If you choose that the men left behind should amuse themselves in your absence by building a small craft, I am certain they will meet with no opposition from me. There is but one place where a vessel can be launched, and that is the spot in the cove where we beached your schooner. There it might possibly be done, though I think not without a great deal of trouble, and possibly not without more means than are to be picked up along shore in this group. But there is a very important fact that you overlook, Daggett, which it may be as well to mention here as to delay it. *Your* craft, or *mine*, must be used as fuel this winter, or we shall freeze to death to a man. I have made the calculations closely : and, certain as our existence, there is no alternative between such a death and the use of the fuel I have mentioned."

"Not a timber of mine shall be touched. I do not believe one-half of these stories about the antarctic winter, which cannot be much worse than what a body meets with up in the Bay of Fundy."

"A winter in the Bay of Fundy without fuel must be bad enough; but it is a mere circumstance to one here. I should think that a man who has tasted an antarctic *summer* and *autumn* must get a pretty lively notion of what is to come after them."

"The men can keep in their berths much of the time, and save wood. There are many other ways of getting through a winter than burning a vessel. I shall never consent to a stick of this good craft's going into the galley-fire as long as I can see my way clear to prevent it. I would burn *cargo* before I would burn my *craft*."

Roswell wondered at this pertinacity; but he trusted to the pressure of the coming season, and changed the subject. Certainly the thought of breaking up his own craft did not cross his mind; though he could see no sufficient objection to the other side of the proposition. As discussion was useless, however, he continued to converse with Daggett on various practical subjects, on which his companion was rational and disposed to learn.

It had been ascertained by experiment that the water, at a considerable depth, was essentially warmer beneath the ice than at its surface. A plan had been devised by which the lower currents of the water could be pumped up for the purposes of the bath; thus rendering the process far more tolerable than it had previously been. Bathing in extremely cold weather, however, is not so formidable a thing as is generally supposed, the air being at a lower temperature than the water. As the greatest importance was attached to these daily ablutions, the subject was gone over between the two masters in all its bearings. There were no conveniences for the operation at the wreck; and this was one reason why Roswell suggested that a residence there ought to be abandoned. Daggett dissented, and invited his companion to take a walk in his caverns.

A promenade in a succession of caves formed of ice, with the thermometer at zero, would naturally strike one as a somewhat chilling amusement. Gardiner did not find it so. He was quite protected from the wind, which gives so much pungency to bitter cold, rendering it insupportable. Completely protected from this, and warmed by the exertion of clambering among the cakes, Roswell's blood was soon in a healthful glow; and, to own the truth, when he left the wreck, it was with a much better opinion of it, as a place of residence, than when he had arrived to pay his visit.

As there was now nothing for the men to do in the way

of preparation, modes of amusement were devised that might unite activity of body with that of the mind. The snows ceased to fall as the season advanced, and there were but few places on which heavy burdens might not have been transported over their crusts. It was, indeed, easier moving about on the surface of the frozen snow than it had been on the naked rocks ; the latter offering obstacles that no longer showed themselves. Sliding down the declivities, and even skating, were practised ; few northern Americans being ignorant of the latter art. Various other sources of amusement were resorted to ; but it was found, generally, that very little exercise in the open air exhausted the frame, and that a great difficulty of breathing occurred. Still, it was thought necessary to health that the men should remain as much as possible out of the crowded house ; and various projects were adopted to keep up the vital warmth while exposed. Ere the month of July had passed, which corresponds to our January, it had been found expedient to make dresses of skins, for which fort- unately the materials abounded.

As the season advanced the idea of preserving more than the lives of his men was gradually abandoned by Gardiner, though Daggett still clung to his wreck, and actually had wood transported back to it, that he might stay as much as possible near his property. There was no longer any thawing, though there were very material gra- dations in the intensity of the frosts. Occasionally it was quite possible to remain in the open air an hour or two at a time ; then again there were days in which it exceeded the powers of human endurance to remain more than a few minutes removed to any distance from heat artificially procured. On the whole, however, it was found that the comparatively moderate weather predominated, and it was rare, indeed, that all the people did not pursue their avocations and amusements outside, at what was called the middle of the day.

And what a meridian it was! The shortest day had passed some time, when Roswell and Stimson were walk- ing together on the terrace, then, as usual, as clear from snow as if swept by a broom, but otherwise wearing the aspect of interminable winter, in common with all around it. They were conversing as had been much their wont of late, and were watching the passage of the sun as he stole along the northern horizon, even at high noon rising but a very few degrees above it!

"It has a cold look, sir, but it does give out some heat," said Stephen, as he faced the luminary in one of his turns. "I can feel a little warmth from it just now, sheltered as we are here under the cliffs, and with a background of naked rock to throw back what reaches us. To me all these changes in the movements of the sun seem very strange, Captain Gar'ner; but I know I am ignorant, and that others may well know all about what I do not understand."

Here Gardiner undertook to explain the phenomena that have been slightly treated on in our own pages. There are few Americans so ignorant as not to be fully aware that the sun has no sensible motion, or any motion that has an apparent influence on our own planet; but fewer still clearly comprehend the reasons of those very changes that are occurring constantly before their eyes. We cannot say that Captain Gardiner succeeded very well in his undertaking, though he imprinted on the old boat-steerer's mind the fact that the sun would not be seen at all were they only a few degrees further south than they actually were.

"And now, sir, I suppose he'll get higher and higher every day," put in Stephen, "until he comes quite up above our heads?"

"Not exactly that at noon; though abeam, as it might be, mornings and evenings."

"Still the coldest of our weather is yet to come, or, I have no exper'ence in such things. Why does not the heat come back with the sun—or what seems to be the sun coming back? though, as you tell me, Captain Gar'-ner, it's only the 'arth sheering this-a-away and that-a-way in her course."

"One may well ask such a question—but cold produces cold, and it takes time to wear it out. February is commonly the coldest month in the year, even in America; though days occur in other months that may be colder than any one in February. March, and even April, are months I dread here; and that so much the more, Stephen, because our fuel goes a good deal faster than I could wish."

"What you say is very true, sir. Still the people must have fire. I turned out this morning, while all hands were still in their berths, and looked to the stove, and it was as much as human natur' could bear to be about without my cap and skin-covering, though in-doors the whole time.

If the weather goes on as it has begun, we shall have to keep a watch at the stove ; nor do I think one stove will answer us much longer. We shall want another in the sleeping-room."

"Heaven knows where the wood is to come from ! Unless Captain Daggett gives up the wreck, we shall certainly be out long before the mild season returns."

"We must keep ourselves warm, sir, by reading the Bible," answered Stimson, smiling ; though the glance he cast at his officer was earnest and anxious. "You must not forget, Captain Gar'ner, that you've promised one who is praying for you daily to go through the chapters she has marked, and give the matter a patient and attentive thought. No sealin', sir, can be half so important as this reading of the good book in the right spirit."

"So you believe that Jesus was the Son of God!" exclaimed Roswell, half inquiringly, and half in a modified sort of levity.

"As much as I believe that we are here, sir. I wish I was half as certain of ever getting away."

"What has caused you to believe this, Stimson ?—reason, or the talk of your mother and of the parson ?"

"My mother died afore I could listen to her talk, sir ; and very little have I had to do with parsons, for the want of being where they are to be found. *Faith* tells me to believe this ; and Faith comes from God."

"And I could believe it, too, were Faith imparted to me from the same source. As it is, I fear I shall never believe in what appears to me to be an impossibility."

Then followed a long discussion, in which ingenuity, considerable command of language, human pride, and worldly sentiments, contended with that clear, intuitive, deep conviction which it is the pleasure of the Deity often to bestow on those who would otherwise seem to be unfitted to become the respositories of so great a gift. As we shall have to deal with this part of our subject more particularly hereafter, we shall not enlarge on it here ; but pursue the narrative as it is connected with the advance of the season, and the influence the latter exerted over the whole party of the lost sealers.

CHAPTER XXV.

" Beyond the Jewish ruler, banded close,
    A company full glorious, I saw
    The twelve apostles stand. Oh, with what looks
Of ravishment and joy, what rapturous tears,
What hearts of ecstasy, they gazed again
On their beloved Master."—HILLHOUSE'S JUDGMENT.

It has become necessary to advance the season to the beginning of the month of October, which corresponds to our own April. In a temperate climate this would mark the opening of spring ; and the reviving hopes of a new and genial season would find a place in every bosom. Not so at Sealer's Land. So long as the winter was at its height, and the clear, steady cold continued, by falling into a system so prepared as to meet the wants of such a region, matters had gone on regularly, if not with comfort ; and, as yet, the personal disasters were confined to a few frozen cheeks and noses, the results of carelessness and wanton exposure, rather than of absolute necessity. But one who had seen the place in July, and who examined it now, would find many marks of change, not to say of deterioration.

In the first place, a vast deal of snow had fallen ; fallen, indeed, to such a degree, as even to cover the terrace, block up the path that communicated with the wreck, and nearly to smother the house and all around it. The winds were high and piercing, rendering the cold doubly penetrating. The thermometer now varied essentially, sometimes rising considerably above zero, though oftener falling far below it. There had been many storms in September, and October was opening with a most blustering and wintry aspect. In one sense, however, the character of the season had changed : the dry, equal cold, that was generally supportable, having been succeeded by tempests that were sometimes a little moist, but oftener of intense frigidity. Of course the equinox was past, and there were more than twelve hours of sun. The great luminary showed himself well above the northern horizon ; and though the circuit described an arc that did not promise soon to bring him near the zenith at meridian, it was a circuit that seemed about to inclose Sealer's Land, by carrying the orb of day so far south, morning and evening, as to give it an air of travelling round the spot.

These changes had not occurred without suffering and danger. Enormous icicles were suspended from the roof of the house, reaching to the ground, the third and fourth successions of these signs of heat and cold united, the earlier formations having been knocked down and thrown away. Mountains of drifted snow were to be seen in places, all along the shore ; and wreaths that threatened fearful avalanches were suspended from the cliffs, waiting only for the increase of the warmth, to come down upon the rocks beneath. Once already had one of these masses fallen on the wreck ; and the Oyster Pond men had been busy for a week digging into the pile, in order to go to the rescue of the Vineyarders. There was much generosity and charitable feeling displayed in this act ; for, owing to the obstinate adherence of Daggett and his people to what they deemed their rights, Roswell had finally been compelled to cut to pieces the upper works of his own schooner to obtain fuel that might prevent his own party from freezing to death. The position of the Sea Lion of Oyster Pond was to be traced only by a high mound of snow, which had been arrested by the obstacle she presented to its drift ; but her bulwarks, planks, deck, top-timbers, stern-frame—in short, nearly all of the vessel above water, had actually been taken to pieces, and carried within the covering of the veranda mentioned, in readiness for the stoves !

To render the obstinacy of the other crew more apparent, Daggett had been obliged to do the same ! Much of his beloved craft had already disappeared in the caboose, and more was likely to follow. This compelled destruction, however, rather increased than lessened his pertinacity. He clung to the last chip ; and no terms of compromise would he now listen to at all. The stranded wreck was his, and his people's ; while the other wreck belonged to the men from Oyster Pond. Let each party act for itself, and take care of its own. Such were his expressed opinions, and on them he acted.

This state of things had not been brought about in a day. Months had passed ; Roswell had seen his last billet of wood put in the caboose ; had tried various experiments for producing heat by means of oil, which so far succeeded as to enable the ordinary boiling to be done, thereby saving wood ; but, when a cold turn set in, it was quickly found that the schooner must go, or all hands perish. When this decree went forth, every one understood that the final preservation of the party depended on that of the boats. For one entire day the question had been up in general council, whether or not the two whale-boats should be burnt, with their oars and appurtenances, before the attack was made on the schooner itself. Stimson settled this point, as he did so many others, Roswell listening to all he said with a constantly increasing attention.

" If we burn the boats first," said the boat-steerer, " and then have to come to the schooner a'ter all, how are we ever to get away from this group ? Them boats wouldn't last us a week, even in our best weather ; but they may answer to take us to some Christian land, when every rib and splinter of the Sea Lion is turned into ashes. I would begin on the upper works of the schooner first, Captain Gar'ner, resarvin' the spars, though they would burn the freest. Then I would saw away the top-timbers, beams, decks, transoms, and everything down within a foot of the water ; but I wouldn't touch anything below the copper, for this here reason : unless Captain Daggett sets to work on his craft and burns her up altogether, we may find mater'als enough in the spring to deck over ag'in the poor thing down there in the cove, and fit her out a'ter a fashion, and make much better weather of it in her than in our boats. That's my opinion, sir."

It was decided that this line of conduct should be pursued. The upper works of the schooner were all taken out of her as soon as the weather permitted, and the wood was carried up and stored in the house. Even with this supply, it was soon seen that great economy was to be used, and that there might be the necessity of getting at the vessel's bottom. As for the schooner, as the people still affectionately called the hull, or what was left of the hull, everything had been taken out of her. The frozen oil was carried up to the house in chunks, and used for fuel and lights. A good deal of heat was obtained by making large wicks of canvas, and placing them in vessels that contained oil ; though it was very far from sufficing to keep life in the men during the hardest of the weather. The utmost economy in the use of the fuel that had been so dearly obtained, was still deemed all-essential to eventual preservation. Happily, the season advanced all this time, and the month of October was reached. The intercourse between the crews had by no means been great during the two solemn and critical months that were just passed. A few visits had been exchanged at noon-day, and when the thermometer was a little above zero ; but the snow was filling the path, and as yet there were no thaws to produce a crust on which the men might walk.

About a month previously to the precise time to which it is our intention now to advance the more regular action of the legend, Macy had come over to the house, attended by one man, with a proposal on the part of Daggett for the two crews to occupy his craft, as he still persisted in calling the wreck, and of using the house as fuel. This was previously to beginning to break up either vessel. Gardiner had thought of this plan in connection with his own schooner, a scheme that would have been much more feasible than that now proposed, on account of the difference in distance ; but it had soon been abandoned. All the material of the building was of pine, and that well seasoned ; a wood that burns like tinder. No doubt there would have been a tolerably comfortable fortnight or three weeks by making these sacrifices ; then would have come certain destruction.

As to the proposal of Daggett, there were many objections to it. A want of room would be one ; want of provisions another ; and there would be the necessity of transporting stores, bedding, and a hundred things that were almost as necessary to the people as warmth ; and which indeed contributed largely to their warmth. In addition was the objection just mentioned, of the insufficiency of the materials of the building ; an objection which was just as applicable to a residence in one vessel as a residence in the other. Of course the proposition was declined.

Macy remained a night with the Oyster Ponders, and left the house after breakfast next morning ; knowing that Daggett only waited for his return with a negative, to commence breaking up the wreck. The mate was attended by the seaman, returning as he had arrived. Two days later, there having been a slight yielding of the snow under the warmth of the noonday sun, and a consequent hardening of its crust in the succeeding night, Roswell and Stimson undertook to return this visit, with a view to make a last effort to persuade Daggett to quit the wreck and come over to the house altogether. When they had got about half-way between the two places, they found the body of the seaman, stiff, frozen, hard, and dead. A quarter of a mile further on, the reckless Macy, who it was supposed greatly sustained Daggett in his obstinacy, was found in precisely the same state. Both had fallen in the path, and stiffened under the terrible power of the climate. It was not without difficulty that Roswell reached the wreck, and reported what he had seen. Even this terrible admonition did not change Daggett's purpose. He had begun to burn his vessel, for there was now no alternative ; but he was doing it on a system which, as he explained it to Roswell, was not only to leave him materials with which to construct a smaller craft in the spring, but which would allow of his inhabiting the steerage and cabin as long as he pleased.

In some respects the wreck certainly had its advantages over the house. There was more room for exercise, the caverns of the ice being extensive, while they completely excluded the wind, which was now the great danger of the season. It was doubtless owing to the wind that Macy and his companion had perished. As the spring approached, these winds increased in violence ; though there had been slight symptoms of their coming more blandly, even at the time when their colder currents were really frightful.

A whole month succeeded this visit of Roswell's, during which there was no intercourse. It was September, the March of the antarctic circle, and the weather had been terrific during most of the period. It was during these terrible four weeks that Roswell completed his examination of the all-important subject Mary had marked out for him, and which Stimson had so earnestly and so often placed before his mind. The sudden fate of Macy and his companion, the condition of his crew, and all the serious circumstances with which he was surrounded, conspired to predispose him to inquiry ; and what was equally important in such an investigation, to humility. Man is a very different being in high prosperity from what he becomes when the blows of an evil fortune, or the visitations of Divine Providence alight upon him. The scepticism of Roswell was more the result of human pride, of confidence in himself, than of any precept derived from others, or of any deep reasoning process whatever. He conceived that the theory of the incarnation of the Son of God was opposed to philosophy and experience, it is true ; and, thus far, he may be said to have reasoned in the matter, though it was in his own way, and with a very contracted view of the subject ; but pride had much more to do with even this conclusion, than a knowledge of physics or philosophy. It did not comport with the respect he entertained for his

21

own powers, to lend his faith to an account that conflicted
with so many of the opinions he had formed on evidence
and practice.   Credulous women might have their convictions on the truth of this history, but it was not necessary
for men to be as easily duped.   There was something even
amiable and attractive in this weakness of the other sex,
that would ill comport, however, with the greater sternness of masculine judgment.   Roswell, as he once told
Stimson, hesitated to believe in anything that he could not
comprehend.   His God must be worshipped for the obvious truth of his attributes and existence.   He wished to
speak with respect of things that so many worthy people
reverenced ; but he could not forget that Providence had
made him a reasoning creature ; and his reason must be
convinced.   Stephen was no great logician, as the reader
will easily understand ; but Newton possessed no clearer
demonstration of any of his problems than this simple, nay
ignorant, man enjoyed in his religious faith, through the
divine illumination it had received in the visit of the Holy
Spirit.

That gloomy month, however, had not been thrown
away.   All the men were disposed to be serious ; and the
reading of the Bible, openly and aloud, soon became a
favorite occupation with every one of them.   Although
Roswell's reading was directed by the marks of Mary, all
of which had reference to those pages that touched on the
divinity of the Saviour, he made no comments that betrayed his incredulity.   There is a simple earnestness in
the narrative portions of the Gospel that commends its
truth to every mind, and it had its effect on that of Roswell Gardiner ; though it failed to remove doubts that had
so long been cherished, and which had their existence in
pride of reason, or what passes for such, with those who
merely skim the surface of things, as they seem to exist
around them.

On the evening of that particular day in October, to
which we desire now to advance the time, and after the
most pleasant and cheerful afternoon and sunset that any
on the island had seen for many months, Roswell and Stimson ventured to continue their exercise on the terrace, then
again clear of impediments, even after the day had closed.
The night promised to be cold, but the weather was not
yet so keen as to drive them to a shelter.   Both fancied
there was a feeling of spring in the wind, which was from
the northeast, a quarter that brought the blandest currents

of air into those seas, if any air of that region deserved such a term at all.

"It is high time we had some communications with the Vineyarders," said Roswell, as they turned at the end of the terrace which was nearest to the wreck. "A full month has passed since we have seen any of them, or have heard a syllable of their doings or welfare."

"It's a bad business this separation, Captain Gar'ner," returned the boat-steerer; "and every hour makes it worse. Think how much good might have been done them young men had they only been with us while we've been reading the book of books, night and morning, sir!"

"That good book seems to fill most of your thoughts, Stephen; I wish I could have your faith."

"It will come in time, sir, if you will only strive for it. I'm sure no heart could have been harder than mine was, until within the last five years. I was far worse as a Christian, Captain Gar'ner, than I consider you to be; for while you have doubts consarning the divinity of our Blessed Lord, I had no thought of any one of the Trinity. My only God was the world; and sich a world, too, as a poor sailor knows. It was being but little better than the brutes."

"Of all the men with me, you seem to be the most contented and happy. I cannot say I have seen even a sign of fear about you, when things have been at the worst."

"It would be very ungrateful, sir, to mistrust a Providence that has done so much for me."

"I devoutly wish I could believe with you that Jesus was the Son of God!"

"Excuse me, Captain Gar'ner; it's jist because you do not *devoutly* wish this that you do not believe. I think I understand the natur' of your feelin's, sir. I had some sich once, myself; though it was only in a small way. I was too ignorant to feel much pride in my own judgment, and soon gave up every notion that went ag'in Scriptur'. I own it is not accordin' to natur', as we know natur', to believe in this doctrine; but we know too little of a thousand things to set up our weak judgments in the very face of revelation."

"I am quite willing to believe all I can understand, Stephen; but I find it difficult to credit accounts that are irreconcilable with all that my experience has taught me to be true."

"They who are of your way of thinkin', sir, do not deny

that Christ was a good man and a prophet; and that the apostles were good men and prophets; and that they all worked miracles."

"This much I am willing enough to believe; but the other doctrine seems contrary to what is possible."

"Yet you have seen, sir, that these apostles believed what you refuse. One thing has crossed my mind, Captain Gar'ner, which I wish to say to you. I know I'm but an ignorant man, and my idees may be hardly worth your notice; but sich as they be, I want to lay 'em afore you. We are told that these apostles were all men from a humble class in life, with little l'arnin', chosen, as it might be, to show men that faith stood in need of no riches, or edication, or worldly greatness of any sort. To me, sir, there is a wholesome idee in that one thing."

"It gives us all a useful lesson, Stephen, and has often been mentioned, I believe, in connection with the doctrines of Christianity."

"Yes, sir—so I should think; though I don't remember ever to have heard it named from any pulpit. Well, Captain Gar'ner, it does not agree with our notions to suppose that God himself, a part of the Ruler and Master of the Universe, should be born of a woman, and come among sinners in order to save 'em from his own just judgments."

"That is just the difficulty that I have in believing what are called the dogmas of Christianity on that one point. To me it has ever seemed the most improbable thing in the world."

"Just so, sir—I had some sort of feelin' of that natur' myself once. When God, in his goodness, put it into my heart to believe, however, as he was pleased to do in a fit of sickness from which I never expected to rise, and in which I was led to pray to Him for assistance, I began to think over all these matters in my own foolish manner. Among other things, I said to myself, 'is it likely that any mortal man would dream of calling Christ the Son of God, unless it was put into *his* mind to say so?' Then comes the characters of them men, who all admit were upright and religious. How can we suppose that they would agree in giving the same account of sich a thing unless what they said had been told to them by some tongue that they believed?"

Roswell smiled at Stephen's reasoning, which was not without a certain point, but which an ingenious man might find the means of answering in various ways.

"There is another thing, sir, that I've read in a book," resumed the boat-steerer, "which goes a great way with me. Jesus allowed others to call him the Son of God, without rebuking them for doing so. It does really seem that they who believe he was a good man, as I understand is the case with you, Captain Gar'ner, must consider this a strong fact. We are to remember what a sin idolatry is ; how much all ra'al worshippers abhor it ; and then set that feelin' side by side with the fact that the Son did not think it robbery to be called the equal of the Father. To me that looks like a proof that our belief has a solid foundation."

Roswell did not reply. He was aware that it would not be just to hold any creed responsible for the manner in which a person like Stimson defended it. Still, he was struck with both of this man's facts. The last he had often met in books ; but the first was new to him. Of the two, this novel idea of the improbability of the apostles inventing that which would seem to be opposed to all men's notions and prejudices, struck him more forcibly than the argument adduced from the acquiescence of the Redeemer in his own divinity. The last might be subject to verbal criticism, and could possibly be explained away, as he imagined ; but the first appeared to be intimately incorporated with the entire history of Christ's ministrations on earth. These were the declarations of John the Baptist, the simple and unpretending histories of the Gospels, the commentaries of St. Paul, and the venerable teachings of the Church through so many centuries of varying degrees of faith and contention, each and all going to corroborate a doctrine that, in his eyes, had appeared to be so repugnant to philosophy and reason. Wishing to be alone, Roswell gave an order to Stimson to execute some duty that fell to his share, and continued walking up and down the terrace alone for quite an hour longer.

The night was coming in cold and still. It was one of those last efforts of winter in which all the terrible force of the season was concentrated ; and it really appeared as if nature, wearied with its struggle to return to a more genial temperature, yielded in despair, and was literally returning backward through the coldest of her months. The moon was young, but the stars gave forth a brightness that is rarely seen, except in the clear cold nights of a high latitude. Each and all of these sublime emblems of the power of God were twinkling like bright torches glowing

in space ; and the mind had only to endow each with its
probable or known dimensions, its conjectural and reasonable uses, to form a picture of the truest sublimity in which
man is made to occupy his real position.   In this world,
where, in a certain sense, he is master ; where all things
are apparently under his influence, if not absolutely subject to his control ; where little that is distinctly visible is
to be met with that does not seem to be created to meet his
wants, or to be wholly at his disposal, one gets a mistaken
and frequently a fatal notion of his true place in the scale
of the beings who are intended to throng around the foot-
stool of the Almighty.   As the animalculæ of the atmospheric air bear a proportion to things visible, so would this
throng seem to bear a proportion to our vague estimates
of the spiritual hosts.   All this Roswell was very capable
of feeling, and in some measure of appreciating ; and
never before had he been made so conscious of his own
insignificance, as he became while looking on the firmament that night, glowing with its bright worlds and suns,
doubtless the centres of other systems in which distance
swallowed up the lesser orbs.

Almost every one has heard or read of that collection of
stars which goes by the name of the Southern Cross. The
resemblance to the tree on which Christ suffered is not
particularly striking, though all who navigate the southern
hemisphere know it, and recognize it by its imputed appellation.   It now attracted Roswell's gaze ; and coming
as it did after so much reading, so many conversations with
Stephen, and addressing itself to one whose heart was softened by the fearful circumstances that had so long en-
vironed the sealers, it is not surprising that it brought our
young master to meditate seriously on his true condition
in connection with the atonement that he was willing to admit had been made for him, in common with all of earth,
at the very moment he hesitated to believe that the sufferer
was, in any other than a metaphorical sense, the Son of God.

It is not our intention to describe more of the religious
feelings of Mary and her suitor, or to enter farther into
any disquisition on subjects of this nature, than may be
absolutely necessary to elucidate the facts of our history.
In order to do the last distinctly, however, we shall endeavor to make a very brief analysis of the process of
reasoning, and we may add of feeling too, that was at work
in Roswell Gardiner's mind and heart, as he paced the
terrace that night, after Stimson had left him.

We suppose that a sense of humility is the first healthful symptom that shows itself in every man's moral regeneration. A meek appreciation of his own station and
character disposes him to receive revelation with respect,
and to have faith in things that are not seen. Perhaps
no one over whom the sword of fate was not actually
suspended by a hair, was ever better placed to admit the
lessons of humility than was Roswell Gardiner at that very
moment. Modest he always was, in the ordinary accepta-
tion of the term, and this without professions or grimaces ;
but he had a high idea of the human understanding, and
revolted at believing that which did violence to all his experience and preconceived opinions. This was the weak
spot in his character, which time, with an increasing
knowledge of men and things, or some merciful teaching
of Divine Providence, could alone remove.

Roswell certainly did not converse with Stimson in the
expectation of being much instructed ; but the humble
and uneducated boat-steerer had been at a school that
raises the dullest intellect far above all the inferences of
philosophy. He had faith, without which no man is truly
wise ; no man learned, in the highest interest of his being.
Under the guidance of this leader, Stephen occasionally
threw out an idea that struck the mind of his officer by its
simplicity and force, and helped to complete that change
for which circumstances, reading and reflection had now
been many months preparing the way. The day preceding this walk on the terrace, Roswell observed to
Stimson that he had difficulty in believing in a Deity he
could not comprehend ; meaning merely that his reason
must be satisfied with a doctrine like that of the incarnation.

"Well, sir, that's not my feelin'," answered Stephen,
earnestly. "A Deity I could understand would be no God
for me. Where there is the same knowledge, there is too
much companionship like, for worship and reverence."

"But we are told that man was created after the image
of God."

"In his likeness, Captain Gar'ner—with *some* of the
Divine Spirit, but not with all. That makes him different
from the brutes, and immortal. I have convarsed with a
clergyman who thinks that the angels, and archangels, and
other heavenly beings, are far even before the saints in
heaven, such as have been only men on 'arth."

The idea of not having a Deity that he could not comprehend, had long been one of Roswell Gardiner's favor-

ite rules of faith. He did not understand by this pretending dogma, that he was, in any respect, of capacity equal to comprehend with that of the Divine Being, but simply that he was not to be expected or required to believe in any theory which manifestly conflicted with his knowledge and experience, as both were controlled by the powers of induction he had derived directly from his Creator. In a word, his exception was one of the most obvious of the suggestions of the pride of reason, and just so much in direct opposition to the great law of regeneration, which has its very gist in the converse of his feeling—Faith.

As our young master paced the terrace alone, that idea of the necessity of the Creator's being incomprehensible to the created, recurred to him. The hour that succeeded was probably the most important in Roswell Gardiner's life. So intense were his feelings, so active the workings of his mind, that he was quite insensible to the intensity of the cold; and his body keeping equal in motion with his thoughts, if one may so express it, his frame actually set at defiance a temperature that might otherwise have chilled it, warmly and carefully as it was clad.

Truly there were many causes existing at that time and place, to bring any man to a just sense of his real position in the scale of created beings. The vault above Roswell was sparkling with orbs floating in space, most of them far more vast than this earth, and each of them doubtless having its present or destined use. What was that light, so brilliant and pervading throughout space, that converted each of those masses of dark matter into globes clothed with a glorious brightness? Roswell had seen chemical experiments that produced wonderful illuminations; but faint, indeed, were the most glowing of those artificial torches, to the floods of light that came streaming out of the void, on missions of millions and millions of miles. Who, and what was the Dread Being—dread in his Majesty and Justice, but inexhaustible in Love and Mercy—who used these exceeding means as mere instruments of his pleasure? and what was he himself, that he should presume to set up his miserable pride of reason, in opposition to a revelation supported by miracles that must be admitted to come through men inspired by the Deity, or rejected altogether?

In this frame of mind Roswell was made to see that Christianity admitted of no half-way belief; it was all true, or it was wholly false.

And why should not Christ be the Son of God, as the Fathers of the Church had perseveringly, but so simply proclaimed, and as that Church had continued to teach for eighteen centuries? Roswell believed himself to have been created in the image of God; and his much-prized reason told him that he could perpetuate himself in successors; and that which the Creator had given *him* the power to achieve, could he not in his own person perform? For the first time, an inference to the contrary seemed to be illogical.

Then the necessity for the great expiation occurred to his mind. This had always been a stumbling-block to Roswell's faith. He could not see it; and that which he could not see he was indisposed to believe. Here was the besetting weakness of his character; a weakness which did not suffer him to perceive that could he comprehend so profound a mystery, he would be raised far above that very nature in which he took so much pride. As he reflected on this branch of the subject, a thousand mysteries, physical and moral, floated before his mind; and he became aware of the little probability that he should have been endowed with the faculties to comprehend this, the greatest of them all. Had not science gradually discovered the chemical processes by which gases could be concentrated and disengaged, the formation of one of those glittering orbs above his head would have been quite as unintelligible a mystery to him, as the incarnation of the Saviour. The fact was, that phenomena that were just as mysterious to the human mind as any that the dogmas of Christianity required to be believed, exist hourly before our eyes without awakening scepticism, or exciting discussion; finding their impunity in their familiarity. Many of these phenomena were strictly incomprehensible to human understandings, which could reason up to a fountain-head in each case; and there it was obliged to abandon the inductive process, purely for the want of power to grapple with the premises which control the whole demonstration.

Could Mary Pratt have known what was going on in Roswell Gardiner's soul that night, her happiness would have been as boundless as her gratitude to God. She would have seen the barrier that had so long interposed itself to her wishes broken down; not by any rude hand, but by the influence of those whisperings of the Divine Spirit, which open the way to men to fit themselves for the presence of God.

CHAPTER XXVI.

" Let winter come ! let polar spirits sweep
     The darkening world, and tempest-troubled deep ! "
                                                —CAMPBELL.

WHILE the bosom of Roswell was thus warming with the new-born faith, of which the germ was just opening in his heart, Stimson came out upon the terrace to see what had become of his officer. It was much past the hour when the men got beneath the coverings of their mattresses ; and the honest boat-steerer, who had performed the duty on which he had been sent, was anxious about Roswell's remaining so long in the open air, on this positively the severest night of the whole season.

"You stand the cold well, Captain Gar'ner," said Stephen, as he joined his officer ; "but it might be prudent, now, to get under cover."

"I do not feel it cold, Stephen," returned Roswell—"on the contrary, I'm in a pleasant glow. My mind has been busy while my frame has kept in motion. When such are the facts, the body seldom suffers. But, hearken—does it not seem that some one is calling to us from the direction of the wreck ? "

The great distance to which sounds are conveyed in intensely cold and clear weather, is a fact known to most persons. Conversations in the ordinary tone had been heard by the sealers when the speakers were nearly a mile off ; and, on several occasions, attempts had been made to hold communications, by means of the voice, between the wreck and the hut. Certain words *had* been understood ; but it was found impossible to hold anything that could be termed conversation. Still, the voice had been often heard, and a fancy had come over the mind of Roswell that he heard a cry like a call for assistance, just as Stimson joined him.

" It is so late, sir, that I should hardly think any of the Vineyarders would be up," observed the boat-steerer, after listening some little time in the desire to catch the sound mentioned. "Then it is so cold, that most men would like to get beneath their blankets as soon as they could."

"I do not find it so very cold, Stephen. Have you looked at the thermometer lately ? "

" I gave it a look in coming out, sir ; and it tells a terrible story to-night ! The mercury is all down in the ball, which is like givin' the matter up, I do suppose, Captain Gar'ner."

" 'Tis strange ! I do not *feel* it so very cold ! The wind seems to be getting round to the northeast too ; give us enough of that, and we shall have a thaw. Hark ! there is the cry again."

This time there could be no mistake. A human voice had certainly been raised amid the stillness of that almost polar night, clearly appealing to human ears, for succor. The only word heard or comprehended was that of " help ;" one well enough adapted to carry the sound far and distinctly. There was a strain of agony in the cry, as if he who made it uttered it in despair. Roswell's blood seemed to flow back to his heart ; never had he before felt so appalling a sense of the dependence of man on a Divine Providence, as at that moment.

" You heard it ? " he said, inquiringly, to Stephen, after an instant of silent attention, to make sure that no more was to reach his ears just then.

"Sartain, sir—no man could mistake *that*. It was the voice of the nigger, Joe ; him that Captain Daggett has for a cook."

" Think you so, Stephen ? The fellow has good lungs, and they may have set him to call upon us in their distress. What can be the nature of the assistance they ask ? "

" I've been thinking of that, Captain Gar'ner ; and a difficult p'int it is to answer. Food they must have still ; and was they in want of their rations, hands would have been sent across to get 'em. They may have let their fire go out, and be without the means to relight it. I can think of nothing else that is likely to happen to men so sarcumstanced."

The last suggestion struck Roswell as possible. From the instant he felt certain that he was called on for aid, he had determined to proceed to the wreck, notwithstanding the lateness of the hour, and the intense severity of the weather. As he had intimated to Stephen, he was not at all conscious how very cold it was ; exercise and the active workings of his mind having brought him to an excellent condition to resist the sternness of the season. The appeal had been so sudden and unexpected, however, that he was at first somewhat at a loss how to proceed. The matter was now discussed between him and Stimson, when the following plan was adopted :

The mates were to be called and made acquainted with what had occurred, and put on their guard as to what might possibly be required of them. It was not thought necessary to call any of the rest of the men. There was always one hand on the watch in the house, whose duty it was to look to the fires, for the double purpose of security against a conflagration, and to prevent the warmth within from sinking too near to the cold without. It had often occurred to Roswell's mind that a conflagration would prove quick destruction to his party. In the first place, most of the provisions would be lost; and it was certain that, without a covering and the means of keeping warm within it, the men could not resist the climate eight-and-forty hours. The burning of the hut would be certain death.

Roswell took no one with him but Stimson. Two were as good as a hundred, if all that was asked were merely the means to relight the fire. These means were provided, and a loaded pistol was taken also, to enable a signal-shot to be fired, should circumstances seem to require further aid. One or two modes of communicating leading facts were concerted, when our hero and his companion set forth on their momentous journey.

Taking the hour, the weather, and the object before him into the account, Roswell Gardiner felt that he was now enlisted in the most important undertaking of his whole life, as he and Stephen shook hands with the two mates, and left the point. The drifts rendered a somewhat circuitous path necessary at first; but the moon and stars shed so much of their radiance on the frozen covering of the earth that the night was quite as light as many a London day. Excitement and motion kept the blood of our two adventurers in a brisk circulation, and prevented their becoming immediately conscious of the chill intensity of the cold to which they were exposed.

"It is good to think of Almighty God, and of his many marcies," said Stephen, when a short distance from the house, "as a body goes forth on an expedition as serious as this. We may not live to reach the wrack, for it seems to me to grow colder and colder!"

"I wonder we hear no more of the cries," remarked Roswell, who was thinking of the distress he was bent on relieving. "One would think that a man who could call so stoutly would give us another cry."

"A body can never calculate on a nigger," answered

Stephen, who had the popular American prejudice against the caste that had so long been held in servitude in the land. "They call out easily, and shut up uncommon quick, if there's nothin' gained by yelling. Black blood won't stand cold like white blood, Captain Gar'ner, any more than white blood will stand heat like black blood."

"I have heard this before, Stephen; and it has surprised me that Captain Daggett's cook should be the only one of that party who seems to have had any voice to-night."

Stimson had a good deal to say now as the two picked their way across the field of snow, always walking on the crust, which in most places would have upheld a loaded vehicle; the subject of his remarks being the difference between the two races as respects their ability to endure hardships. The worthy boat-steerer had several tales to relate of cases in which he had known negroes freeze when whites have escaped. As the fact is one pretty well established, Roswell listened complacently enough, being much too earnest in pressing forward toward his object to debate any of his companion's theories just then. It was while thus employed that Roswell fancied he heard one more cry resembling those which had brought him on this dangerous undertaking on a night so fearful. This time, however, the cry was quite faint; and what was not so easily explained, it did not appear to come from the precise direction in which the wreck was known to lie, but from one that diverged considerably from that particular quarter. Of course, the officer mentioned this circumstance to the boat-steerer; and the extraordinary part of the information caused some particular discussion between them.

"To me that last call seemed to come from up yonder nearer to the cliffs than the place where we are, and not at all from down there, near to the sea, where the wrack is," said Stimson, in the course of his remarks. "So sartain am I of this, that I feel anxious to change our course a little, to see if it be not possible that one of the Vine-yarders has got into some difficulty in trying to come across to us."

Roswell had the same desire, for he had made the same conjecture; though he did not believe the black would be the person chosen to be the messenger on such an occasion.

"I think Captain Daggett would have come himself or have sent one of his best men," he observed, "in preference to trusting a negro with a duty so important."

"We do not know, sir, that it was the nigger we heard. Misery makes much the same cries, whether it comes from the throat of white or black. Let us work upward, nearer to the cliffs, sir ; I see something dark on the snow, hereaway, as it might be on our larboard bow."

Roswell caught a glimpse of the same object, and thither our adventurers now bent their steps, walking on the crust without any difficulty, so long as they kept out of the drifts. One does not find it so easy to make any physical effort in an intensely cold atmosphere, as he does when the weather is more moderate. This prevented Roswell and his companion from moving as fast as they otherwise might have done ; but they got along with sufficient rapidity to reach the dark spot on the snow in less than five minutes after they had changed their course.

"You are right, Stephen," said Gardiner, as he came up to this speck, amid the immensity of the white mantle that covered both sea and land, far as the eye could reach ; "it is the cook ! The poor fellow has given out here, about half way between the two stations."

"There must be life in him yet, sir—nigger as he is. It's not yet twenty minutes since he gave that last cry. Help me to turn him over, Captain Gar'ner, and we will rub him, and give him a swallow of brandy. A little hot coffee, now, might bring the life back to his heart."

Roswell complied, first firing his pistol as a signal to those left behind. The negro was not dead, but so near it that a very few more minutes would have sealed his fate. The applications and frictions used by Gardiner and the boat-steerer had an effect. A swallow of the brandy probably saved the poor fellow's life. While working on his patient, Captain Gardiner found a piece of frozen pork, which, on examination, he ascertained had never been cooked. It at once explained the nature of the calamity that had befallen the crew of the wreck.

So intent were the two on their benevolent duty that a party arrived from the house, in obedience to the signal, in much less time than they could have hoped for. It was led by the mate, and came provided with a lamp burning beneath a tin vessel filled with sweetened coffee. This hot drink answered an excellent purpose with both well and sick. After a swallow or two, aided by a vigorous friction, and closely surrounded by so many human bodies, the black began to revive ; and the sort of drowsy stupor which is known to precede death in those who die by

freezing having been in a degree shaken off, he was enabled to stand alone, and by means of assistance to walk.
The hot coffee was of the greatest service, every swallow
that he got down appearing to set the engine of life into
new motion. The compelled exercise contributed its part ;
and by the time the mate, to use his own expression, "had
run the nigger into dock," which meant when he had got
him safe within the hut, his senses and faculties had so
far revived as to enable him to think and to speak. As
Gardiner and Stimson returned with him, everybody was
up and listening, when the black told his story.

It would seem that during the terrible month which had
just passed, Daggett had compelled his crew to use more
exercise than had been their practice of late. Some new
apprehension had come over him on the subject of fuel,
and his orders to be saving in that article were most strin-
gent, and very rigidly enforced. The consequence was that
the caboose was not as well attended to as it had been
previously, and as circumstances required, indeed, that it
should be. At night the men were told to keep themselves
warm with bedclothes, and by huddling together ; and
the cabin being small, so many persons crowded together
in it, did not fail to produce an impression on its atmosphere.

Such was the state of things, when, on going to his caboose, in order to cook the breakfast, this very black found
the fire totally extinguished ! Not a spark could he discover, even among the ashes ; and, what was even worse,
the tinder-box had disappeared. As respects the last, it
may be well to state here, that it was afterward discovered
carefully bestowed between two of the timbers of the wreck,
with a view to particular safe keeping ; the person who
had made this disposition of it forgetting what he had
done. The loss of the tinder-box, under the circumstances, was almost as great a calamity as could have befallen men in the situation of the Vineyarders. As against
the cold, by means of bedclothes, exercise and other precautions, it might have been possible to exist for some
time, provided warm food could be obtained ; but the
frost penetrated the cabin, and every one soon became sensitively alive to the awkwardness, not to say danger, of
their condition. A whole day was passed in fruitless attempts to obtain fire by various processes. Friction did
not succeed ; it probably never does with the thermometer
at zero. Sparks could be obtained, but by this time every

thing was stiff with the frost. The food already cooked
was soon as hard as bullets, and it was found that on the
second night brandy that was exposed was converted into
a lump of ice. Not only did the intensity of the cold increase, but everything, even to the human system, seemed
to be gradually congealing, and preparing to become converted into receptacles for frost. Several of the men began to suffer in their ears, noses, feet, and other extremities, and the bunks were soon the only places in which it
was found possible to exist in anything like comfort. No
less than three men had been sent, at intervals of a few
hours, across to the house, with a view to obtain fire, or
the means of lighting one, along with other articles that
were considered necessary to the safety of the people.
The cook had been the third and last of these messengers.
He had passed his two shipmates, each lying dead on the
snow,—or, as he supposed, lifeless ; for neither gave the
smallest sign of vitality, on an examination. It was in the
agony of alarm produced by these appalling spectacles,
that the negro had cried aloud for help, sending the
sounds far enough to reach the ears of Roswell. Still he
had persevered ; until chilled, as much with terror as with
the cold and the want of warm nourishment, the cook had
sunk into what would have soon proved to be his last long
sleep, when the timely succor arrived.

It was some two hours after the black had been got into
the hut, and was strengthened with a good hot supper,
ere he had communicated all the facts just related. Roswell succeeded, however, in getting a little at a time from
him ; and when no more remained to be related, the plan
was already arranged for future proceedings. It was quite
clear no unnecessary delay should be permitted to take
place. The cold continued to increase in intensity, notwithstanding it was the opinion of the most experienced
among the men that a thaw, and a great spring thaw, was
approaching. It often happens, in climates of an exaggerated character, that these extremes almost touch each
other, as they are said to meet in man.

Roswell left the house for the second time that eventful
night, just at the hour of twelve. He now went accompanied by the second mate and a foremast-hand, as well as
by his old companion, the boat-steerer. Each individual
drank a bowl of hot coffee before he set out, and a good
warm supper had also been taken in the interval between
the return and this new sortie. Experience shows that

there is no such protector against the effect of cold as a full stomach, more especially if the food be warm and nourishing. This was understood by Roswell; and not only did he cause the whole party that set forth with him at that late and menacing hour to receive this sustenance, but he ordered the kettle of boiling coffee to be carried with them, and kept two lamps burning for the double purpose of maintaining the heat, and of having a fire ready on reaching the wreck. The oil of the sea-elephant, together with pieces of canvas prepared for the purpose, supplied the necessary materials.

So intensely severe was the weather that Roswell had serious thoughts of returning when he reached the spot where the black had been found. But the picture of Daggett's situation that occurred to his mind, urged him on, and he proceeded. Every precaution had been taken to exclude the cold, as it is usually termed, which, as it respects the body, means little less than keeping the vital heat in, and very useful were these provisions found to be. Skins formed the principal defence, though the men had long adopted the very simple but excellent expedient of wearing two shirts. Owing to this, and to the other measures taken, neither of the four was struck with a chill, and they all continued on.

At the place mentioned by the black, the body of one of Daggett's best men, a boat-steerer, was found. The man was dead, of course, and the corpse was as rigid as a billet of wood. Every particle of moisture in it had congealed, until the whole of what had been a very fine and manly frame, lay little more than a senseless lump of ice. A few degrees to the southward of the spot where it was now seen, it is probable that this relic of humanity would have retained its form and impression, until the trump sounded to summon it to meet its former tenant, the spirit, in judgment.

No time was lost in useless lamentations over the body of this man, who was much of a favorite among the Oyster Ponders. Twenty minutes later the second corpse was found; both the bodies lying in what was the customary track between the house and the wreck. It was the last that had died; but, like that of the unfortunate man just described, it was in a state to be preserved ten thousand years without the occurrence of a thaw. Merely glancing at the rigid features of the face, in order to identify the person, Roswell passed on, the chill feelings of every individual of his party now admonishing them all of the necessity of getting as soon as possible to some place where they could feel the influence of a fire. In ten minutes more, the whole were in the caverns of the ice, and presently, the cabin of the wreck was entered. Without turning to the right hand or to the left, without looking for one of the inmates of the place, every man among the new-comers turned his attention instantly to getting the fire lighted. The caboose had been filled with wood, and it was evident that many efforts had been made to produce a blaze, by those who had put it there. Splinters of pine had been inserted among the oak of the vessel, and nothing was wanting but the means of kindling. These, most fortunately for themselves, the party of Roswell had, and eagerly did they now have recourse to their use.

There was not a man among the Oyster Ponders who did not, just at that moment, feel his whole being concentrated in that one desire to obtain warmth. The cold had slowly, but surely, insinuated itself among their garments, and slight chills were now felt even by Roswell, whose frame had been most wonderfully sustained that night, through the force of moral feeling. Stimson was the individual who was put forward at the caboose, others holding the lamps, canvas saturated with oil, and some prepared paper. It was found to be perceptibly warmer within the cabin, with its doors closed, and the external coverings of sails, etc., that had been made to exclude the air, than without ; nevertheless, when Roswell glanced at a thermometer that was hanging against the bulk-head, he saw that all the mercury was still in the ball !

The interest with which our party now watched the proceedings of Stephen, had much of that intensity that is known to attend any exhibition of vital importance. Life and death were, however, to be dependent on the issue ; and the manner in which every eye was turned on the wood, and Stephen's mode of dealing with it, denoted how completely the dread of freezing had got possession of the minds of even these robust and generous men. Roswell alone ventured, for a single moment, to look around the cabin. Three of the Vineyarders only were visible in it ; though it struck him that others lay in the berths, under piles of clothes. Of the three who were up, one was so near the lamp he held in his hand, that its light illumined his face, and all that could be seen of a form enveloped in skins. This man sat leaning against a transom. His

eyes were open, and glared on the party around the caboose ; the lips were slightly parted, and, at first, Roswell
expected to hear him speak. The immovable features,
rigid muscles, and wild expression of the eyeballs, however, soon told him the melancholy truth. The man was
dead. The current of life had actually frozen at his heart.
Shuddering, as much with horror as with a sharp chill that
just then passed through his own stout frame, our young
master turned anxiously to note the success of Stimson, in
getting the wood of the caboose in a blaze.

Every one, in the least accustomed to a very severe climate, must have had frequent occasions to observe the reluctance with which all sorts of fuel burn, in exceedingly
cold weather. The billet of wood that shall blaze merrily,
on a mild day, moulders and simmers, and seems indisposed to give out any heat at all, with the thermometer at
zero. In a word, all inanimate substances that contain the
elements of caloric appear to sympathize with the prevailing state of the atmosphere, and to contribute to render
that which is already too cold for comfort, even colder.
So it was now, notwithstanding the preparations that had
been made. Baffled twice in his expectations of procuring
a blaze, Stephen stopped and took a drink of the hot
coffee. As he swallowed the beverage, it struck him that
it was fast losing its warmth.

A considerable collection of canvas, saturated with oil,
was now put beneath the pile, in the midst of splinters of
pine, and one of the lamps was forced into the centre of
the combustibles. This expedient succeeded ; the frosts
were slowly chased out of the kindling materials ; a sickly
but gradually increasing flame strove through the kindling
stuff and soon began to play among the billets of the oak,
the only fuel that could be relied on for available heat.
Still there was great danger that the lighter wood would
all be consumed ere this main dependence could be aroused
from its dull inactivity. Frost appeared to be in possession of the whole pile ; and it was expelled so slowly, clung
to its dominion with so much power, as really to render
the result doubtful, for a moment or two. Fortunately,
there was found a pair of bellows ; and by means of a
judicious use of this very useful implement, the oak wood
was got into a bright blaze, and warmth began to be given
out from the fire. Then came the shiverings and chills,
with which intense cold consents even to abandon the human frame ; and, by their number and force, Roswell was

made to understand how near he and his companions had
been to death. As the young man saw the fire slowly
kindle to a cheerful blaze, a glow of gratitude flowed
toward his heart, and mentally he returned thanks to God.
The cabin was so small, had been made so tight by artificial means, and the caboose was so large, that a sensible
influence was produced on the temperature, as soon as the
wood began to burn a little freely. As none of the heat
was lost, the effect was not only apparent, but most grateful. Roswell had looked into the vessels of the caboose,
while the fire was gathering head. One, the largest, was
filled, or nearly so, with coffee frozen to a solid mass! In
the other, beef and pork had been set over to boil, and
there the pieces now were, embedded in ice, and frozen to
blocks. It was when these two distinct masses of ice began
to melt, that it was known the fire was beginning to prevail, and hope revived in the bosoms of the Oyster Ponders. On taking another look at the thermometer, it was
found that the mercury had so far expanded as to be leaving the ball. It soon after ascended so high as to denote
only forty degrees below zero!

Everything, even to life, depending on maintaining and
increasing the power of the fire, the men now looked
about them for more fuel. There was an ample stock in
the cabin, however, the fire having become extinguished,
not for want of wood, but in the usual way. It were need-
less to describe the manner in which those who stood
around the stove watched the flames, or how profound was
their satisfaction when they saw that Stimson had finally
succeeded.

"God be praised for this and for all his marcies!" exclaimed Stephen, laying aside the bellows at last. "I can
feel warmth from the fire, and that will save such of us as
have not yet been taken away." He then lifted the lids,
and looked into the different vessels that were on. The
ice was melting fast, and the steams of coffee became apparent to the senses. It was at this instant that a feeble
voice was heard issuing from beneath the coverings of a
berth.

"Gar'ner," it said, imploringly, "if you have any feelin'
for a fellow-creatur' in distress, warm me up with one
swallow of that coffee! Oh! how pleasantly it smells, and
how good it must be for the stomach! For three days
have I tasted nothing—not even water."

This was Daggett, the long-tried sealer; the man of iron

nerves and golden longings ; he who had so lately concentrated within himself all that was necessary to form a pertinacious, resolute, and grasping seeker after gain. How changed, now, in all this ! He asked for the means of preserving life, and thought no more of skins, and oils, and treasures on desert keys.

Roswell was no sooner apprised of the situation of his brother-master, than he bestowed the necessary care on his wants. Fortunately, the coffee brought by the Oyster Ponders, and which retained some of its original warmth, had been set before the fire, and was now as hot as the human stomach could bear it. Two or three swallows of this grateful fluid were given to Daggett, and his voice almost instantaneously showed the effect they produced.

"I'm in a bad way, Gar'ner," resumed the Vineyard-master. "I fear we're all in a bad way, that are here. I held out ag'in the cold as long as human natur' could bear it, but was forced to give in at last."

"How many of your people still remain, Daggett ? tell us that we may look for them, and attend to their wants."

"I'm afraid, Gar'ner, they'll never want anything more in this life ! The second mate and two of the hands were sitting in the cabin when I got into this berth, and I fear 'twill be found that they're dead. I urged them to turn in, too, as the berths were the only place where anything like warmth was to be found ; but drowsiness had come on 'em, and, when that is the case, freezin' soon follows."

"The three men in the cabin are past our assistance, being actually frozen into logs ; but there must be several more of you. I see the signs of two others in the berths —ah ! what do you say to that poor fellow, Stephen ?"

"The spirit is still in the body, sir, but about to depart. If we can get him to swallow a little of the coffee, the angel of death may yet loosen his hold on him."

The coffee was got down this man's throat, and he instantly revived. He was a young man named Lee, and was one of the finest physical specimens of strength and youth in the whole crew. On examining his limbs, none were found absolutely frozen, though the circulation of the blood was so near being checked that another hour of the great cold which had reigned in the cabin, and which was slowly increasing in intensity, must have destroyed him. On applying a similar process to Daggett, Roswell was startled at the discovery he made. The feet, legs, and forearms of the unfortunate Vineyarder were all as stiff and rigid as icicles. In these particulars there could be no mistake, and the men were immediately sent for snow, in order to extract the frost by the only safe process known to the sealers. The dead bodies were carried from the cabin, and laid decently on the ice, outside, the increasing warmth within rendering the removal advisable. On glancing again at the thermometer, now suspended in a remote part of the cabin, the mercury was found risen to two above zero. This was a very tolerable degree of cold, and the men began to lay aside some of their extra defences against the weather, which would otherwise be of no service to them when exposed outside.

The crew of the Vineyard Lion had consisted of fifteen souls, one less than that of her consort. Of these men, four had lost their lives between the wreck and the house ; two on a former, and two on the present occasion. Three bodies were found sitting in the cabin, and two more were taken out of the berths, dead. The captain, the cook, and Lee, added to these, made a dozen, leaving but three of the crew to be accounted for. When questioned on the subject, Lee said that one of those three had frozen to death in the caverns several days before, and the other two had set out for the hut in the last snow-storm, unable to endure the cold at the wreck any longer. As these two men had not arrived at the house when Gardiner and his companions left it, they had perished, out of all doubt. Thus, of the fifteen human beings who had sailed together from Martha's Vineyard, ready to encounter every hazard in order to secure wealth, or what in their estimation was wealth, but three remained ; and of these, two might be considered in a critical condition. Lee was the only man of the entire crew who was sound and fit for service.

CHAPTER XXVII.

"Bid *him* bow down to that which is above him,—
The overruling Infinite,—the Maker,—
Who made him not for worship,—let him kneel,
And we will kneel together."—BYRON.

WHEN the bodies had been removed from the cabin, and the limbs of Daggett were covered with snow, Roswell Gardiner took another look at the thermometer. It had risen already to twenty degrees above zero. This was absolutely warmth, compared with the temperature from which the men had just escaped, and it was felt to be so, in their persons. The fire, however, was not the only cause of this most acceptable change. One of the men who had been outside soon came back and reported a decided improvement in the weather. The wind, which had been coquetting with the northeast point of the compass for several hours, now blew steadily from that quarter. An hour later it was found, on examination, that a second thermometer, which was outside, actually indicated ten above zero! This sudden and great change came altogether from the wind, which was now in the warm quarter. The men stripped themselves of most of their skins, and the fire was suffered to go down, though care was taken that it should not again be totally extinguished.

We have little pleasure in exhibiting pictures of human suffering; and shall say but little of the groans and pains that Daggett uttered and endured, while undergoing that most agonizing process of having the frost taken out of his system by cold applications. It was the only safe way of treating his case, however, and as he knew it, he bore his sufferings as well as man could bear them. Long ere the return of day he was released from his agony, and was put back into his berth, which had been comfortably arranged for him, having the almost unheard-of luxury of sheets, with an additional mattress.

Stephen remarked, when the men were told to try and get a little sleep, "There's plenty of berths empty, and each on us can have as many clothes and as warm a bed as he can ask for, now that so many have hastened away to their great account, as it might be, in the pride of their youth and strength."

Activity, the responsibility of command, and the great necessity there had been for exertion, prevented Roswell from reflecting much on what had happened, until he lay down to catch a little sleep. Then, indeed, the whole of the past came over him in one sombre, terrible picture, and he had the most lively perception of the dangers from which he had escaped, as well as of the mercy of God's providence. Surrounded by the dead, as it might be, and still uncertain of the fate of the living, his views of the past and future became much lessened in confidence and hope. The majesty and judgment of God assumed a higher place than common in his thoughts, while his estimate of himself was fast getting to be humbled and searching. In the midst of all these changes of views and feelings, however, there was one image unaltered in the young man's imagination. Mary occupied the background of every picture, with her meek, gentle, but blooming countenance. If he thought of God, *her* eyes were elevated in prayer; if the voyage home was in his mind, and the chances of success were calculated, *her* smiles and anxious watchfulness stimulated him to adventure; if arrived and safe, her downcast but joyful looks betrayed the modest happiness of her inmost heart. It was in the midst of some such pictures that Roswell now fell asleep.

When the party turned out in the morning, a still more decided change had occurred in the weather. The wind had increased to a gale, bringing with it torrents of rain. Coming from the warm quarter, a thaw had set in with a character quite as decided as the previous frost. In that region the weather is usually exaggerated in its features, and the change from winter to spring is quite as sudden as that from autumn to winter. We use the terms "spring" and "autumn" out of complaisance to the usages of men; but in fact these two seasons have scarcely any existence at all in the antarctic seas. The change commonly is from winter to summer, such as summer is, and from summer back to winter.

Notwithstanding the favorable appearances of things when Roswell walked out into the open air next morning, he well knew that summer had not yet come. Many weeks must go by ere the ice could quit the bay, and even a boat could put to sea. There were considerations of prudence, therefore, that should not be neglected, connected with the continuance of the supplies and the means of subsistence. In one respect, the party now on the island had been gainers by the terrible losses it had sustained in Daggett's crew. The provisions of the two vessels might now virtually be appropriated to the crew of one; and Roswell, when he came to reflect on the circumstances, saw that a Providential interference had probably saved the survivors from great privations, if not from absolute want.

Still there was a thaw, and one of that decided character which marks a climate of great extremes. The snows on the mountain soon began to descend upon the plain in foaming torrents, and increased by the tribute received from the last, the whole came tumbling over the cliffs in various places in rich water-falls. There was about a mile of rock that was one continuous cataract, the sheet being nearly unbroken for the whole distance. The effect of this deluge from the plain above was as startling as it was grand. All the snow along the rocky shore soon disappeared, and the fragments of ice began rapidly to diminish in size, and to crumble. At first Roswell felt much concern on account of the security of the wreck; his original apprehension being that it would be washed away. This ground of fear was soon succeeded by another of scarcely less serious import—that of its being crushed by the enormous cakes of ice that made the caverns in which it lay, and which now began to settle and change their positions, as the water washed away their bases. At one time Roswell thought of setting the storm at defiance, and of carrying Daggett across to the house by means of the handbarrow; but when he came to look at the torrents of water that were crossing the rocks, so many raging rivulets, the idea was abandoned as impracticable. Another night was therefore passed in the midst of the tempest.

The northeast wind, the rain, and the thaw, were all at work in concert, when our adventurers came abroad to look upon the second day of their sojourn in the wreck. By this time the caverns were dripping with a thousand little streams, and every sign denoted a most rapid melting of the ice. On carrying the thermometer into the open air it stood at sixty-two, and the men found it necessary to lay aside their second shirt, and all the extraordinary defences of their attire. Nor was this all; the wind that crosses the salt water is known to have more than the usual influence on the snows and ice; and such was the effect now produced by it on Sealer's Land. The snow, indeed, had mostly disappeared from all places but the drifts, while the ice was much diminished in its size and outlines. So grateful was the change from the extreme cold that they had so lately endured, that the men thought nothing of the rain at all; they went about in it just as if it did not stream down upon them in little torrents. Some of them clambered up the cliffs and reached a point whence it was known that they could command a view of the house. The return of this party, which Roswell did not accompany, was waited for with a good deal of interest. When it got back it brought a report that was deemed important in several particulars. The snow had gone from the plain, and from the mountain, with the exception

of a few spots where there had been unusual accumula-
tions of it. As respected the house, it was standing, and
the snow had entirely disappeared from its vicinity. The
men could be seen walking about on the bare rocks, and
every symptom was that of settled spring.

This was cheering news ; and the torrents having much
diminished in size, some having disappeared altogether,
Roswell set out for the cape, leaving the second mate in
charge of the wreck. Lee, the young Vineyarder who
had been rescued from freezing by the timely arrival of
our hero, accompanied the latter, having joined his fortunes to those of the Oyster Ponders. The two reached
the house before dark, where they found Hazard and his
companions in a good deal of concern touching the fate
of the party that was out. A deep impression was made
by the report of what had befallen the other crew ; and
that night Roswell read prayers to as attentive a congregation as was ever assembled around a domestic hearth.
As for fire, none was now needed, except for culinary purposes, though all the preparations to meet cold weather
were maintained, it being well known that a shift of wind
might bring back the fury of the winter.

The following morning it was clear, though the wind
continued warm and balmy from the north. No such
weather, indeed, had been felt by the sealers since they
reached the group ; and the effect on them was highly
cheering and enlivening. Before he had breakfasted,
Roswell was down in the cove, examining into the condition of the vessel, or what remained of her. A good deal
of frozen snow still lay heaped on the mass, and he set the
hands at work to shovel it off. Before noon the craft was
clear, and most of the snow was melted, it requiring little
more than exposure to the air in order to get rid of it.

As soon as the hulk was clear, Roswell directed his men
to take everything out of it ; the remains of cargo, water-
casks, and some frozen provisions, in order that it might
float as light as possible. The ice was frozen close to
every part of the vessel's bottom to a depth of several feet,
following her mould, a circumstance that would necessarily
prevent her settling in the water below her timbers ; but,
as there was no telling when this ice might begin to recede
by melting, it was deemed prudent to use this precaution.
It was found that the experiment succeeded, the hulk
actually rising, when relieved from the weight in it, not
less than four inches.

A consultation was held that night, between Gardiner, his officers, and the oldest of the seamen. The question presented was whether the party should attempt to quit the group in the boats, or whether they should build a little on the hulk, deck her over, and make use of this altered craft to return to the northward. There was a good deal to be said on both sides. If the boats were used, the party might leave as soon as the weather became settled, and the season a little more advanced, by dragging the boats on sledges across the ice to the open water, which was supposed to be some ten or twenty miles to the northward, and a large amount of provisions might thus be saved. On the other hand, however, as it regarded the provisions, the boats would hold so little, that no great gain would be made by going early in them, and leaving a sufficient supply behind to keep all hands two or three months. This was a consideration that presented itself, and it had its weight in the decision. Then there was the chance of the winter's returning, bringing with it the absolute necessity of using a great deal more fuel. This was a matter of life and death. Comparatively pleasant as the weather had become, there was no security for its so continuing. One entire spring month was before the sealers, and a shift of wind might convert the weather into a wintry temperature. Should such be the case, it might become indispensable to burn the very materials that would be required to build up and deck over the hulk. There were, therefore, many things to be taken into the account; nor was the question settled without a great deal of debate and reflection.

After discussing all these points, the decision was as follows: It was at least a month too soon to think of trusting themselves in that stormy ocean, on the high seas and in the open boats; and this so much the more because nature, as if expressly to send back a reasonable amount of warm air into the polar regions, with a view to preserve the distinction of the seasons, caused the wind to blow most of the time from the northward. As this month, in all prudence, must be passed on the island, it might as well be occupied with building upon the hulk, as in any other occupation. Should the cold weather return, the materials would still be there, and might be burned, in the last extremity, just as well, or even with greater facility, after being brought over to the cove, as if left where they then were, or at the wreck. Should the winter not return, the work done on the vessel would be so much gained, and they would be ready for an earlier start, when the ice should move.

On this last plan the duty was commenced, very little interrupted by the weather. For quite three weeks the wind held from points favorable to the progress of spring, veering from east to west, but not once getting any southing in it. Occasionally it blew in gales, sending down upon the group a swell that made great havoc with the outer edges of the field-ice. Every day or two a couple of hands were sent up the mountain to take a look-out, and to report the state of matters in the adjacent seas. The fleet of bergs had not yet come out of port, though it was in motion to the southward, like three-deckers dropping down to outer anchorages, in roadsteads and bays. As Roswell intended to be off before these formidable cruisers put to sea, their smallest movement or change was watched and noted. As for the field-ice, it was broken up, miles at a time, until there remained very little of it, with the exception of the portion that was wedged in and jammed among the islands of the group. From some cause that could not be ascertained, the waves of the ocean, which came tumbling in before the northern gales, failed to roll home upon this ice, which lost its margin, now it was reduced to the limits of the group, slowly and with great resistance. Some of the sealers ascribed this obstinacy in the bay-ice to its greater thickness ; believing that the shallowness of the water had favored a frozen formation below, that did not so much prevail off soundings. This theory may have been true, though there was quite as much against it as in its favor, for polar ice usually increases above and not from below. The sea is much warmer than the atmosphere, in the cold months, and the ice is made by deposits of snow, moisture, and sleet, on the surfaces of the fields and bergs.

In those three weeks, which carried forward the season to within ten days of summer, a great deal of useful work was done. Daggett was brought over to the house, on a handbarrow, for the second time, and made as comfortable as circumstances would allow. From the first, Roswell saw that his state was very precarious, the frozen legs, in particular, being threatened with mortification. All the expedients known to a sealer's *materia medica* were resorted to, in order to avert consequences so serious, but without success. The circulation could not be restored, as nature required it to be done, and, failing of the support derived from a healthful condition of the vital current, the fatal symptoms slowly supervened. This change, however, was so gradual, that it scarce affected the regular course of the duty.

It was a work of great labor to transport the remaining timbers and plank of the wreck to the cove. Without the wheels, indeed, it may be questioned whether it could have been done at all, in a reasonable time. The breaking up of the schooner was, in itself, no trifling job, for fully one half of the frame remained to be pulled to pieces. In preparing the materials for use, again, a good deal of embarrassment was experienced in consequence of the portions of the two vessels that were left being respectively their lower bodies, all the upper works of each having been burned, with the exception of the after part of Daggett's craft, which had been preserved on account of the cabin. This occasioned a good deal of trouble in moulding and fitting the new upper works on the hulk in the cove. Roswell had no idea of rebuilding his schooner strictly in her old form and proportions; he did not, indeed, possess the materials for such a reconstruction. His plan was, simply, to raise on the hulk as much as was necessary to render her safe and convenient, and then to get as good and secure a deck over all as circumstances would allow.

Fortunately for the progress of the work, Lee, the Vineyard man, was a ship-carpenter, and his skill essentially surpassed that of Smith, who filled the same station on board the Oyster Pond craft. These two men were now of the greatest service; for, though neither understood drafting, each was skilful in the use of tools, and a certain readiness that enabled him to do a hundred things that he had never found it necessary to attempt on any former occasion. If the upper frame that was now got on the Sea Lion was not of a faultless mould, it was securely fastened, and rendered the craft even stronger than it had been originally. Some regard was had to resisting the pressure of ice, and experience had taught all the sealers where the principal defences against the effects of a " nip " ought to be placed. The lines were not perfect, it is true ; but this was of less moment, as the bottom of the craft, which alone had any material influence on her sailing, was just as it had come from the hands of the artisan who had originally moulded her.

By the end of a fortnight the new top-timbers were all in their places and secured, while a complete set of bends were brought to them, and were well bolted. The caulking-irons were put in requisition as soon as a streak was on, the whole work advancing, as it might be, *pari passu.* Planks for the decks were much wanted, for, in the terrible strait for fuel which had caused the original assault on the schooner, this portion of the vessel had been the first burned, as of the most combustible materials. The quarter-deck of the Vineyard craft, luckily, was entire, and its planks so far answered an excellent purpose. They served to make a new quarter-deck for the repairs, but the whole of the main-deck and forecastle remained to be provided for. Materials were gleaned from different parts of the two vessels, until a reasonably convenient, and a perfectly safe deck was laid over the whole craft, the coamings for the hatches being taken from Daggett's schooner, which had not been broken up in those parts. It is scarcely necessary to say that the ice had early melted from the rocks of the coast. The caverns all disappeared within the first week of the thaw, the attitudes into which the cakes had been thrown greatly favoring the melting process, by exposing so much surface to the joint action of wind, rain, and sun. What was viewed as a favorable augury, the seals began to reappear. There was a remote portion of the coast, from which the ice had been driven by the winds around the northwest cape, that was already alive with them. Alas! these animals no longer awakened cupidity in the breasts of the sealers. The last no longer thought of gain, but simply of saving their lives, and of restoring themselves to the humble places they had held in the world previously to having come on this ill-fated voyage.

This reappearance of the seals produced a deep impression on Roswell Gardiner. His mind had been much inclined of late to dwell more and more on religious subjects, and his conversations with Stephen were still more frequent than formerly. Not that the boat-steerer could enlighten him on the great subject, by any learned lore, for in this Stimson was quite deficient; but his officer found encouragement in the depth and heartiness of his companion's faith, which seemed to be raised above all doubts and misgivings whatever. During the gloomiest moments of that fearful winter, Stephen had been uniformly confiding and cheerful. Not once had he been seen to waver, though all around him were desponding and anticipating the worst.

His heart was light exactly in proportion as his faith was strong.

"We shall neither freeze nor starve," he used to say, "unless it be God's will ; and, when it is his pleasure, depend on it, friends, it will be for our good." As for Daggett, he had finally given up his hold on the wreck, and it seemed no longer to fill his thoughts. When he was told that the seals had come back, his eyes brightened, and his nature betrayed some of its ardent longings. But it was no more than a gleaming of the former spirit of the man, now becoming dim under the darkness that was fast encircling all his views of the world.

"It's a pity, Gar'ner, that we have no craft ready for the work," he said, under the first impulse of the intelligence. "At this early time in the season, a large ship might be filled !"

"We have other matters on our hands, Captain Daggett," was the answer ; "they must be looked to first. If we can get off the island at all, and return safe to those who, I much fear, are now mourning us as dead, we shall have great reason to thank God."

"A few skins would do no great harm, Gar'ner, even to a craft cut down and reduced."

"We have more cargo now than we shall be able to take with us. Quite one half of all our skins must be left behind us, and all of the oil. The hold of the schooner is too shallow to carry enough of anything to make out a voyage. I shall ballast with water and provisions, and fill up all the spare room with the best of our skins. The rest of the property must be abandoned."

"Why abandoned ? Leave a hand or two to take care of it, and send a craft out to look for it as soon as you get home. Leave me, Gar'ner, I am willing to stay."

Roswell thought that the poor man would be left, whether he wished to remain or not, for the symptoms that are known to be so fatal in cases like that of Daggett's were making themselves so apparent as to leave little doubt of the result. What rendered this display of the master-passion somewhat remarkable was the fact that our hero had on several occasions conversed with the invalid, concealing no material feature of his case, and the latter had expressed his expectation of a fatal termination, if not an absolute willingness to die. Stimson had frequently prayed with Daggett, and Roswell had often read particular chapters of the Bible to him, at his own request,

creating an impression that the Vineyarder was thinking
more of his end than of any interest connected with this
life.   Such might have been, probably *was* the case, until
the seeming return of what had once been deemed good
luck awakened old desires, and brought out traits of
character that were about to be lost in the near views of a
future world.   All this Roswell saw and noted, and the
reflection produced by his own perilous condition, the
certain loss of so many companions, the probable death of
Daggett, and the humble but impressive example and
sympathy of Stimson, were such as would have delighted
the tender spirit of Mary Pratt, could she have known of
their existence.

But the great consideration of the moment, the centre of
all the hopes and fears of our sealers, was the rebuilding of
the mutilated Sea Lion.   Although the long thaw did so
much for them, the reader is not to regard it as such a spell
of warm weather as one enjoys in May within the temperate
zone.   There were no flowers, no signs of vegetation, and
whenever the wind ceased to blow smartly from the northward, there was frost.   At two or three intervals cold
snaps set in that looked seriously like a return to winter,
and at the end of the third week of pleasant weather mentioned, it began to blow a gale from the southward, to
snow, and to freeze.   The storm commenced about ten in
the forenoon ; ere the sun went down, the days then being
of great length, every passage around the dwelling was
already blocked up with banks of snow.   Several times
had the men asked permission to remove the sails from
the house, to admit air and light ; but it was now found
that the tent-like verandah they formed was of as much
use as it had been at any time during the season.   Without it, indeed, it would not have been possible for the
people to quit their dwelling during three entire days.
Everything like work was, of course, suspended during
this tempest, which seriously menaced the unfortunate
sealers with the necessity of again breaking up their
schooner, now nearly completed, with a view again to
keep themselves from freezing.   The weather was not so
intensely cold as it had been, continuously, for months
during the past winter ; but, coming as it did, after so
long a spell of what might be considered as a balmy
atmosphere in that region, it found the people unbraced,
and little prepared for it.   At no time was the thermometer lower than twenty degrees below zero ; this was near

morning, after a sharp and stinging night ; nor was it for
any succession of hours much below zero. But zero was
now hard to bear, and fires, and good fires too, were absolutely necessary to keep the men from suffering, as well as
from despondency. Perhaps the spectacle of Daggett, dying from the effects of frost, before their eyes, served to increase the uneasiness of the people, and to cause them to
be less sparing of the fuel than persons in their situations
ought to have been. It is certain that a report was
brought to Roswell, in the height of the tempest, and
when the thermometer was at the lowest, that there was
not wood enough left from the plunder of the two vessels,
exclusively of that which had been worked up in the
repairs, to keep the fires going eight-and-forty hours
longer ! It was true, a little wood, intended to be used
in the homeward passage, enough to last as far as Rio
possibly, had been used in stowing the hold ; and that
might be got at first, if it ever ceased to snow. Without
that addition to the stock in the house, it would not be
within the limits of probability to suppose the people
could hold out against the severity of such weather a
great while longer.

Every expedient that could be devised to save wood,
and to obtain warmth from other sources, was resorted to,
of course, by Roswell's orders. Lamps were burned with
great freedom ; not little vessels invented to give light, but
such torches as one sees at the lighting up of a princely
court-yard on the occasion of a *fête*, in which wicks are
made by the pound, and unctuous matter is used by the
gallon. Old canvas and elephants' oil supplied the materials ; and the spare caboose, which had been brought
over to the house to be set up there, while the other galley
was being placed on board, very well answered the purpose
of a lamp. Some warmth was obtained by these means,
but much more of a glaring and unpleasant light.

It was during the height of this tempest that the soul of
Daggett took its flight toward the place of departed spirits, in preparation for the hour when it was to be summoned before the judgment-seat of God. Previously to
his death, the unfortunate Vineyarder held a frank and
confidential discourse with Roswell. As his last hour approached, his errors and mistakes became more distinctly
apparent, as is usual with men, while his sins of omission
seemed to crowd the vista of by-gone days. Then it was
that the whole earth did not contain that which, in his

23

dying eyes, would prove an equivalent for one hour passed in a sincere, devout, and humble service of the Deity!

"I'm afraid that I've loved money most too well," he said to Roswell, not an hour before he drew his last breath; "but I hope it was not so much for myself as for others. A wife and children, Gar'ner, tie a man to 'arth in a most unaccountable manner. Sealers' companions are used to hearing of misfortunes, and the Vineyard women know that few on 'em live to see a husband at their side in old age. Still, it is hard on a mother and wife to l'arn that her chosen friend has been cut off in the pride of his days, and in a distant land. Poor Betsey! It would have been better for us both had we been satisfied with the little we had; for now the good woman will have to look to all matters for herself."

Daggett now remained silent for some time, though his lips moved, most probably in prayer. It was a melancholy sight to see a man in the vigor of his manhood, whose voice was strong, and whose heart was still beating with vigor and vitality, standing, as it were, on the brink of a precipice, down which all knew he was to be so speedily hurled. But the decree had gone forth, and no human skill could arrest it. Shortly after the confession and lamentation we have recorded, the decay reached the vitals, and the machine of clay stopped. To avoid the unpleasant consequences of keeping the body in so warm a place, it was buried in the snow a short distance from the house, within an hour after it had ceased to breathe.

When Roswell Gardiner saw this man, who had so long adhered to him like a leech, in the pursuit of gold, laid a senseless corpse among the frozen flakes of the antarctic seas, he felt that a lively admonition of the vanity of the world was administered to himself. How little had he been able to foresee all that had happened, and how mistaken had been his own calculations and hopes! What, then, was that intellect of which he had been so proud, and what reason had he to rely on himself in those matters that lay equally beyond the cradle and the grave—that incomprehensible past, and the unforeseen future toward which all those in existence were hastening! Roswell had received many lessons in humility, the most useful of all the lessons that man can receive in connection with the relation that really exists between the Deity and himself. Often had he wondered, while reading the Bible Mary Pratt had put into his hand, at the stubborn manner in which the chosen people of God had returned to their "idols," and their "groves," and their "high places;" but he was now made to understand that others still erred in this great particular, and that of all the idols men worship, that of self was perhaps the most objectionable.

CHAPTER XXVIII.

"Long swoln in drenching rains, seeds, germs, and buds,
    Start at the touch of vivifying beams.
    Moved by their secret voice, the vital lymph
    Diffusive runs, and spreads o'er wood and field
    A flood of verdure."—WILCOX.

AT length it came to be rumored among the sealers that the fires must be permitted to go out, or that the materials used for making the berths, and various other fixtures of the house, must be taken to supply the stove. It was when it got to be known that the party was reduced to this sad dilemma that Roswell broke through the bank of snow that almost covered the house, and got so far into the open air as to be able to form some estimate of the probable continuance of the present cold weather. The thermometer, within the bank of snow, but outside of the building, then stood at twenty below zero; but it was much colder in the unobstructed currents of as keen and biting a south wind as ever came howling across the vast fields of ice that covered the polar basin. The snow had long ceased, but not until an immense quantity had fallen; nearly twice as much, Roswell and Hazard thought, as they had seen on the rocks at any time that winter.

"I see no signs of a change, Mr. Hazard," Roswell remarked, shivering with the intensity of the cold. "We had better go back into the house before we get chilled, for we have no fire now to go to, to warm ourselves. It is much warmer within doors than it is in the open air, fire or no fire."

"There are many reasons for that, Captain Gar'ner," answered the mate. "So many bodies in so small a space, the shelter from the outer wind and outer air, and the snow-banks, all help us. I think we shall find the thermometer in-doors at a pretty comfortable figure this morning."

On examining it, it was found to stand at only fifteen below zero, making a difference of five degrees in favor of

the house, as compared with the sort of covered gallery
under the tent, and probably of five more, as compared
with the open air.

On a consultation, it was decided that all hands should
eat a hearty meal, remove most of their clothes, and get
within the coverings of their berths, to see if it would not
be possible to wear out the cold spell, in some tolerable
comfort, beneath rugs and blankets. On the whole it was
thought that the berths might be made more serviceable
by this expedient, than by putting their materials into the
stoves. Accordingly, within an hour after Roswell and
his mate had returned from their brief out-door excursion,
the whole party was snugly bestowed under piles of rugs,
clothes, sails, and whatever else might be used to retain
the animal heat near the body, and exclude cold. In this
manner six-and-thirty hours were passed, not a man of
them all having the courage to rise from his lair, and encounter the severity of the climate, now unrelieved by anything like a fire.

Roswell had slept most of the time during the last ten
hours, and in this he was much like all around him. A
general feeling of drowsiness had come over the men, and
the legs and feet of many among them, notwithstanding
the quantity of bedclothes that were, in particular, piled
on that part of their person, were sensitively alive to the
cold. No one ever knew how low the thermometer went
that fearful night ; but a sort of common consciousness
prevailed, that nothing the men had yet seen, or felt,
equalled its chill horrors. The cold had got into the
house, converting every article it contained into a mass of
frost. The berths ceased to be warm, and the smallest
exposure of a shoulder, hand, or ears, soon produced pain.
The heads of very many of the party were affected, and
breathing became difficult and troubled. A numbness began to steal over the lower limbs ; and this was the last
unpleasant sensation remembered by Roswell, when he
fell into another short and disturbed slumber. The propensity to sleep was very general now, though many struggled against it, knowing it was the usual precursor of death
by freezing.

Our hero never knew how long he slept in the last nap
he took on that memorable occasion. When he awoke,
he found a bright light blazing in the hut, and heard some
one moving about the caboose. Then his thoughts reverted to himself, and to the condition of his limbs. On

trying to rub his feet together, he found them so nearly
without sensation as to make the consciousness of their
touching each other almost out of the question. Taking
the alarm at once, he commenced a violent friction, until
by slow degrees he could feel that the nearly stagnant
blood was getting again into motion. So great had been
Roswell's alarm, and so intent his occupation, that he took
no heed of the person who was busy at the caboose,
until the man appeared at the side of his berth, holding
a tin pot in his hand. It was Stimson, up and dressed,
without his skins, and seemingly in perfect preservation.

"Here's some hot coffee, Captain Gar'ner," said the
provident boat-steerer, "and then turn out. The wind has
shifted, by the marcy of God, and it has begun to rain.
Now, I think we may have summer in 'arnest, as summer
comes among these sealin' islands."

Roswell took six or eight swallows of the coffee, which
was smoking hot, and instantly felt the genial influence
diffused over his whole frame. Sending Stephen to the
other berths with this timely beverage, he now sat up in
his berth, and rubbed his feet and legs with his hands.
The exercise, friction, and hot coffee, soon brought him
round ; and he sprang out of his berth, and was quickly
dressed. Stimson had lighted a fire in the caboose,
using the very last of the wood, and the warmth was
beginning to diffuse itself through the building. But the
change in the wind, and the consequent melioration of
the temperature, probably alone saved the whole of the
Oyster Pond crew from experiencing the dire fate of that
of the Vineyard craft.

Stephen got man after man out of his berth, by doses of
the steaming coffee ; and the blood being thus stimulated,
by the aid of friction, everybody was soon up and stirring.
It was found, on inquiry, that all three of the blacks had
toes or ears frozen, and with them the usual application of
snow became necessary ; but the temperature of the house
soon got to be so high as to render the place quite comfortable Warm food being deemed very essential, Stephen
had put a supply of beans and pork into his coppers ; and,
the frost having been extracted from a quantity of the
bread by soaking it in cold water, a hearty meal of good,
hot, and most nourishing food, was made by all hands.
This set our sealers up, no more complaints of the frost
being heard.

It was, indeed, no longer very cold. The thermometer

was up to twenty-six above zero in the house when Roswell turned out ; and the cooking process, together with Stephen's fires and the shift of wind, soon brought the mercury up to forty. This was a cheering temperature for those who had been breathing the polar air ; and the influence of the northeast gale continued to increase. The rain and thaw produced another deluge ; and the cliffs presented, for several hours, a sight that might have caused Niagara to hide her head in mortification. These sublime scenes are of frequent occurrence amid the solitudes of the earth ; the occasional phenomena of nature often surpassing in sublimity and beauty her rarest continued efforts.

The succeeding day the rain ceased, and summer appeared to have come in reality. It is true that at midday the thermometer in the shade stood at only forty-eight ; but in the sun it actually rose to seventy. Let those who have ever experienced the extremes of heat and cold imagine the delight with which our sealers moved about under such a sun! All excess of clothing was thrown aside ; and many of the men actually pursued their work in their shirt-sleeves.

As the snow had vanished quite as suddenly as it came, everything and everybody was now in active motion. Not a man of the crew was disposed to run the risk of encountering any more cold on Sealer's Land. Roswell himself was of opinion that the late severe weather was the dying effort of the winter, and that no more cold was to be expected ; and Stimson agreed with him in this notion. The sails were taken down from around the house, and those articles it was intended to carry away were transferred to the schooner as fast as the difficulties of the road would allow. While his mates were carrying on this duty, our young master took an early occasion to examine the state of matters generally on the island. With this view he ascended to the plain, and went half-way up the mountain, desiring to get a good look into the offing.

It was soon ascertained that the recent deluge had swept all the ice and every trace of the dead into the sea. The body of Daggett had disappeared with the snow-bank in which it had been buried ; and all the carcasses of the seals had been washed away. In a word, the rocks were as naked and as clean as if man's foot had never passed over them. From the facts that skeletons of seals had been found strewed along the north shore, and the present void, Roswell was led to infer that the late storm had been one of unusual intensity, and most probably of a character to occur only at long intervals.

But the state of the ice was the point of greatest interest. The schooner could now be got ready for sea in a week, and that easily ; but there she lay, imbedded in a field of ice that still covered nearly the whole of the waters within the group. As Roswell stood on the cliffs which overlooked the cove, he calculated the distance it would be necessary to take the schooner through the ice by sawing and cutting, and that through a field known to be some four feet thick, and five good miles at least. So Herculean did this task appear to be, that he even thought of abandoning his vessel altogether, and of setting out in the boats, as soon as the summer was fairly commenced. On reflection, however, this last plan was reserved as a *dernier ressort*, the danger of encountering the tempests of those seas in a whale-boat, without covering or fire, being much too great to be thought of, so long as any reasonable alternative offered.

The bergs to the southward were in motion, and a large fleet of them was putting to sea, as it might be, coming in from those remote and then unknown regions in which they were formed. From the mountain our hero counted at least a hundred, all regularly shaped, with tops like that of table-land, and with even, regular sides, and upright attitudes. It was very desirable to get ahead of these new maritime Alps, for the ocean to the northward was unusually clear of ice of all kinds, that lodged between the islands excepted.

So long as it was safe to calculate on the regular changes of the seasons, Roswell knew that patience and vigilance would serve his turn, by bringing everything round in its proper time and place. But it was by no means certain that it was a usual occurrence for the Great Bay to be crammed with field-ice, as had happened the past winter ; if the actual state of the surrounding waters were an exception instead of the rule. On examining the shores, however, it was found that the rain and melted snow had created a sort of margin, and that the strong winds which had been blowing, and which in fact were still blowing, had produced a gradually increasing attrition, until a space existed between the weather-side of the field and the rocks that was some thirty fathoms wide. This was an important discovery, and brought up a most grave question for decision.

Owing to the shape of the surrounding land, it would
not be possible for the ice to float out in a body for two
or three months to come; or until so much had melted as
to leave room for the field to pass the capes and headlands.
It never could have entered the bay for the same reason,
but for the resistless power of a field that extended leagues
out into the ocean, where, acted on jointly by wind and
tide, it came down with a momentum that was resistless,
ripping and tearing the edges of the field as if they had
been so much freshly turned-up mould. It was, then, a
question how to get the schooner out of her present bed,
and into clear water.

The reader will probably remember that, on her first arrival at the group, the Sea Lion had entered the Great Bay
from the southward; while, in her subsequent effort to get
north, she had gone out by the opposite passage. Now, it
occurred to Roswell that he might escape by the former of
these routes more readily than by the latter, and for the
following reasons: No field-ice had ever blocked up the
southern passage, which was now quite clear, though the
approach to it just then was choked by the manner in which
the northeast gale, that was still blowing, pressed home
against the rocks the field that so nearly filled the bay. A
shift of wind, however, must soon come; and, when that
change occurred, it was certain that this field would move
in an opposite direction, leaving the margin of open water,
that has already been mentioned, all along the rocks. The
distance was considerable, it is true—not less than fifteen
miles—and the whole of it was to be made quite close to
sharp angular rocks that would penetrate the schooner's
sides almost as readily as an axe, in the event of a nip; but
this danger might be avoided by foresight, and a timely
attention to the necessities of the case. Seeing no more
available plan to get the vessel out of her present duress,
the mates came readily into this scheme, and preparations
were made to carry it out. As the cove was so near the
northeast end of Sealer's Land, it may be well to explain
that the reason this same mode of proceeding could not be
carried out in a northern direction, was the breadth of the
field seaward, and the danger of following the north shore
when the solid ice did leave it, on account of the quantities of broken fragments that were tossing and churn-
ing in its front, far as the eye could reach from the
cliffs themselves.

The third day after the commencement of the thaw, the

wind came around again from the southwest, blowing heavily. As was expected, this soon began to set the field in motion, driving it over toward the volcano, and at the same time northerly. About six in the morning, Hazard brought a report to Roswell that a margin of open water was beginning to form all along under the cliffs, while there was great danger that the channel which had been cut from the schooner to the nearest point beneath the rocks, in readiness for this very contingency, might be closed by the pressure of the ice without on that within the cove. No time was to be lost, therefore, if it was intended to move the craft on this shift of wind. The distance that had been sawed through to make the channel just named did not exceed a hundred yards. The passage was not much wider than the schooner's breadth ; and it will be easily understood that it was to the last degree important to carry her through this strait as soon as possible. Although many useful articles were scattered about on the ice, and several remained to be brought over the rocks from the house, the order was given to get out lines, and to move the vessel at once : the men set to work with hearty good-will, another glimpse of home rising before their imaginations ; and, in five minutes after Hazard had made his communication, the Sea Lion had gone six or eight times her length toward the cliffs. Then came the pinch ! Had not the ice been solid between the cape and the berth just before occupied by the schooner, she would have been hopelessly nipped by the closing of the artificial channel. As it was, she was caught, and her progress was arrested, but the field took a cant, in consequence of the resistance of the solid ice that filled the whole cove to the eastward of the channel ; and, before any damage was done, the latter began to open even faster than it had come together. The instant the craft was released, the sealers manned their hauling lines again, and ran her up to the rocks with a hurrah ! The margin of water was just opening, but so prompt had been the movement of the men that it was not yet wide enough to permit the vessel to go any further ; and it was found necessary to wait until the passage was sufficiently wide to enable her to move ahead. The intervening time was occupied in bringing to the craft the articles left behind.

By nine o'clock everything was on board ; the winding channel that followed the sinuosities of the coast could be traced far as the eye could see ; the lines were manned ;

and the word was again given to move. Roswell now felt
that he was engaged in much the most delicate of all his
duties. The desperate run through the fleet of bergs, and
the second attempt to get to sea, were not in certain particulars as hazardous as this. The field had been setting
back and forth now for several weeks ; the margin of clear
water increasing by the attrition at each return to the
rocks ; and it was known by observation that these changes
often occurred at very short notices. Should the wind haul
round with the sun, or one of the unaccountable currents
of those seas intervene before the southeast cape was
reached, the schooner would probably be broken into splinters, or ground into powder, in the course of some two or
three hours. It was all-important, therefore, to lose not a
moment.

Several times in the course of the first hour the movement of the schooner was arrested by the want of sufficient
room to pass between projecting points in the cliffs and the
edge of the ice. On two of these occasions passages were
cut with the saw, the movement of the field not answering
to the impatience of the sealers. At the end of that most
momentous hour, however, the craft had been hauled ahead
a mile and a half, and had reached a curvature in the coast
where the margin of open water was more than fifty
fathoms wide, and the tracking of the vessel became easy
and rapid By two o'clock the Sea Lion was at what might
be called the bottom of the Great Bay, some three or four
leagues from the cove, and at the place where the long
low cape began to run out in a southeasterly direction. As
the wind could now be felt over the rocks, the foretopsail
was set, as well as the lower sails, the latter being mainly
becalmed, however, by the land, when the people were
all taken on board, the craft moving faster under her canvas than by means of the hauling lines. The wind was very
fresh, and in half an hour more the southeast cape came in
sight, close as were the navigators to the rocks. Ten
minutes later the Sea Lion was under reefed sails, stretching off to the southward and eastward, in perfectly clear
water !

At first Roswell Gardiner was disposed to rejoice, under
the impression that his greatest labor had been achieved.
A better look at the state of things around him, however,
taught the disheartening lesson of humility, by demon-
strating that they had in truth but just commenced.

Although there was scarcely any field-ice to the southward of the group, and in its immediate neighborhood, there was a countless number of bergs. It is true, these floating mountains did not come near the passage, for the depth of water just there usually brought them up ere they could get into it; nevertheless, a large fleet of them was blockading the entire group, as far as the eye could reach, looking east, west, and south, or along the whole line of the southern coast. It was at first questionable whether, and soon after it became certain, that the schooner could never beat through such dangers. Had the wind been fair, the difficulty would have been insurmountable; but ahead, and blowing a little gale, the matter was out of the question. Some other course must be adopted.

There was a choice of alternatives. One was to go entirely round the whole group, passing to the eastward of the volcano, where no one of the party had ever been; and the other was to follow the eastern margin of the bay, keeping inside of it, and trusting to find some opening by which the schooner could force her way into clear water to the northward. After a very brief consultation with his mates, Roswell decided on attempting the last.

As the course now to be steered was almost dead before the wind, the little craft, lightened of so much of her upper works, almost flew through the water. The great source of apprehension felt by our young men in attempting this new expedient was in the probability that the field would drift home to the rocks in the northeast quarter of the bay, which, with a southwest wind, was necessarily a quarter to leeward. Should this prove to be the case, it might be found impossible to pass ahead, and the schooner would be caught in a *cul de sac;* since it would not be in the power of her people to track her back again in the teeth of so strong a wind. Notwithstanding these probabilities, on Roswell went; for he saw plain enough that at such a moment almost anything was better than indecision.

The rate at which the little craft was flying before a fresh gale, in perfectly smooth water, soon put our sealers in a better condition to form closer estimates of their chances. The lookouts aloft, one of whom was Hazard, the first officer, sent down on deck constant reports of what they could see.

"How does it look ahead now, Mr. Hazard?" demanded Roswell, about five in the afternoon, just as his schooner was coming close under the smoking sides of the volcano, which had always been an object of interest to him, though he had never found time to visit it before. "Is there no danger of our touching the ground, close in as we are to this island?"

"I think not, sir; when I landed here, we kept the lead going the whole time, and we got two fathoms quite up to the shore. In my judgment, Captain Gar'ner, we may run down along this land as bold as lions."

"And how does it look ahead? I've no wish to get jammed here, close aboard of a volcano, which may be choking us all with its smoke before we know where we are."

"Not much danger of that, sir, with this wind. These volcanoes are nothin' but playthings, a'ter all. The vapor is driving off toward the northeast—That was a crack, with a vengeance!"

Just as Hazard was boasting of the innocuous character of a volcano, that near them fired a gun, as the men afterward called it, casting into the air a large flight of cinders and stones, accompanied by a sharp flash of flame. All the lighter materials drove away to leeward, but the heavier followed the law of projectiles, and scattered in all directions. Several stones of some size fell quite close to the schooner, and a few smaller actually came down on her decks.

"It will never do to stop here to boil our pot," cried Roswell to the mate. "We must get away from this, Mr. Hazard, as fast as the good craft can travel!"

"Get away it is, sir. There is nothing very near ahead to stop us; though it does look more toward the east cape as if the field was jammed in that quarter."

"Keep all your eyes about you, sir; and look out especially for any opening among the smaller islands ahead. I am not without hope that the currents which run among them may give us a clear passage in that quarter"

These words explain precisely that which did actually occur. On went the schooner, almost brushing the base of the volcano, causing Roswell many a bound of the heart, when he fancied she must strike; but she went clear. All this time it was crack, crack, crack, from the crater, rumbling sounds and heavy explosions; the last attended by flames, and smoke of a pitchy darkness. A dozen times the Sea Lion had very narrow escapes when nearer to the danger, stones of a weight to pass through her decks and bottom falling even on the ice outside of her; but that Hand which had so benevolently stayed various other evils, was stretched forth to save, and nothing touched the schooner of a size to do any injury. These escapes made a deep impression on Roswell. Until the past winter he had been accustomed to look upon things and events as matters of course. This vacant indifference, so common to men in prosperity, was extended even to the sublimest exhibition of the Almighty power; our hero seeing nothing in the firmament of heaven, of a clear night, but the twinkling lights that seemed to him to be placed there merely to garnish and illumine the darkness of this globe. Now, how differently did he look upon natural objects, and their origin! If it were only an insect, his mind presented its wonderful mechanism, its beauty, its uses. No star seemed less than what science has taught us that it is; and the power of the Dread Being who had created all, who governed all, and who was judge of all, became an inseparable subject of contemplation, as he looked upon the least of his works. Feelings thus softened and tempered by humility, easily led their subject to the reception of those leading articles of the Christian faith which have been consecrated by the belief of the Church catholic since the ages of miraculous guidance, and which are now venerable by time. Bold and presuming is he who fancies that his intellect can rectify errors of this magnitude and antiquity, and that the Church of God has been permitted to wallow on in a most fatal idolatry for centuries, to be extricated by the pretending syllogisms of his one-sided and narrow philosophy!

The people of the Sea Lion were less affected by what they saw than their young commander. Their hearts were light with the prospect of a speedy release from the hardships and dangers they had undergone; and, at each explosion of the volcano, as soon as out of reach of the falling stones, they laughed, and asserted that the mountain was firing a salute in honor of their departure. Such is the difference between men whose hearts and spirits have submitted to the law of faith, and those who live on in the recklessness of the passing events of life.

The schooner was racing past a rocky islet, beginning to haul more on a wind, as she made the circuit of the bay, just as Hazard came to the conclusion that the field had drifted home on the outer island of the group, and that it would be impossible to pass into clear water by going on. Turning his head in quest of some bay, or other secure place in which the craft might wait for a favorable change, he saw a narrow opening to leeward of the islet he had passed but a minute before, and, so far as he could perceive, one that led directly out to sea.

It was too late to keep away for the entrance of the passage, the ice being too close at hand to leeward; but, most fortunately, there was room to tack. A call to Roswell soon caused the schooner to be close on a wind; down went her helm, and round she came like a top. Sail was shortened in stays, and by the time the little craft was ready to fall off for the passage, she had nothing on her but a fore-topsail, jib, and a close-reefed mainsail. Under this canvas she glided along, almost brushing the rocks of the islet, but without touching. In twenty minutes more she was clear of the group altogether, and in open water.

That night some embarrassment was encountered from broken field-ice, of which the ocean was pretty full; but by exercising great vigilance, no serious thump occurred. Fortunately the period of darkness was quite short, the twilight being of great length, both mornings and evenings; and the reappearance of the sun cast a cheerful glow on the face of the troubled waters.

The wind held at southwest for three days, blowing heavily the whole time. By the second night-fall the sea was clear of ice, and everything was carried on the schooner that she could bear. About nine o'clock on the morning of the fourth day out, a speck was seen rising above the ragged outline of the rolling waves; and each minute it became higher and more distinct. An hour or two later, the Sea Lion was staggering along before a westerly gale, with the Hermit of Cape Horn on her larboard beam, distant three leagues. How many trying scenes and bitter moments crowded on the mind of young Roswell Gardiner as he recalled all that had passed in the ten months which intervened since he had come out from behind the shelter of those wild rocks! Stormy as was that sea, and terrible as was its name among mariners, coming, as he did, from one still more stormy and terrible, he now regarded it as a sort of place of refuge. A winter there he well knew would be no trifling undertaking; but he had just passed a winter in a region where even fuel was not to be found, unless carried there.

Twenty days later the Sea Lion sailed again from Rio, having sold all the sea-elephant oil that remained, and bought stores; of which, by this time, the vessel was much in want. Most of the portions of the provisions that were left had been damaged by the thawing process ; and food was getting to be absolutely necessary to her people, when the schooner went again into the noble harbor of the capital of Brazil. Then succeeded the lassitude and calms that reign about the imaginary line that marks the circuit of the earth, at that point which is ever central as regards the sun, and where the days and nights are always equal. No inclination of the earth's axis to the plane of its orbit affected the climate there, which knew not the distinctions of summer and winter ; or which, if they did exist at all, were so faintly marked as to be nearly imperceptible.

Twenty days later the schooner was standing among some low sandy keys under short canvas, and in the south-east trades. By her movements, an anchorage was sought ; and one was found at last, where the craft was brought up, boats were hoisted out, and Roswell Gardiner landed.

CHAPTER XXIX.

"If every ducat in six thousand ducats
Were in six parts, and every part a ducat,
I would not draw them ; I would have my bond."
—SHAKESPEARE.

THE earth had not stopped in its swift race around the sun at Oyster Pond, while all these events were in the course of occurrence in the antarctic seas. The summer had passed, that summer which was to have brought back the sealers; and autumn had come to chill the hopes as well as the body. Winter did not bring any change. Nothing was heard of Roswell and his companions, nor *could* anything have been heard of them short of the intervention of a miracle.

Mary Pratt no longer mentioned Roswell in her prayers. She fully believed him to be dead ; and her puritanical creed taught her that this, the sweetest and most endearing of all the rites of Christianity, was allied to a belief that it was sacrilege to entertain. We pretend not to any distinct impressions on this subject ourselves, beyond a sturdy Protestant disinclination to put any faith in the abuses of purgatory at least ; but most devoutly do we wish that such petitions *could* have the efficacy that so large a portion of the Christian world impute to them. But

Mary Pratt, so much better than we can lay any claim to be in all essentials, was less liberal than ourselves on this great point of doctrine. Roswell Gardiner's name now never passed her lips in prayer, therefore, though scarce a minute went by without his manly person being present to her imagination. He still lived in her heart, a shrine from which she made no effort to expel him.

As for the deacon, age, disease, and distress of mind had brought him to his last hours. The passions which had so engrossed him when in health, now turned upon his nature, and preyed upon his vitals, like an ill-omened bird. It is more than probable that he would have lived some months, possibly some years longer, had not the evil spirit of covetousness conspired to heighten the malady that wasted his physical frame. As it was, the sands of life were running low ; and the skilful Doctor Sage, himself, had admitted to Mary the improbability that her uncle and protector could long survive.

It is wonderful how the interest in a rich man suddenly revives among his relatives and possibly heirs, as his last hour draws near. Deacon Pratt was known to be wealthy in a small way ; was thought to possess his thirty or forty thousand dollars, which was regarded as wealth among the east-enders thirty years since ; and every human being in Old Suffolk, whether of its overwhelming majority or of its more select and wiser minority, who could by legal possibility claim any right to be remembered by the dying man, crowded around his bedside. At that moment Mary Pratt, who had so long nursed his diseases and mitigated his sufferings, was compelled to appear as a very insignificant and secondary person. Others who stood in the same degree of consanguinity to the dying man, and two, a brother and sister, who were even one degree closer, had *their* claims, and were by no means disposed to suffer them to be forgotten. Gladly would poor Mary have prayed by her uncle's bedside ; but Parson Whittle had assumed this solemn duty, it being deemed proper that one who had so long filled the office of deacon, should depart with a proper attention to the usages of his meeting. Some of the relatives who had lately appeared, and who were not so conversant with the state of things between the deacon and his divine, complained among themselves that the latter made too many ill-timed allusions to the pecuniary wants of the congregation ; and that he had, in particular, almost as much as asked the deacon to make a legacy that would enable those who were to stay behind to paint the meeting-house, erect a new horse-shed, purchase some improved stoves, and reseat the body of the building. These modest requests, it was whispered—for all passed in whispers then—would consume not less than a thousand dollars of the deacon's hard earnings; and the thing was mentioned as a wrong done him who was about to descend into the grave, where naught of earth could avail him in any way.

Close was the siege that was laid to Deacon Pratt during the last week of his life. Many were the hints given of the necessity of his making a will, though the brother and sister, estimating their rights as the law established them, said but little on the subject, and that little was rather against the propriety of annoying a man, in their brother's condition, with business of so perplexing a nature. The fact that these important personages set their faces against the scheme had due weight, and most of the relatives began to calculate the probable amount of their respective shares under the law of distribution as it stood in that day. This excellent and surpassingly wise community of New York had not then reached the pass of exceeding liberality toward which it is now so rapidly tending. In that day, the debtor was not yet thought of as the creditor's next heir, and that plausible and impracticable desire of a false philanthropy, which is termed the Homestead Exemption Law—impracticable as to anything like a just and equitable exemption of equal amount in all cases of indebtedness—was not yet dreamed of. New York was then a sound and healthful community; making its mistakes, doubtless, as men ever will err; but the control of things had not yet passed into the hands of sheer political empirics, whose ignorance and quackery were stimulated by the lowest passion for majorities. Among other things that were then respected were wills; but it was not known to a single individual among all those who thronged the dwelling of Deacon Pratt, that the dying man had ever mustered the self-command necessary to make such an instrument. He was free to act, but did not choose to avail himself of his freedom. Had he survived a few years, he would have found himself in the enjoyment of a liberty so sublimated, that he could not lease, or rent a farm, or collect a common debt, without coming under the harrow of the tiller of the political soil.

The season had advanced to the early part of April, and

24

that is usually a soft and balmy month on the sea-shore, though liable to considerable and sudden changes of temperature. On the day to which we now desire to transfer the scene, the windows of the deacon's bedroom were open, and the soft south wind fanned his hollow and pallid cheek. Death was near, though the principle of life struggled hard with the King of Terrors. It was now that that bewildered and Pharisaical faith which had so long held this professor of religion in a bondage even more oppressive than open and announced sins, most felt the insufficiency of the creed in which he had rather been speculating than trusting all his life, to render the passing hour composed and secure. There had always been too much of self in Deacon Pratt's moral temperament to render his belief as humble and devout as it should be. It availed him not a hair, now that he was a deacon, or that he had made long prayers in the market-places, where men could see him, or that he had done so much, as he was wont to proclaim, for example's sake. All had not sufficed to cleanse his heart of worldly-mindedness, and he now groped about him, in the darkness of a faith obscured, for the true light that was to illume his path to another world.

The doctor had ordered the room cleared of all but two or three of the dying man's nearest relatives. Among these last, however, was the gentle and tender-hearted Mary, who loved to be near her uncle in this his greatest need. She no longer thought of his covetousness, of his griping usury, of his living so much for self and so little for God. While hovering about the bed, a message reached her that Baiting Joe wished to see her in the passage that led to the bedroom. She went to this old fisherman and found him standing near a window that looked toward the east, and which consequently faced the waters of Gardiner's Bay.

"There she is, Miss Mary," said Joe, pointing out of the window, his whole face in a glow between joy and whiskey. "It should be told to the deacon at once, that his last hours might be happier than some that he has passed lately. That's she—though at first I did not know her."

Mary saw a vessel standing in toward Oyster Pond, and her familiarity with objects of that nature was such as to tell her at once that it was a schooner; but so completely had she given up the Sea Lion that it did not occur to her that this could be the long-missing craft.

"At what are you pointing, Joe?" the wondering girl asked, with perfect innocence.

"At that craft—at the Sea Lion of Sterling, which has been so long set down as missing, but which has turned up just as her owner is about to cast off from this 'arth altogether.''

Joe might have talked for an hour : he did chatter away for two or three minutes, with his head and half his body out of the window, uninterrupted by Mary, who sank into a chair to prevent falling on the floor. At length the dear girl commanded herself, and spoke.

"You cannot possibly be certain, Joe," she said ; "that schooner does not look, to me, like the Sea Lion."

"Nor to me, in some things, while in other some she does. Her upper works seem strangely out of shape, and there's precious little on 'em. But no other fore-taw-sail schooner ever comes in this-a-way, and I know of none likely to do it. Ay, by Jupiter, there goes the very blue peter I helped to make with my own hands, and it was agreed to set it as the deacon's signal. There's no mistake now!"

Joe might have talked half an hour longer without any fear of interruption, for Mary had vanished to her own room, leaving him with his body and head still out of the window, making his strictures and conjectures for some time longer ; while the person to whom he fancied he was speaking, was, in truth, on her knees, rendering thanks to God! An hour later all doubts were removed, the schooner coming in between Oyster Pond and Shelter Island, and making the best of her way to the well-known wharf.

"Isn't it wonderful, Mary," exclaimed the deacon, in a hollow voice, it is true, but with an animation and force that did not appear to have any immediate connection with death—"isn't it wonderful that Gar'ner should come back, a'ter all ! If he has only done his duty by me, this will be the greatest ventur' of my whole life ; it will make the evening of my days comfortable. I hope I've always been grateful for blessings, and I'm sure I'm grateful, from the bottom of my heart, for this. Give me prosperity, and I'm not apt to forget it. They've been asking me to make a will, but I told 'em I was too poor to think of any such thing ; and, now my schooner has got back, I s'pose I shall get more hints of the same sort. Should anything happen to me, Mary, you can bring out the sealed paper I gave you to keep, and that must satisfy 'em all. You'll remember it is addressed to Gar'ner. There isn't much in it, and it won't be much thought of, I fancy ; but, such as it is, 'tis the last instrument I sign, unless I get better. To think of Gar'ner's coming back, a'ter all! It has put new life in me, and I shall be about ag'in in a week if he has only not forgotten the key and the hidden treasure!"

Mary Pratt's heart had not been so light for many a weary day, but it grieved her to be a witness of this lingering longing after the things of the world. She knew that not only her uncle's days, but his very hours, were numbered; and that notwithstanding this momentary flickering of the lamp, in consequence of fresh oil being poured into it, the wick was nearly consumed, and that it must shortly go out, let Roswell's success be what it might. The news of the sudden and unlooked-for return of a vessel so long believed to be lost spread like wildfire over the whole Point, and greatly did it increase the interest of the relatives in the condition of the dying man. If he was a subject of great concern before, doubly did he become so now. A vessel freighted with furs would have caused much excitement of itself; but, by some means or other, the deacon's great secret of the buried treasure had leaked out, most probably by means of some of his lamentations during his illness, and, though but imperfectly known, it added largely to the expectations connected with the unlooked-for return of the schooner. In short, it would not have been easy to devise a circumstance that should serve to increase the liveliness of feeling that just then prevailed on the subject of Deacon Pratt and his assets, than the arrival of the Sea Lion at that precise moment.

And arrive she did, that tempest-tossed, crippled, ice-bound, and half-burned little craft, after roaming over an extent of ocean that would have made up half-a-dozen ordinary sea voyages. It was, in truth, the schooner so well known to the reader, that was now settling away her mainsail and jib, as she kept off, under her fore-topsail alone, toward the wharf, on which every human being who could, with any show of propriety, be there at such a moment, was now collected, in a curious and excited crowd. Altogether, including boys and females, there must have been not less than a hundred persons on that wharf; and among them were most of the anxious relatives who were in attendance on the vessel's owner, in his last hours. By a transition that was natural enough, perhaps, under the circumstances, they had transferred their interest in the deacon to this schooner, which they looked upon as an inanimate portion of an investment that would soon have little that was animate about it.

Baiting Joe was a sort of oracle, in such circumstances. He had passed his youth at sea, having often doubled the Horn, and was known to possess a very respectable amount of knowledge on the subject of vessels of all sorts and sizes, rig and qualities. He was now consulted by all who could get near him, as a matter of course, and his opinions were received as *res adjudicata*, as the lawyers have it.

"That's the boat," said Joe, affecting to call the Sea Lion by a diminutive, as a proof of regard; "yes, that's the craft, herself; but she is wonderfully deep in the water! I never seed a schooner of her tonnage, come in from a v'y'ge, with her scuppers so near a-wash. Don't you think, Jim, there must be suthin' heavier than skins in her hold, to bring her down so low in the water?"

Jim was another loafer, who lived by taking clams, oysters, fish, and the other treasures of the surrounding bays. He was by no means as high authority as Baiting Joe; still he was always authority on a wharf.

"I never seed the like on't," answered Jim. "That schooner must ha' made most of her passage under water. She's as deep as one of our coasters comin' in with a load of brick!"

"She's deep; but not as deep as a craft I once made a cruise in. I was aboard of the first of Uncle Sam's gunboats, that crossed the pond to Gibraltar. When we got in, it made the Mediterranean stare, I can tell you! We had furrin officers aboard us, the whull time, lookin' about, and wonderin', as they called it, if we wasn't amphibbies."

"What's that?" demanded Jim, rather hastily. "There's no sich rope in the ship."

"I know that well enough; but an amphibby, as I understand it, is a new sort of whale, that comes up to breathe, like all of that family, as old Dr. Mitchell, of Cow Neck, calls the critturs. So the furrin officers thought we must be of the amphibby family, to live so much under water, as it seemed to them. It was wet work, I can tell you, boys; I don't think I got a good breath more than once an hour, the whull of the first day we was out. One of the furrin officers asked our captain how the gunboat steered. He wasn't a captain, at all—only a master, you see, and we all called him Jumpin' Billy. So Jumpin' Billy says, 'Don't know, sir.' 'What! crossed the Atlantic in her, and don't know how your craft steers!' says the furrin officer, says he—and well he might, Jim, since nothin' that ever lived could go from Norfork to Gibraltar without *some* attention to the helm—but Jumpin' Billy had another story to tell. 'No, sir; don't know,' he answered. 'You see, sir, a nor-wester took us right aft, as we cleared the capes, and down she dove, with her nose under and her starn out, and she came across without having a chance to try the rudder.'"

This story, which Joe had told at least a hundred times before, and which, by the way, is said to be true, produced the usual admiration, especially among the crowd of legatees-expectant, to most of whom it was quite new. When the laugh went out, which it soon did of itself, Joe pursued a subject that was of more interest to most of his auditors, or rather to the principal personages among them.

"Skins never brought a craft so low, that you may be sartin of!" he resumed. "I've seed all sorts of vessels stowed, but a hundred press-screws couldn't cram in furs enough to bring a craft so low! To my eye, Jim, there's suthin' unnat'ral about that schooner, a'ter all."

The study is scarce worthy of a diploma, but we will take this occasion to say, for the benefit of certain foreign writers, principally of the female sex, who fancy they represent Americanisms, that the vulgar of the great republic, and it is admitted there are enough of the class, never say "summat" or "somethink," which are low English, but not low American, dialect. The in-and-in Yankee says "suth-in." In a hundred other words have these ambitious ladies done injustice to our vulgar, who are not vulgar, according to the laws of Cockayne, in the smallest degree. "*The* Broadway," for instance, is no more used by an American than "*the* Congress," or "the United States of *North* America."

"Perhaps," answered Jim, "'tisn't the Sea Lion, a'ter all. There's a family look about all the craft some men build, and this may be a sort of relation of our missin' schooner."

"I'll not answer for the craft, though that's her blue peter and them's her mast-heads, and I turned in that tawsail halyard-block with my own hands. I'll tell you what, Jim, there's been a wrack, or a nip, up yonder, among the ice, and this schooner has been built anew out of that there schooner. You see if it don't turn out as I tell you. Ay, and there's Captain Gar'ner himself, alive and well, just comin' forrard."

A little girl started with this news, and was soon pouring it into the willing ears and open heart of the weeping and grateful Mary. An hour later, Roswell held the latter in his arms ; for at such a moment it was not possible for the most scrupulous of the sex to affect coldness and reserve, where there was so much real tenderness and love. While folding Mary to his heart, Roswell whispered in her ears the blessed words that announced his own humble submission to the faith which accepted Christ as the Son of God. Too well did the gentle and ingenuous girl understand the sincerity and frankness of her lover's nature to doubt what he said, or in any manner to distrust the motive. That moment was the happiest of her short and innocent life !

But the welcome tidings had reached the deacon, and ere Roswell had an opportunity of making any other explanations but those which assured Mary that he had come back all that she wished him to be, both of them were summoned to the bedside of the dying man. The effect of the excitement on the deacon was so very great as almost to persuade the expectant legatees that their visit was premature, and that they might return home, to renew it at some future day. It is painful to find it our duty to draw sketches that shall contain such pictures of human nature ; but with what justice could we represent the loathsome likeness of covetousness, hovering over a grave, and omit the resemblances of those who surrounded it ? Mary Pratt, alone, of all that extensive family connection, felt and thought as Christianity, and womanly affection, and reason, dictated. All the rest saw nothing but the possessor of a considerable property, who was about to depart for that unknown world, into which nothing could be taken from this, but the divine and abused spirit which had been fashioned in the likeness of God.

"Welcome, Gar'nen—welcome home, ag'in !" exclaimed the deacon, so heartily as quite to deceive the young man as to the real condition of his owner ; a mistake that was, perhaps, a little unfortunate, as it induced him to be more frank than might otherwise have been the case. " I couldn't find it in my heart to give you up, and have all along believed that we should yet have good news from you. The Gar'ners are a reliable family, and that was one reason why I chose you to command my schooner. Them Daggetts are a torment, but we never should have known anything about the islands, or the key, hadn't it been for one on 'em."

As the deacon stopped to breathe, Mary turned away from the bed, grieved at heart to see the longings of the world thus clinging to the spirit of one who probably had not another hour to live. The glazed but animated eye, a cheek which resembled a faded leaf of the maple laid on a cold and whitish stone, and lips that had already begun to recede from the teeth, made a sad, sad picture, truly, to look upon at such a moment; yet, of all present, Mary Pratt alone felt the fulness of the incongruity, and alone bethought her of the unreasonableness of encouraging feelings like those which were now uppermost in the deacon's breast. Even Minister Whittle had a curiosity to know how much was added to the sum total of Deacon Pratt's assets by the return of a craft that had so long been set down among the missing. When all eyes, therefore, were turned in curiosity on the handsome face of the fine manly youth who now stood at the bedside of the deacon, including those of brother and sister, of nephews and nieces, of cousins and friends, those of this servant of the most high God were of the number, and not the least expressive of solicitude and expectation. As soon as the deacon had caught a little breath, and had swallowed a restorative that the hired nurse had handed to him, his eager thoughts reverted to the one engrossing theme of his whole life.

"These are all friends, Gar'ner," he said; "come to visit me in a little sickness that I've been somewhat subject to of late, and who will all be glad to hear of our good fortune. So you've brought the schooner back, a'ter all, Gar'ner, and will disapp'int the Sag Harbor shipowners, who have been all along foretelling that we should never see her ag'in:—brought her back—ha! Gar'ner?"

"Only in part, Deacon Pratt We have had good luck and bad luck since we left you, and have only brought home the best part of the craft."

"The best part!" said the deacon, gulping his words in a way that compelled him to pause; "the best part! What, in the name of property, has become of the rest?"

"The rest was burned, sir, to keep us from freezing to death." Roswell then gave a brief but very clear and intelligible account of what had happened, and of the manner in which he had caused the hulk of the deacon's Sea Lion to be raised upon by the materials furnished by the Sea Lion of the Vineyard. The narrative brought Mary Pratt back to the side of the bed, and caused her calm eyes to become riveted intently on the speaker's face. As for the deacon, he might have said, with Shakespeare's Wolsey:

> "Had I but served my God with half the zeal
> I served my king, he would not, in mine age,
> Have left me naked to mine enemies."

His fall was not that of a loss of power, it is true, but it was that of a still more ignoble passion—covetousness. As Roswell proceeded, his mind represented one source of wealth after another released from his clutch, until it was with a tremulous voice, and a countenance from which all traces of animation had fled, that he ventured again to speak.

" Then I may look upon my ventur' as worse than nothing ? " he said. " The insurers will raise a question about paying for a craft that has been rebuilt in this way, and the Vineyard folks will be sartain to put in a claim of salvage, both on account of two of their hands helping you with the work, and on account of the materials—and we with no cargo, as an offset to it all ! "

" No, deacon, it is not quite so bad as that," resumed Roswell. "We have brought home a good lot of skins ; enough to pay the people full wages, and to return you every cent of outfit, with a handsome advance on the venture. A sealer usually makes a good business of it, if she falls in with seals. Our cargo in skins can't be worth less than $20,000 ; besides half a freight left on the island, for which another craft may be sent."

"That is suthin', the Lord be praised ! " ejaculated the deacon. "Though the schooner is as bad as gone, and the outlays have been awfully heavy ; I'm almost afraid to go any further. Gar'ner,—did you—I grow weak very fast—did you stop—Mary, I wish *you* would put the question."

" I am afraid that my uncle means to ask if you stopped at the Key, in the West Indies, according to your instructions, Roswell ? " the niece said, and most reluctantly ; for she plainly saw it was fully time her uncle ceased to think of the things of this life, and to begin to turn all his thoughts on the blessed mediation, and another state of being.

" I forgot no part of your orders, sir," rejoined Roswell. "It was my duty to obey them, and I believe I have done so to the letter——"

" Stop, Gar'ner," interrupted the dying man—" one question, while I think of it. Will the Vineyard men have any claim of salvage on account of them skins ? "

"Certainly not, sir. These skins are all our own—were taken, cured, stowed, and brought home altogether by ourselves. There is a lot of skins belonging to the Vineyarders stowed away in the house, which is yours, deacon, and

which it would well pay any small craft to go and bring
away. If anybody is to claim salvage, it will be ourselves.
No salvage was demanded for the loss off Cape Henlopen,
I trust ? "

" No, none—Daggett behaved what I call *liberal* in that
affair,"—half the critics of the day would use the adjective
instead of the adverb here, and why should Deacon Pratt's
English be any better than his neighbors ?—" and so I have
admitted to his friends over on the Vineyard. But, Gar'-
ner, our great affair still remains to be accounted for. Do
you wish to have the room cleared before you speak of
that—shall we turn the *key* on all these folks, and then settle accounts ?—he ! he ! he !"

The deacon's facetiousness sounded strangely out of
place to Roswell ; still, he did not exactly know how to
gainsay his wishes. There might be an indiscretion in pur-
suing his narrative before so many witnesses, and the
young man paused until the room was cleared, leaving no
one in it but the sick man, Mary, himself, and the nurse.
The last could not well be gotten rid of on Oyster Pond,
where her office gave her an assumed right to know all
family secrets ; or, what was the same thing to her, to *fancy*
that she knew them. Among all the sayings which the experience of mankind has reduced to axioms, there is not
one more just than that which says, " There are secrets in
all families." These secrets the world commonly affects to
know all about ; but we think few will have reached the
age of threescore without becoming convinced of how
much pretending ignorance there is in this assumption of
the world. " *Tot ou tard tout se scait,*" is a significant saying of our old friends, the French, who know as much of
things in practice as any other people on the face of the
earth ; " *tot ou tard tout ne se scait pas.*"

" Is the door shut ?" asked the deacon, tremulously, for
eagerness united to debility was sadly shaking his whole
frame. " See that the door is shut tight, Mary ; this is our
own secret, and nurse must remember that."

Mary assured him that they were alone, and turned away
in sorrow from the bed.

" Now, Gar'ner," resumed the deacon, " open your whole
heart, and let us know all about it."

Roswell hesitated to reply ; for he, too, was shocked at
witnessing this instance of a soul's clinging to mammon
when on the very eve of departing for the unknown world.
There was a look in the glazed and sunken eyes of the old

man that reminded him unpleasantly of that snapping of
the eyes which he had so often seen in Daggett.

"You didn't forget the key, surely, Gar'ner?" asked the
deacon, anxiously.

"No, sir; we did our whole duty by that part of the
voyage."

"Did you find it—was the place accurately described?"

"No chart could have made it better. We lost a month
in looking for the principal landmark, which had been
altered by the weather; but that once found, the rest was
easy. The difficulty we met with in starting has brought
us home so late in the spring."

"Never mind the spring, Gar'ner; the part that is past
is sartain to come round ag'in, in due time. And so you
found the very key that was described by Daggett?"

"We did, sir; and just where he described it to be."

"And how about the tree, and the little hillock of sand
at its foot?"

"Both were there, deacon. The hillock must have grown
a good deal, by reason of the shifting sand; but, all things
considered, the place was well enough described."

"Well—well—well—you opened the hillock, of course?"

"We did, sir; and found the box mentioned by the pirate."

"A good large box, I'll warrant ye! Them pirates seldom do things by halves—he! he! he!"

"I can't say much for the size of the box, deacon—it
looked to me as if it had once held window-glass, and that
of rather small dimensions."

"But, the contents—you do not mention the contents."

"They are here, sir," taking a small bag from his
pocket, and laying it on the bed, by the deacon's side.
"The pieces are all of gold, and there are just one hundred
and forty-three of them.—Heavy doubloons, it is true, and
I dare say well worth their sixteen dollars each."

The deacon gave a gulp, as if gasping for breath, at the
same time that he clutched the bag. The next instant he
was dead; and there is much reason to believe that the de-
mons who had watched him, and encouraged him in his
besetting sin, laughed at his consummation of their ma-
lignant arts! If angels in heaven did not mourn at this
characteristic departure of a frail spirit from its earthly
tenement, one who had many of their qualities did. Heavy
had been the load on Mary Pratt's heart, at the previous
display of her uncle's weakness, and profound was now her
grief at his having made such an end.

CHAPTER XXX.

"*4th Cit.* We'll hear the will : Read it, Mark Antony.
  Cit. The will, the will ; we will hear Cæsar's will.
  Ant. Have patience, gentle friends, I must not read it ;
It is not meet you know how Cæsar loved you."—*Julius Cæsar.*

THERE is usually great haste, in this country, in getting
rid of the dead.   In no other part of the world, with which
we are acquainted, are funerals so simple, or so touching ;
placing the judgment and sins which lead to it, in a far
more conspicuous light than rank, or riches, or personal
merits. Scarfs and gloves are given in town, and gloves in
the country, though scarfs are rare ; but, beyond these, and
the pall, and the hearse, and the weeping friends, an American funeral is a very unpretending procession of persons
in their best attire ; on foot, when the distance is short ; in
carriages, in wagons, and on horseback, when the grave is
far from the dwelling. There is, however, one feature connected with a death in this country, that we could gladly
see altered.   It is the almost indecent haste, which so
generally prevails, to get rid of the dead.   Doubtless the
climate has had an effect in establishing this custom ; but
the climate, in no means, exacts the precipitancy that is
usually practised.

As there were so many friends from a distance present,
some of whom took the control of affairs, Mary shrinking
back into herself, with a timidity natural to her sex and
years, the moment her care could no longer serve her
uncle, the funeral of the deacon took place the day after
that of his death. It was the solemn and simple ceremony
of the country. The Rev. Mr. Whittle conceived that he
ought to preach a sermon on the occasion of the extinguish-
ment of this " bright and shining light," and the body was
carried to the meeting-house, where the whole congregation
assembled, it being the Sabbath. We cannot say much for
the discourse, which had already served as eulogiums on
two or three other deacons, with a simple substitution of
names.   In few things are the credulous more imposed on
than in this article of sermons. A clergyman shall preach
the workings of other men's brains for years, and not one
of his hearers detect the imposition, purely on account of
the confiding credit it is customary to yield to the pulpit.

In this respect, preaching is very much like reviewing,—
the listener, or the reader, being too complaisant to see
through the great standing mystifications of either. Yet
preaching is a work of high importance to men, and one
that doubtless accomplishes great good, more especially
when the life of the preacher corresponds with his doctrine ;
and even reviewing, though infinitely of less moment,
might be made a very useful art, in the hands of upright,
independent, intelligent, and learned men. But nothing
in this world is as it should be, and centuries will probably
roll over it ere the " good time" shall really come !

The day of the funeral being the Sabbath, nothing that
touched on business was referred to. On the following
morning, however, " the friends" assembled early in the
parlor, and an excuse for being a little pressing was made,
on the ground that so many present had so far to go. The
deacon had probably made a remove much more distant
than any that awaited his relatives.

" It is right to look a little into the deacon's matters before we separate," said Mr. Job Pratt, who, if he had the
name, had not the patience of him of old, " in order to
save trouble and hard feelings. Among relatives and
friends there should be nothing but confidence and affection, and I am sure I have no other sentiments toward any
here. I suppose "—all Mr. Job Pratt knew, was ever on
a supposition—" I suppose I am the proper person to administer to the deacon's property, though I don't wish to do
it, if there's the least objection."

Every one assented that he was the most proper person,
for all knew he was the individual the surrogate would be
the most likely to appoint.

" I have never set down the deacon's property as anything like what common report makes it," resumed Mr.
Job Pratt ; " though I do suppose it will fully reach ten
thousand dollars."

" La !" exclaimed a female cousin, and a widow, who
had expectations of her own, " I'd always thought Deacon
Pratt worth forty or fifty thousand dollars ! Ten thousand
dollars won't make much for each for us, divided up
among so many folks ! "

" The division will not be so very great, Mrs. Martin,"
returned Mr. Job, " as it will be confined to the next of
kin and their representatives. Unless a will should be
found—and, by all I can learn, there is *none* "—emphasiz-
ing the last word with point—" unless a will be found, the

whole estate, real and personal, must be divided into just five shares, which, accordin' to my calculation, would make about two thousand dollars a share. No great fortin', to be sure, though a comfortable addition to small means. The deacon was cluss (Anglicé, close); yes, he was cluss—all the Pratts are a little given to be cluss; but I don't know that they are any the worse for it. It is well to be curful (careful) of one's means, which are a trust given to us by Divine Providence."

In this manner did Mr. Job Pratt often quiet his conscience for being as "curful" of his own as of other person's assets. Divine Providence, according to his morality, made it as much a duty to transfer the dollar that was in his neighbor's pocket to his own, as to watch it vigilantly after the transposition had been effected.

"A body should be curful, as you say, sir," returned the Widow Martin; "and for that reason I should like to know if there isn't a will. I *know* the deacon set store by me, and I can hardly think he has departed for another world without bethinking him of his cousin Jenny, and of her widowhood."

"I'm afraid he has, Mrs. Martin—really afraid he has. I can hear of no will. The doctor says he doubts if the deacon could ever muster courage to write anything about his own death, and that he has never heard of any will. I understand Mary, that she has no knowledge of any will, and I do not know where else to turn in order to inquire. Rev. Mr. Whittle thinks there *is* a will, I ought to say."

"There *must* be a will," returned the parson, who was on the ground again early, and on this very errand; "I feel certain of that from the many conversations I have held with the deceased. It is not a month since I spoke to him of divers repairs that were necessary to each and all of the parish buildings, including the parsonage. He agreed to every word I said—admitted that we could not get on another winter without a new horse-shed; and that the east end of the parsonage ought to be shingled this coming summer."

"All of which may be very true, parson, without the deacon's making a will," quietly, and we may now add *patiently*, observed Mr. Job.

"I don't think so," returned the minister, with a warmth that might have been deemed indiscreet, did it not relate to the horse-shed, the parsonage, and the meeting-house, all of which were public property, rather than to anything in which he had a more direct legal interest. "A pious member of the church would hardly hold out the hopes that Deacon Pratt has held out to me for more than two years, without meaning to make his words good in the end. I think all will agree with me in that opinion."

"Did the deacon, then, go so far as to promise to do anything?" asked Mr. Job, a little timidly, for he was by no means sure the answer might not be in the affirmative, in which case he anticipated the worst.

"Perhaps not," answered Minister Whittle, too conscientious to tell a downright lie, though sorely tempted so to do. "But a man may promise indirectly as well as directly. When I have a thing much at heart, and converse often about it with a person who can grant all I wish, and that person listens as attentively as I could wish him to do, I regard that as a promise, and, in church matters, one of a very solemn nature."

All the Jesuits in the world do not get their educations at Rome, or acknowledge Ignatius Loyola as the great founder of their order. Some are to be found who have never made a public profession of their faith and zeal, have never assumed the tonsure, or taken the vows.

"That's as folks think," quietly returned Mr. Job Pratt, though he smiled in a manner so significant as to cause Mrs. Martin a new qualm, as she grew more and more apprehensive that the property was, after all, to go by the distribution law. "Some folks think a promise ought to be expressed, while others think it may be understood. The law, I believe, commonly looks for the direct expression of any binding promise; and, in matters of this sort, one made in writing, too, and that under a seal, and before three responsible witnesses."

"I wish a full inquiry might be made, to ascertain if there be no will," put in the minister, anxiously.

"I'm quite willing so to do," returned Mr. Job, whose confidence and moral courage increased each instant. "Quite willing; and am rather anxious for it, if I could only see where to go to inquire."

"Does no one present know of any will made by the deceased?" demanded Minister Whittle, authoritatively.

A dead silence succeeded to the question. Eye met eye, and there was great disappointment among the numerous collaterals present, including all those who did not come in as next of kin, or as their direct representatives. But the Rev. Mr. Whittle had been too long and too keenly on the scent of a legacy, to be thrown out of the hunt, just as he believed the game was coming in sight.

"It might be well to question each near relative directly," he added. "Mr. Job Pratt, do *you* know nothing of any will?"

"Nothing whatever. At one time I did think the deacon meant to make his testament; but I conclude that he must have changed his mind."

"And you, Mrs. Thomas," turning to the sister—"as next of kin, I make the same inquiry of you?"

"I once talked with brother about it," answered this relative, who was working away in a rocking-chair as if she thought the earth might stop in its orbit, if she herself ceased to keep in motion; "but he gave me no satisfactory answer—that is, nothin' that I call satisfactory. Had he told me he *had* made a will, and given me a full shear (share), I should have been content; or had he told me that he had *not* made a will, and that the law would give me a full shear, I should have been content. I look upon myself as a person easily satisfied."

This was being explicit, and left little more to be obtained from the deacon's beloved and only surviving sister.

"And you, Mary; do you know anything of a will made by your uncle?"

Mary shook her head; but there was no smile on her features, for the scene was unpleasant to her.

"Then no one present knows of any paper that the deacon left specially to be opened after his death?" demanded Rev. Mr. Whittle, putting the general question pretty much at random.

"A paper!" cried Mary, hastily. "Yes, I know something of a *paper*—I thought you spoke of a will."

"A will is commonly written on paper, nowadays, Miss Mary—but, you have a *paper*?"

"Uncle gave me a *paper*, and told me to keep it till Roswell Gardiner came back; and, if he himself should not then be living, to give it to him." The color now mounted to the very temples of the pretty girl, and she seemed to speak with greater deliberation and care. "As I was to give the paper to Roswell, I have always thought it related to him. My uncle spoke of it to me as lately as the day of his death."

"That's the will, beyond a doubt!" cried Rev. Mr. Whittle, with more exultation than became his profession and professions. "Do you not think this may be Deacon Pratt's will, Miss Mary?"

Now Mary had never thought any such thing. She knew that her uncle much wished her to marry Roswell, and had all along fancied that the paper she held, which indeed was contained in an envelope addressed to her lover, contained some expression of his wishes on this to her the most interesting of all subjects, and nothing else. Mary Pratt thought very little of her uncle's property, and still less of its future disposition, while she thought a great deal of Roswell Gardiner and of his suit. It was, consequently, the most natural thing in the world that she should have fallen into some such error as this. But, now that the subject was brought to her mind in this new light, she arose, went to her own room, and soon reappeared with the paper in her hand. Both Mr. Job Pratt and Rev. Mr. Whittle offered to relieve her of the burden ; and the former, by a pretty decided movement, did actually succeed in getting possession of the documents. The papers were done up in the form of a large business letter, which was duly sealed with wax, and addressed to " Mr. Roswell Gardiner, Master of the Schooner Sea Lion, now absent on a voyage." The superscription was read aloud, a little under the influence of surprise ; notwithstanding which, Mr. Job Pratt was very coolly proceeding to open the packet, precisely as if it had been addressed to himself. In this decided step, Mrs. Martin, and Mrs. Thomas, and Rev. Mr. Whittle, might be set down as accessories before the act ; for each approached ; and so eager were the two women that they actually assisted in breaking the seal.

" If that letter is addressed to me," said Roswell Gardiner, with firmness and authority, " I claim the right to open it myself. It is unusual for those to whom a letter is *not* addressed to assume this office."

" But, it comes *from* Deacon Pratt," cried the widow Martin, "and may contain his will."

" In which case, a body would think I have some rights concerned," said Mr. Job Pratt, a little more coolly, but with manifest doubts.

" Sartain ! " put in Mrs. Thomas. " Brothers and sisters, and even cousins, come before strangers, any day. Here we are, a brother and sister of the deacon, and we ought to have a right to read his letters."

All this time Roswell had stood with an extended arm, and an eye that caused Mr. Job Pratt to control his impatience. Mary advanced close to his side, as if to sustain him, but she said nothing.

25

"There is a law, with severe penalties, against knowingly opening a letter addressed to another," resumed Roswell steadily ; "and it shall be enforced against any one who shall presume to open one of mine. If that letter has my address, sir, I demand it ; and I will have it, at every hazard."

Roswell advanced a step nearer Mr. Job Pratt, and the letter was reluctantly yielded ; though not until the widow Martin had made a nervous but abortive snatch at it.

"At any rate, it ought to be opened in our presence," put in this woman, "that we may see what is in it."

"And by what right, ma'am ? Have I not the privilege of others, to read my own letters when and where I please ? If the contents of this, however, do really relate to the late Deacon Pratt's property, I am quite willing they should be made known.   There is nothing on this superscription to tell me to open the packet in the presence of witnesses ; but, under all the circumstances, I prefer it should be done."

Hereupon Roswell proceeded deliberately to look into the package.   The seal was already broken, and he exhibited it in that state to all in the room, with a meaning smile, after which he brought to light and opened some written instrument, that was engrossed on a single sheet of foolscap, and had the names of several witnesses at its bottom.

"Ay, ay, that's it," said Baiting Joe, for the room was crowded with all sorts of people ; "that's the dockerment. I know'd it as soon as I laid eyes on it!"

"And what do *you* know about it, Josy ?" demanded the widow, eagerly.   "Cousin Job, this man may turn out a most important and considerable witness!"

"What do I know, Mrs. Martin ? Why, I seed the deacon sign for the seals, and execute.   As soon as I heard Squire Craft, who was down here from Riverhead on that 'ere very business, talk so much about seals, I know'd Captain Gar'ner must have suthin' to do with the matter. The deacon's very heart was in the schooner and her v'y'ge, and I think it was the craft that finished him, in the end."

"Won't that set aside a codicil, cousin Job, if so be the deacon has r'ally codicilled off Captain Gar'ner and Mary ?"

"We shall see, we shall see.   So you was present, Josy, at the making of a will ?"

"Sartain—and was a witness to the insterment, as the squire called it. I s'pose he sent for me to be a witness, as I am some acquainted with the sealin' business, having made two v'y'ges out of Stunnin'tun, many years since. Ay, ay ; that's the insterment, and pretty well frightened was the deacon when he put his name to it, I can tell you ! "

"Frightened ! " echoed the brother—"that's ag'in law, at any rate. The instrument that a man signs because he's frightened, is no instrument at all, in law. As respects a will, it is what we justices of the peace call ' dies non,' or, don't die : that is, in law."

"Can that be so, Squire Job ? " asked the sister, who had said but little hitherto, but had thought all the more.

"Yes, that's Latin, I s'pose, and good Latin, too, they tell me. A man may be dead in the flesh, but living in law."

"La ! how cur'ous ! Law is a wonderful thing, to them that understands it."

The worthy Mrs. Thomas expressed a much more profound sentiment than that of which she was probably aware herself. Law *is* a wonderful thing, and most wonderful is he who can tell what it is to-day, or is likely to be to-morrow The law of testamentary devises, in particular, has more than the usual uncertainty, the great interest that is taken by the community in the large estates of certain individuals who are placed without the ordinary social categories by the magnitude of their fortunes, preventing anything from becoming absolutely settled, as respects *them*. In Turkey, and in America, the possession of great wealth is very apt to ruin their possessors ; proscription, in some form or other, being pretty certain to be the consequences. In Turkey, such has long and openly been the fact, the bow-string usually lying at the side of the strong box ; but, in this country, the system is in its infancy, though advancing toward maturity with giant strides. Twenty years more, resembling the twenty that are just past, in which the seed recently sown broadcast shall have time to reach maturity, and, in our poor opinion, the great work of demoralization, in this important particular, will be achieved. We are much afraid that the boasted progress, of which we hear so much, will resemble the act of the man who fancied he could teach his horse to live without food—just as he believed the poor beast was perfect, it died of inanition !

Roswell read Baiting Joe's " insterment " twice, and then

he placed it, with manly tenderness, in the hands of Mary. The girl read the document, too, tears starting to her eyes ; but a bright flush suffused her face, as she returned the will to her lover.

"Ah ! do not read it now, Roswell," she said, in an undertone ; but the stillness and expectation were so profound, that every syllable she uttered was heard by all in the room.

"And why not read it now, Miss Mary !" cried the Widow Martin. "Methinks *now* is the proper time to read it. If I'm to be codicilled out of that will, I want to know it."

"It is better, in every respect, that the company present should know all that is to be known, at once," observed Mr. Job Pratt. "Before the will is read, if that be the will, Captain Gar'ner——"

"It is the will of the late Deacon Pratt, duly signed, sealed, and witnessed, I believe, sir."

"One word more, then, before it is read. I think you said, Josy, that the deceased was *frightened* when he signed that will ? I do not express any opinion until I hear the will ; perhaps a'ter it is read, I shall think or say nothin' about this fright ; though the instrument that a man signs because he is frightened, if the fright be what I call a legal fright, is no instrument at all."

"But such was not the deacon's case, Squire Job," put in Baiting Joe, at once. "He did not sign the insterment because he was frightened, but was frightened because he signed the insterment. Let the boat go right eend foremost, squire "

"Read the will, Captain Gar'ner, if you have it," said Mr. Job Pratt, with decision. "It is proper that we should know who is executor. Friends, will you be silent for a moment ? "

Amid a death-like stillness, Roswell Gardiner now read as follows :

"In the name of God, amen. I, Ichabod Pratt, of the town of Southold, and county of Suffolk, and State of New York, being of failing bodily health, but of sound mind, do make and declare this to be my last will and testament.

"I bequeath to my niece, Mary Pratt, only child of my late brother, Israel Pratt, all my real estate, whatsoever it may be and wheresoever situate, to be held by her, her heirs, and assigns, forever, in fee.

"I bequeath to my brother, Job Pratt, any horse of which

I shall die possessed, to be chosen by himself, as a compensation for the injury inflicted on a horse of his, while in my use.

"I bequeath to my sister, Jane Thomas, the large looking-glass that is hanging up in the east bedroom of my house, and which was once the property of our beloved mother.

"I bequeath to the widow Catherine Martin, my cousin, the big pin-cushion in the said east chamber, which she used so much to praise and admire.

"I bequeath to my said niece, Mary Pratt, the only child of my late brother, Israel Pratt, aforesaid, all of my personal estate, whether in possession or existing in equity, including money at use, vessels, stock on farm, all other sorts of stock, furniture, wearing apparel, book-debts, money in hand, and all sorts of personal property whatever.

"I nominate and appoint Roswell Gardiner, now absent on a sealing voyage, in my employment, as the sole executor of this my last will, provided he return home within six months of my decease ; and should he not return home within the said six montns, then I appoint my above-mentioned niece and heiress, Mary Pratt, the sole executrix of this my will.

"I earnestly advise my said niece, Mary Pratt, to marry the said Roswell Gardiner ; but I annex no conditions whatever to this advice, wishing to leave my adopted daughter free to do as she may think best."

The instrument was, in all respects, duly executed, and there could not be a doubt of its entire validity. Mary felt a little bewildered, as well as greatly embarrassed. So perfectly disinterested had been all her care of her uncle, and so humble her wishes, that she did not for some time regard herself as the owner of a property that she had all her life been accustomed to consider as a part of her late uncle. The heirs expectant, "a'ter reading the insterment," as Baiting Joe told his cronies, when he related the circumstances over a mug of cider that evening, "fore and aft, and overhauling it from truck to keelson, give the matter up, as a bad job. They couldn't make nawthin' out of oppersition," continued Joe, "and so they took the horse, and the looking-glass, and the pin-cushion, and cleared out with their cargo. You couldn't get one of that breed to leave as much as a pin behind, to which he thought the law would give him a right. Squire Job went off very unwillingly ; for so strong was his belief in his claim, that he had made up his mind, as he told me himself, to break up the north meadow, and put it in corn this coming season."

"They say that Minister Whittle took it very hard that nawthin' was said about him, or about meetin', in the deacon's will," observed Jake Davis, one of Baiting Joe's cronies.

"That he did ; and he tuck it so hard that everybody allows that the two sermons he preached the next Sabba' day to be the very two worst he ever *did* preach."

"They must have been pretty bad, then," quaintly observed Davis ; "I've long set down Minister Whittle's discourses as being a *leetle* the worst going, when you give him a chance."

It is unnecessary to relate any more of this dialogue, nor should we have given the little we have, did it not virtually explain what actually occurred on the publication of the contents of the will. Roswell met with no opposition in proving the instrument ; and the day after he was admitted to act as executor he was married to Mary Pratt, and became tenant, by the courtesy, to all her real estate ; such being the law *then*, though it is so no longer. *Now*, a man and wife may have a very pretty family quarrel about the ownership of a dozen teaspoons, and the last, so far as we can see, may order the first out of one of her rocking-chairs, if she sees fit ! Surely domestic peace is not so trifling a matter that the law should seek to add new subjects of strife to the many that seem to be nearly inseparable from the married state.

Let this be as it may, no such law existed when Roswell Gardiner and Mary Pratt became man and wife. One of the first acts of the happy young couple, after they were united, was to make a suitable disposition of the money found buried at the foot of the tree, on the so-much-talked-of key. Its amount was a little more than two thousand dollars ; the pirate who made the revelation to Daggett having, in all probability, been ignorant himself of the real sum that had been thus secreted. By a specific bargain with the crew, all this money belonged to the deacon ; and, consequently, it had descended to his niece, and through her was now legally the property of Roswell. The young man was not altogether free from scruples about using money that had been originally taken as booty by pirates, and his conscientious wife had still greater objections. After conferring together on the subject, however, and seeing the impossibility of restoring the gold to those from whom it had been forced in the first place, the doubloons were distributed among the families of those who had lost their lives at Sealer's Land. The shares did not amount to much, it is true, but they did good, and cheered the hearts of two or three widows and dependent sisters.

Nor did Roswell Gardiner's care for their welfare stop here. He had the Sea Lion put in good order, removed her decks, raised upon her, and put her in her original condition, and sent her to Sealer's Land again, under the orders of Hazard, who was instructed to take in all the oil and skins that had been left behind, and to fill up, if he could, without risking too much by delay. All this was successfully done, the schooner coming back after a very short voyage, and quite full. The money made by this highly successful adventure had the effect to console several of those who had great cause to regret their previous losses.

As to Roswell and Mary, they had much reason to be contented with their lot. The deacon's means were found to be much more considerable than had been supposed. When all was brought into a snug state, Roswell found that his wife was worth more than thirty thousand dollars, a sum which constituted wealth on Oyster Pond in that day. We have, however, already hinted that the simplicity, and we fear with it the happiness, of the place has departed. A railroad terminates within a short distance of the deacon's old residence, bringing with it the clatter, ambition, and rivalry of such a mode of travelling. What is even worse, the venerable and expressive name of "Oyster Pond," one that conveys in its very sound the ideas of savory dishes, and an abundance of a certain and a very agreeable sort, has been changed to "Orient." Heaven save the mark! Long Island has hitherto been famous, in the history of New York, for the homely piquancy of its names, which usually conveyed a graphic idea of the place indicated. It is true, "Jerusalem" cannot boast of its Solomon's Temple, nor "Babylon" of its Hanging Gardens; but, by common consent, it is understood that these two names, and some half-a-dozen more of the same quality, are to be taken by their opposites.

Roswell Gardiner did not let Stimson pass out of his sight, as is customary with seamen when they quit a vessel. He made him master of a sloop that plied between New York and Southold, in which employment the good old man fulfilled his time, leaving to a widowed sister who dwelt with him the means of a comfortable livelihood for life.

The only bit of management of which Mary could be accused, was practised by her shortly after Stimson's death, and some six or eight years after her own marriage. One of her school friends, and a relative, had married a person who dwelt "west of the bridge," as it is the custom to say of all the counties that lie west of Cayuga Lake. This person, whose name was Hight, had mills, and made large quantities of that excellent flour that is getting to enjoy its merited reputation even in the Old World. He was disposed to form a partnership with Roswell, who sold his property and migrated to the great West, as the country " west of the bridge " was then termed, though it is necessary now to go a thousand miles farther in order to reach what is termed "the western country." Mary had an important agency in bringing about this migration. She had seen certain longings after the ocean, and seals, and whales, in her husband ; and did not consider him safe so long as he could scent the odors of a salt marsh. There is delight in this fragrance that none can appreciate so thoroughly as those who have enjoyed it in youth : it remains as long as human senses retain their faculties. An increasing family, however, and el dorado of the West, which, in that day, produced wheat, were inducements for a removal there, and, aided by Mary's gentle management, produced the desired effect ; and for more than twenty years Roswell Gardiner has been a very successful miller, on a large scale, in one of the western counties of what is called " the Empire State." We do not think the *sobriquets* of this country very happy, in general, but shall quarrel less with this than with the phrase of "commercial emporium," which is much as if one should say, " a townish town."

Roswell Gardiner has never wavered in his faith, from the time when his feelings were awakened by the just view of his own insignificance, as compared to the power of God. He then learned the first great lesson in religious belief, that of humility ; without which no man can be truly penitent, or truly a Christian. He no longer thought of measuring the Deity with his narrow faculties, or of setting up his blind conclusions, in the face of positive revelations. He saw that all must be accepted, or none ; and there was too much evidence, too much inherent truth, a morality too divine, to allow a mind like his to reject the gospel altogether. With Mary at his side, he has continued to worship the Trinity, accepting its mysteries in an humble reliance on the words of inspired men.